A FRIEND OF THE EARTH

BY THE SAME AUTHOR

A FRIEND
OF THE EARTH

T. C. Boyle

BLOOMSBURY

First published in Great Britain 2000
This paperback edition published 2001

Copyright © 2000 by T.C. Boyle

The moral right of the author has been asserted

Bloomsbury Publishing Plc, 38 Soho Square, London W1D 3HB

A CIP catalogue record for this book
is available from the British Library

ISBN 0 7475 5668 7 .

10 9 8 7 6 5 4 3 2 1

Typeset by Hewer Text Ltd, Edinburgh
Printed in Great Britain by Clays Limited, St Ives plc

For Alan Arkawy

ACKNOWLEDGMENTS

The author would like to thank Marie Alex, Russell Timothy Miller and Richard Goldman for their advice and assistance.

Every spirit builds itself a house, and beyond
its house a world, and beyond its world, a heaven.
Know then that the world exists for you.

Ralph Waldo Emerson, 'Nature'

The earth died screaming
While I lay dreaming . . .

Tom Waits, 'The Earth Died Screaming'

Prologue
Santa Ynez, November 2025

I'M OUT FEEDING the hyena her kibble and chicken backs and doing what I can to clean up after the latest storm, when the call comes through. It's Andrea. Andrea Knowles Cotton Tierwater, my ex-wife, my wife of a thousand years ago, when I was young and vigorous and relentlessly virile, the woman who routinely chained herself to cranes and bulldozers and seven-hundred-thousand-dollar Feller Buncher machines back in the time when we thought it mattered, the woman who helped me raise my daughter, the woman who made me crazy. Jesus Christ. If somebody has to come, why couldn't it be Teo? He'd be easier — him I could just kill. Bang-bang. And then Lily would have something more than chicken backs for dinner.

Anyway, there are trees down everywhere and the muck is tugging at my gum boots like a greedy sucking mouth, a mouth that's going to pull me all the way down eventually, but not yet. I might be seventy-five years old and my shoulders might feel as if they're attached at the joint with fishhooks, but the new kidney they grew me is still processing fluids just fine, thank you, and I can still outwork half the spoonfed cretins on this place. Besides, I have skills, special skills — I'm an animal man and there aren't many of us left these days, and my boss, Maclovio Pulchris, appreciates that. And I'm not name-dropping here, not necessarily — just stating the facts. I manage the man's private menagerie, the last surviving one in this part of the world, and it's an important — scratch that, vital — reservoir for zoo-cloning and the distribution of what's left of the major mammalian species. And you can say what you will about pop stars or the quality of his music or even the way he looks when he takes his hat and sunglasses off and you can see what a ridiculous little crushed nugget of a head he was born with, but I'll say this – he's a friend of the animals.

Of course, there isn't going to be anything left of the place if the weather doesn't let up. It's not even the rainy season – or what we used to qualify as the rainy season, as if we knew anything about it in the first place – but the storms are stacked up out over the Pacific like pool balls on a billiard table and not a pocket in sight. Two days ago the wind came up in the night, ripped the roof off of one of the back pens and slammed it like a giant Frisbee into the Lupine Hill condos across the way. Mac didn't particularly care about that – nobody's insured for weather anymore and any and all lawsuits are automatically thrown out of court, so don't even ask – but what hurt was the fact that the Patagonian fox got loose, and that's the last native-born individual known to be in existence on this worn-out planet, and we still haven't found the thing. Not a clue. No tracks, no nothing. She just disappeared, as if the storm had picked her up like Dorothy and set her down in the place where the extinct carnivores of all the ages run riot through fields of hobbled game – or in the middle of a freeway, where to the average motorist she'd be nothing more than a dog on stilts. The pangolins, they're gone too. And less than fifty of them out there in the world. It's a crime, but what can you do – call up the search and rescue? We've all been hit hard. Floods, winds, thunder and lightning, even hail. There are plenty of people without roofs over their heads, and right here in Santa Barbara County, not just Los Andiegoles or San Jose Francisco.

So Lily, she's giving me a long steady look out of the egg yolks of her eyes, and I'm lucky to have chicken backs what with the meat situation lately, when the pictaphone rings (think *Dick Tracy,* because the whole world's a comic strip now). The sky is black – not gray, black – and it can't be past three in the afternoon. Everything is still, and I smell it like a gathering cloud, death, the death of everything, hopeless and stinking and wasted, the pigment gone from the paint, the paint gone from the buildings, cars abandoned along the road, and then it starts raining again. I talk to my wrist (no picture, though – the picture button is set firmly and permanently in the off position – why would I want to show this wreck of a face to anybody?). 'Yeah?' I shout, and the rain is heavier, wind-driven now, snapping in my face like a wet towel.

'Ty?'

The voice is cracked and blistered, like the dirt here when the storms move on to Nevada and Arizona and the sun comes back to pound us with all its unfiltered melanomic might, but I recognize it right away, twenty years notwithstanding. It's a voice that does something physical to me, that jumps out of the circumambient air and seizes hold of me like a thing that lives off the blood of other things. 'Andrea? Andrea Cotton?' Half a beat. 'Jesus Christ, it's you, isn't it?'

Soft and seductive, the wind rising, Lily fixing me from behind the chicken wire as if I'm the main course: 'No picture for me?'

'What do you want, Andrea?'

'I want to see you.'

'Sorry, nobody sees me.'

'I mean in person, face to face. Like before.'

Rain streams from my hat. One of the sorry inbred lions starts coughing its lungs out, a ratcheting, oddly mechanical sound that drifts across the weedlot and ricochets off the monolithic face of the condos. I'm trying to hold back a whole raft of feelings, but they keep bobbing and pitching to the surface, threatening to break loose and shoot the rapids once and for all. 'What for?'

'What do you think?'

'I don't know – to run down my debit cards? Fuck with my head? Save the planet?'

Lily stretches, yawns, shows me the length of her yellow canines and the big crushing molars in back. She should be out on the veldt, cracking up giraffe bones, extracting marrow from the vertebrae, gnawing on hoofs. Except that there is no veldt, not anymore, and no giraffes either. Something unleashed in my brain shouts, IT'S ANDREA! And it is. Andrea's voice coming back at me. 'No, fool,' she says. 'For love.'

I am a fool, a fool in a thousand hats and guises, and the proof of it is that I agree to see her, with hardly any argument and the paltriest spatter of foreplay, the old voice banging around inside my head like a fist with a gnawed bone in it. And how long has it been –

exactly, now? Since '02 or '03, anyway. We used to climb mountains together, dance till the music went deaf in our ears, fuck till the birds woke up and sang and died of old age. Once we spent thirty days naked together in the Sierra Nevada, and even if it wasn't exactly like *The Blue Lagoon,* it was an experience you could never forget. And, yes, all my working parts are still in order, no Viagra Supra or penile implants needed here, thank you very much, and I wonder what she looks like after all this time. She was eight years younger than me, and unless the laws of mathematics have broken down like everything else, that would make her sixty-seven, which from my perspective can be a very interesting age for a woman. So, yes, I am going to see her.

But not here. No, I'm not that much of a fool. I've arranged an assignation at Swenson's Catfish and Sushi House in Solvang for six this evening, despite the torrents and the washed-out roads, because I've got Mac's 4x4 and whatever she's got or how she's going to get there isn't exactly my problem. Not yet, anyway.

She'll be there, though – you can bet on that. She wants something – money, a place to crash, clothes, a nice bottle of wine, my last can of Alaskan snow crab (now extinct, like everything else that swims or crawls in the sea, except maybe zebra mussels) – and she always gets what she wants. I try to picture her as she was back then, in her mid-forties, and all I can see is her eyes, eyes that took hold of you and wouldn't let go, as hot and hard and punishing as a pair of torches. And her breasts. I remember them too. I don't think she ever went out of the house a day in her life in anything that didn't cling to them like a fresh coat of paint, except for the month in the Sierras when she wore nothing but bug bites and dirt.

Andrea. Yeah, sure, it'll be good to see her, even if nothing happens – and as I say, I haven't gone over the horizon as far as sex is concerned, not yet, and even if I haven't actually participated in anything remotely sexual since Lori died in the *mucosa* epidemic that hit here three years ago, I still think about it all the time. I look at the women Mac's bodyguards bring in and reconfigure how they're built under their rain clothes, and I watch the lean-legged things in khaki dresses wheeling their carts around the forlorn aisles of the supermarket when I take the 4x4 in for kibble and whatever they've got by way of half-rotten vegetable matter for the spectacled bear and the peccaries. Sex. It's a good thing. Even if I don't think I could stand it more than maybe once a month, and only then if all the attachment that comes with it – the hand-wringing and nose-wiping, the betrayals and shouting matches and the animal intimacy that isn't a whit higher on the emotional scale than the licking, sucking and groveling of the hyenas – is strictly exiled from the process.

Love, she said. *For love.* And despite myself, despite everything I've learned and suffered and the claw marks etched into my back, I feel myself soften for that fatal instant, and I know she's got me.

I'm standing there gazing into Lily's pen, all the rain in the universe dripping from the brim of my silly yellow rain-hat and the jutting overgrown humiliation of my old man's nose, when a windblown shout comes to me across the yard. It's Chuy, lit by a fantastic tendril of lightning that brings me back to my tie-dye days, blotter acid, strobe lights in a dance club and Jane, my first wife and first love, but Chuy isn't Jane, he's Chuy, who has no surname because he can't remember it since the crop-dusting accident that took his hair, his manhood and half his brain and left him as jittery as a cockroach on a griddle. He's dragging some-thing, a bundled wet rug, old newspapers, the rain intercepting him in broad gray sheets that are just like the flung buckets of the old comedy routines – like special effects, that is.

'It's a dog,' Chuy says, panting up to me through the ocean of the air, and sure enough, that's what it is, a dog. Two, three days dead, bloated a bit in the belly, collie-shepherd mix, never seen him before and at least it's not the Patagonian fox, because that's all we need. 'Found him dead in the bushes, Mr. Ty, and what I'm thinking is maybe he is the kind of something Lily can *comer,* no?'

Me, judicious, old, scrawny, rain-beaten: 'Poison? Because if it is – '

Chuy is squinting up at me, my personal reclamation project, his eyes loopy, no control of his jaws or tongue, every nerve fried and sizzling still. 'No poison, Mr. Ty, road tracks.' And he lifts the hind end of the thing to show the mangled legs and crushed spine.

Well, and this is good, a real bonus, and as the two of us hoist the sodden carcass to the level of our armpits and heave it up over the chicken wire to where Lily, interested, lurches up out of the mud, I can't help thinking of Andrea and what shirt I'll wear and whether or not I should bother with a sportcoat. I'm picturing us there at the bar at Swenson's, her irreducible eyes and deep breasts, no change in her at all because change is inconceivable, Andrea at forty-three, a knockout, a killer, hello, look at me, and then Lily gets hold of the dog and all I can hear is the crunch of bone.

The lions have had their horsemeat and the giant anteaters *(Myrmecophaga tridactyla)* are busy with some half-rotted beams full of Formosa termites, lunch enough, I expect, when finally I develop the sense to come in out of the wet. By this time – it must be four, four-thirty – the rain has slackened off a bit and the wind, which always seems to be peaking at Force 10 lately, seems a bit quieter too. What would you call it? – hat-extracting velocity. A strike and a spare and eight more frames to go. Gusty. Blustery. Not-quite-gale-force. It rattles the hood of my slicker, slapping my cheeks with wet vinyl, thwack-thwack, and my glasses are riding up and down the bridge of my nose as if it's been greased. Things are a mess, and no doubt about it, every step a land mine, the shrubs tattered like old sails, the trees snapped in two and then snapped in two again. But what can I do? I leave all that to Mac's gardeners and the masochistic pup of a landscape architect who keeps popping up, unfazed, whenever the rain lets up for an hour – though with all the topsoil running off and the grass gone to seed, I can see we'll be living in the middle of a desert here in the dry season. If it ever comes.

As part of my arrangement with Mac, I occupy a two-room guesthouse on the far verge of the estate, just under the walls of Rancho Seco, the gated community to the east of us. It was built back in the nineties, with all the modern conveniences, and it's a cozy-enough place but for the fact that the winds have long since torn off the gutters and three-quarters of the shingles and the fireplace is bricked up, as per state law. Still, I have a space heater, and it never gets too cold here, not like in the old days – never below sixty, anyway – and I'm field marshal over an army of old pots and paint cans that catch at least half the rain at least half the time. Yet how can I account for the fact that I'm shivering like a cholera victim by the time I actually shrug off the slicker and stamp out of my boots and take a towel to my head? Because I'm old, that's how. Because sixty degrees and wet at my age is like the temperature water turned to ice when I was thirty-nine, the year I met Andrea.

The place smells of mold – what else? – and rats. The rats – an R-selected species, big litters, highly mobile, selected for any environment – are thriving, multiplying like there's no tomorrow (but of course there is, as everybody alive now knows all too well and ruefully, and tomorrow is coming for the rats too). They have an underlying smell, a furtive smell, old sweat socks balled up on the floor of the high-school locker room, drains that need cleaning, meat sauce dried onto the plate and then reliquefied with a spray of water. It's a quiet stink, nothing like the hyena when she's wet, which is all the time now, and I forgive the rats that much. I'm an environmentalist, after all – or used to be; not much sense in using the term now – and I believe in Live and Let Live, Adat, Deep Ecology, No Compromise in Defense of Mother Earth.

Andrea. Oh, yes, Andrea. She burned me in that crucible, with her scorching eyes and her voice of ash, and her body, her beautiful hard backpacker's body, stalwart legs, womanly hips and all the rest. She's on her way to Swenson's to meet me. Maybe there already, the *sake* cup like a thimble in her big female hands, leaning into the bar to show off what she has left, stupefying Shigetoshi Swenson, the bartender, who can't be more than sixty-four or - five. The thought of that scenario wakes me up, just as surely as it ever did, and the next minute I'm in the bedroom pulling a sweater from the bureau drawer (black turtleneck, to hide the turkey wattles under my chin), thinking, No time for a shower and I'm wet enough as it is. I find a semi-clean pair of jeans hanging from a hook in the closet, step into my imitation-leather cowboy boots and head for the door – but not before I finish off the ensemble with the crowning touch: the red beret she sent me the second time I went to jail. I pull it down low over the eyebrows, like a watchcap. For old times' sake.

There's a whole crowd out on the road, storm or no storm, commuters, evening shoppers, repair crews, teenagers jazzed on a world turned to shit, and I have to be careful with the wind rocking the car and the jolts and bumps and washed-out places.

This used to be open country twenty-five years ago – a place where you'd see bobcat, mule deer, rabbit, quail, fox, before everything was poached and encroached out of existence. I remember stud farms here, fields running on forever, big estates like Mac's set back in the hills, even an emu ranch or two *(Leaner than beef, and half the calories, try an Emu Burger today!)*. Now it's condos. Gray wet canyons of them. And who's in those condos? Criminals. Meat-eaters. Skin-cancer patients. People who know no more about animals – or nature, or the world that used to be – than their computer screens want them to know.

All right. I'll make this brief. The year is 2025, I'm seventy-five years old, my name is Tyrone O'Shaughnessy Tierwater, and I'm half an Irish Catholic and half a Jew. I was born in the richest county in the suburbs of the biggest city in the world, in a time when there were no shortages, at least not in this country, no storms (except the usual), no acid rain, no lack of wild and jungle places to breathe deep in. Right now, I'm on my way to share some pond-raised catfish sushi with my ex-wife Andrea, hoist a few, maybe even get laid for auld lang syne. Or love. Isn't that what she said? *For love?* The windshield wipers are beating in time to my arrhythmic heart, the winds are cracking their cheeks, the big 4x4 Olfputt rocking like a boat at sea – and in my head, stuck there like a piece of gum to the sole of my shoe, the fragment of a song from so long ago I can't remember what it is or how it got there. *Down the alley the ice wagon flew . . . Arlene took me by the hand and said, Won't you be my man?*

This is going to be interesting.

The parking lot is flooded, two feet of gently swirling shit-colored water, and there go my cowboy boots – which I had to wear for vanity's sake, when the gum boots would have done just as well. I sit there a minute cursing myself for my stupidity, the murky penny-pincher lights of Swenson's beckoning through the scrim of the rain-scrawled windshield, the Mex-Chinese take-out place next door to it permanently sandbagged and dark as a cave, while the computer-repair store and 7-Eleven ride high, dry and smug on eight-foot pilings salvaged from the pier at Gaviota. The rain is coming down harder now – what else? – playing timbales on the roof of the 4x4, and the wind rattles the cab in counterpoint, picking up anything that isn't nailed down and carrying it off to some private destination, the graveyard of blown things. All the roofs here, where the storms tend to set down after caroming up off the ocean, have been secured with steel cables, and that's a company to invest in – Bolt-A-Roof, Triple AAA Guaranteed. Of course, everything I ever had to invest, every spare nickel I managed to earn and everything my father left me, went to Andrea and Teo and my wild-eyed cohorts at Earth Forever! (Never heard of it? Think radical enviro group, eighties and nineties. Tree-spiking? Ecotage? Earth Forever! Ring a bell?)

It takes me that long minute, mulling things over and delaying the inevitable in the way of the old (but not that old, not with all the medical advances they've thrust on us, what with our personal DNA codes and telomerase treatments and epidermal rejuvenators, all of which I've made liberal use of, thanks to Maclovio Pulchris' generosity), and then I figure what price dignity, jerk off the boots, stuff my socks deep in the pointed toes of them and roll my pants up my skinny legs. The water creeps up my shins, warm as a bath, and I tuck the boots under my slicker, tug the beret down against the wind and start off across the lot. It's almost fun, the feel of it, the splashing, all that water out of its normal bounds, and the experience takes me back sixty-five years to Hurricane Donna and a day off from school in Peterskill, New York, splash and splash again. (And people thought the collapse of the biosphere would be the end of everything, but that's not it at all. It's just the opposite – more of everything, more sun, water, wind, dust, mud.)

I'm standing under the jury-rigged awning (steel plates welded to steel posts set in concrete), trying to balance on one bare foot and administer a sock and boot to the other, when the door flings open and two drunks, as red in face and bare blistered arm as if they've been baked in a tandoori, trundle out to gape at the rain. 'Shit,' the one to my right says, and I'm squinting past him to the bar, to see if Andrea's there, 'may as well have another drink.' His companion blinks at the deluge as if he's never seen weather before – and maybe he hasn't, maybe he's from Brazil or New Zealand or one of the other desert countries – and then he says,

9

'Can't. Got to get home to' (you fill in the name) 'and the kids and the dog and the rats in the attic . . . but fuck this weather, fuck it all to hell.'

I take a deep breath, dodge around them, and step into the restaurant. I should point out that Swenson's isn't the most elegant place – elegance is strictly for the rich, computer repairmen, movie people, pop stars like Mac – but it has its charms. The entryway isn't one of them. There's an empty fish tank built into the cement block wall on your immediate right, a coat rack and umbrella stand on the left. Music hits you – oldies, the venerable hoary inescapable hits of the sixties, played at killing volume for benefit of the deaf and toothless like me – and a funk of body heat and the kind of humidity you'd expect from the Black Hole of Calcutta. No air-conditioning, of course, what with electrical restrictions and the sheer killing price per kilowatt hour. Go straight on and you're in the bar, turn left and you've got the dining room, paneled in mismatching pine slats recycled from the classic California ranch houses that succumbed to the historical imperative of mini-malls and condos. I go straight on, the bar teeming, Shiggy glancing up from the blender with a nod of acknowledgment, some antiquated crap about riding your pony blistering the overworked speakers.

No Andrea. *Ride your pony, ride your pony.* My elbows find the bar, cheap *sake* (tastes of machine oil, brewed locally) finds me, and I scan the faces to be sure. I even slide off my glasses and wipe them on my sleeve, a gesture as habitual as breathing. Replace them. Study the faces now, in depth, erasing lines and blotches and liver spots, pulling lips and eyes up out of their fissures, smoothing brows and firming up chins, and still no Andrea. (Swenson's, in case you're wondering, caters strictly to the young-old, the fastest-growing segment of the U.S. population, of which I am a reluctant yet grateful part, considering the alternative.)

A woman in red at the end of the bar catches my eye – that is, I catch hers – and my blood surges like a teenager's until I realize she can't be more than fifty. I look again as she turns away and lets out a laugh in response to something the retired dentist at her elbow is saying, and I see she's all wrong: Andrea, and I don't care what age she might be – sixty, eighty-five, a hundred and ten – has twice her presence. Ten times. Yes. Sure. She's not Andrea. Not even close.

But does that make it any less depressing to admit that I'm really standing here on aching knees in a dress-up shirt and with a sopping-wet beret that looks like a chili-cheese omelet laid over my naked scalp, waiting for a phantom? A blood-sucking phantom at that?

Ride your pony, ride your pony. What is it Yeats said about old age? It wasn't ride your pony. An aged man is but a paltry thing, that's what he said. A tattered coat upon a stick. In spades.

But what is this I feel on the back of my neck? Dampness. Water. Ubiquitous water. I'm looking up, the ceiling tiles giving off a gentle ooze, and then down at the plastic bucket between my feet – I'm practically standing in it – when I feel a pressure on my arm. It's her hand, Andrea's hand, the feel of it round my biceps as binding as history, and what can I do but look up into her new face, the face that's been molded like wet clay on top of the one glazed and fired and set on a shelf in my head. 'Hello, Ty,' she says, the bucket gently sloshing, the solid air rent by the blast of the speakers, the crowd gabbling, her unflinching eyes locked on mine. I can't think of what to say, Shiggy moving toward us on the other side of the bar, mountainous in a Hawaiian shirt, the bartender's eternal question on his lips, and then she's smiling like the sun coming up over the hills. 'Nice hat,' she says.

I snatch it off and twist it awkwardly behind me.

'But, Ty – a laugh – 'you're bald!'

'Something for the lady?' Shiggy shouts over the noise, and before I've said a word to her I'm addressing him, a know-nothing I could talk to any day of the week. '*Sake* on the rocks,' I tell him, 'unless she's paying for her own – and I'll take a refill too.' The transaction gives me a minute to collect myself. It's Andrea. It's really her, standing here beside me in the flesh. Pleasure, I remind myself, is inseparable from its lawfully wedded mate, pain. 'We all get older,' I shout, swinging round with the drinks, ' – if we're lucky.'

'And me?' She takes a step back, center stage, lifting her arms in display. For a minute I think she's going to do a pirouette. But I don't want to sound too cynical here, because time goes on and she's looking good, very good, eight or nine on a scale of ten, all things considered. Her mouth settles into a basket of grooves and lines when the smile fades, and her eyes are paler and duller than I remembered – and ever so slightly exophthalmic – but who's to quibble? She was a beauty then and she's a beauty still.

'You look terrific,' I tell her, 'and I'm not just saying that – it's the truth. You look – I don't know – edible. Are you edible?'

The smile returns, but just for a second, flashing across her face as if blown by the winds that are even now rattling the windows – and rattling them audibly, despite the racket of the place and my suspect hearing (destroyed sixty years ago by Jimi Hendrix and The Who). She's wearing a print dress, low-cut of course, frilly sleeves, a quarter-inch of makeup, and her hair – dyed midnight black – bunches at her shoulders. She fixes on my eyes with that half-spacey, half-calculating wide-eyed look I know so well – or used to know. 'Is there someplace we can talk?'

Most people don't relate to hyenas. You say 'hyena' to them and they give you a long stare, as if you're talking about a mythical beast – which it practically is nowadays. The more enlightened might remember the old nature shows where the hyenas gang-pile a corpse or disembowel the newborn wildebeest and devour it in ragged bloody lumps before the awareness has left its eyes, but that's all they remember, the ugliness and the death. I knew an African game-hunter once (Philip Ratchiss, and more on him later) who used to cull elephants for the Zambian government, back when there was a Zambian government, and he'd had some grisly encounters with all three species of hyena. When he retired to California, he brought his Senga gunbearer with him, a man named Mag or Mug – I could never get it straight – who'd had his face removed by a hyena one night as he lay stretched out drunk in front of the campfire. Ratchiss dressed him up in Dockers and polo shirts and got his teeth fixed for him, but Mag – or Mug – didn't want anything to do with plastic surgery. He had an eye left, and a pair of ears. The rest of his face was like a big pitted prune.

The reason I mention it is because people can't understand why Mac wants to save hyenas – in Lily's case, the brown hyena – when the cheetahs, cape buffalo, rhinos and elephants are gone. And what do I tell them? Because they exist, that's why. And if we can't manage to impregnate Lily with sperm from the San Diego Zoo's lone surviving male, we'll clone her – and clone the clones, ad infinitum. 'I want to save the animals nobody else wants,' Mac told me when we entered into our present arrangement. 'The ones nobody but a mother could love. Isn't that cool? Isn't that selfless and cool and brave?' I told him it was. And we got rid of the peacocks and Vietnamese pot-bellied pigs, and the dogs and cats and goats and all the rest, and concentrated on the unglamorous things of the world, the warthogs, peccaries, hyenas and jackals, with the three lions thrown in for the excitement factor. Mac likes to hear them cough and roar when he turns in at night. When he's here, that is. Which is precious little this time of year.

Anyway, Lily looms up in my mind when Andrea leans into the table and asks me what it's like to work for Maclovio Pulchris. We're seated in the candlelit dining room, waiting for our order, deep into the *sake* now and too civilized – or too old – to let all the bitterness of the past spoil our little reunion. I'm rattling on about Mac, how he likes to stay up all night with a bottle of champagne and a favorite lady and sit out in the yard listening to the anteaters snore while Lily roams her cage, sniggering over the rats she traps between her four-toed paws. And then I'm on to Lily, the virtuosity of her digestive tract, her calcified bowel movements (all that pulverized bone), the roadkill we feed her when we get lucky – opossums mostly, another R-species – when Andrea clears her throat in a pre-emptive way.

I duck my head in embarrassment – my shining bald dome of a head *(Flow it, show it/Long as God can grow it/My hair)*. Suck at the metallic patchwork of my old man's teeth. Fumble with the *sake* cup. I haven't shut up since we sat down – and why? Because, for all my bravado back at the house, all my macho notions of remining an old vein, of exploiting her body in some superheated motel room and then writing her off, good night, goodbye and thanks for the masterful application of the lips, I find myself riveted by her, racked in body and nerve, ready to be slit open and sacrificed all over again. I'm nervous, that's what it is. And when I'm nervous I can't stop talking.

'Do you remember that girl, April Wind – she was about Sierra's age?' Andrea is watching my face, looking for the crack into which she can drive the first piton and begin her ascent to my poor quivering brain. I give her nothing. Nothing at all. My eyes are glass. My face a sculpture by Oldenburg, monumental, impenetrable. Sierra – the famous Sierra Tierwater, martyr to the cause of the trees – is my daughter. Was my daughter. April Wind I've never heard of. Or at least I hope I haven't.

'She was part of that tree-sitting thing, summer of '01?'

All my danger sensors are on alert – I should have stayed home with my hyena, I knew it. I'm hurt. I'm lonely. I'm old. I haven't got time for this. But Andrea will persist, she will – if there's one thing I know about her, it's that. Something's afoot here, something I'm not going to like one bit, and once she's sprung it she'll get down to more practical matters – she needs to borrow money, food, clothes, medical supplies, she absolutely has to stay with me a while, a couple of weeks, a month, she needs me, wants me, and suddenly she'll lean forward and we'll kiss with sushi on our lips and her hand will snake out under the table and take hold of me in the one place that's even more vulnerable than my brain.

Her lips, I'm watching her lips – I know she's had collagen implants, and her face is too shining and perfect to be natural, but who wants natural at my age? 'You remember her,' she insists, picking at her food with an absent squeeze of her chopsticks (she's having the spicy catfish roll, tilapia sushi, smoked crappie and koi sashimi, a good choice – or the best available, anyway. And it's not going to be cheap, but, knowing Andrea, I came prepared with a new five-hundred-dollar debit card). 'She came straight to us from Teo's Action Camp? Tiny, she couldn't have weighed more than a hundred pounds? Asian. Or half Asian? She swore the trees talked to her, remember?'

I'm beginning to remember, but I don't want to. And the mention of Teo shoots a flaming brand into my gut, where it ignites the wasabi lurking there in a gurry of carp roe and partially digested tilapia. 'What about Teo?' I say, just as the wind comes up in a blast that shakes the place as if it were made of straw.

'I hate this,' she hisses, bracing for the next blast. A sound of rending, some essential piece of the roof above us scraping across the tiles and plucking briefly at the strings of steel cable before hurtling off into the night. People have been decapitated by roofing material, crushed, poleaxed, impaled – you hear about

14

it every day on the news. A woman in the Lupine Hill condos was taking out the trash last year when a flagpole came down out of the sky like a javelin and pinned her to the Dumpster like an insect to a mounting board. And then there are the eye and lung problems associated with all the particulate matter in the air, not to mention allergies nobody had heard of twenty years ago. A lot of people – myself included – wear goggles and a gauze mask during the dry season, when the air is just another kind of dirt. But what can I say? I told you so?

This is the world we've made. Live in it.

'You get used to it,' I say, and give her a shrug. 'But you've got your own problems in Arizona – that's where you've been living, right?'

She nods, a tight economical dip of the chin that says, Ask no more.

'So Teo,' I persist, trying to sound casual though I'm chewing up my insides and wishing I were home in front of the tube with a bottle of Gelusil and the lions coughing me to sleep. 'Is he still in the picture, or what?'

Right then is when I begin to notice that my feet are wet, and when I lift first one, then the other from the floor, the rug gives like a sponge. Out of the corner of my eye I can see one of Shiggy's daughters busy at the rear door with a mop and a mountain of napkins, furious activity, but not enough to stanch the flow of water seeping inexorably into the room. Shiggy should have built on pilings and he knows it, but he inherited the place from his father, who ran a successful smorgasbord out of the location for forty years, and the expense of jacking up the building was prohibitive. And Shiggy, like everyone else, kept waiting for the weather to break. 'No problem, sir, no problem,' Shiggy's daughter is saying to a solitary diner in the corner, 'we'll have this mopped up in a minute.'

Distracted – my boots are ruined for sure – I've forgotten all about the question I left hanging in the dank air of the place, forgotten where I am or why or even who I am, one of those little lapses that make life tolerable at my age, ginkgo biloba, caffeine and neuroboosters notwithstanding. For a whole ten seconds I've managed to disconnect my gut from my brain. 'He's dead,' Andrea says into the silence.

'Who?'

'Teo.'

Dead? Teo dead? Well, and now I'm back in the moment, as alert as Lily when she sees me reach into the big greasy plastic bag for another chicken back. I'm beginning to enjoy myself. I feel expansive suddenly. I want details. Did he suffer? Was it lingering? Did he lose control of his bowels, his dick, his brain? 'I thought it would take a silver bullet,' I hear myself say. 'Or a stake through the heart.'

Her eyes draw down, drop the curtains and pull the shades. Her smallest voice: 'It was quick.'

'How quick?'

Whoa, shouts the wind, *whoa, whoa, whoa,* and now there's a steady drip of water – the ghost of Teo, his slick aqueous heartbeat – thumping down on the table, just to the left of my chopsticks. I'm watching her, feeding on this, but my back hurts – it always hurts, will always hurt, has hurt without remit since I was in my mid-thirties – and the arthritis in my right foot isn't being helped any by the dampness of the floor. I have a premature hard-on. I resist the impulse to snatch a look at my watch. 'How quick?' I repeat.

'I don't want to talk about it,' she says, 'because that's not why I – that's not what I wanted to . . . It was a meteor, all right?'

I can't pull my laugh in. Sharp and resounding, it explodes from my runaway lips and startles the couple two tables over. 'You're putting me on.'

'Eleven and a half billion people on the earth, Ty, sixty million of them right here in California. Meteors hit the earth, okay? They've got to land somewhere.'

'You mean it actually hit him? How big? And when? When was this – ten years ago, yesterday or what?'

'I won't lie to you, Ty: I loved him. Or at least I thought I did.'

'Yeah, and you thought you loved me too. That did me a lot of good.'

'Listen, I don't want to get into this, all right? This is not why I came – '

'What, did it hit him like a bullet? Go through the roof of his house?'

'He was making a soft-boiled egg. In the kitchen. He was living in one of those group homes for people like me who never saved for retirement – and don't ask, because I'm not going to say a word about my present circumstances, so don't.' Patting at her lips with the napkin, pausing to take a doleful sip of faintly greasy *sake,* the best the house has to offer. (Have I mentioned that grapes are a thing of the past? Napa-Sonoma is all rice paddies now, the Loire and Rhine Valleys so wet they'd be better off trying to grow pineapples – though on the plus side I hear the Norwegians are planting California rootstock in the Oslo suburbs.)

'He never knew what hit him,' she's saying, chasing me down with her eyes. 'His son told me they found the thing – it was the size of a golf ball – embedded in the concrete in the basement, still smoldering.'

I'm in awe. Sitting there over my *sake* and a plate of cold fish, holding that picture in my head – a soft-boiled egg! The world is a lonely place.

'Ty?'

I look up, still shaking my head. 'You want another drink?'

'No, no – listen. The reason I came is to tell you about April Wind – '

I do everything I can to put some hurt and surprise in my face, though I'm neither hurt nor surprised, or not particularly. 'I thought you said you wanted to see me for love – isn't that what you said? Correct me if I'm wrong, but my impression was you wanted to, well, get together – '

'No,' she says. 'Or yes, yes, I do. But the thing that got me here, the reason I had to see you, is April Wind. She wants to do a book. On Sierra.'

I don't get angry much anymore, no point in it. But with all I've been through – not just back then, but now too, and who do you think is going to have to track down the Patagonian fox and the slinking fat pangolins on feet that are like cement blocks? – I can't help myself. 'I don't want to hear it,' I say, and somehow I'm standing, the carpet squelching under my feet, the whole building vibrating under the assault of another gust. My arm, my right arm, seems to be making some sort of extenuating gesture, moving all on its own, *I come to bury Caesar, not to praise him.* 'She's dead, isn't

17

that enough? What do you want – to make some sort of Joan of Arc out of her? Open the door. Look around you. What the fuck difference does it make?'

She's a big woman, Andrea, big still – in her shoulders, the legs tucked up under her skirt, those hands – but she reduces herself somehow. She's a waif. She's put-upon. She's no threat to anybody and this isn't her idea but April Wind's, the woman who talks to trees. 'I think it's a good idea,' she says. 'For posterity.'

'What posterity?' My arm swings wide. 'This is your posterity.'

'Come on, Ty – do it for Sierra. Let the woman interview you, tell your story – what'll it hurt?'

Everything compresses to rush into the vacuum inside me, the winds dying as if on the downstroke of a baton, the rain taking a time-out, the mop finally prevailing at the door. Andrea is standing now too, and we're a matching pair of the young-old, as rejuvenant as any couple you'd see in New York or Paris or in those TV ads for transplants, poised over the table as if we're about to sweep off across the floor in some elaborate dance routine. 'What's it in for you? A finder's fee?'

No response.

'And how *did* you track me down, anyway?'

There's no malice in her smile – a hint of smugness, maybe, but no malice. She holds up her fingers, all ten of them. 'The Internet. Search for Maclovio Pulchris and you'd be amazed at what turns up – and as far as what's in it for me, that's easy: you. You're what I want.'

I'm stirred, and there's no denying it. But I'm not taking her home with me, never, no matter what. I'm grinning, though – a grin so glutinous you could hang wallpaper on it. 'You want to go to a motel?'

'You don't have to do that.'

Still grinning, all my dental enhancements on display, my naked gums anaesthetized with *sake* fumes and my eyes on fire behind the twin discs of my glasses: 'I want to.'

The wind comes back for an encore. Snatches of music drift in from the bar. Everything is roaring, the whole world, noise and more noise. 'I won't stay long,' she says. 'And I'll help with the animals. You know how I love animals – '

PART ONE

Bring 'Em Back Alive

The Siskiyou, July 1989

THIS IS THE way it begins, on a summer night so crammed with stars the Milky Way looks like a white plastic sack strung out across the roof of the sky. No moon, though – that wouldn't do at all. And no sound, but for the discontinuous trickle of water, the muted patter of cheap tennis sneakers on the ghostly surface of the road and the sustained applause of the crickets. It's a dirt road, a logging road, in fact, but Tyrone Tierwater wouldn't want to call it a road. He'd call it a scar, a gash, an open wound in the body corporal of the forest. But for the sake of convenience, let's identify it as a road. In daylight, trucks pound over it, big D7 Cats, loaders, wood-chippers. It's a road. And he's on it.

He's moving along purposively, all but invisible in the abyss of shadow beneath the big Douglas firs. If your eyes were adjusted to the dark and you looked closely enough, you might detect his three companions, the night disarranging itself ever so casually as they pass: now you see them, now you don't. All four are dressed identically, in cheap tennis sneakers blackened with shoe polish, two pairs of socks, black tees and sweatshirts and, of course, the black watchcaps. Where would they be without them?

Tierwater had wanted to go further, the whole nine yards, stripes of greasepaint down the bridge of the nose, slick rays of it fanning out across their cheekbones – or, better yet, blackface – but Andrea talked him out of it. She can talk him out of anything, because she's more rational than he, more aggressive, because she has a better command of the language and eyes that bark after weakness like hounds – but then she doesn't have half his capacity for paranoia, neurotic display, pessimism or despair. Things can go

21

wrong. They do. They will. He tried to tell her that, but she wouldn't listen.

They were back in the motel room at the time, on the unfledged strip of the comatose town of Grants Pass, Oregon, where they were registered under the name of Mr. and Mrs. James Watt. He was nervous – butterflies in the stomach, termites in the head – nervous and angry. Angry at the loggers, Oregon, the motel room, her. Outside, three steps from the door, Teo's Chevy Caprice (anonymous gray, with the artfully smudged plates) sat listing in its appointed slot. He came out of the bathroom with a crayon in one hand, a glittering, shrink-wrapped package of Halloween face paint in the other. There were doughnuts on the bed in a staved-in carton, paper coffee cups subsiding into the low fiberboard table. 'Forget it, Ty,' she said. 'I keep telling you, this is nothing, the first jab in a whole long bout. You think I'd take Sierra along if I wasn't a hundred percent sure it was safe? It's going to be a stroll in the park, it is.'

A moment evaporated. He looked at his daughter, but she had nothing to say, her head cocked in a way that indicated she was listening, but only reflexively. The TV said, ' – and these magnificent creatures, their range shrinking, can no longer find the mast to sustain them, let alone the carrion.' He tried to smile, but the appropriate muscles didn't seem to be working. He had misgivings about the whole business, especially when it came to Sierra – but as he stood there listening to the insects sizzle against the bug zapper outside the window, he understood that 'misgivings' wasn't exactly the word he wanted. Misgivings? How about crashing fears, terrors, night sweats? The inability to swallow? A heart ground up like glass?

There were people out there who weren't going to like what the four of them were planning to do to that road he didn't want to call a road. Bosses, underbosses, heavy-machine operators, CEOs, power-lunchers, police, accountants. Not to mention all those good, decent, hardworking and terminally misguided timber families, the men in baseball caps and red suspenders, the women like tented houses, people who spent their spare time affixing loops of yellow ribbon to every shrub, tree, doorknob, mailbox and car antenna in every town up and down the coast. They had mortgages, trailers, bass boats, plans for the future, and the dirt-blasted bumpers of their pickups sported stickers that read *Save a Skunk, Roadkill an Activist* and *Do You Work for a Living or Are You an Environmentalist?* They were angry – born angry – and they didn't much care about physical restraint, one way or the other. Talk about misgivings – his daughter is only thirteen years old, for all her Gothic drag and nose ring and the cape of hair that drapes her shoulders like an advertisement, and she's never participated in an act of civil disobedience in her life, not even a daylit rally with minicams whirring and a supporting cast of thousands. 'Come on,' he pleaded, 'just under the eyes, then. To mask the glow.'

Andrea just shook her head. She looked good in black, he had to admit it, and the watchcap, riding low over her eyebrows, was a very sexy thing. They'd been married three months now, and everything about her was a novelty and a revelation, right down to the way she stepped into her jeans in the morning or pouted over a saucepan of ratatouille, a thin strip of green pepper disappearing between her lips while the steam rose witchily in her hair. 'What if the police pull us over?' she said. 'Ever think of that? What're you going to say – "The game really ran late tonight, officer"? Or "Gee, it was a great old-timey minstrel show – you should have been there."' She was the one with the experience here – she was the organizer, the protestor, the activist – and she wasn't giving an inch. 'The trouble with you,' she said, running a finger under the lip of her cap, 'is you've been watching too many movies.'

Maybe so. But you couldn't really call the proposition relevant, not now, not here. This is the wilderness, or what's left of it. The night is deep, the road intangible, the stars the feeblest mementos of the birth of the universe. There are nine galaxies out there for each person alive today, and each of those galaxies features a hundred billion suns, give or take the odd billion, and yet he can barely see where he's going, groping like a sleepwalker, one foot stabbing after the other. This is crazy, he's thinking, this is trouble, like stumbling around in a cave waiting for the bottom to fall out. He's wondering if the others are having as hard a time as he is, thinking vaguely about beta-carotene supplements and night-vision goggles, when an owl chimes in somewhere ahead of them, a single wavering cry that says it has something strangled in its claws.

His daughter, detectable only through the rhythmic snap of her gum, asks in a theatrical whisper if that could be a spotted owl, 'I mean hopefully, by any chance?'

He can't see her face, the night a loose-fitting jacket, his mind ten miles up the road, and he answers before he can think: 'Don't I wish.'

Right beside him, from the void on his left, another voice weighs in, the voice of Andrea, his second wife, the wife who is not Sierra's biological mother and so free to take on the role of her advocate in all disputes, tiffs, misunderstandings, misrepresentations and adventures gone wrong: 'Give the kid a break, Ty.' And then, in a whisper so soft it's like a feather floating down out of the night, 'Sure it is, honey, that's a spotted owl if ever I heard one.'

Tierwater keeps walking, the damp working odor of the nighttime woods in his nostrils, the taste of it on his tongue – mold transposed to another element, mold ascendant – but he's furious suddenly. He doesn't like this. He doesn't like it at all. He knows it's necessary, knows that the woods are being raped and the world stripped right on down to the last twig and that somebody's got to save it, but still he doesn't like it. His voice, cracking with the strain, leaps out ahead of him: 'Keep it down, will you? We're supposed to be stealthy here – this is illegal, what we're doing, remember? Christ, you'd think we were on a nature walk or something – *And here's where the woodpecker lives, and here the giant forest fern.*'

A chastened silence, into which the crickets pour all their Orthopteran angst, but it can't hold. One more voice enters the mix, an itch of the larynx emanating from the vacancy to his right. This is Teo, Teo Van Sparks, aka Liverhead. Eight years ago he was standing out on Rodeo Drive, in front of Sterling's Fur Emporium, with a slab of calf's liver sutured to his shaved head. He'd let the liver get ripe – three or four days or so, flies like a crown of thorns, maggots beginning to trail down his nose – and then he'd tear it off his head and lay it at the feet of a silvery old crone in chinchilla or a starlet parading through the door in white fox. Next day he'd be back again, with a fresh slab of meat. Now he's a voice on the E.F.! circuit (*Eco-Agitator,* that's what his card says), thirty-one years old, a weightlifter with the biceps, triceps, lats and abs to prove it, and there isn't anything about the natural world he doesn't know. At least not that he'll admit. 'Sorry, kids,' he says, 'but by most estimates they're down to less than five hundred breeding pairs in the whole range, from B.C. down to the southern Sierra, so I doubt – '

'Fewer,' Andrea corrects, in her pedantic mode. She's in charge here tonight, and she's going to rein them all in, right on down to the finer points of English grammar and usage. If it was just a question of giving out instructions in a methodical, dispassionate voice, that would be one thing – but she's so supercilious, so self-satisfied, cocky, bossy. He's not sure he can take it. Not tonight.

'Fewer, right. So what I'm saying is, more likely it's your screech or flammulated or even your great gray. Of course, we'd have to hear its call to be sure. The spotted's a high-pitched hoot, usually in groups of fours or threes, very fast, crescendoing.'

'Call, why don't you,' Sierra whispers, and the silence of the night is no silence at all but the screaming backdrop to some imminent and catastrophic surprise. 'So you can make it call back. Then we'll know, right?'

Is it his imagination, or can he feel the earth slipping out from under him? He's blind, totally blind, his shoulders hunched in anticipation of the first furtive blow, his breath coming hard, his heart hammering at the walls of its cage. And the others? They're moving down the road in a horizontal line like tourists on a pier, noisy and ambling, heedless. 'And while we're at it,' he says, and he's surprised by his own voice, the vehemence of it, 'I just want to know one thing from you, Andrea – did you remember the diapers? Or is this going to be another in a long line of, of – '

'*At* what?'

'It. The subject of stealth and preparedness.'

He's talking to nothing, to the void in front of him, moving down the invisible road and releasing strings of words like a street gibberer. The owl sounds off again, and then something else, a rattling harsh buzz in the night.

'Of course I remembered the diapers.' The reassuring thump of his wife's big mannish hand patting the cross-stitched nylon of her daypack. 'And the sandwiches and granola bars and sunblock too.

You think I don't know what I'm doing here? Is that what you're implying?'

He's implying nothing, but he's half a beat from getting excruciatingly specific. The honeymoon is over. He's out here risking arrest, humiliation, physical abuse and worse – and for her, all for her, or because of her, anyway – and her tone irritates him. He wants to come back at her, draw some blood, get a good old-fashioned domestic dispute going, but instead he lets the silence speak for him.

'What kind of sandwiches?' Sierra wants to know, a hushed and tremulous little missive inserted in the envelope of her parents' bickering. He can just make out the moving shape of her, black against black, the sloped shoulders, the too-big feet, the burgeoning miracle of tofu-fed flesh, and this is where the panic closes in on him again. What if things turn nasty? What then?

'Something special for you, honey. A surprise, okay?'

'Tomato, avocado and sprouts on honey wheatberry, don't spare the mayo?'

A low whistle from Andrea. 'I'm not saying.'

'Hummus – hummus and tabouleh on pita. Whole-wheat pita.'

'Not saying.'

'Peanut butter – marshmallow? Nusspli?'

A stroll in the park, isn't that what she said? Sure, sure it is. And we're making so much racket we might as well be shooting off fireworks and beating a big bass drum into the bargain. What fun, huh? The family that monkeywrenches together stays together? But what if they ARE listening? What if they got word ahead of time, somebody finked, ratted, spilled the beans, crapped us out? 'Look, really,' he hears himself saying, trying to sound casual but getting nowhere with that, 'you've got to be quiet. I'm begging you – Andrea, come on. Sierra. Teo. Just for my peace of mind, if nothing else – '

Andrea's response is clear and resonant, a definitive nonwhisper. 'They don't have a watchman, I keep telling you that – so get a grip, Ty.' A caesura. The crickets, the muffled tramp of sneakered feet, the faintest soughing of a night breeze in the doomed expanse of branch and bough. 'Tomorrow night they will, though – you can bet on it.'

*　　*　　*

It's ten miles in, and they've given themselves three and a half hours at a good brisk clip, no stops for rest or scholarly dissertations on dendrology or Strigidae calls, their caps pulled down tight, individual water rations riding their backs in bota bags as fat and supple as overfed babies. They're carrying plastic buckets, one apiece, the indestructible kind that come with five gallons of paint at Dunn-Edwards or Colortone. The buckets are empty, light as nothing, but tedious all the same, rubbing against their shins and slapping at the outside of his bad knee just over the indentation where the arthroscope went in, scuffing and squeaking in a fabricated, not-made-for-this-earth kind of way. But there's no talking, not anymore, not once they reach the eight-mile mark, conveniently indicated by a tiny Day-Glo E.F.! sticker affixed to the black wall of a doomed Douglas fir – a tree that took root here five hundred years before Columbus brought the technological monster to a sunny little island in the Caribbean.

But Tierwater wouldn't want to preach. He'd just want to explain what happened that night, how it stuck in him like a barbed hook, like a bullet lodged too close to the bone to remove, and how it was the beginning, the real beginning, of everything to come.

All right.

It's still dark when they arrive, four-fifteen by his watch, and the concrete – all thirty bags of it – is there waiting for them, not ten feet off the road. Andrea is the one who locates it, with the aid of the softly glowing red cap of her flashlight – watchman or no, it would be crazy to go shining lights out here, and the red, she explains, doesn't kill your night vision like the full glare of the white. Silently, they haul the concrete up the road – all of them, even Sierra, though sixty pounds of dead weight is a real load for her. 'Don't be ridiculous, Dad,' she says when he asks if she's okay – or whispers, actually, whispers didactically – 'because if Burmese peasants or coolies or whatever that hardly weigh more than I do can carry hundred-and-twenty-pound sacks of rice from dawn to dusk for something like thirty-two cents a day, then I can lift this.'

He wants to say something to relieve the tension no one but him seems to be feeling, something about the Burmese, but they're as alien to him as the headhunters of the Rajang Valley – don't some of them make thirty-six cents a day, the lucky ones? – and the best he can do is mutter 'Be my guest' into the sleeve of his black sweatshirt. Then he's bending for the next bag, snatching it to his chest and rising out of his crouch like a weightlifter. The odd grunt comes to him out of the dark, and the thin whine of the first appreciative mosquitoes.

In addition to the concrete, there are two shovels and a pickax secreted in the bushes. Without a word, he takes up the pick, and once he gets his hands wrapped round that length of tempered oak, once he begins raising it above his head and slamming it down into the yielding flesh of the road, he feels better. The fact that the concrete and the tools were here in the first place is something to cheer about – they have allies in this, confederates, grunts and foot soldiers – and he lets the knowledge of that soothe him, his shoulders working, breath coming in ragged gasps. The night compresses. The pick lifts and drops. He could be anywhere, digging a petunia bed, a root cellar, a grave, and he's beginning to think he's having an out-of-body experience when Andrea takes hold of his rising arm. 'That's enough, Ty,' she whispers.

Then it's the shovels. He and Teo take turns clearing the loose dirt from the trench and heaving it into the bushes, and before long they have an excavation eighteen inches deep, two feet wide and twelve feet across, a neat black line spanning the narrowest stretch of the road in the roseate glow of Andrea's flashlight. It may not be much of a road by most standards, but still it's been surveyed, dozed, cleared and tamped flat, and it brings the machines to the trees. There's no question about it – the trucks have to be stopped, the line has to be drawn. Here. Right here. *Our local friends have chosen well,* he thinks, leaning on the shovel and gazing up into the night, where two dark fortresses of rock, discernible now only as the absence of stars, crowd in over the road: block it here and there's no way around.

They're tired, all of them. Beat, exhausted, zombified. Though they dozed away the afternoon at the Rest Ye May Motel and fueled themselves with sugar-dipped doughnuts and reheated diner coffee, the hike, the unaccustomed labor and the lateness of the hour are beginning to take their toll. Andrea and Teo are off in the bushes, bickering over something in short, sharp explosions of breath that hit the air like body blows. Sierra, who has an opinion on everything, is uncharacteristically silent, a shadow perched on a rock at the side of the road – she may want to save the world, but not at this hour. He can hardly blame her. He's sapped too, feeling it in his hamstrings, his shoulders, his tender knee, and when he tries to focus on anything other than the stars, random spots and blotches float across his field of vision like paramecia frolicking under the lens of a microscope. But they're not done yet. Now it's the water. And again, their comrades-in-arms have chosen well. Shut your eyes and listen. That's right. That sound he's been hearing isn't the white noise of traffic on a freeway or the hiss of a stylus clogged with lint – it's water, the muted gargle of a stream passing into a conduit not fifty feet up the road. This is what the buckets are for – to carry the water to the trench and moisten the concrete. They're almost home.

But not quite. There seems to be some confusion about the concrete, the proportion of water to mix in, and have any of them – even he, son of a builder and thirty-nine years on this earth – ever actually worked with concrete? Have any of them built a wall, smoothed out a walk, set bricks? Teo once watched a pair of Mexican laborers construct a deck round the family pool, but he was a kid then and it was a long time ago. He thinks they just dumped the bags into a hand-cranked mixer and added water from the hose. Did they need a mixer, was that the problem? Andrea thinks she can recall setting fenceposts with her father on their ranch in Montana, and Tierwater has a vague recollection of watching his own father set charges of dynamite on one of his job sites, stones flung up in the air and bang and bang again, but as far as concrete is concerned, he's drawing a blank. 'I think we just dump the bags in the trench, level it out and add water to the desired consistency,' he concludes with all the authority of a man who flunked chemistry twice.

Andrea is dubious. 'Sounds like a recipe for cake batter.'

Teo: 'What consistency, though? This is quick-set stuff, sure, but if we get it too runny it's never going to set up in two hours, and that's all we've got.'

A sigh of exasperation from Sierra. 'I can't believe you guys – I mean, three adults, and we come all the way out here, with all this planning and all, and nobody knows what they're doing? No wonder my generation is going to wind up inheriting a desert.' He can hear the plaintive, plangent sound of her bony hands executing mosquitoes. 'Plus, I'm tired. Really like monster-tired. I want to go home to bed.'

He's giving it some thought. How hard could it be? The people who do this for a living – laying concrete, that is – could hardly be confused with geniuses. 'What does it say on the package? Are there any directions?'

'Close one eye,' Andrea warns, 'because that way you don't lose all your night vision, just in case, I mean, if anybody – ' and then she flicks on the flashlight. The world suddenly explodes in light, and it's a new world, dun-colored and circumscribed, sacks of concrete like overstuffed brown pillows, the pipestems of their legs, the blackened sneakers. He's inadvertently closed his good eye, the one that sees up close, and he has to go binocular – and risk a perilous moment of night-blindness – to read what it says on the bag.

King Kon-Crete, it reads, over the picture of a cartoon ape in sunglasses strutting around a wheelbarrow, *Premium Concrete. Mix Entire Bag with Water to Desired Consistency. Keep Away from Children.*

'Back to consistency again,' Teo says, shuffling his feet round the bag, and that's all that can be seen of him, his feet – his diminutive feet, feet no bigger than Sierra's – in the cone of light descending from Andrea's hand. Tierwater can picture him, though, squat and muscular, his upper body honed from pumping iron and driving his longboard through the surf, his face delicate, his wrists and ankles tapered like a girl's. He's so small and pumped he could be a special breed, a kind of human terrier, fearless, indefatigable, tenacious, and with a bark like – But enough. They need him here. They need him to say, 'Shit, let's just dump the stuff and get it over with.'

And so they do. They slit the bags and let the dependable force of gravity empty them. They haul the water in a thickening miasma of mosquitoes, swatting, cursing, unceremoniously upending the buckets atop the dry concrete. And then they mix and slice and chivy till the trench is uniformly filled with something like cold lava, and the hour is finally at hand. 'Ready, everybody?' Tierwater whispers. 'Teo on the outside, Andrea next to Teo – and, Sierra, you get in between me and Andrea, okay?'

'Aren't you forgetting something?' This is Andrea, exhausted, but reclaiming the initiative.

He looks round him in the dark, a wasted gesture. 'No, what?'

A slight lilt to the tone, an edge of satisfaction. She's done her homework, she's seen the movie, memorized the poem, got in touch with her inner self. She has the information, and he doesn't. 'The essential final step, the issue you've been avoiding all week except when you accused me of forgetting it – *them*, I mean?'

Then it hits him. 'The diapers?'

Eighteen per package, at $16.99. They've had to invest in three different sizes – small, medium and large, for Sierra, Andrea and Teo, and himself, respectively – though Andrea assures him they'll use them up during the next direct action, whenever and wherever that may be. Either that, or give them away to volunteers. They're called, comfortingly enough, Depends, and on her advice they've chosen the Fitted Briefs for Extra Absorbency. He can't help thinking about that for just the smallest slice of a moment – *Extra Absorbency* – and about what it is the diapers are meant to absorb.

There's a moment of silence there in the dark, the naked woods crepitating round them, the alertest of the birds already calling out for dawn, when they're all communally involved in a very private act. The sound of zippers, the hopping on one foot, arms jerked out for balance, and then they're diapered and the jeans rise back up their legs to grab at their bellies and buttocks. He hasn't worn diapers – or pads, as the professionals euphemistically call them so as not to offend the Alzheimer's patients and other walking disasters who have to be swathed in them day and night – since he was an infant, and he doesn't remember much of that. He remembers Sierra, though, mewling and gurgling, kicking her shit-besmeared legs in the air, as he bent to the task on those rare occasions when Jane, the perfect mother, was either absent or unconscious. They feel – not so bad, not yet anyway. Like underwear, like briefs, only thicker.

And now, finally, the time has come to compete the ritual and settle down to slap mosquitoes, slumber fitfully and await the first astonished Freddies (Forest Service types) and heavy-machine operators. They join hands for balance, sink their cheap tennis sneakers into the wet concrete as deep as they'll go and then ease themselves down on the tapered bottoms of their upended buckets. He will be miserable. His head will droop, his back will scream. He will bait mosquitoes and crap in his pants. But it's nothing. The smallest thing, the sacrifice of one night in bed with a book or narcotized in front of the tube – that, and a few hours of physical discomfort. And as he settles in, the concrete gripping his ankles like a dark set of jaws, the stars receding into the skullcap of the silvering sky and every bird alive in every tree, he tells himself, *Somebody's got to do it.*

He must have dozed. He did doze – or sleep, would be more accurate. He slumped over his knees, put his head to rest and drifted into unconsciousness, because there was no sense in doing anything else, no matter his dreads and fears – nothing was going to happen till seven-thirty or eight at the earliest, and he put all that out of his mind and orchestrated his dreams to revolve around a man in bed, a man like him, thin as grass but big across the shoulders, with no gut or rear end to speak of and the first tentative fingers of hair loss massaging his skull, a man in an air-conditioned room in blissful deep non-REM sleep with something like Respighi's 'The Birds' playing softly in the background.

And what does he wake to? Is it the coughing wheeze of a poorly tuned pickup beating along the road, the single mocking laugh of a raven, the low-threshold tocsin of his daughter's voice, soft and supple and caught deep in her throat, saying, 'Uh . . . Dad. Dad, wake up?' Whatever it is, it jerks him up off the narrow stool of the bucket in one explosive motion, like a diver surging up out of the deepest pool, and he tries to lift his feet, to leap, to run, to escape the hammering in his chest. But his feet are locked in place. And his body, his upper body, is suddenly floundering forward without support, even as the image of the burnt-orange pickup with its grinning bumper and the swept-back mask of the glassed-in cab comes hurtling down the road toward him, toward *them* . . . but the knee joint isn't designed to give in that direction, and even in the moment of crisis – *Jesus Christ, the shithead's going to hit us!* – he lurches back and sits heavily and ignominiously on the bucket that even now is squirting out from under him. 'Stop,' he roars, 'stop!,' against a background of shrieks and protests, and somehow he's on his feet again and reaching out to his left, for his daughter, to pull her to him and cradle her against the moment of impact . . . which, mercifully, never comes.

He wouldn't want to talk about the diapers, not in this context. He'd want to address the issue of the three intensely bearded, red-suspendered timber people wedged into the cab of that pickup, that scorching-orange Toyota 4x4 that comes to rest in a demon-driven cloud of dust no more than ten feet from them. And the looks on their faces – their seven-thirty-in-the-*a.m.* faces, Egg McMuffins still warm in their bellies, searing coffee sloshed in their laps, the bills of their caps askew and their eyes crawling across their faces like slugs. This is the look of pure, otherworldly astonishment. *(Don't blame these men – or not yet, anyway. They didn't expect us to be there – they didn't expect anything, other than maybe a tardy coyote or a suicidal ground squirrel – and suddenly there we were, like some manifestation of the divine, like the lame made to walk and the blind to see.)*

'Oh, God,' Andrea murmurs, and it's as if the air has been squeezed out of her lungs, and they're all standing now, erect and trembling and holding hands for lack of anything better to do. Tierwater cuts a swift glance from the stalled pickup to the face of his daughter. It's a tiny little dollop of a face, shrunken and drawn in on itself, the face of the little girl awake with the terror of the night and the scratchy voice and the need for reason and comprehension and the whispered assurance that the world into which she's awakened is the ancient one, the imperturbable one, the one that will go on twisting round its axis whether we're here to spin it or not. That face paralyzes him. What are they thinking? What are they doing?

'Christ *Jes*us, what is goin' on here?' comes the voice of the pickup, the unanimous voice, concentrated in the form of the pony-tailed and ginger-bearded head poking through the open window of the wide-swinging driver's-side door. 'You people lost or what?' A moment later, the rest of the speaker emerges, workboots, rolled-up jeans, a flannel shirt in some bleached-out shade of tartan plaid. His face is like an electric skillet. Like a fuse in the moment of burning out. 'What in Christ's name is wrong with you? I almost – you know, I could of – ' He's trembling too, his hands so shaky he has to bury them in his pockets.

Tierwater has to remind himself that this man – thirty-five, flat dead alcoholic eyes, the annealed imprint of a scar like a brand stamped into the flange of his nose – is not the enemy. He's just earning his paycheck, felling and loading and producing so many board feet a year so middle-class Americans can exercise their God-given right to panel their family rooms and cobble together redwood picnic tables from incomprehensible sets of plans. He's never heard of Arne Naess or Deep Ecology or the mycorrhizal fungi that cling to the roots of old growth trees and make the forest possible. Rush Limbaugh wrote his bible, and the exegesis of it too. He has a T-shirt in a drawer at home that depicts a spotted owl in a frying pan. He knows incontrovertibly and with a kind of unconquerable serenity that all members of the Sierra Club are 'Green Niggers' and that Earth Forever! is a front for Bolshevik terrorists with homosexual tendencies. But he's not the enemy. His bosses are.

'We're not letting you through,' Teo announces, and there he is, a plug of muscle hammered into the ground, anchoring the far end of the human chain. All he needs is a slab of liver.

The other two have squeezed out of the truck by now, work-hardened men, incongruously bellied, looks of utter stupefaction on their faces. They just stare.

'What are you,' the first man wants to know, the driver, the one in faded tartan, 'environmentalists or something?' He's seen house-wives, ministers, schoolchildren, drug addicts, drunks, ex-cons, jockeys, ballplayers, maybe even sexual deviates, but you can tell by the faltering interrogatory lift of the question that he's never in his life been face to face with the devil before.

'That's right,' Tierwater says, radicalized already, gone from suburban drudge to outside agitator in eight months' time, 'and you ought to be one too, if you want to keep your job beyond next year or even next month.' He glances up at the palisade of the trees, needles stitched together like a quilt, the sun stalking

34

through crowns and snags in its slow progress across the sky, and then he's confronting those blunted eyes again. And this is the strange part: he's not in bed dreaming, but actually standing in the middle of a concrete trench in a road in the middle of nowhere, wearing diapers and giving a speech — at seven-thirty in the morning, no less.

'What are you going to cut when all the trees are gone? You think your bosses care about that? You think the junk-bond kings and the rest of the suits in New York give the slightest damn about you or your children or the mills or the trees or anything else?'

'Or retirement,' Teo puts in. 'What about retirement? Huh? I can't hear you. Talk to me. Talk to me, man, come on: *talk to me.*'

He isn't one for debate, this man, or consorting with environmentalists either. For a long moment he just stands there staring at them – at Tierwater, at Sierra, Andrea, Teo, at their linked hands and the alien strip of concrete holding them fast at the ankles. 'Piss on you,' he says finally, and in a concerted move he and his companions roll back into the pickup and the engine fires up with a roar. A screech of tires and fanbelt, and then he's reversing gears, jerking round and charging back down the road in the direction he came from. They're left with dust. With the mosquitoes. And the sun, which has just begun to slash through the trees and make its first radiant impression on their faces and hands and the flat black cotton and polyester that clothe them.

'I'm hungry. I'm tired. I want to go home.'

His daughter is propped up on her bucket, limp as an invertebrate, and she's trying to be brave, trying to be an adult, trying to prove she's as capable of manning the barricades as anybody, but it isn't working. The sun is already hot, though it's just past ten by Tierwater's watch, and they've long since shed their sweatshirts. They've kept the caps on, for protection against the sun, and they've referred to their water bags and consumed the sandwiches Andrea so providentially brought along, and what they're doing now is waiting. Waiting for the confrontation, the climax, the reporters and TV cameras, the sheriff and his deputies. Tierwater can picture the jail cell, cool shadows playing off the walls, the sound of a flushing toilet, a cot to stretch out on. They'll have just long enough to close their eyes, no fears, no problems, events leaping on ahead of them – bailed out before the afternoon is over, the E.F.! lawyers on alert, everything in place. Everything but the sheriff, that is. What could be keeping him?

'How much longer, Andrea? Really. Because I want to know, and don't try to patronize me either.'

He wants to say, *It's all right, baby, it'll be over soon,* but he's not much good at comforting people, even his own daughter – Bear up, that's his philosophy. Tough it out. Think of the Mohawk, whose captives had to laugh in the face of the knife, applaud their own systematic dismemberment, cry out in mirth as their skin came away in bloody tapering strips. He leaves it to Andrea, who coos encouragement in a voice that's like a salve. Numbed, he watches her reach out to exchange Sierra's vampire novel (which, under the circumstances, hasn't proved lurid enough) for a book of crossword puzzles.

Teo, at the opposite end of the line, is a model of stoicism. Hunched over the upended bucket like a man perched on the throne in the privacy of his own bathroom, his eyes roaming the trees for a glimpse of wildlife instead of scanning headlines in the paper, he's utterly at home, unperturbed, perfectly willing to accept the role of martyr, if that's what comes to him. Tierwater isn't in his league, and he'd be the first to admit it. His feet itch, for one thing – a compelling, imperative itch that brings tears to his eyes – and the concrete, still imperceptibly hardening, has begun to chew at his ankles beneath the armor of his double socks and stiffened jeans. He has a full-blown headache too, the kind that starts behind the eyes and works its way through the cortex to the occipital lobe and back again in pulses as rhythmic and regular as waves beating against the shore. He has to urinate. Even worse, he can feel a bowel movement coming on.

Another hour oozes by. He's been trying to read – Bill McKibben's *The End of Nature* – but his eyes are burning and the relentless march of dispirited rhetoric makes him suicidal. Or maybe homicidal. It's hot. Very hot. Unseasonably hot. And though they're all backpackers, all four of them, exposed regularly to the sun, this is something else altogether, this is like some kind of torture – like the sweat box in *The Bridge on the River Kwai* – and when he lifts the bota bag to his lips for the hundredth time, Andrea reminds him to conserve water. 'The way it's looking,' she says, and here is the voice of experience, delivered with a certain grim satisfaction, 'we could be here a long time yet.'

And then, far off in the distance, a sound so attenuated they can't be sure they've heard it. It's the sound of an internal-combustion engine, a diesel, blat-blatting in the interstices between dips in the road. The noise grows louder, they can see the poisoned billows of black exhaust, and all at once a bulldozer heaves into view, scuffed yellow paint, treads like millwheels, a bulbous face of determination and outrage at the controls. The driver lumbers straight for them, as if he's blind, the shovel lowered to reap the standing crop of them, to shear them off at the ankles like a row of dried-out cornstalks. Tierwater is on his feet suddenly, on his feet again, reaching out instinctively for his daughter's hand, and 'Dad,' she's saying, 'does he know? Does he know we can't move?'

It's the pickup truck all over again, only worse: the four of them shouting till the veins stand out in their necks, Andrea and Teo waving their arms over their heads, the sweat of fear and mortal tension prickling at their scalps and private places, and that's exactly what the man on the Cat wants. He knows perfectly well what's going on here – they all do by now, from the supervisors down to the surveying crews – and his object is intimidation, pure and simple. All those gleaming, pumping tons of steel in motion, the big tractor treads burning up the road and the noise of the thing, still coming at them at full-speed, and Tierwater can't see the eyes of the lunatic at the controls – *shades, he's wearing mirror shades that give him an evil insectoid look, no mercy, no appeal* – and suddenly he's outraged, ready to kill: this is one sick game. At the last conceivable moment, a raw-knuckled hand jerks back a lever and the thing rears like a horse and swivels away from them with a kind of mechanized grace he wouldn't have believed possible.

But that's only the first pass, and it carries the bulldozer into the wall of rock beside them with a concussive blast, sparks spewing from the blade, the shriek of one unyielding surface meeting another, and Tierwater can feel the crush of it in his feet, even as the shards of stone and dirt rain down on him. He's no stranger to violence. His father purveyed it, his mother suffered it, his first wife died of it – the most casual violence in the world, in a place as wild as this. He's new at pacifism or masochism or whatever you'd want to call what they're suffering here, and if he could free his legs for just half a minute, he'd drag that tight-jawed executioner down off his perch and instruct him in the laws of the flesh, he would. But he can't do a thing. He's caught. Stuck fast in the glue of passive resistance, Saint Mahatma and Rosa Parks and James Meredith flashing through his mind in quick review. And he's swearing to himself, *Never again, never,* even as the man with the stick and eight tons of screaming iron and steel swings round for the second pass, and then the third and the fourth.

But that's enough. That's enough right there. Tyrone Tierwater wouldn't want to remember what that did to his daughter or the look on her face or the sad sick feeling of his own impotence. The sheriff came, with two deputies, and he took his own sweet time about it. And what did he do when he finally did get there? Did he arrest the man on the Cat? Close down the whole operation and let the courts decide if it's legal to bulldoze a dead zone through a federally designated roadless area? No. He handcuffed the four of them – even Sierra – and his deputies had a good laugh ripping the watchcaps off their heads, wadding them up and flinging them into the creek, and they caught a glimpse of the curtains parting on redneck heaven when they cut the straps of the bota bags and flung them after the hats. And then, for good measure, smirking all the while, these same deputies got a nice little frisson out of kicking the buckets out from under Tierwater and his wife and daughter and good friend, one at a time, and then settling in to watch them wait three interminable hours in the sun for the men with the sledgehammers.

Andrea cursed the deputies, and they cursed her back. Teo glared from the cave of his muscles. Tierwater was beside himself. He raged and bellowed and threatened them with everything from aggravated assault to monetary damages and prosecution for police brutality – at least until the sheriff, Sheriff Bob Hicks of Josephine County, produced a roll of duct tape and shut his mouth for him. And his daughter, his tough, right-thinking, long-haired, tree-hugging, animal-loving, vegetarian daughter – she folded herself up like an umbrella over the prison of her feet and cried. Thirteen years old, tired, scared, and she just let herself go. *(They shuffled their workboots and looked shamefaced then, those standard-issue badge-polishers and the Forest Service officials who drove up in a green jeep to join them — they probably had daughters themselves, and sons and dogs and rabbits in a hutch — but there was nothing any of them could do about my little girl's grief. Least of all me.)*

Grateful for a day's reprieve, the Pacific salamanders curled up under the cover of their rocks, the martens retreated into the leaves and the spotted owls winked open an eye at the sound of that thin disconsolate wail of human distress. Tierwater's hands were bound, his mouth taped. Every snuffle, every choked-back sob, was a spike driven into the back of his head.

Yes. And here's the irony, the kicker, the sad, deflating and piss-poor denouement. For all they went through that morning, for all the pain and boredom and humiliation, there wasn't a single reporter on hand to bear witness, because Sheriff Bob Hicks had blocked the road at the highway and wouldn't let anyone in — and so it was a joke, a big joke, the whole thing. He can remember sitting there frying like somebody's meal with a face, no ozone layer left to protect them from the sun, no water, no hat and no shade and all the trees of the world under the ax, while he worked out the conundrum in his head: if a protest falls in the woods and there's no one there to hear it, does it make a sound?

Santa Ynez, November 2025

IT'S STILL RAINING when we wake up – or when
I wake up, anyway. I'm awake before her, long before her,
and why wouldn't I be? I'm feeling historical here. Eggs and
bacon, that's how I'm feeling, but you don't see much of those
commodities any more (eggs maybe, but you can forget bacon)
and there's her purse on the table, big as the head of an elephant
and stuffed with used Kleenex, debit slips, gum wrappers, key-
chains full of keys to doors in houses that no longer exist. I'm an
archaeologist, that's what I am, prising one potsherd after another
out of the dung heap of my life. Andrea sleeps late. I knew that.
I've lived with that. But for twenty-odd years until now, it didn't
operate, not in my sphere. We've had, let's say, an interesting
night, highly stimulating, drenched in nostalgia and heartbreak, a
night that was finally, if briefly, sexual, and I've got no complaints
on that score. I think I'm actually whistling as I dodge round the
splootching cans and buckets in the living room/kitchen, pre-
paratory to fixing something nice for her to eat when she gets
around to it.

How am I feeling? Moist. Moist in the tear ducts and gonads,
swelled up like a lungfish that's been buried in the sand through a
long desiccated summer till the day the sky breaks apart and the
world goes wet again. The smell of coffee is taking me back – I
don't drink it myself anymore, too expensive and it raises hell
with my stomach – and I feel myself slipping so far into the past
I'm in danger of disappearing without making a ripple. She's
snoring. I can hear it – no delicate insuck and outhale, but a real
venting of the airways, a noise as true in its way as anything Lily
could work up. The rain slaps its broad hand on the roof,
something that wasn't tied down by somebody somewhere hits

the wall just above the window, the world shudders, Andrea sleeps. It's a moment.

Unfortunately, our idyll doesn't last much longer than that moment, because, before I can think whether to serve her the tuna salad I've been storing in the food compressor the past three years for a special occasion or just to go ahead and open up that last can of crab because life doesn't last forever, especially if you're a crab, Chuy is at the door. He's agitated. Dancing on his feet, working his jaws and lips and tongue and generally trying, without success, to communicate something to me. He's hatless and slickerless, the hair glued to his scalp, his eyes so naked you can almost see through them to his Dursban-dusted brain. How old is he? He doesn't know – doesn't even remember what town he was born in, though the country, he's pretty sure – almost 'a hunerd and ten percent, or maybe a hunerd and twenty' – was Guatemala. I'm not as good at judging people's ages as I once was, because everybody looks young to me except the old-old, but I'd figure him for forty, forty-five. Anyway, he's on my doorstep, and this is what he says, more or less: 'Some people . . . some people, Mr. Ty – '

'What people?' I'm standing there at the open door, the sky like an inverted fishbowl, big propellers of wind chasing sticks, papers, leaves across the swamp of the yard, the immemorial coffee smell behind me, the heater, the bed, Andrea. Chuy might as well be standing under Niagara Falls. My slippers are wet. The fringe of my bathrobe. Everything is wet, always – molding and wet – books falling apart on the shelves, slugs climbing out of the teapot, the very chairs turning green under our hind ends and sprouting again. Exasperated, I take Chuy by the collar and drag him into the room. I'm not a patient man.

'The, the people – ' A gesture, mostly spastic, in the direction of the condos.

'The people at Lupine Hill?'

'*Ellos, sí,* the ones *sobre* the hill, they, they – they *encuentran* Petunia. In the laundry.'

Petunia is the Patagonian fox. She stands two and a half feet tall at the shoulder, thin red ribbons for legs, a black shag of bristling hair laid over her back like a rug. The laundry rooms, as I understand these things, are communal to every ten units at

Lupine Hill. As for the Spanish, this is the language Chuy reverts to when the pesticide clogs up the pathways scored in his brain by the contortions of English.

'She have, what do you call, some catch in her mouth. Maybe *un gato*. And maybe they shut the door. So we, we – '

'We need to get over there ASAP.'

Streaming, grinning, flicking the hair out of his eyes: 'Yes, Ess-A-Pee.'

That's the moment Andrea chooses to emerge from the back room, hair in her face, eyes vacant, legs bare to the follicles – and good legs, because legs are the last thing to go in a beautiful woman, hardly any cellulite and no varicosities to speak of. She's wearing one of my shirts, I notice (black silk, fanciest thing I own, a gift from Mac, of course, because Tyrone Tierwater the animal man is strictly no frills), and there's nothing underneath that but what she was born with. Or evolved into. I follow Chuy's eyes to the black shirt and the place in front, down low, where she hasn't bothered with the bottom two buttons. I can see her private hair, and it's white, white as a winter ptarmigan (now extinct), and then we're both staring at the glossy dyed black marvel of her head. I have to admit it: I'm embarrassed. And before I can think, I'm crossing the room and moving into her, fastening the buttons like a doting husband. Or maybe a lovesick dog – one with bad breath and the mange and a habit of getting whipped and liking it. 'Andrea,' I say, 'Chuy. Chuy, Andrea.'

Chuy is giving her a watery stare of amazement, as if she's materialized out of one of the animal pens, and he's looking hard at me too, re-evaluating everything we've said and done together over the past decade in an entirely new light – the revivifying beers, meat cooked out in the open, animals dying on us in a welter of shit and blood, the bites, bruises and festering claw-wounds and the breakneck trips to the emergency room, Lori and her melting smile and love of high-end *sake,* the rare '95 Qupé Chardonnay out of Mac's cellars the three of us would share on special occasions, Mac – Mac himself – all of it. And Andrea – she just gives him a bright-eyed look and says, 'You staying for breakfast?'

I can see Chuy wrestling with the response to that one, and I'm right on the verge of answering for him, my George to his Lennie, when there comes a fearsome thumping at the door. Who is it? Delbert Sakapathian, of #1002B, Avenida Lupine Hill, Santa Ynez, California. He's a big man with a cueball head, younger than the young-old, sixty maybe, and with the kind of gut you used to see a lot more of around the turn of the century, when junk food was a staple. Now people crave meat and fish and broccoli, sweet potatoes, chard, wheat germ, the things they can't get the way they used to, and forget the Ho-Ho's and Pop Tarts and Doritos Extra-Spicy Meat-Flavored Tortilla Chips – that crap they can't give away. 'You him?' Delbert Sakapathian says, poking a finger the size of a souvenir bat in my face.

I don't have time for this sort of thing, I really don't, but if it'll get me Petunia back, I guess I'll see if my secretarial staff can cancel one of my morning appointments and work Mr. Sakapathian in. I nod. 'I'm him,' I say.

The doorframe isn't big enough to contain him, besides which the rain isn't doing much for my carpet, not to mention the reddish muck melting off his gum boots and the steady divestiture of water from his slicker (and there's another business to invest in – Slickers, Inc., or maybe Slickers 'R' Us). 'Well, goddamnit,' he spits. 'Goddamnit to hell.'

And then a voice zeroes in over my shoulder, as accurate as a smart bomb. 'Lighten up,' Andrea says, and I know that tone, though it hasn't been directed at me, not this time around, not yet anyway. 'And shut the door, clod – you're ruining the carpet.'

The big streaming cueball ducks, chin to chest, and then Delbert Sakapathian is in the room, the door thundering shut behind him. He's chastened, but not for long. 'You got to get that thing, whatever it is, out of there, because it's got my, my' – and here a wave of emotion peaks in his eyes and I think he's going to break down – 'Pitty-Sing, my cat, and I think, I mean, by Christ you better, because, if anything happens to her, I'll, I'll – '

And then we're fighting the wind, all four of us, slickered and booted and hatted like tars rounding the Horn on a clipper ship, except that this is dry land – or should be, or used to be – and I've got the shock-stick in one hand and Andrea's big warm mitt clenched in the other, Chuy leading the way with the wire net and

Delbert Sakapathian bringing up the rear with an asthmatic wheeze. I'm hopeful. Not so much for the cat – let's face it, if Petunia got hold of it more than thirty seconds ago, it's history – but for my fox and Patagonia and the barren pampas Mac and I are going to repopulate one day in the not-too-distant future. (By the way, I'm not the one responsible for the asinine names of the animals around here – give them a little dignity, that's what I say. No, it's Mac. He thought it would be nice – 'utterly and fantastically groovy' – if they all had the names of flowers. One of the lions, to my everlasting embarrassment, is called Dandelion.)

When we get there – up the hill, through the claws of the blasted trees and the crazy growth of invasives and into the perpetually flooded basement of Building B, or 'Sunshine House,' as the plaque out front identifies it – we find a group of condo-dwellers gathered expectantly outside a rotting plywood door marked *laundry* in fading green letters. There are a couple of kids there, their faces so small and featureless they might have been painted right on the skin, and women in bare feet, braving ankle-deep water the color of graveyard seepage. No one says a word. But they all step back when I slosh past them and brandish the shock-stick. 'Unkink that net, Chuy,' I say, about 90 percent certain I'm going to get bitten at least once, but hopefully not to the bone, and Andrea – my Andrea, newly restored to me and conjugal as all hell – whispers, 'Be careful, Ty.'

Of course, this is a fox we're talking about here. Not a normal fox, maybe – a fox the size of a wolf – but a fox for all that. It's not as if one of the lions got loose. Or Lily, who could crush your spine and rip out your intestines with a single bite. Still, here we are, and you never can tell what's going to happen. 'Petunia,' I croon in my sweetest and-here's-a-chicken-back-for-you-too voice, gently pushing the door open with the stick, and then I'm in the room, washers, dryers, a couple of sinks, and somebody's socks and brassieres tumbled out of a straw basket to the (very wet) floor.

Nothing. A drip of water, cheap fluorescents flickering, the inescapable hiss of the storm outside. And then, from behind the sink to my right, the sound of a chainsaw if a chainsaw had a tongue, a palate and a set of lips to muffle it: *RRRRRrrrrrrrrrrr!*

Chuy, I should say, is a master of stating the obvious, and he gives me a demonstration of his uncanny talent at this very crucial moment. '*Yo pienso que* he's up under the sink, Mr. Ty, is what I am thinking, *verdad?*'

Verdad. A pair of flaming eyes, the red paws, the scrabble of claws digging into the buckling linoleum, and why is the theme to *Born Free* running through my head like mental diarrhea? Sure enough, she's got the limp white carcass of a Siamese cat (lilac-point) clenched in her jaws, and that's good, I'm thinking, because she can't chew and bite at the same time, can she? 'Okay, Chuy,' I hear myself say, and though my knee doesn't like it or my back either, I'm down there poking the stick in the thing's face, afraid to use the electric shock for fear of electro-cuting her and maybe myself into the bargain. No fear. All I have to do is touch her and she launches herself out from under the sink like a cruise missile to perforate my forearm with her canines and the dainty cutting teeth in front of them, me on my posterior in the water, the corpse of the cat floating free, Chuy fumbling with the net and Andrea wading in to grab hold of Petunia by the ears. Which she does. And this is a good move, from my point of view. An excellent move. Because Petunia, cornered, lets go of my arm for just the quarter of a second it takes Chuy to wrap the wire net round the most dangerous part of her, and after that, it's all she wrote.

'Ty,' Andrea says.

'Andrea,' Ty says.

And then we're on the way to the emergency room, where they've got a stretcher and an IV unit named in honor of me, snuggling, actually snuggling (though Andrea's got her right hand clamped round the pressure point in front of my elbow and Chuy is jerking at the wheel like a Dursban-addled stock-car driver), and for the life of me I just can't seem to recall the name of that woman who talks to the trees. She'll be here tomorrow, though. 'I invited her for tomorrow,' is the way Andrea puts it, Chuy slithering all over the road as if the car were a big Siamese walking catfish, traffic stalled all the way to Monterey and here we go up on the shoulder – look out, we're coming through. 'What do you mean, "tomorrow"?' I say, and she tightens her grip on the artery running up my arm.

She says – and the wind is raging, the Olfputt pitching, the blood flowing free – 'I mean the day after today. Honey.'

Mexico City, São Paulo, Shanghai, Buenos Aires, Seoul, Tokyo, Dhaka, Cairo, Calcutta, Reykjavík, Caracas, Lagos, Guadalajara, Greater Nome, Sakhalinsky, Nanking, Helsinki – all bigger than New York now. Forty-six million in Mexico City. Forty in São Paulo. New York doesn't even rank in the top twenty. And how does that make me feel? Old. As if I've outlived my time – and everybody else's. Because the correction is under way – has been under way for some time now. Let's eat each other, that's what I propose – my arm tonight and yours tomorrow – because there's precious little of anything else left. Ecology. What a joke.

I'm not preaching. I'm not going to preach. It's too late for that, and besides which, preaching never did anybody any good any-way. Let me say this, though, for the record – for the better part of my life I was a criminal. Just like you. I lived in the suburbs in a three-thousand-square-foot house with redwood siding and oak floors and an oil burner the size of Texas, drove a classic 1966 Mustang for sport and a Jeep Laredo (red, black leather interior) to take me up to the Adirondacks so I could heft my three-hundred-twenty-dollar Eddie Bauer backpack and commune with the squirrels, muskrats and fishers. I went to the gym. Drank in fern bars. Bought shoes, jackets, sweaters and hair-care products. I guess I was dimly aware – way out there on the periphery of my consciousness – of what I was doing to the poor abused corpus of old mother earth, and I did recycle (when I got around to it, which was maybe twice a year), and I thought a lot about packaging. I wore a sweater in the house in winter to conserve energy and turn the flame down on global warming, and still I burned fuel and more fuel, and the trash I generated plugged its own hole in the landfill like a permanent filling in a rotten tooth.

Worse, I accumulated things. They seemed to stick to me, like filings to a magnet, a whole polarized fur of objects radiating from my fingertips in slavish attraction. Paper clips, pins, plastic bags, ancient amplifiers, rusted-out cooking grills. Clothes, books, records, CDs. Cookware, Ginzu knives, food processors, popcorn poppers, coffeemakers, my dead father's overcoats and my dead mother's shoes. I kept a second Mustang, graffitied with rust, out behind the garage, on blocks. There were chairs in the attic that hadn't been warmed by a pair of buttocks in fifty years, trunks of neatly folded shorts and polo shirts I hadn't worn since I was five.

I drove fast, always in a hurry, and stuffed the glove box so full of tickets it looked like a napkin dispenser in a restaurant. I dated (women, whole thundering herds of them, looking – in vain – for another Jane). I parented. Cooked. Cleaned. Managed my dead father's crumbling empire – you've heard of him, Sy Tierwater, developer of tract homes in Westchester and Dutchess Counties? – and paid bills and collected rents and squeezed down the window of my car to add my share of Kleenex, ice-cream sticks and cigarette wrappers to the debris along the streaming sides of the blacktop roads.

Want more? I drank wine, spent money, spoiled my daughter and watched her accumulate things in her turn. And just like you – if you live in the Western world, and I have to assume you do, or how else would you be reading this? – I caused approximately two hundred fifty times the damage to the environment of this tattered, bleeding planet as a Bangladeshi or Balinese, and they do their share, believe me. Or did. But I don't want to get into that.

Let's just say I saw the light – with the help of a good nudge from Andrea, Teo (may he rot in hell or interplanetary space or wherever) and all the other hard chargers down at Earth Forever! Forces were put in motion, gears began to grind. I sold the house, the cars, the decrepit shopping center my father left me, my wind surfer and Adirondack chair and my complete set of bootleg Dylan tapes, all the detritus left behind by the slow-rolling glacier of my old life, my criminal life, the life I led before I became a friend of the earth. Friendship. That's what got me into the movement and that's what pushed me way out there on the naked edge of nothing, beyond sense or reason, or even hope. Friendship for the earth. For the trees and shrubs and the native grasses and the antelope on the plain and the kangaroo rats in the desert and everything else that lives and breathes under the sun.

Except people, that is. Because to be a friend of the earth, you have to be an enemy of the people.

*　　*　　*

I've got no health care, of course – nobody does, the whole system long since gone bankrupt, and don't bother to ask about Social Security – but they're happy to see a paying customer hustling through the emergency-room doors. Whatever it takes – and in this case it won't be much – they know Mac is good for it. Maclovio Pulchris. It's a magical name, better than cash, because you can only carry so much of that – Mac's my Medicare and Social Security, all wrapped up in one. And now I've got Andrea too, a woman who breeds emergencies, one night of love and here we are. She's lending me support – literally – as we crabwalk through the doors, Chuy somewhere behind us, hurtling up the ramp of the parking structure as if he's trying to launch the 4x4 out of the atmosphere. 'What's the problem?' the attendant wants to know, a monster of a man who looks vaguely familiar (Swenson's? last night?), his nose, lips, scalp and forearms a patchwork of skin cancers past and present. 'It's nothing, moron,' Andrea says, and there's that snarl again – 'he's just bleeding to death, that's all.'

Then it's the ordeal of the forms – there must be twenty, twenty-five pages of them. Andrea squeezes up close beside me, her big thumb still locked in place over the wound, the woman behind the desk yawning, the intercom hissing, somebody strolling off to find a ligature of some sort and wake one of the doctors out of his trance. All the windows are boarded up because they got tired of replacing them every third or fourth day, and the quality of the light is what you might expect from a high-end mausoleum. Depressing. Depressing in the extreme. Just to lighten things up, I make a joke about how it's a good thing Petunia got my left arm or I'd be up shit creek as far as checking off the relevant box is concerned. Nobody laughs. And even here, deep in the recesses of the bleach-rubbed and almost spanking-clean corridors, with six floors of steel and concrete and body fluids above us, I can hear the rain. *Sssssss, it hisses, background music to every mortal drama, sssssss.*

What does it take? Thirty-two stitches and half a mile of gauze, no big deal and no offense, I tell the doctor, but I've been hurt worse. A whole lot worse. I give Andrea a meaningful glance, but her mind is off someplace else. With each stitch, that little burn and the bigger hurt to follow, I study her, first in profile and then from the rear as she moves across the room to gaze out the window that isn't a window at all but the naked whorled face of some sort of artificial plywood with predrilled holes for easy application (and *there's* another business). I still can't get used to her. How can that old lady's face belong to those shoulders and legs? That's what I'm thinking as the doctor – an infant of twenty-and-something who probably doesn't even shave yet – sticks his needle in me, and more: If you want to start gauging degrees of pain, what does it mean that she's finally come back?

April Wind is sunk deep in the dog-stinking couch I inherited with this place ten years ago. I don't own dogs. Never have. When you've got hyenas, Patagonian foxes and spectacled bears, what do you need dogs for? The fact is, one of Mac's roadies died here – right here, on the floor under the window, where you can still see the stains if you look closely enough – after an unfortunate and wholly preventable accident involving a noose, a plastic bag, two women and three twenty-four-ounce squeeze bottles of ketchup; his effects, as they say, came down to me. Or is it *on* me? Anyway, there she is, and forget the thrill in my arm, the stoked fires raging away in my lower back (expertly jammed against the open door of one of the dryers when Petunia went for me) or the fact that I've had a satisfactory and highly reminiscent sexual experience for the second night in a row – I'm a stranger in my own house, and my house is getting crowded.

Yesterday I was whistling, today I'm in no mood. Breakfast (oatmeal with bran and brewer's yeast spooned in for ballast, the crab already sacrificed for love), is barely settled, I haven't seen the paper or suffered over the toilet yet, and this wind from the past blows in. A wind with a face. All I can think of is a Peter Max poster, with Helios in one corner, Aeolus in the other, battling over the weather. Back then, of course, the sun always won out.

'You remember April, Ty,' Andrea says, and she's not making a question of it. I watch her as she pulls one of the mold-spattered kitchen chairs across the room and perches girlishly on the edge of it, her bare feet splayed over the rungs. The way she does it, the way she maneuvers the chair and settles herself – and more, the tone of her voice, the smell of her – plumbs some deep inversion layer in the unstirred lake of my memory. But that's what this is all about, isn't it? Memory? *In Memoriam, Sierra Tierwater, 1976–2001. Requiescat in Pace.* Fat chance.

'I said, you remember April, don't you, Ty?'

Ah: and now it's a question. I can stall. I can put on my old-man-with-a-postnasal-drip-and-a-glued-up-brain act, but what will it get me – a sixty-second reprieve? Andrea's tough. She wants something here – I'm not exactly sure what it is yet, but I know she'll get it. Besides which, I'm not really that old, not in the way my grandparents were – or Andrea's decrepit father and foot-shuffling old withered wreck of a mother, who for the final two years of her life thought Andrea was the cleaning lady's cat – because my generation never let go of its (pharmaceutically and surgically assisted) youth, till death do us part. April Wind knows that. And Andrea especially knows it. Of course, I could duck into the bedroom, bad back and chewed-up arm notwithstanding, dig out the .470 Nitro Express elephant gun I stole from Philip Ratchiss a thousand years ago and make the two of them into hyena food, but, despite reports to the contrary, I've never been a violent man. Or not especially. Or excessively. 'Yeah,' I mumble, 'sure.'

A bright look comes into the eyes of the woman who talks to trees, the kind of look you see in a serval when it detects movement in the high grass. She must be about Sierra's age, I suppose – the age Sierra would be now, that is, if she were still among those of us who pass for the living. Forty-nine, fifty maybe. I can't begin to see Sierra's face in hers, though, and I wouldn't want to, because there's an exercise in futility and unquenched sorrow if you ever wanted one: My daughter? Now? She'd be beautiful, a head-turner still, nothing at all like this wizened little buck-toothed poppet of a woman in rotting Doc Martens and a dress a sixth-grader couldn't get into.

'Nice to see you again,' April Wind says, and she has to crank up her voice just a notch to be heard over the blow outside (storm number three in the latest succession hit down about an hour ago). 'And thanks for granting me this interview. I really appreciate it.'

Look out, here it comes: *Saint Sierra.* 'I didn't grant it.'

The look on April Wind's face – you'd think I'd just punched her in the stomach. I give her my best impression of a bitter glare, clenching my jaw and hard-cooking my eyes, but what I'm really doing is looking over her shoulder to where the snails are riding their slime trails up and down the windowpane, fully prepared to inherit the earth we've made for them. I remember her, all right. The woo-woo queen. Endless nights in a drafty teepee, the pitilessly chirpy voice, totems in a bag strung round her neck – she couldn't sit down to eat without some loopy prayer to the earth goddess. *I can totally see your aura, and it's blue shading to magenta on the edges, and I already know I'm attracted to you in a like major way because our birth planets are in the same house.*

'But I thought, like – '

'Still wearing your totems? What was that one – the toad, wasn't it? Weren't you a toad?' Pause, one beat, listen to the buckets catch the eternal drip. 'So what do you do when your totem animal's not just dead but extinct?'

Andrea into the breach: 'April? Would you like a cup of tea?'

The child's fingers go to something under the neck of the dress, the little muslin bag there, quick nervous fingers. She smoothes the damp cotton over her thighs, throws a tentative glance at Andrea, then me. *Mama told me there'd be days like this.* 'No, thanks, I'm fine. Really.'

'You sure?'

'No, really.'

But Andrea, who didn't exist two days ago and now owns me, the house and everything in it, is selling tea here this morning. 'It warms you,' she says. 'I mean, not that it's cold out, not the way it used to be this time of year – remember the Stanislaus River, the way it rained and then we froze our butts off for, what was it, two days out there in the woods? But when you're wet all the time – '

'What have you got?'

'Lapsang souchong.' A glance for me. 'I brought it with me.'

Somehow, the women find this funny, as if I'm some sort of barbarian who couldn't be trusted to have a teabag in the house, and all the tension I'd been trying to inject into the moment evaporates. This is the laughter of relief, of camaraderie and nostalgia, but of something else too, something conspiratorial. I recognize this – I'm the target with the bull's-eye painted on it here, and let's not forget it – but Andrea's back, I tell myself, *Andrea,* and you may as well ride with it wherever it's going to go. So I laugh too. And it's a genuine laugh, it is, the unstoppered whinny that always used to get me in trouble in redneck bars, because I'm caught up in it too. I was there at the Headwaters and Mono Lake and a dozen other places, just like them. I can laugh. I can still laugh. Why not? You never forget how to ride a bicycle, do you? Ha-ha, ha-ha.

'Screw the tea,' I hear myself saying, my miserable cramped two-room shack with the splootching buckets and the stink of terminal mold and animal feces suddenly alive and musical with the laughter of women. 'Let's just break out a bottle of *sake.'*

The Siskiyou, July 1989

THE ONE HE has the clearest recollection of is the one named Boehringer. There were three of them, their names stenciled in black above the right breast pockets of their camouflage fatigues: Boehringer, Butts and Jerpbak. They climbed out of the jeep with faces that said, *This is no joke,* the sledgehammers slung over their shoulders like rifles, Sheriff Bob Hicks of Josephine County nodding his approval even as he fished the dark slim tube of a twenty-ounce Pepsi out of a cooler in the police cruiser and pressed it to his lips. 'Pot commandos,' Teo said under his breath.

So these are pot commandos, Tierwater was thinking, but the thought didn't go much further than that. He watched them dispassionately, tired to the bone, tired of the sun, the trees, the hard dirt road he'd been sitting on for what seemed half his life. At this point, he was thinking nothing, dwelling deep inside himself, his lips raw beneath the tape, each breath tugged through his nostrils like an overinflated balloon, no thought but to get this over with and take his daughter and his wife and go back home and bury his head in the sand. Or maybe he wasn't quite so whipped as he appeared. Maybe he was thinking of Thoreau, his hero of the moment (along with Messrs. Muir, Leopold and Abbey): *The authority of government can have no pure right over my person and property but what I concede to it.* Yes. Sure. Sure, he was. But of course he was right at the very beginning of a fool's progress that was to be like no other.

Collectively, Boehringer, Butts and Jerpbak had never heard of Thoreau, Muir, Leopold or Abbey – or Jefferson, for that matter. And even if they had, it wouldn't have mattered much more than a flea on an elephant. They were part of an elite force of five hundred paramilitary gun-loving whipcrack Marine Corps rejects who'd been organized to interdict clandestine marijuana operations on Forest Service lands. That was their stated purpose, but in fact – since all but the most oblivious and terminally stoned potheads had long since taken their plants indoors to escape detection – they were actually being used to intimidate people like Tyrone Tierwater and his wife and daughter: that is, anybody who dared to get in the way of the profits to be made in the plunder of the national forests. Not that he'd want to preach.

(They used sledgehammers to break us loose – did I mention that? – and they didn't much concern themselves with the delicacy of the operation. If a blow went astray and an iron fist struck an ankle or a shinbone, so much the worse. The reasoning went like this, rhetorical flourishes and all: What else did you expect? If you didn't want your ankle broke, then why didn't you stay down there in California with the rest of the faggots and environmentalists? People work for a living around here, and that might just come as a surprise to you, huh? You could put all the owls in the world in a meat grinder for all I care, and I still say they aren't worth one American job.)

They looked at nothing, these men, and nothing fazed them – it was all the same to them whether they were torching marijuana plants or hauling activists off to jail. What they hadn't counted on, though, was Andrea. As soon as they filed out of the jeep, her face hardened. And this was no ordinary face – it was a movie screen in miniature, able to leap at you in startling close-up and quick-cut from the soft focus of the love scene in the candlelit restaurant to the raging harsh light of confrontation. She was especially good at confrontation, as Tierwater could testify. Her eyes swelled up pneumatically, and a ridge of three ascending V's formed between her eyebrows, hovering there like birds of prey. Her chin became Mount Rushmore. And her mouth – the mouth that kissed, nibbled, licked, leaked words of tenderness and erotic encouragement – turned parsimonious suddenly, shriveled up like a strip of jerky.

Needless to say, she didn't intimidate easily. And when the blows started to fall and Sierra shielded her eyes against the sudden sharp spray of concrete fragments, she opened up on them in a voice that was like an air-raid siren. 'I can't believe you people. You call yourselves men? Or do you think it's a big-dick manly thing to brutalize women and children? Huh, you sons of bitches? I don't hear you. And don't give me that look, you – yes, I'm talking to you, you with the air between your legs and that mongoloid smirk on your lips – Ow! – because if you have a wife, which I doubt because what woman would go for a sack of shit like – OW! – or a sister, you must have a sister, everybody's got at least one – because this is wrong, what you're doing here, all of you, and you know it. If you don't stop this now, right here and now, the whole fucking – Ow!, and will you get the fuck off me? – the whole fucking biosphere is going to collapse like a balloon with a pin stuck in it, and then where're you going to be with your let's-dress-up-and-play-soldier suits? Huh? Where are you going to go? What are you going to eat? Ever think about that? When they – Ow! – close down the grocery stores? Huh? What then?'

It hurt. It hurt more than Tierwater could ever have imagined when he sank his sneakered feet into that yielding plastic medium, now hard as stone – stone, in fact – but he gritted his teeth and thought of the Mohawk. The hammers dropped again and again, the dull reverberative thump sucked up in the baffle of the trees. A crack would appear, and they'd go after it, beating a wedge loose here, levering up a section there. He tried to remain calm through all of this, tried to choke down the rage rising in his throat – passive resistance, that was the ticket, the strategy that brought the British Empire to its knees, stopped the war in Vietnam, humbled George Wallace and Bull Connor – but when his daughter let out a gasp, the smallest exhalation of pained surprise, the faintest whisper built round the thump of the hammer at her ankle, it went right to him.

Before he could think, he rose up off the concrete like a leashed animal and hit the nearest man to him – Boehringer, as it turned out, he of the vacant eyes and narrow, pinched-up shoulders – with everything he had. Which admittedly wasn't much, since his hands were cuffed behind his back, his feet locked in place and his mouth sealed with duct tape beyond even the possibility of bringing his teeth into play. Still, the man who'd made his daughter gasp – Boehringer – heaved into the next man, Butts, who was just then raising his hammer, and the two of them embraced briefly and tentatively, just learning the steps, before they went down in a heap of khaki and camouflage.

They didn't stay down long, though. And when they untangled their limbs and pushed themselves up from the dirt of the road, their faces had changed. No more the tight mask of duty and restraint, the averted eyes and diligently clamped jaws, but something looser, more brutal and habitual. One braced the other while Teo cried out to distract them in the high anxious voice of a man selling peanuts at the ballpark, 'Hey, officers! Officers, would you please find the people that did this to us and arrest them? We'll even press charges – I mean, we were just standing here minding our business when these, these gang members come out of the woods and pour all this concrete on our feet – '

They ignored him. Nor did they take up the sledgehammers again, not right away. It was Butts who grabbed hold of Tierwater's rigid arms and jammed them high up into the wings of his shoulders while Boehringer, the offended party, drove his right fist into the exposed gut – once, twice, then the left, then the right again – till Tierwater the pacifist was back down on the road that wasn't a road sucking at the air through two wholly inadequate nostrils. He couldn't breathe. They'd knocked the wind out of him, which was bad enough – and frightening too; he thought his lungs would never reinflate – but all the worse because his mouth was taped shut. Flat out on his back, arms twisted beneath him, the concrete jerking at his ankles, he thrashed like a freshly caught trout (or a sucker – wouldn't that be more appropriate?), asphyxiating in the clean sweet untainted air of the Oregon woods.

The third man – this was Jerpbak – paused to watch for the briefest moment before bringing his sledge down on Teo's left ankle, while the sheriff drank Pepsi and the Freddies looked the other way. Andrea was screaming, nothing wrong with her lungs, a sound that rang rapturously through the ravine, feeding on itself until there was no other sound in the world. And his daughter – he couldn't focus on her, but he can remember her shrinking into herself, dwindling, growing smaller and ever smaller, a puddle of black, a spot, an insignificant vanishing little speck caught between the mighty legs of the trees and the crushing stupendous lid of the sky.

He woke in a bed, in a room with a TV suspended from the ceiling and stiff white sanitary curtains on the windows. No bars. No toilet clamped to the floor, no must of fermenting bodies, no muttering, no retching, no shadows rising to greet him from a concrete bench bolted to the wall. He wasn't in jail, that much was clear, but he wasn't in the Rest Ye May Motel either. The ceiling tiles were perforated, like ceiling tiles everywhere, and the walls were painted in a clean no-nonsense shade of pale institutional green. But what was this? An IV. Inserted in his left arm and taped in place. So that was it. He was in a hospital. The thought of that froze him a moment: Was it a heart attack? At thirty-nine? He thought of his Uncle Sol, the world-beater who'd worked with Frank Buck in Singapore and been mauled and bitten by half the species on earth at one time or another, with a heart so strong it could have pumped blood for ten men, a heart that would have been pumping still, but for the fact that a coronary thrombosis cut him down while he was bending over the bulbul cages one fine sunny morning, and then he thought of his daughter: if he was here, in the hospital, then where was she? For that matter, where was Andrea? Teo?

All these mysteries were resolved for him in the next moment, when Deputy Sheets, of the Josephine County Sheriff's Department, stuck his head in the door, looked round him twice, as if checking the water before taking the plunge, and stepped into the room. Tierwater saw a man as tall and attenuated as a gusher, the uniform shrinking away from his wrists and ankles, his glasses shedding light. 'Well,' the deputy said, 'awake at last.'

'I think so,' Tierwater murmured, going through a mental checklist of his body parts, just to be sure everything was still there. Since childhood, he'd had a fear of waking up in a hospital bed (not this one – a grainy, grayish, black-and-white-movie bed) with a doctor standing over him saying, I'm afraid the other leg's going to have to go too. 'I mean, I don't remember – '

'You're in the Ida P. Klipspringer Memorial Hospital. You passed out. Heat exhaustion is what the doctor called it.' The deputy's eyes were the same color as the walls. He screwed them up and gave Tierwater a look that had no hint of sympathy in it.

'Heat exhaustion? Your friends or colleagues or whoever punched me in the goddamned stomach – and with my hands tied behind my back and, and duct tape over my mouth, for

Christ's sake – punched me till I was out cold. You listen here' –
and he was up on his elbows now, stoked with the recollection –
'we're talking police brutality, we're talking a methodical,
premeditated . . . and your sheriff was right there drinking a Pepsi
and he never said a word.'

'That's right,' the deputy said, nodding his head on the long
stalk of his neck till it was like a hand at the end of a wrist, waving
goodbye. 'And that's a violation of the penal code – two of 'em,
actually. Resisting arrest, and assault and battery on a peace officer.
That's in addition to the charge of disturbing the peace – and
trespassing.'

'Trespassing? Are you out of your mind? The Siskiyou National
Forest is public property and you know it as well as I do – '

'Listen, mister – *sir* – and I tell you it really rankles me to have to
be professional with people like you, but what I know or don't
know isn't the issue here – it's what the judge knows. And you'll
be seeing him soon enough.'

At this juncture of his life, Tyrone Tierwater was prone to
volatility, and he would have been the first to admit it. The term
'slow burn' meant nothing to him. He was a pile of mesquite
branches on a windy day, a rag soaked in paint thinner. What did
he know? He thought things mattered, believed in the power of
individuals to influence events, illuminate issues, effect change,
resuscitate the earth. None of this did his digestion any good. Or
his bank account either. Now, in the face of intransigence and
stupidity, in the face of Deputy Sheets, he sat up, all the way up,
and tore the IV from his arm as if he were swatting a mosquito.
'Where's my wife and daughter?' he demanded. Or no: he roared,
his voice erupting from the deepest cavity of his chest to boom off
the walls and evoke a responsive tinkle from the instruments on
the metal shelf in the corner.

Deputy Sheets never flinched. He gave Tierwater a tight,
encapsulated smile. He was wearing his firearm, and he let his
right hand go to it, as much to reassure himself as to let Tierwater
know exactly what the parameters were here. His lips barely
moved as he spoke. 'In custody,' he said.

'What do you mean, "in custody"? Where?'

He didn't answer, not right away. Just squared his shoulders and turned his head to the side, as if to spit, but then he caught himself, all the linoleum tiles agleam from his boots to the foot of the bed. 'No worries on that score. Soon as the doctor says so, friend,' he breathed, letting his eyes go cold, 'you'll be joining 'em.'

This hospital room wasn't the first Tierwater had inhabited. He'd had his tonsils out at the Peterskill Municipal Hospital when he was six, and he was back again a few years later with a fractured arm – after an ill-fated decision to intervene in one of his parents' more physical discussions. Oh, his father was destroyed – never has there been such sorrow, not since Abraham offered up Isaac – and his mother was a fragrant sink of pity and consolation and he pushed his face of greed into gallon after gallon of the butter-brickle ice cream proffered as compensatory damages. Sure. But violence breeds violence, and though neither parent ever laid a finger on him again, there it was, a rotten seed, festering. He was in the hospital again for the birth of his daughter, though the venue was a theater of pain and confusion, women crying out from behind the thin trembling walls of curtains on sliding hooks – *Oh, God! Oh, my God!* shrieked one anonymous soprano voice for forty-five solid minutes – and he made it as far as the emergency room in Whitefish, Montana, with Jane, but she wasn't breathing by then, and all the king's horses and all the king's men couldn't – what? They couldn't do shit.

There was nothing wrong with him, but the doctor – a pale, towering bald-headed man with a pelt of laminated black hair climbing out of the V-neck of his scrubs – wanted to run some tests. Just to be sure. Deputy Sheets stood at the door, a look of disgust pressed into his skeletal features, scrutinizing the doctor's every move. 'I'm all right, really,' Tierwater insisted while the doctor studied his chart and paced back and forth, a broad-beamed scurrying nurse at his elbow. 'I feel fine, I do. I just want to get out of here, okay?'

All three of them – Tierwater, the doctor and his nurse – turned to look at Deputy Sheets. 'I don't like your blood pressure,' the doctor said, swinging back round again. His arms were unnaturally long, ape's arms, the knuckles all but grazing his knees, and even in his extremity, Tierwater couldn't help puzzling over a species so recently come down from the trees and yet so intent on destroying them. 'It's dangerously elevated. And I'm going to have to ask you not to interfere with the intravenous drip. You've been dehydrated. We need to replenish your fluids.'

That put a scare into him – *dangerously elevated,* Uncle Sol, where are you? – but he fought it down. 'What do you expect? I've been gagged and beaten and left out in the sun all day by your, your – '

Sheets' voice, from the door: 'Nobody laid a finger on him. He's one of those activists is what he is. From California.'

The doctor gave Tierwater a cold look. Josephine County was a timber county, replete with timber families, and timber families paid the bills. 'Yes, well,' the doctor said, and he was practically scraping the ceiling with the big shining globe of his head, 'you're not going anywhere' – peering at the chart – 'Mr. Tierwater. Not to jail and not to California either – not till we stabilize you.'

'But what about my daughter?' he demanded, and his blood pressure was going up, through the roof, sure, and what did they expect, the sons of bitches? He hadn't been away from Sierra for a single night since her mother died – and if he hadn't been away from her then, if he and Jane had just stayed put, stayed home where they belonged, then Jane would be alive today. 'Don't I get a phone call at least? I mean, what is this, the gulag?'

No one bothered to answer, least of all the doctor, whose looming hairy frame was already passing through the door, on his way out, but the nurse lingered long enough to reinsert the IV with the abraded tips of her cold, rough fingers. The stab of it was no more than a bee sting, the merest prick, but he couldn't help thinking they were taking something from him – draining him, drop by drop – instead of putting something back in.

When he woke again, he checked his watch, and his watch told him it was morning. There was no confusion about where he was, none of the dislocation he'd experienced a hundred times in pup tents and motel rooms or on the unforgiving couch at a friend's house – he woke to full consciousness and saw everything in the room as if it were an oil painting he'd spent the whole night composing. Central to the composition was Deputy Sheets, seated, thin cloth pressed to narrow shanks, skull thrown back against the wall behind him, mouth agape. Long shadows. Early light. Deputy Sheets was asleep. Stationed by the door, it's true, but lost in the wilderness of dreams.

Stealthily, Tierwater slipped the IV from his arm. His thoughts, at this juncture, were uncomplicated. He was getting out of here, that's all he knew, vacating this place, sidestepping the emaciated arm of the law and making his way to his daughter, his wife, the outraged and militant cadre of E.F! lawyers who would make everything right. And the reporters too – don't forget them. They had to hear about this, about the desecration of the forest, the complicity of the sheriff and the brutality of Boehringer and Butts, and he did want to preach, yes, he did – preach, proclaim and testify. His feet were on the floor, the papery hospital gown rustling at his shoulders. And where were his clothes – his wallet, his keys, his belt? They took those things away from you in jail, that much he knew, but were they as scrupulous at the hospital?

Across the room to the closet. Nothing there. The bathroom. Easing the door shut, one eye on Deputy Sheets, the whir of the fan cyclonic, and he was sure the noise of it would rouse his jailer – *Just taking a leak, officer, and I suppose you're going to tell me that's against the law too* – but no, Sheets slept on. In his gown, on silent feet, Tierwater vacated the bathroom, slipped past the innocuous lump of creased and pleated matter that was the deputy and out into the corridor. He was dimly aware of adding yet another offense to the list Sheets had recited for him, but the great hardwood forests of the East and Midwest had been decimated by men like Sheriff Bob Hicks and Boehringer and their ilk, and the redwoods and Doug firs were going fast – this was no time for indecision.

The corridor was deserted. Cadaverous light, eternally fluorescent – nobody could look healthy here. His powers of observation told him he was on the second floor, judging from the view to the middle reaches of the trees just beyond the windows at the far end of the hall, and he understood – from the movies, primarily, or maybe exclusively – that the elevator would be a mistake. Nurses, orderlies, gurneys transporting the near-dead and partially alive, anxious relatives and loved ones, interns, candy stripers – they'd all be packed into that elevator, and all wondering aloud about his bare feet and bare legs and the disposable paper gown that left his rear exposed. And that was another thing – what had become of the diapers? The thought shrank him. He pictured the blocky nurse cutting the things off of him, her nose wrinkled in disgust, and then he changed channels and headed down the corridor, looking for the stairwell.

Twice he had to duck into occupied rooms – a subterranean light, tubes, hoses, the electric winking eyes of the machines that took note of every fluctuation and discharge – to avoid detection by prowling nurses. No one seemed to notice. They were busy with their tubes and monitors, busy trying to breathe, a collection of tired old beaks and chins grimly relaxing into death – or so he imagined, secreted behind the door as the nurses soft-stepped up the hallway. Then, a cold draft playing off his genitals, he flung open the door marked *stairwell* and plunged through it.

In the process, he startled a morose-looking woman sneaking a smoke, but she dropped her eyes and never said a word, and the stairs vibrated under his feet. He cracked the door on the ground floor – early yet, very early, but there was more traffic here – and waited for the golden moment when everybody seemed to disappear simultaneously through separate doorways. Freedom glowed in the glass panels of the door at the main entrance, just past the gift shop and reception desk. What was it – fifty feet, seventy-five? Now or never. He pinched the gown closed behind him and made for the door, deaf to the startled cries of the two women at the desk (young nursey types, with hamburger faces and plasticized hair, and *Sir!* they cried; *Sir! Can I help you, sir?*), the sweet, fresh, as-yet-uncorrupted Oregon air in his face and an endless field of scrub and weed heaving into view just beyond the dead expanse of the parking lot.

If this were a movie, he was thinking – and his every move to this point had been dictated by what he'd witnessed repeatedly on the big screen – he would slip into a late-model sports sedan, punch the ignition with a screwdriver, hotwire the thing and be gone in a glorious roil of smoke and gravel. Or the heroine, looking a lot like Andrea, with a scoop neckline and killer brassiere, would at that moment wheel up to the curb and he'd say, *Let's move it.* Or *Let's rock and roll.* Isn't that what they said in every definable moment of heroic duress? But this was no movie, and he had no script. In the end, he had to settle for making his way on all fours through the briars and poison oak, awaiting the inevitable clash of sirens and uproar of excited voices.

(How long was I out there – at large, that is? Let me tell you, I don't know, but it was the longest better part of a morning I ever spent in my life. And then it was the dogs – or dog – and the humiliation of that on top of the concrete and the diapers and the tight shit-eating smirks of the Freddies and their sledgehammering minions. I gave myself up. Of course I did. How far was I going to get in a hospital gown?)

Tierwater had plenty of time to nurse his grievances and contemplate the inadvisability – the sheer unreconstructed foo-lishness, the howling idiocy – of what he'd done that morning in extricating himself from the personal jurisdiction of Deputy Sheets and, by extension, the Josephine County Sheriff's Department. He sat there in the heavy brush, not five hundred yards from the hospital entrance, scraped and begrimed, his feet bleeding in half a dozen places, the paper gown bunched up around his hips, thinking of what they would do to him now, on top of everything else. If he'd been tentative two nights ago in the fastness of the Siskiyou and purely outraged when they went after his daughter, now he was almost contrite. Almost. But not quite. They'd humiliated him and terrorized his wife and daughter – there was no coming back from that.

He listened to the wail of the sirens in the distance, and, more immediately, to the songbirds in the trees and the insects in the grass. His breathing slowed. After a while, the sun burned through the early-morning haze and warmed him. He laid his head back in the cradle of his hands and became an observer, for lack of anything better to do. The tracery of the plants – saxifrage, corn lily, goldenrod – stood illuminated against the sky, every leaf and stem trembling with animate life. Grasshoppers, moths, ants, beetles, spiders, they were the gazelles here and the lions, prowling a miniature veldt that was plenty big enough for them – at least until the hospital needed a new wing or a developer threw up a strip mall. He tried not to think about mites, chiggers, ticks, though he itched in every part and scratched till his flesh was raw and his fingernails bloody. He had no plan. He was here, couched in the bushes, instead of sitting up in bed and addressing a plate of eggs or waffles while CNN droned on about Polish Solidarity or the turmoil in Iran, but why? Because he had to do something, anything – he couldn't just roll over and become their whipping boy. Could he?

For a long while – hours, it seemed – there were the distant sights and sounds of confusion emanating from the front of the hospital. The clash of sirens, raised voices, a flurry of activity centering on two police cruisers. It wasn't until the K-9 Corps arrived, and the first eager lusty deep-chested woofs of the police dog began to ring out over the scrub, that Tierwater developed a plan. He wasn't about to let the dog come careening through the bushes to take hold of his ankle and drag him thrashing out into the open, where the local reporter would snap action shots of his flailing legs and unclothed buttocks for the edification of the local timber families. No way. It simply wasn't a viable scenario. Beyond that, he was hungry, thirsty, sunburned, fed up. He'd made his point. Enough was enough. He stood up and waved his arms. 'Over here!' he shouted.

And this was where things got interesting. The dog, dragging a cop who might have been Sheets' brother (thin as a wading bird, a stick of an arm at the end of the leash), made a show of it, barking ferociously, hysterically even, and right behind cop and dog was the inevitable reporter, camera flashing away. She was a female, this reporter, a little blonde with bangs, short skirt and running shoes, and Tierwater couldn't help trying to smooth his hair down and maybe even work up a smile for her. Say 'cheese.' Behind her was Sheets, looking hangdog, and the stomping, massive, outraged figure of Sheriff Bob Hicks himself.

The dog was encouraged to come in close and to nip at the ankles without drawing any evidentiary blood, the cops dutifully produced service revolvers and handcuffs and Tierwater was led out of the bush and across the lot, wincing on bare feet. A crowd was gathered to watch the sheriff consummate his duty by shoving the cuffed and subdued desperado into the back of the patrol car – *Publicity, that's what we came here for,* Tierwater kept telling himself, trying to transmute defeat into victory, humiliation into triumph, but he was half naked, his hair was a mess and he felt less like a crusader than a figure out of the Opéra Bouffe.

'Get in there, shithead,' the sheriff said under his breath as he spread a big hand over the crown of Tierwater's head and forced him into the car, where Deputy Sheets sat awaiting him. For an instant, everything confused in his mind, Tierwater thought of kicking open the door and making a hobbled run for it, because things were out of hand here – a peaceful protest, and look what it had led to – and it tore his heart out to give them the satisfaction of beating him down like this. Better to die than submit. His jaw ached from gritting his teeth. He was sweating. His heart was pounding, his eyes were crazy, there were twigs and bits of seed and chaff in his hair. *Kick the door!* screamed a voice in his head. *Kick the door!*

He didn't kick the door. He didn't have to. Andrea was there – Andrea and an attorney with beard and briefcase – and Teo, shadowing them on a pair of crutches. 'We've come to bail him out,' Andrea said, and through the window of the cruiser Tierwater could see the winged creases ascending her forehead.

Officious, already moving round the front of the car while the door slammed shut like the lid of a coffin, Sheriff Bob Hicks let out a short mocking bark of a laugh. 'Bail? Bail hasn't been set yet – he hasn't even been arraigned.'

The lawyer, in high dudgeon, countered with something Tierwater couldn't hear. Andrea bent to peer in the window, and Tierwater the desperado pressed his fingers to the glass, and it was just like the movies, exactly – visiting hour at the penitentiary, time's up, boys, this way, ladies. She was saying something, her lips moving, the police dog barking for the sheer love of it, the crowd jeering, something about Sierra –

' – too sick to go to jail,' the sheriff was saying, pointing a finger in the lawyer's face, 'and then he pulls this crap, this escape from custody, and what do you have to say to that, Fred, huh?'

Fred had plenty to say, most of which escaped Tierwater, but during the course of the ensuing debate, he was able to lean forward to where the Plexiglas divider gave onto the front seat and the convenient flap there for purposes of criminal/peace-officer communication. 'Where's Sierra?' he shouted into his wife's hovering face.

'Child Protective Services.'

'What? What do you mean?'

This was where Deputy Sheets, seated beside him on the hard serviceable seat, got into the act. Deputy Sheets had been embarrassed professionally, and he wasn't amused. 'Juvenile Hall,' he said, giving a jerk at the handcuffs to get Tierwater's attention. 'She's in there with your runaways, your shoplifters, your junkies and murderers. And she's going to stay there till the judge makes his ruling.'

'His ruling?' Tierwater's heart was pounding. 'Ruling on what?'

'What do you think? On whether you're a fit parent or not.'

He jerked back round to read Andrea's face, a black gulf of despair and regret opening up inside him, limitless, unbreachable. He knew it. He'd known it all along. Trouble is a given in a world ruled by accident, sure, and lightning hits too, but only a fool – strike that: an inveterate idiot – goes looking for it.

Deputy Sheets cleared his throat. 'Got two more charges for you,' he said, and his voice was so rich with triumph he sounded as if he were announcing the winners of the Fourth of July sack race. 'Attempted escape and contributing to the delinquency of a minor.'

Eight months earlier, Tierwater was busy leading his life of quiet desperation, aimless, asleep at the wheel, watching his father's empire fall away into dust like all the geriatric empires before it – *Look on my works, ye Mighty, and despair!* It was December, bleak and wind-knifed. Ice one day, slush the next, then refrozen slush the day after that. Pathetic cardboard Santas and cutout menorahs clung to the dirty windows of the stores in the shopping center – the ones that hadn't gone dark for lack of tenants – and half the bulbs were burned out in the relict strings of Christmas lights he'd looped over the bent and rusting nails his father had hammered into the stucco fascia twenty years earlier. Sierra was twelve, insufferably motherless, inappropriately dressed (Jodie Foster, *Taxi Driver*), addicted to TV, gloom and doom, vegetarianism. Her face was a falling ax, and it fell on him twice a day: in the morning, when he drove her to school in the Jeep Laredo, and in the evening, when he got home from work and she was there infesting the house with her evil friends.

For his part, Tierwater tried to do his best, puzzling over geography and the *Golden Book of Literary Treasures* with her, taking her out for a weekly bonding ritual at the Mongolian Barbecue in the shopping center, withholding judgment when she came home with a nose ring from the brand-new sixty-seven-shop enclosed mall that was killing him, tearing his heart out, flattening his feet and destroying his digestion. His love life was null and void. A month earlier he'd withdrawn as tactfully as possible from a six-month affair with a skinny ungenerous woman named Sherry who wore her weedy hair kinked out in a white-blond corona that grazed the lintel of every door she passed through (to his secretary: 'Tell her it was a mountaineering accident and they never recovered my body'). He hadn't met anyone since. In fact, during all that time, no woman so much as gave him a glance – not even in Cappelli's, the bar in the shopping center that was the only place that seemed to be doing any business at all. Single mothers clustered around shrinking tables and hung off the shoulders of single fathers as if all they needed were crampons and rope, cosmetologists wept over the thunderous hits of the sixties, aerobics instructors showed off their tightly clamped buttocks round the pool table, but none of them had time for Tierwater. He was depressed, and he wore his depression like a lampshade over his head.

But then fate intervened. (*'We are turned round and round in this world, and Fate is the handspike.' I don't know exactly what a handspike is, but I like the quote – and Melville had it right, especially if a handspike is something you can drive into the back of somebody's head.*) Reflexively, without giving it much thought, Tierwater had sent a check to the Sierra Club, a year's membership. Before his parents died – they were stopped in traffic, 44th and Lexington, when a crane hoisting steel girders capitulated to the force of gravity – he'd been chasing down a B.S. in wildlife biology, after having dropped out twice in his drug-tranced days, and nature had always glimmered somewhere out there on the horizon of his consciousness. This little gesture, this check delivered in a good cause, was like a Band-Aid slapped over a big gaping crater in his psyche, and he knew that, but there it was. He was a member of the Sierra Club. And as a member, he got onto a mailing list that entitled him to receive whole cordilleras of junk mail – talk about conserving paper – including, but not limited to, invitations to attend meetings, swim with the dolphins, save whales and remember the Himalayas. He felt guilty, but he never accepted any of these high-minded invitations, and worse, he never recycled a scrap of them.

Then, one day, a postcard slipped out of the pile of bills, letters, invitations, solicitations, violations, entreaties and threats his secretary mounded on his desk each morning. It featured a logo he'd never seen before – a crimson circle with a raised fist in the center of it (his first thought was the Black Panthers – but weren't they all dead, in jail or running Nike outlets?). It wasn't the Black Panthers. It was E.F.! – Earth Forever! – inviting him to attend a powwow/chili cookoff/apocalyptic lecture/slide show at the home of Linda D'Piqua-Hoover in Croton. He turned the postcard over in his hand. *Dear Mr. or Ms. Tierwater,* it read, *Are you concerned about the environment? Do you care about the rape of our forests, the pollution of our streams and rivers, the acid rain killing off the pristine lakes of the Adirondacks? Are you tired of promises? Fed up? Ready for Direct Action? Then come to our,* etc.

He went. Why? Boredom, curiosity, the desire to duck the Sherrys of the world and meet some environmentally minded women who might just want to share a freeze-dried entrée and a sleeping bag on the shore of an acidic lake somewhere. And more – and he wouldn't want to make light of this – because he believed. He did. He genuinely did. He needed an awakening, a cause, a call to arms – and here it was.

It was raining the night of the powwow, a cold soulless wintry rain that wrung out the sky like an old cloth and found its way into the seams of his boots and down the collar of his jacket. He stepped out of the office and into a world from which every trace of light had been relentlessly squeezed, the moon imploded, the stars erased – there was no illumination without electricity, and electricity lit his path from the office to the car. The car itself was another kind of environment, a sort of rolling sarcophagus. It spat its fumes into the air, coughed and shook, gave off its stink of incinerated metal. Beyond the rain-scrawled windows lay the shopping center – the Copper Beech Shopping Center – curled into the killing night like the architecture of his nightmares. He sat there breathing the carbon monoxide coming through the floor-boards till his classic 1966 Mustang could be coaxed into moving without stalling, and then he was off, rocketing over the potholes like a master of nature and machine alike.

He made an uncanny series of wrong turns, U-turns and gravel-churning retreats, all the while consulting the map reproduced on the back of the card, until finally the D'Piqua-Hoover house loomed up out of a dark lane, lit like a supernova. Import cars clustered around it, sleek and menacing in their steel skins. The black lawn glittered in the light of a hundred windows. His feet found the flagstone path, and then a tall woman in post-hippie Birkenstocks was greeting him at the door, so good of him to come and did he know Mrs. Somebody, chair of the Something Committee? He took Mrs. Somebody's limp hand in his own – she must have been seventy – and then made his way toward the bar, the scents of woodsmoke, body heat, perfume and warring chilies rising up to envelop him as he inserted himself into the crowd. A man in cummerbund and bow tie handed him a glass of wine. He wanted scotch. But he accepted the wine, sipped it and took a moment to get his bearings.

That was when he first noticed Andrea. She was in the corner, hunkered over a bowl of yogurt dip with a handful of carrot sticks and broccoli florets, gathering faces round her like a puppet master. Her free hand (ringless, chapped, the nails bitten down to trans-lucent slivers) was in constant motion, underscoring each point she made, and she made a lot of them. She was talking with animation and confidence, lecturing, though he couldn't hear what she was saying from where he stood with his nose in a long-stemmed glass. He must have watched her for a full five minutes, picture only, the sound muted, before he found himself moving toward her – and he wasn't moving consciously, not at all; it was more in the way of a moth following a pheromone trail. He fluttered his wings and sailed across the room.

(I need to describe her as she was then – and none of this black hair dye

71

and she looks pretty good for a sixty-seven-year-old and all the rest of an old man's twice-burned revisionism — because you have to experience this for yourself. Be there. Step into the room, feel the heat of the big hardwood fire carbonizing the air, smell the simmering pots of chili and the burned-dust odor of the slide projector, inhale the aroma of coffee — decaf and espresso — and the perfume of forty women who want to give the impression that they're wearing nothing at all but the scent they were born with. 'Natural' is the word here. Earnest. Committed. And quick now, what's an environmentalist? Somebody who already has their mountain cabin.)

She gave him a look — the quickest snatch of her eyes — and admitted him to her circle. She was talking about logging in the West, some forest in Oregon he'd never heard of, old growth going down, weep for the animals, weep for the earth. He wasn't listening. Or not particularly. He was too busy studying her, enjoying her lips and the intensity of her eyes, trying to break her code and assimilate it. She might have been a steelworker or glass blower, her face shining with a light that seemed to radiate from a place just under her chin, the light of hammered ingots, molten silica, fire, and her hands were big and mannish, hands that had done things, accomplished things — *An activist's hands,* he told himself, as he clutched the glass of wine and moved in still closer, already sick with the romance of it — *Save the world, sure, and get laid too.*

Her hair was blond in those days — then, and for all the time he knew her, but for those special occasions when they went out in the night to strike back at the machine and she dyed it dirt brown or fish-belly gray — and it was cut and parted in a way that allowed it to fall across her face whenever she tilted her head. The hair would fall — good hair, healthy hair, *California* hair — and then she would push it back, and you saw her hands, or she'd give her chin a flick so that her hair would grab the light and drop unerringly into place, and you saw her eyes. Tierwater saw them. He saw her. And even before he understood she was the main attraction of the evening — along with Teo, that is — he pushed his way through the scrim of faces hanging at her shoulder and introduced himself. 'Hi,' he said, showing his teeth in his best imitation of a grin, 'I'm Ty Tierwater, and you're — '

What was he wearing? He wouldn't remember. Certainly

nothing that could be described as environmentally chic – no Gore-Tex or Bion II or anything like that. He looked like a bum, most likely. And why not? He wasn't going anywhere. Give him a three-day growth of prematurely graying beard (graying to the chin only, and no higher), blue jeans spattered with paint and spackle and other accoutrements of the building-management trade, a bomber jacket so crosshatched with age it looked as if it had been varnished over by one of the Italian masters. Style he didn't have. He would have been the first to admit it. But he wasn't bad-looking, depending on your taste. Thin. Skinny, actually – but at least he hadn't gone to fat like every other thirty-nine-year-old in America. He had most of his hair and a good proportion of his teeth and he could lift anything, throw it over his shoulder and walk to hell and back with it if the right woman were to ask him. And he was a patient, tireless and tender lover, a combination of adjectives and a resonant noun he should have had printed up on a T-shirt. It couldn't have hurt his chances.

Her hand was in his. He felt a roughness there, callus, the horn of work and worry, but a frankness too – no bullshit here, her handshake said. Her lips were moving too. 'Andrea,' she said, in answer to his question, and her voice surprised him, so high and piping, so pure, when he'd expected a rasp, a growl deep in the throat – *Let's get down on all fours and fight over the meat* – 'Andrea Cotton.'

Teo's car was cramped on the way back to Los Angeles, but not as cramped as it had been on the way up. Tierwater sat up front, next to Teo, because of the length of his legs, and Andrea stretched out across the back seat because of the length of hers. Sierra was represented by a pink over-the-shoulder bag with the grinning face of a Disney character impressed on the front flap, a relic of her childhood. It was tucked away on the floor behind Tierwater's seat, and it contained a pair of cut-off jeans, a spandex top, socks, underwear, cosmetics, seven home-made gloom-and-doom tapes in cracked plastic cases and a backup vampire novel the size of a pocket dictionary. Though they'd been on the road for two hours – in California now, Mount Shasta appearing and vanishing through first one window, then another, like a conjuror's illusion – Tierwater hadn't said a word. He stared straight ahead, his jaw clenched so hard his teeth hurt.

Andrea and Teo talked around him, the truncated vowels of Teo's glad-handing surfer's voice banging up against the country inflections of her Montana drawl, on and on, and the only subject was tactics. Not Sierra. Not how they were going to wrest her away from the judge – Judge Duermer, fat as a rutting sea lion and twice as belligerent – and the slab-faced puritans down at Child Protective Services. Because this was the fact: Sierra's lawyer, assigned by the state, had filed a dependency petition in the Name of the People against Tierwater as an unfit parent, a parent who endangers his child and contributes to her delinquency, and she was in Juvenile Hall with the hard cases and he was heading home to California. On fifty thousand dollars' bail and facing a plea bargain negotiated by Fred – 'They'll drop all the charges if you plead to assault on a peace officer' – that could, that would, put him in jail for as much as three months. And then what would his daughter do?

'I say we go for the jugular, man – like play up Ty as *Father Knows Best* and Siskiyou Lumber and the Josephine County Sheriff's Department like a cross between the KGB and the Ayatollah.'

The worn tires sang on the pavement, cars clustered round them, fell back, moved ahead, the radio coughed up static. Tierwater was paralyzed. He was a fragile thing in a soft container. He'd forgotten how to blink. How to swallow. Andrea's voice came to him from a thousand miles away: 'Sure, sure, of course. This is worth fifty protests. If we can just figure a way to get it into the papers – and you're on to it, Teo, you're totally right, I mean, separating a father from his daughter, it's like dropping a nuclear bomb on a Girl Scout picnic – '

Teo, muscles working the wheel, jaws pounding gum to a private beat, left ankle wrapped in gauze: 'Yeah, but all I've seen so far is that thing in their Mickey Mouse newspaper – you know, Ty going berserk on an officer of the law, escaping from the hospital and all that. All that *shit,* I mean. Because that's what it is. It's like the Chicago Seven or the Jonesboro Boys or something. People can see that. They're not stupid.'

Andrea came forward suddenly, her head floating over the seat like a satellite drifting into orbit. 'Oh, yes, they are. Stupid as dirt. But we've got to give this to Shep and Suzie – they'll run with it, they'll spin it and spin it again. We need the *L.A. Times*, *Newsweek*, *Woman's Day*, *Time*.'

'CBS News – TV, that's the way to go.'

Tierwater took all this in – not consciously, not alertly, but in the way of a sponge absorbing a slow trickle of water. This was his wife speaking, the woman he loved, the woman who set him on fire, and the man who'd stepped in to win the role of his best friend in the abbreviated space of a few short months. This was his life talking here, a life so radically altered he couldn't have imagined it a year ago. Get married, draw down the bank accounts, sell off the movables and put the house and the shopping center on the market and never mind whether you take a beating or not – just get out, all the way out, all the way to the San Fernando Valley in the Jeep Laredo, and then sell that too, find a school for Sierra and stare at the palm trees rising up out of the smog like the tapering, reticulated necks of Mesozoic beasts. Sure. And commit criminal acts in the night.

What about Sierra? he wanted to say. *What about me?*

He hadn't responded, even to a direct question, for hours, and he couldn't blame them if they went on as if he weren't there. Or yes, he could. And he did. They talked over him, around him, through him, as if he were laid out on a gurney in the trauma ward. Their voices rose and fell. They were pillars of outrage, righteous, scheming, Trotsky and Lenin plotting to bring down Kerensky, Woodward and Bernstein with their heads together in the back room. Tierwater stared straight ahead. The rattling Caprice sliced through the apparent world and for the longest time he saw nothing at all. But then –

Then things slowed down and the real world coalesced for him with the dull rolling thunder of epiphany. Up ahead, on the right, was a construction site. They – the anonymous, omnipresent and ever-industrious – were apparently constructing an overpass here, slabs of concrete studded with rebar, steel beams, survey stakes trailing their raggled banners of pink and orange plastic, dirt in a violent state of disarrangement. And a Cat. A big solid D7 Cat, sitting idle beneath the gray film of dusk, the sun drawn down the sink of the sky, dead brush, the crippled fingers of the scarified trees. Tierwater saw this picture, a murky still-life, and in the same instant saw himself at the center of it, and suddenly he was snatching at the steering wheel. 'Pull over,' he said.

Teo, his jaws working beneath the blond stubble of his head, looked alarmed. But just for a moment. Tierwater watched the light come into his eyes, saw his hands relax on the wheel. 'You need to take a leak, Ty?' A glance back to Andrea, the makings of a grin. 'Is that it?'

Nothing. Tierwater just looked out the window, but he kept his hand locked on the wheel, and in the next moment they were slowing and the tires began to sing a new song on the raw corrugations of the exit ramp. 'Over there,' Tierwater heard himself say, 'on the crossroad, just behind the Cat there.'

'Wait a minute, Ty,' Andrea said, her hands on his shoulders, sweet breath and her look of concern, 'you're not thinking – ?'

But Tierwater was already out of the car, the heat rising in his face, lizards scuttling for cover, already fingering the matches he'd idly lifted from the ashtray in the Rest Ye May Motel. They had his daughter, that's what he was thinking – they had *him,* had him by the balls – and now they were going to start paying for it, right now, now and forever. 'Ty!' she was calling, Andrea, out of the car already, a wind coming up out of nowhere to whip that perfect sheet of hair across her face while the gray cars hunted along the freeway behind the steady pulse of their headlights. Everything was gray now, washed out, rinsed of color and definition. Could they see him? Could they see what he was doing, what he was about to do? *(At that point, I have to tell you, I honestly didn't care – they'd hit me, hard, and I was going to hit them back, and damn the consequences.)*

His head was down, looking for something, a scrap of paper to stuff into the fuel tank, the fuse that would give him ten seconds, because that was all he was going to need, and 'Ty!' Andrea was calling, 'Ty, don't be crazy!' There was trash everywhere. Of course there was – what else would you expect? He bent to it mechanically, paper, take-out coffee cups, cans, bottles, and found what he was looking for – a rust-colored rag stained with machine

76

oil. It took him a minute to locate the fuel tank and wrench the cap off of it – she was back in the car now, in the rear seat, her face drawn down to nothing, a pale bulb preserved behind the dark glass and you'd better plant it now and hope for flowers in the spring – and then he touched a match to the rag and the thinnest, blackest little coil of smoke crawled up into the air.

He was running by then, thirty-nine years old and mortgaged to the eyeballs, his right knee tender, teeth aching, hair undergoing a daily transmigration from head to comb, and he never stopped running till he was in the car and the car was slamming down the road and the shining big new D7 Cat was breathing fire like a dragon, yellow, orange and red.

Santa Ynez, November 2025

SO WE LAUGH. It feels good, feels good to be looped on cheap *sake* at quarter past ten in the morning too, even though my nose is dripping and my head seems to be waterlogged. (It's the weather, of course, everybody indoors all the time, the great biomass of humanity a juicy, snuffling, shuffling culture medium for the sly and patient viruses, and I just pray it's not the *mucosa* plague making a comeback. But that's the thrill of life on this blistered planet: you never know which sniffle is going to be your last.) And my arm – they injected it, dusted it, stitched and wrapped it, and there's no hint of pain from that quarter. Not yet, anyway. In fact, it doesn't even feel attached to me, and here I am resting my haunches on the kitchen table and draining one tiny glass after another of fermented rice wine, casual as an amputee, my guard down – definitely down – and the women laughing along with me. Things could be worse.

Plus, we got Petunia back, and that's cause for celebration. Chuy rigged up a plywood enclosure at the corner of her pen where the chicken wire had been torn loose in the storm, and he buried the bottom end of it three feet in the ground so she can't dig under it, or wouldn't want to. Not that she isn't hot to get loose – all the animals are – but she's got to be the laziest Patagonian fox in the world (of course, since the set of Patagonian foxes is tiny and dwindling, the subset of lazy ones must be infinitesimal). At any rate, she's there, hunkered over a bowl of dog meal and the freshly trapped corpses of a couple of rats Chuy tossed her as a welcome-home present, and I know all about it because I was out in the pens myself before the sun came up, scattering straw over the mud to make her comfortable. And Delbert Sakapathian is satisfied too, because I got Mac's secretary to hand-deliver him a check for a thousand bucks, to make up for the loss of his cat. Everything wraps up neatly, doesn't it?

Still, that's April Wind over there sunk into the couch, and I might be laughing now, but I know that sooner or later a perforated chuckle or premoistened guffaw is going to stick in my throat like a catfish bone. 'Remember the time,' Andrea's saying, and we're all remembering, grinning wide, a day in the Tehachapis, dry and hot and with a sky so blue it was like somebody's eye — all right, God's eye, if He wants to exist — and the shock of that creek, instant deep-freeze. We were eluding the Freddies, and somebody — Teo? me? — insisted on the creek, throw them off the scent, and how deep is it, somebody else asked, knee-deep, that's all, knee-deep. ' — And then Ty stepped off that rock and came up sputtering like a polar bear?' Oh, yes. Yes. Ha-ha.

'So that was, like, when?' April Wind is wondering. 'Before or after Sierra . . . Because I don't remember her there, correct me if I'm wrong — '

Boom! goes the wind, choosing the perfect moment to rattle my shack [*Enter* Ghost; *Exeunt* Peace, Sanity and Determination.] They're both looking at me, Andrea with her reconstructed face and midnight hair, eyes so glassy and opaque you could lather up and shave in them, and April Wind, the amazing dwarf woo-woo woman with a stare like two screws boring into a four-by-four. 'After,' I say, and listen to the hiss of the rain swelling to fill the silence.

But what am I seeing? Sierra Tierwater, twenty-four years old, staring down at me out of Jane's fleshed-in circle of a face (perfectly round, round as the Doughboy's), the long braid of her hair dangling like a bell pull and a fine rain of particles sifting down from the weathered platform high up in her tree. Her redwood tree. Her one-thousand-year-old, two-hundred-foot-tall redwood that weighed something like a hundred tons and contained an estimated twenty thousand board feet of lumber, four hundred thousand dollars stacked up in the middle of an old-growth forest and there for the taking. That tree. The one that made her famous. Artemis, she called it, the Lady of Wild Things.

Sure. That's what I'm seeing, Sierra, my daughter, perched up there halfway to the sky in a blizzard of mystical, earth-mothering, New Wave crap, woo-woo on parade, and every ravening nutball with a grudge and a chainsaw stalking round down below.

'So you were pretty broken up by that,' April Wind inserts into the howling silence – literally howling, Force 8 at least, a whole universe of untethered objects hurtling in a dismal blur past the only window that hasn't been boarded up yet. 'Is that when you really, like, started to, you know – '

'Broken up?' I throw it back it at her on the heels of two quick burning hits of *sake*, and forget the delicate little cups, it's my lips now and the wet viridian throat of the bottle. 'Is that what you came to hear about? This is the interview, right? We're not laughing anymore, are we, anything for the cold naked page and let's take down the last ten trees in the world for the paper to print it on. But what's the angle, what's the deal – does anybody really give a shit anymore? Because I don't. I really don't.'

Oh, they look uncomfortable now, the shifting buttocks and nervous little flicks of the head, fingers twirling twists of hair, eyes left, eyes right, eyes crawling up the walls. And what a coincidence that Andrea should come back to me the day before the little reporter shows up. It's money, sure, some publisher's money – we always need the next hagiography – but there's more to it than that, and I can see it glittering in their eyes. Andrea and April Wind. Am I crazy to think they don't have an agenda?

'All right, Ty, we'll be straight with you.' Andrea is up out of the chair now, at the stove, all brisk elbows and saluting shoulders, rattling the teapot. 'Maybe we've had enough *sake* – it's too early for me. Tea, anyone?' And she swings round with a smile.

And me? I just perch there, buttock to table, my mouth grim, waiting.

A sigh. The smile flutters and flaps off. 'First of all,' she says, 'I came to you because I missed you and I need you, so don't think – and plus, as I'm sure you suspected all along, I've got nowhere else to go. And nothing. I mean nothing. April and I thought – well, a book, you know? I need the money – *we* need the money – yes, that's true, but we really felt it was time to tell Sierra's story – and yours – so people can see that we tried, and that we can try again.'

'Not that they would care,' I say, bitter to the dregs. Another hit of *sake,* straight from the bottle, and it tastes like machine oil.

'They would, you know they would.' This from the little face of April Wind, clenched round her conviction.

'I may as well tell you, Ty – we're starting up E.F.! again. For the survivors, I mean.' Andrea lights the stove with a soft whoosh of gas, sets the teapot on the burner. She can't look me in the eye.

For the survivors. That was the kind of thinking that got me crazy, that got me put in prison, not to mention reviled and caricatured and labeled 'a human hyena' by the *San Francisco Chronicle* and half a dozen other papers. 'You know something I don't?'

This has got to be the worst of the storms yet – the rain is nearly horizontal now, roofing nails shot out of a gun, and the yard seems to be in motion, one soupy swirl of muck and water. I need to get out there and see to the animals. I need to get hold of Chuy. Mac. The National Guard. But here I am, drunk on *sake,* a withered, rapier-nosed, hunched-over relic, holding my breath and listening to hear the worst of the bad news.

Andrea ducks her head and lets her voice go soft. 'They've got the *mucosa* on the East Coast. A new strain.'

That hits me in the stomach, all right. Up comes Lori's face, bobbing to the surface, and then it's gone. Of course, I knew it – could have predicted it – and why not? If not the *mucosa,* then something else. 'No vaccine?'

A shake of her newly minted head. 'Not yet.'

'So, then, why . . . I don't understand why you'd – ?'

'Sit down, Ty,' Andrea says, and April Wind is so wired I think she's going to rocket up off the dog-stinking couch, leap out the window and parachute to safety.

'I am sitting.'

'Look, Ty, there's one more thing – '

I'm an old man. My teeth hurt, my knee hurts, my back – and there's a dull inchoate intimation of pain just starting to make its presence known deep in the intertwined muscles of my stitched-up forearm. I just gape at her.

'Maclovio Pulchris. We need him. His money, anyway. Earth Forever! is going to fly again, in a big way. If this new *mucosa* strain is what we think it is, then the crash we've been talking about all these years is here, here right now.' How did she get across the room so fast? Because here she is, right in my face, looming over me, Andrea, all of her, ready to put the screws to me all over again. 'You hear me, Ty? Because you're coming with us.'

No time for a snappy comeback, no time to reflect on being used yet again, no time for volition or even protest. 'I am?'

When I was younger – young, that is – everybody I knew was alive. Now pretty much everybody I know, or knew, is dead, and the odd thing is that none of them died a natural death – *He expired in his sleep, never knew what hit him,* that sort of thing. Uncle Sol was the exception, though his death seemed unnatural too, in the way that all death seems unnatural – I was a teenager then, working with him on his safari ranch in San Diego, both of us up to our elbows in urine-drenched straw and the exotic shit of exotic beasts, and as I say, he was leaning over the bulbul cages one morning and felt the jab of mortality up under his rib cage. Tell me, is that natural? I've had friends succumb to cancer, and Lori – Lori died in my arms, both of us wearing gauze masks, the *mucosa* so thick in her lungs and throat she couldn't draw a breath, tracheotomy or no, and that's natural, nothing more natural than the disease we spread in our sticky, promiscuous way. But what about my parents, my wife, my daughter, what about Teo? They say that if all disease was cured (and what a joke that fond promise has turned out to be) people wouldn't get much past the age of ninety or so anyway, what with the chances of accident. Actuarial tables? Take it to Las Vegas.

Accident rules the universe, I know that, and there's no escaping it, science or no. But accident gives rise to the concept of luck – and if you believe in luck, you might as well break out your juju beads and get your mojo working, you might as well borrow a totem from April Wind and go out and talk to the trees. Go ahead and pray to the gods, pray to God and Jehovah, pray to Newton and Kepler and Oppenheimer. See what good it does you.

My mother, Bernadette O'Shaughnessy, believed in the mystery with a divine face, believed in heaven, spirits, angels on high. She was the one who sat me in a pew in the hushed, candlelit vaults of the Church of the Assumption in Peterskill, New York, when I was so small I couldn't see over the rail. Every Sunday morning imploded on the sleepy, dreary, mind-numbing ritual that was mass, nothing left of it now but a welter of reworked sensory impressions misfiring in my septuagenarian brain: my mother's gloved hand like silk in my own, the power of her perfume to drive back the narcotic musk of the incense, the icy dip of the holy water – icy even in summer – and the music of the organ like some exotic feast that fills you to bursting with something that isn't food at all. I attended religious instructions. I was conversant with nuns and priests. I was eight, ten, twelve years old, I was communed and confirmed, bore the mystery of Latin, knew that masturbation was a sin and that God was watching. It was He who created the universe, the gnatcatcher, the canyon wren, the brown hyena and all those fifty-four billion galaxies, and He who created me and created Santa Claus and his elves too and the mountain of foil-wrapped gifts under the tree.

Yeah, sure. And then came science.

Science – empiricism, skepticism, the spirit of inquiry, doubt, debate and outright derision – was a gift of my Jewish father, Seymour Tierwater, the man everyone called Sy *(Get it? Sy and Ty?)* and I called Daddy. He was an MP during the war, a man who cracked heads as casually as he cracked walnuts, an angry man, a big man. He drank vodka. My mother drank scotch. With the backing of my mother's father, a roaring, barking, rock-headed, neo-Cretaceous presence looming large in the dining room and den of my early years, Seymour Tierwater took his brand-new architectural degree from City College and built the development I grew up in. And how did you build a housing development? With divine help and guidance? With incense and magic? With elves? No. You built it with orthogonal angles and real things, concrete things, things made and scavenged by man out of a harsh, alien and godless universe that existed because it existed, and for no other discernible reason.

My father and I never had discussions along the lines of 'If God is so good and wise and all-knowing and all-powerful, then why did He create ticks and tapeworms and let all the Jews die in the ovens?' For him, there was no god but science, and never had been. But there must have been an ironclad quid pro quo in my parents' marriage contract – my grandfather's money, my grandfather's religion – because my father never objected to my early indoctrination, or not that I knew of, anyway. He just bided his time, a look of bemusement or mockery on his face whenever the sacerdotal words – Jesus, God the Father, the Holy Spirit – dropped from his son's lips. Was this a happy marriage? No. Not after the first ten years, anyway, but it lasted, held together by a king-size bed and ice cubes in a glass, till a crane buckled and a beam gave way and I became an orphan at the age of twenty-seven.

I mention all this because it gives me a context for evaluating what Andrea's just told me. If I'm getting it straight, it's this: the world is ending, so we have to write *The Lives of the Environmental Saints* and fleece Maclovio Pulchris so that we can run off and hide till such time as we can use the booty to rebuild it again. The world, that is.

'You're coming with us,' she repeats.

'I'm going nowhere. Or scratch that – I'm going to the bathroom. *Sake* in the morning, you know what I mean?' A look for April Wind. 'And *you* must know, right, April? You're getting to that age now, aren't you? Just wait,' I tell them, tell them both, and I'm so worked up I can hear the blood singing in my ears, 'just wait till you get to be my age.'

And then I'm ducking around the eternally overspilling buckets, my shoes sloshing on the sodden carpet, the pyrotechnics in my bowels a direct consequence of being seventy-five years old and foolish enough to think you can imbibe *sake* at ten o'clock in the morning and get away with it. Cheap *sake*, at that. My need is urgent, but still I can't help stopping at the bathroom door to turn a withering look on my ex-wife and current bed-partner. 'Did you really say "Earth Forever! is going to fly again"? Am I hearing right? *"Fly again"?* I mean, how deluded can you get?' Oh, yes, and now I'm full of it, full of myself and gas pains too. 'If it ever flew, and don't tell me it ever really did, not in any way that mattered to anybody except maybe Sierra and a bunch of dis-affected lunatics and bush-beaters, then I'm sorry it did, heartily sorry, and I wish I'd been there to cut the wings off of it with a rusty pair of scissors. Or shears. Carpet shears. And a bag of salt to rub in the wounds.

'And don't try to rattle me with this bullshit about the *mucosa,* because I know that's what it is: bullshit.'

I slam the door for punctuation, and then I'm alone in the bathroom. The dimmest of light here – a single amber-shaded fluorescent miser oozing just enough illumination to make me feel like I'm back in prison again – but I dig out my glasses reflexively and pick up the thin crumbling copy of the newspaper I keep on hand to get me through my more punishing bouts on the toilet. We don't see newspapers much anymore, I should tell you that – everybody gets their news electronically now, and the cost of paper, even newsprint, is prohibitive. Still, some of us like the physical feel of the thing, and the *Los Andiegoles Times* prints up a thin sheet every two weeks for the nostalgic and the deluded, not to mention the constipated. Rattle, rattle. Smooth out the pages. What am I reading? An account of a football game played in an empty leaking dome, the details as irrelevant as the outcome, page three of four, and the rest is about the weather. What's in store for us – or what was in store for us, two, or no, three weeks ago? Rain. Wind. Flooding in the low-lying and mid-lying areas. Hundred-percent chance of tornadoes, waterspouts, tsunamis.

There's a fire down below, no doubt about it, and I sit here waiting it out, reading about fumbles, interceptions and somebody's stout foot, the wind dragging its claws across the pitted stucco outside, my own familiar odor rising poisonously about me. I'll be here a while, a fact of life at my age (and forget the old-old, they might as well have their rectums sewed up), and I'm not hiding from anybody, least of all the two women in the next room, the ones who seem to have taken over my house. I'm not stupid. No matter how Andrea tries to spin it, love is the smallest part of what's involved here – they want access to Mac, that's what this is all about. They want money. And they want me. Or Sierra, that is. Sierra's ghost. So why do I put up with it? Why don't I run both of them out the door and go back to Lily and my anteaters and peccaries?

Because I'm bored. Because I've got nothing to lose. Because I know I can put the brakes on if I have to. Roll with it. Ride your pony. Oh, yes, indeed.

When I emerge, the two of them have their heads together, two wan little smiles for me, the lord of the house, and there's a smell in the air – fragrant, fecund, seductive – a smell that rings every bell in my olfactory lobe and knocks my defenses right back down to nothing: they're baking cookies. Cookies. The world has been transformed to shit, I'm about to be turned inside out, gutted, spitted, grilled and filleted, and they're baking cookies. It's too much. I just wave my hand feebly, in surrender, and fade away into the very damp bedroom for a nap.

I wake in darkness, to the sound of the rain. It's steady now, the kind of vertical pounding that brings to mind tin roofs, coconut palms and Singapore slings, but at least the wind has died down. I've been dreaming, a standard dream about a too-big house with too many wings and too many doors that lead to nothing but house and more house, and it takes me a good five minutes to resurrect my conscious mind. But what time is it? It feels like midnight, but then it always feels like midnight. My watch says 12:15 – p.m. – and that seems about right. I hold my wrist up to study the glowing numerals against the dim backdrop of the room, my mouth dry, head throbbing, tireder than I was when I staggered in here an hour and a half ago.

For a time I just lie there, putting off the inevitable reaccessing of my dog's life for another sodden minute. (The walls are sweating, I don't need to turn on the light to know that, and the banana slug that lives in the architecturally inconvenient gap under the windowsill will be grazing the algal bloom over the portrait of Thoreau. And the gap itself will have grown perceptibly – subsidence, and with this rain what isn't subsiding?) Want more? There's a new leak in the roof, easily detectable as a kind of snare drumming in the corner over the regular splootching of the bedroom buckets, I'm probably going to have to sandbag the front porch again, and the fullness of the afternoon is going to be spent in a river of muck and hyena shit as Chuy and I try to keep the animals from drowning.

Then the pictaphone is ringing – or speaking, actually: *Incoming call,* a mechanical voice announces – and I'm lifting my other wrist to answer it. 'Yeah?' I say, and I can't help it if my voice lacks enthusiasm – I'm not expecting much out of the day, or for that matter the week, month or year.

'Ty? You there?'

The voice is familiar, soft and sugar-coated, pitched as high as a child's, and I know it, I do, know it as well as my own . . . 'Mac?' I venture.

'Give me a picture, Ty, come on – '

I hit the button, and there he is, Maclovio Pulchris, trapped in a little box on the underside of my wrist. He's wearing the fedora he was born with – it must have been clamped on his head all the way through the birth canal – and there are three strands of slick processed hair (his eel whips, he calls them) clinging to his mirror shades just over the place where his left eye would be. If he ever took his shades off, that is. 'Jesus, Ty, you look like shit.'

'Thanks. It's the look I'm after. I've been putting a lot of work into it.'

'Are you in bed? At this hour?' A pause. All you can see of him, really, is his lips, nose and cheekbones. It's a disguise, and it makes him appear ageless, I suppose, though he's hardly one of the young-young, or even young. And then, in the softest, breathiest, most forlorn fifth-grader's voice: 'You're not sick, are you?'

What can I say? Andrea's out there in the other room, and she's a kind of sickness. So's April Wind. And Earth Forever! 'Petunia got loose – and don't worry, she's all right, we got her back' – bringing my bandaged arm into view – 'but she chewed up my arm and plus it's raining like holy hell here and I was up before dawn scattering straw in the cages, checking on the sandbags, that sort of thing.'

'I know.'

I'm just looking at his face, and there's no more flexibility to it than you'd find in a carved wooden mask, but I know what my face is showing on his end: befuddlement, age and decrepitude, uncertainty, incompetence, a doddering around the eyes and a pronounced dwindling of the mouth and chin. 'What do you mean?'

'I'm here. Back from sunny North Carolina and all those sweet tropical drinks. And it's a gas, it is – up in the nineties every day, sunshine like you wouldn't believe . . . but Ty, you know what?'

Here I am, the champion of the young-old, in full possession of my faculties and fresh from my latest sexual triumph, and what do I say? Something penetrating, like 'Huh?'

The fifth-grader's voice again, pinched and whispery with concern: 'I'm worried about the animals.'

Well, so am I, I want to tell him, *what do you think you're paying me for?* Unfortunately, I never get the chance. Because at that moment, Chuy comes banging through the door – the bedroom door, and I wonder where my peace and dignity have fled to – and he's waving his arms and opening and closing his mouth on nothing, so excited he can't seem to form the words to tell me about it in either of the two languages at war in his brain. I can see it in his eyes, though – trouble, big trouble – and of course he's dripping and his hair and mustache have just been recovered from the bottom of the sea. 'Sorry, Mac,' I say to my wrist, 'gotta go, talk to you later,' and break the connection.

'What?' I throw at Chuy, bolt upright in bed now, the light from the other room shining sick and weak on the mossy walls and the banana slug fixed like a lamprey to the image of Thoreau's face. *('Morning air! If men will not drink of this at the fountain head of the day, why, then, we must even bottle up some and sell it in the shops, for the benefit of those who have lost their subscription ticket to morning time in this world.')* 'What's the matter?'

'*Los edificios,* they, they – '

'What *edificios?*' I'm up now, pulling on my jeans, the anxious faces of Andrea and April Wind hanging on cords in the distance.

'*Los, los condos,* and Rancho Seco – them too – they are what I think is falling down, I mean like in the *corriente,* you know, like boom, boom, boom – '

When Frank Buck wanted elephants – that is, when some zoo or circus placed an order – he would cruise over to Ceylon, hire a couple hundred natives and cut down a whole forest's worth of tropical hardwoods to build a pen with a four-hundred-foot chute in front of it. Fifteen-foot-tall logs were set in the ground eighteen inches apart throughout the pen – or *kraal,* as it was called – and then, using tame elephants to lure the wild ones in close, Buck and his men would stampede the whole lot of them down the chute and into the enclosure as if they were sheep. Uncle Sol, who was there, informed me about this and other peculiarities of the animal trade when I was fifteen, a skinny kid with a mop and shovel, overwhelmed by the sheer amount of ordure – shit, that is – his eight Indian elephants produced daily. There was the dust, he said, that was the first thing you noticed, a roiling river of dust fifty feet high, and then you felt the concussion through the soles of your shoes – fifty or sixty panicked animals weighing up to five tons apiece punishing the ground. But it was the screaming he remembered most, like a brass band hitting nothing but high notes, right off the scale, a noise that shivered and humbled you till the big gate dropped and all that ocean of flesh was just one more commodity for sale and export. The elephants went to Cincinnati, Cleveland, Chicago, Central Park, the big timbers of the *kraal* rotted and tumbled over and the jungle sprang back up to conceal the next generation of pachyderms.

That was ninety years ago. Now the elephants are gone, and the forest too – Ceylon, last I heard, was 100 percent deforested, a desert of unemployable mahouts and third-generation twig-gatherers. Uncle Sol had it easy – all he had to do was go out into the wilderness and catch things, and it was a deep wilderness, a jungle full of sights unseen and sounds unheard, raffalii and dorango in the trees, chevrotains, tapirs and yes, pangolins poking through the leaves. It's a little different for me and Chuy. There is no wilderness, and there's nothing left to catch, except maybe rats. Our job, as it turns out on this very wet sixth-consecutive day of rain, is to subdue a menagerie of disgruntled, penned-up and reeking animals named after flowers and escort them to higher ground.

Andrea's going to help. So are April Wind and Mac's two bodyguards. We need all the help we can get, because chaos has been unleashed here, two whole sections of the Lupine Hill condos collapsed like wet cardboard (and where are Delbert Sakapathian and his thousand-dollar check now, I wonder), Rancho Seco gone wet suddenly and looking less like a gated community and more like a riverbed every minute, and my own humble abode flooded right up to the high-water mark on my gum boots. At some point, not long after Chuy's revelation in my darkened bedroom, Mac himself appeared at the front door, wrapped up and hooded in a black slicker that might have been a body bag in another incarnation, his eel whips hanging limp, shades misted over. The bodyguards bookended him. The sky was close. My carpets were fishbait and the *Titanic* was going down fast. 'Everybody,' he shouted, and even in his extremity his voice was as breathy and sweet as a kindergarten teacher's, 'everybody up the hill to my house!'

We're coming, I want to tell him, Andrea scooping up floating paperbacks and doing triage on the kitchen appliances, and you don't have to ask twice − but, first, the animals. Out there in the thick of it, Chuy and I discover that one of the giant anteaters has drowned. I don't know if you can picture a giant anteater offhand − this is the kind of creature that never looked quite real anyway, what with the Mohawk haircut, the underslung bear's feet and the three lengths of hose stuffed into its snout − but it looks even less convincing now. Just dead. Dead and gone. And probably no more than thirty or forty of them left on earth. Even with the rain, even with Andrea and my knee and Mac and the threat of the *mucosa,* I want to sit down and cry.

Lily, fortunately, is all right − she's dug herself a mound big as a tumulus, and there she is, curled up on top of it like a wet rug. The lions we find stacked up on the roof of the concrete-block structure at the back of their cage, roaring their guts out. Dandelion, the male, looks as if he's been drowned twice and twice resuscitated, the mane drooping round his jowls like some half-finished macramé project. Amaryllis and Buttercup, the lionesses Mac ordered through a breeding-facility catalogue from some place in Ohio, don't look much better. Their eyes tell me they want to be pacing neurotically up and down the length of the chain-link fence that encloses their half-acre savanna, but the whole thing is a three-foot-deep stew of phlegm-colored water and Siamese walking catfish (have I mentioned that some environmental anarchist let half a dozen of them go in Carpinteria twenty years back, just as the weather started to turn?).

'Chuy,' I announce, swinging round on him and the two hopeless-looking bodyguards, 'the lions are going to be a problem. If we dart them, they're liable to fall into the slop and drown, and if we just wade in there with the wire net, they'll just as likely chew our heads off.'

The bodyguards – both of them are named Al, I think – don't look as if they like the sound of this. They're the ones who are going to have to drag a four-hundred-pound cat bristling with claws and teeth through three feet of water and sling it in the back of the Olfputt, and that's no mean feat, whether it's unconscious or not. And then – stirring news – they'll have to go back for the lionesses.

Chuy, meanwhile, is blinking back the rain, hunched and stringy, considering the problem. His slicker, which is at least three sizes too long for him in the arms, is a pale, faded orange in color, liberally stained with Rorschach blots of oil, mold and animal blood. 'They can swim, Mr. Ty, *nadan estos gatos,* and maybe I think we can tie them like *caballos,* you know, around the neck, and maybe we hook the rope up to the back of the truck, and, you know – '

I'm dazed. Old and dazed. The rain is like a trillion hammers, blow after blow, staggering me. 'You mean, we drag them?'

'Sure. And when they see *la puerta* open wide to that dry warm basement at Mr. Mac's, then maybe *yo pienso que* where they want to go, *verdad?*'

Or we could just leave them. The water's probably not going to get up that high, I tell myself, but even so it can't be good for them to be soaked through for days on end – they'll catch cold, won't they? What about in Africa, though – or Africa as it once was? They didn't have lion pens to snuggle in – or multimillionaire pop stars' carpeted, paneled and Ping-Pong–tabled basements either. Yes. Sure. And they died, every last one of them, flagged, skinned and eaten right down to the bone by the pullulating masses of our own degraded species. Africa doesn't matter anymore. Nature doesn't matter anymore – it's not even nature, just something we created out of a witches' brew of fossil-fuel emissions and defor-estation. These lions live here, in the Santa Ynez Valley – this is their natural habitat now. And if the valley floods, then we'll move them to higher ground, a new habitat for the infinitely adaptable New Age lion: Maclovio Pulchris' twelve-thousand-square-foot basement.

And you know what I say? Hallelujah and praise the Lord.

Los Angeles/Titusville, July 1989

WHAT HE WANTED, more than anything, more than revenge, even – more than Andrea and the trees and the owls – was to get his daughter back. Just that. Just walk her down the steps of Juvenile Hall, put her in the car and drive back to New York with his tail between his legs – and it wasn't too late to go back, the house in escrow, the shopping center on the market still, the old blanket of his old life neatly folded and all ready and waiting to be pulled up over his head again. And Andrea? Forget Andrea, forget sex, forget life. He didn't want to be alive, because if you were alive you hurt, and this hurt worse than anything he'd ever known or imagined. His daughter. They'd taken his daughter away. And why? Because he was an unfit parent.

An unfit parent. That set him on fire, all right, that set him off like a Scud missile, all thrust and afterburners and calamitous rage. There was no fitter parent. Show me one – that was his attitude – just show me one. He'd been father and mother to Sierra since she was three years old and he had to rescue her from her grandmother and tell her that her mommy wasn't coming back anymore because she'd just vanished from the face of this earth like a ghost or a breath of wind. Try that one on for size. Try climbing out of the cavern of sleep to the screams and night alarms of an inconsolable thirty-seven-pound ball of confusion and rage, try dropping her off at nursery school, a single father on his way to mind-numbing, soul-crushing work, and she won't let go of the door handle, no joke, no cajoling, the drooping faces of the nursery-school teachers and pitying mothers hanging over the fenders of the car like fruit withered on the vine. A motherless kindergartner, a motherless ten-year-old, a motherless teenager.

Tierwater put his *life* into fixing that – or assuaging it, bandaging it, kissing the hurt to make it better – and no one could tell him different. Not Judge Duermer or the Josephine County Child Protective Services or the Supreme Court either.

But here was the fact: he was in Los Angeles, trapped in a blistering funk of heat and smog and multicultural sweat, and she was in Oregon, where the trees stood tall and the air was cool and sweet – in Oregon, in jail. Or Juvenile Hall. Same difference. They wouldn't let him see her, wouldn't let him correspond with her, wouldn't even let him speak with her on the phone – he was too evil and corrupting an influence. He was a monster. A criminal. A freak. Three and a half weeks had gone by now, and he'd done nothing but lie on the couch and stare at the ceiling. He wanted to be in Oregon, close to her, just to tread the same soil and breathe the same air, but Fred wouldn't hear of it. You'll do more harm than good, he insisted. Stay out of it. Don't go near the state line except for court appearances – don't even think about it. And don't worry: we'll get her released to Andrea, no problem – no matter what happens with you.

The sad fact was that since the day he made bail he'd been back just once – up and down the coast in the space of forty-eight hours – with Andrea and Fred, for a dependency hearing before the judge.

Judge Duermer (triple-chinned, rolling in his robes, the great bulging watery sea lion's eyes): Can you show cause why this juvenile – Sierra Sarah Tierwater – should be returned to the custody of her father and stepmother, both of whom are facing criminal charges in this county?

Fred (short and bald, a blazing wick of vital energy, appalled for all the world to see): But, Your Honor, with all due respect, this is a matter of peaceable civil protest, an exercise of my clients' rights to free speech and assembly –

Judge Duermer (reading from a sheet in front of him, Sierra nowhere to be seen): Assault on a peace officer, resisting arrest, escape from custody, child endangerment, contributing to the delinquency of a minor? Come on, counsel, these are serious charges, and until such time as they have been adjudicated, I can't see fit to release this child to the parents.

Sierra's Lawyer (Cotton Mather in a three-piece suit, no nose or chin to speak of): Your honor, on behalf of Child Protective Services, I move to have Sierra Sarah Tierwater placed with a foster family until such time as the parents can show that they have taken appropriate measures – parenting classes, for instance, and refraining from further criminal conduct – to assure the court that they are indeed fit to raise this child.

The upshot? Tierwater, still facing up to a year in jail on the criminal charge, was ordered to take approved parenting classes and to keep his own very prominent nose clean for a period of twelve months, after which the court would make its decision. Back again to Los Angeles, doom and gloom and seething hate. He stared out the window of the car and into the trees, and even the shell of the burned-out Cat glimpsed somewhere between Cottonwood and Red Bluff gave him no pleasure. Criminal conduct. The sons of puritanical high-and-mighty bitches – they haven't seen anything yet. That's what Tierwater was thinking, but it came and went. Revenge fantasies got you nowhere. Despair did, though. Despair got you to submit to the gravitational force and become one with the cracked leather couch in front of the eternally blipping TV in a rented house on a palm-lined street in suburbia. *(Give me my daughter back and I will pluck the owls and drop them in the frying pan myself, no questions asked, that's how I felt, because I was all about giving up then, a victim, a schmuck, ground under the iron heel of Judge Duermer and Sheriff Bob Hicks.)*

'Come on, Ty,' Andrea said, trying for a smile but looking grim underneath it, 'snap out of it. We're fighting this, okay? It'll be all right. It will.'

It was a morning of common heat, a hundred and three by eleven o'clock, the San Fernando Valley baking like cheap pottery. The dry wind they called Santa Ana was rattling the leaves of the grapefruit trees in the desiccated backyard – nothing there, not a spike of grass, not even a gopher mound – and knocking the dead fronds out of the palms out front with a sound like sabers rattling. This was in a place called Tarzana, named for the Lord of the Jungle, whose steady earning power had allowed his creator to buy it all up at one time and make it his ranch, his spread, his dusty, spottily irrigated, citrus-tree-studded estate and manor in the New

World – and there was a transformation for you. Now it was part of the stinking, creeping, blistered megalopolis – Teo's home-town, incidentally – and E.F! had chosen it as the location for their Los Angeles chapter. Why? Because Teo knew it, and because it was quiet and dull, a place where people had jobs and foreign cars and repainted their classic 1950s ranch houses every other year in the same two basic colors. Ecotage? Never heard of it.

Teo and Andrea didn't have jobs. Neither, any longer, did Tierwater. Teo and Andrea were supported by E.F.! contributions, the money they made stumping in places like Croton, and, ultimately, by Tierwater. And Tierwater was supported by his dead father. This is called the food chain. 'Yeah, I know,' he said, his voice buried in a swamp of misery and depression, 'but it's killing me. It's like going to a shrink when you're a kid – did you ever go to a shrink?'

She was sitting beside him on the couch. Phones were ringing, people moving incessantly from room to room, sweating and conspiratorial. She just lifted her eyebrows, noncommittal.

'Just because you know what the problem is, just because you can express it in so many words, that doesn't mean you can do anything about it. I feel impotent. Castrated. Fucked. I think I'm having a nervous breakdown here. I mean, I've dealt with grief before – *grieving* – but this is different. Nobody died.' The effort of talking was giving him a headache. He was in a hyperbaric chamber, that's what it was, and they'd screwed down the pressure so he could feel it in every pore. 'Except maybe me.'

She slipped down beside him, the curves and hollows of her body seeking his, holding him, mothering him, but it was no good. For one thing, it must have been ten degrees hotter inside than out. For another, the phones were ringing, a natural irritant, and the voices whispering. And then there was this, the issue he really hadn't dealt with yet: resentment. How could he let himself be soothed by her when she was the one who'd dragged him into this, when she was the one to blame? 'Listen,' and she was whispering now, her breath sour, the smell of her underarms and the sweat sliding down her temples, one more weight crushing him, 'Fred says – '

And here was where the violence spurted out like bad blood,

where push came to shove, Andrea on the floor suddenly, Tierwater up off the couch in a single snaking motion. He was shouting. Standing over her and shouting. 'Fuck Fred!' he shouted. 'Fuck him! And fuck you too!'

And then the letter came. It was in a stained envelope, invitation-size, and it wasn't from his ex-secretary, his realtor in New York or any of the legal or social-service departments of Josephine County, Oregon. The handwriting – a random conjunction of block letters and an undisciplined, wobbling cursive – brought him out of his slumber. With trembling fingers, he tore open the flap – tore the letter inside into two curling strips, in fact – and saw Sierra's hasty scrawl there on the back of a fast-food napkin. *Dad,* he read, *they've got me at this farmers house in this town called i think Titansville or something come get me I'm going to die here Sierra.*

'I'm not going to do anything rash,' he told Andrea in a kitchen full of volunteers, the wind flailing branches against the windows, flyers running hot off the Canon copier on the table, Teo on the phone in the corner, rubbing the unfashionable stubble of his athlete's head as if the harder he rubbed, the more money he could conjure up out of the wires. It was two in the afternoon. He wouldn't let her take the letter from him – the napkin, that is, already damp with his sweat – but he spread it across his palm for her to read.

He watched her eyes.

'I mean,' and he dropped his voice, 'I'm not going to kidnap her or anything. I just want to see her, that's all – just for a minute. Give her some money. Reassure her – '

'No, Ty. Uh-uh. No way in the world.'

'She's scared, don't you understand that? Can you even imagine it? She doesn't know what's going on here. Maybe she thinks we abandoned her, maybe that's what she thinks. I want my daughter. I miss her. I can't even sleep, for Christ's sake.'

'Forget it, Ty. No.'

'You know something, Andrea' – and they were all listening now, the three Pierce College students in their Pierce College sweatshirts, the housewife with the spiked hair and bruised mascara, the unemployed stockboy of forty with the beard, ponytail and multiple earrings – 'nobody tells me no, because I don't like to hear that word, not from you, not from Fred, not from anybody. I'm going up there.'

'You're out of your mind, Ty. Flat-out crazy.' She gestured to Teo, an urgent swipe of the hand, and he whispered something into the phone and hung up. 'This is no joke – they're trying to make an example of us up there – of you, and you're the one who had to go and try to escape, and from a hospital, no less – '

'What's the problem?' Teo wanted to know. His face was suddenly interposed between Tierwater's and his wife's, the face of Liverhead, severe and uncompromising. Both of them had to look down at him.

Andrea, her eyes cold as crystal. 'Ty wants to go up and rescue Sierra. Show him the letter, Ty.'

Tierwater brought his hand out from behind his back, where it had gone instinctively, and held out the limp napkin. Teo scanned the message while Andrea made her case: 'I don't think Ty understands just how serious this is – I mean, we could lose her for good, permanently, till she's of legal age anyway. They'll put her in a foster home, they will. In a heartbeat.'

Tierwater couldn't appreciate the logic of this. 'She's in a foster home now. With some farmer. Imagine that? Some farmer. Who the hell is he? Maybe he's a pedophile or something – sure, why wouldn't he be? Aren't they all?'

Teo: 'What, farmers?'

'These people that take in kids. Why else would they do it?'

'Come on, Ty – what planet are you living on? For money, for one thing. Because they like kids. Because they have a social conscience.' Andrea was turning over one of the flyers in her hand – in a week they'd be staging a protest in the Arizona desert against yet another power plant. 'Listen, Ty, I know you're upset – I miss her too, and I regret this whole thing, it's tearing me up, it is – but you've got to stay above ground with this one. Fred'll have her back in a week, trust me, he will.'

The Santa Anas tapped at the windowpane and Tierwater looked up to see a tumbleweed (Russian thistle, *Salsola kali,* another invasive species) hurtle across the yard. The college students, three boys so alike they might have been triplets, shared a laugh over something, their breathless snorts of amusement a counterpoint to the rasp of the wind outside. 'A week? You heard what the judge said.'

'Fred's working on it.'

'Bullshit he is. I'm out the door, I'm telling you – and if you want to come, that's fine with me, but I'm going whether you like it or not.' Tierwater's voice got away from him for a minute, and the students' laughter died in their throats. He looked round the room. Nobody said a word. Even the telephones stopped ringing. 'This is my *daughter* we're talking about here.'

Tierwater didn't like traffic. He didn't like freeways. He hated the constant nosing for position at seventy, seventy-five, eighty, the big eighteen-wheelers thundering along on either side of you like moving walls, the exhaust, the noise, the heat. He'd come to Los Angeles with his new bride, with Andrea, because that was what she wanted – and it was what Sierra wanted too, or seemed to want. ('This place? You mean, like Peterskill? You've got to be joking, Dad – you really think there's a kid in America that wouldn't choose L.A. over *Peterskill?*') He wouldn't kid himself – he wanted out too – and though Andrea moved in with him in the house he shared with his daughter, it was understood that she was a California girl, and once he got his affairs in order (read: sold everything at rock-bottom prices) and Sierra's school let out, they were heading west, as an environmentally correct, newly nuclear family. It might have been different if they'd got there in February, when the sun was pale as milk and the days were long cool tunnels full of light and bloom, but they arrived on the first of June – after truncating Sierra's seventh-grade experience by three and a half weeks – and it was hot. And smoggy. And the freeways were burning up.

And now he was out on the freeway again, in an unfamiliar car, looking to feed into the 405 North from the 101 East – and why couldn't they call the freeways by their proper names, the San Diego and Ventura? – a very pale and bristling Andrea at his side. Trucks swerved, cars shot randomly across lanes, engines coughed and roared and spat out fumes, oleander flashing red and white along the dividers, the palms gone shabby, garbage everywhere. 'Jesus Christ,' Tierwater swore, crushing the accelerator, 'there's too many people in the world, that's what it is, and they're all going the same place we are – all the time. That's what gets to me – you can't even take a crap without six hundred people in line ahead of you.'

'And I suppose Peterskill's better?'

'At least you could see the road. At least you felt like you were in control.'

He swerved and lurched, hit the horn, hit the brakes, randomly punching buttons on the radio, swearing all the while. He was letting the little things get to him, because the big thing – Sierra – was something he didn't want to think about, not yet, not until the 405 became the 5 and he followed it all the long way up the spine of California to Oregon, where he wasn't welcome, definitely wasn't welcome. He had no plan. None whatever. He didn't even know what town she was in, though 'Titansville' seemed a pretty good match for Titusville, ten or fifteen miles south of Grants Pass, and that was good enough for him.

They spent the night at a public campground near Yreka, Tierwater dropping off into a dense dreamless sleep the minute he'd unfurled his groundcloth and sleeping bag. It was 3:00 a.m. The sky was open to the stars, not a light showing anywhere, out of the car, low whispers, and that was all till he opened his eyes on ten o'clock in the morning and Andrea sitting cross-legged beside him. Her face was a deep drenched blue, the color imparted to it by the light sifting through the walls of the tent, and she was studying a map. 'You slept like a zombie,' she said. 'Or no, not a zombie – zombies don't sleep at all, do they?'

He was almost his usual self, and this was his wife, and he loved her. He was almost in Oregon. He was alive. It was the morning of the day on which he was going to see his daughter, one way or the other.

'Au contraire,' he said, 'they sleep all day, in their graves. Or for weeks or months at a time. Until the *houngan* summons them to rise up and commit acts of mayhem, that is. And can you really blame them – the zombies, I mean?' A jay screeched from someplace nearby. He smelled coffee. Heard children –

high, colliding voices and running feet. 'What does the map say?'

The map said what he already knew: that Titusville was in Josephine County. Period. It didn't indicate whether there was a school there, a gas station, a firehouse or a café where some innocuous tourist or long-lost relative could inquire about farmers who took in foster children. That was all right. He felt good for the first time since he'd stuck his feet in that dark trough of cement – at least he was moving, at least he was doing something. He'd find her. He knew he would. It was the next step he was foundering on: what then? He pictured her out in some cinematic barnyard, all the colors true, geese bobbing, hogs snuffling, and Sierra in the middle of it, pitching hay in a pair of bib overalls in the company of four or five cross-eyed orphans and snub-nosed runaways. And then he saw himself emerging from the car – and he was in her point of view now – emerging from the car in triumph, radiant and tall and unafraid, climbing the fence, striding across the yard and taking her in his arms.

They made Titusville by noon, Tierwater too wrought up to eat breakfast, Andrea placidly munching a stale American cheese on white and washing it down with a Diet Coke as the scenery scrolled by. The town was anonymity itself, fast-food outlets creeping out along the highway, an uneven mouthful of older buildings, hand-lettered signs advertising antiques and going-out-of-business sales, old men on a bench, adolescents clustered around a sleek white convertible. Andrea sauntered into the local gas station and let her halter top do the talking while Tierwater sat hunched in the car, disguised as a timber person (jeans, workboots, plaid shirt and 49ers cap). The car itself was a disguise, a turd-brown Chevy Nova with some damage to both rear fenders, the trunk and the rear bumper, loaned out for the occasion by one of the Los Angeles chapter's volunteers (the housewife, divorced, angry, name of Robin Goldman). He watched Andrea's movements through the crusted window of the garage as she leaned across the counter in black spandex, a refugee from the ballet school in Eugene, and worked the two teenagers there like a fortune-teller. ('You know those foster kids?' 'Who, you mean out the Billrays'?' 'Who'd you think I was talking about? They're out there past the school, aren't they?' 'Uh-huh, second right, Cedar Street.' 'Big white house?' 'Naw, it's blue now.')

It wasn't what Tierwater had been expecting – no farm, no cows, pigs, chickens, goats, not even a dog – just a big shining turquoise house set in a clearing hacked out of the woods. There was a vegetable garden to one side of it, with some sort of plow or rototiller abandoned in the high grass in back of a substantial stand of corn, and a shuttered shed out on the road that advertised SWEET CORN, TOMATOES, SUMMER SQUASH, but nobody, not even a suburban teenager under duress, would describe the place as a farm. A yellow Subaru was parked in the driveway. The windows caught the sun and held it. Nothing moved, not so much as a bird flitting across the lawn or a butterfly suspended over the peonies.

They drove by twice, once at normal speed so as not to arouse suspicion, and then very slowly, falteringly, like the lost tourists they were planning to impersonate. 'Go ahead, Ty,' Andrea prodded him, 'pull into the driveway already – if she's there, maybe we'll see her, signal to her or something. If she's not, she's not. We'll dig some more. Okay? So pull in already.'

Tierwater, in this moment of truth, found himself strangely – and sadly – unable to act. He'd brought the car to a stop on the blacktop road just past the driveway, and when he looked over his shoulder to see about backing it up, discovered that there was another car behind him. Directly behind him – right on his bumper, in fact. The driver was an old lady – sixty, seventy, it was all the same to him, senile no doubt, a puff of white hair and some sort of kerchief round her neck. She was just parked there, staring at him through the outsized lenses of her glasses as if she were at the drive-in waiting for the show to start. He flagged his arm – go on, pass me, I'm just parked here for the rest of my life – but she didn't seem to comprehend the gesture. Out of the corner of his eye he caught movement now up at the house, activity around the Subaru, a kid – not Sierra – and a trim-looking man in a short-sleeved white shirt, slam, slam, the distant soft concussion of both doors shutting simultaneously, followed by the sound of an engine revving. Another gesture for the old lady, but she was planted behind the wheel of the car – a Cadillac of the fin era – and worse, the car was blocking the driveway.

'What now?' Tierwater demanded, his teeth clenched, stomach churning, all the many mountains of shit in the world piled high around him. He was looking at Andrea, looking for someone to blame, and she was the prime candidate. By default. 'That could be them – that could be them right there – what do I do?'

The Subaru had come to a stop at the end of the drive, two mild faces caught behind the untinted glass of the windshield, looks of mild surprise for the old lady in the Cadillac, but no horn-hammering impatience or big-city sneers, the broadest of neighborly grins already blooming. The trim man – and Tierwater was calculating now – looked to be about thirty, blond hair parted on the left side, a pair of smoked discs clamped over prescription lenses, the sort of thing a building inspector might wear on his day off. Next to him was a boy of sixteen or seventeen, eyes gouged into his head as if by the thumbs of a ceramic sculptor, flattop haircut, peach-colored. Andrea stepped out of the car.

'Hello, there,' she said, shading her eyes with one hand and shaking out a conciliatory wave with the other. She was moving forward, along the weed-choked ditch that was the shoulder, addressing the windshield of the Subaru rather than the hunched and frozen form of the old lady. 'I wonder if you could help us – we seem to've gotten lost. We're looking for' – and here she gave a glance with a smile wrapped round it to the old lady, for form's sake, before coming back to the Subaru – 'for the Wilsons' place. Ted and Dodie Wilson?' And then she stopped, just beyond the Cadillac, not five feet from the Subaru's bumper.

The trim man – five eight, one forty-five, ironed right into his clothes – stepped out of the car, the neighborly smile turned up till it could roast meat. The door swung wide, and then the other door creaked open and the boy was standing there on the near side of the car. And what was he? Heavier than Tierwater had thought, meaty arms, the high-school linebacker's neck and shoulders, a look of nullity behind the smile. 'The Wilsons?' the trim man said – but let's call him the building inspector, because that's what he was, then and forever, in Tierwater's mind anyway. 'Wilkersons I know, and Westons, but nobody named Wilson. Not around here anyways.' Turning to the boy. 'You know of any Wilsons at school, Donnie?'

Donnie didn't know of any. Tierwater got out of the car. 'Hi,' he said, the length of his car and the old lady's Cadillac between them. 'Sorry about this, but I guess I stopped to look at the map and the lady' – a gesture for the old lady, white gloves clamped on the steering wheel, eyes locked straight ahead – 'she seemed to just stop here behind me and, well, I don't know – I mean, I can move the car . . .'

Smiling wider. 'Oh, that's Mrs. Toffler. She's all right. A little confused, is all. Nothing to worry about.' And now the building inspector was on the blacktop, moving round the fins and up the long coruscating fender to the driver's-side door – helpful; helpful, friendly and neighborly – the whole world a sweet and peaceable place.

That was when Sierra burst through the gleaming turquoise door of the house behind them and fled out onto the lawn, a dog and two scrawny teenaged girls at her heels. 'Dad!' she screamed. 'Dad, Dad!'

Tierwater froze. He watched as a new look came into the building inspector's eyes, a look that said, *Dad? Who's Dad?* The man was clearly bewildered. He glanced from Tierwater to Andrea and then over his shoulder at the charging trio and the yapping dog, and all the while Sierra kept shouting out that most intimate and filial sobriquet, her bare feet flapping on the lawn like precious white fish, her braces gleaming in the sunlight, her face saturated with a martyr's ecstasy. Tierwater felt his heart move in his chest, a deep-buried tectonic movement that made him shudder in every cell: the imposture was over. Time to improvise.

Meanwhile, the building inspector had begun to show signs of a dawning grasp of the situation, his eyes hardening first with suspicion, then anger and, finally, outrage. Behind him, still poised at the open passenger's door of the Subaru, the bull-necked kid settled into his shoulders as if awaiting the referee's whistle. 'You, you,' sputtered the man, the building inspector, his face gone red suddenly, 'you know you can't, you're not allowed – '

Sierra was coming on, pumping her arms, shouting, the dog – some kind of terrier – making a game of it, the other two girls falling back and jeering in their piping, incomprehensible adolescent voices. Tierwater glanced at Andrea, who hadn't moved a muscle, Andrea, his ally and accomplice, and what was her face telling him? *I told you so,* that's what. Her face was telling him that he was in the biggest trouble of his life, far bigger than anything Judge Duermer or Sheriff Bob Hicks had dished out yet – he was in direct violation of a court order and he'd better get a good long look at his daughter because he wasn't going to see her again till she was eighteen, not even a glimpse, not after this. 'No contact!' the building inspector barked, and he was moving rigidly along the length of the Cadillac and past the sculpture of the old woman locked at the wheel, moving toward Tierwater with what could only be violent intent, and here came the bull-necked kid in a linebacker's trot down the apron of the lawn, even as Sierra, in perfect synchronization with the dog, leapt the ditch and threw herself into her father's arms.

'No!' was all the building inspector could say, and he was vehement on this point of law and order and propriety, into the fray now and one hand locked on Tierwater's right arm and the other on Sierra's, trying to thrust them apart with the sort of effort he might have used on a pair of recalcitrant elevator doors.

(I have to say that I've never really enjoyed strangers taking hold of my arm, and that alone would have been enough to set me off, but this four-square WASP of a child-harboring Oregonian Child Protective Services person was trying to separate me from my daughter – and to what end, I could only imagine. Layer Andrea on top of that and the kid with the flattop and the terminally yapping, heat-seeking dog, and I don't think you could blame me for reacting in a way that would have disappointed Sheriff Bob Hicks.)

At first, Tierwater merely tried to protect his daughter, clutching her to him and interposing the mantle of his upper back between the sticks of her arms and the building inspector's clawing hands, but that was the stratagem of a rapidly dissolving moment. She'd fallen into his arms. He wanted to hold her, wanted to protect her. Was that a crime? He didn't think so, but before he could consider the issue or even draw his breath, the bull-necked kid was there, thick wrists and fat swollen fingers jerking at Sierra's shoulders, tug of war, the dog coming in low to complicate matters by snapping at Tierwater's unprotected shins and drooping socks. For one long suspended moment, they were doing a dance, all four of them, arms wrestling with arms, feet shuffling on the blacktop, grunting and straining while the dog played throat music and Andrea and the two skinny-legged girls shouted instructions from the sidelines, and then Tierwater found himself in another arena altogether.

He looked into the bull-necked kid's swollen face and saw release. That was all. Nothing he'd planned or even thought about, but when he brought his fist in over his daughter's shoulder and planted it in the center of that looming fat-constricted face, he felt himself sail right off the ground, as if gravity no longer operated on him. The kid fell magically away, all two hundred linebacking pounds of him, even as Tierwater turned to the building inspector. The man was still clawing at him, a look of anguish and prayerful appeal on his face, but the elbow Tierwater slashed to his windpipe was like a wing, fluttering and flapping and holding him aloft and out of harm's way.

He was thinking nothing, his posture defensive, but his daughter was behind him now and Andrea somehow in the driver's seat of the turd-brown car, shouting, 'Ty! Ty!' He looked at Sierra. Her face was bloodless and raw. She glanced over her shoulder at Andrea, and then looked back at the girls on the lawn and the turquoise house and the building inspector writhing on the blacktop with both hands wrapped around his throat, and she broke for the car with a tight little smile of triumph on her face. As for Tierwater, high as he was, he had no choice but to sidestep the kid when the kid came back at him in the spastic sort of lunge he might have made at a tackling dummy, and for good measure he gave the dog a deft kick that sent it skittering into the ditch with a yelp of surprise. And so what if he could see the lips of both the skinny girls working as they repeated the license-plate number to fix it in their memories? So what?

He had his daughter back now, and nobody was going to take her away again.

For the first ten miles, no one said a word. Gas fled down the throat of the carburetor, the tires screeched, Andrea hammered the accelerator and fought the wheel with spasmodic jerks of her big hands, and everything – farmhouses, sagging pickups, shirts, faces, clothes on a line, bark, branches, leaves – clapped by the windows like images in a rifled deck. She was going too fast, her eyes jumping at the rearview mirror, the borrowed car rocketing down one country lane after another, and there was nothing to say. Because this was no passive resistance, no peaceful protest, this was no mere violation of a court order or even the willful destruction of private property along the shoulder of Interstate 5 – this was the serious business now. Tierwater knew it, Andrea knew it, and even Sierra, clinging to him in the back seat and struggling to breathe through the muffled hoarse rasp of her sobs, must have known it. There was no coming back from this.

They drove on. A meadow appeared and vanished, two horses, a culvert, a narrow bridge. Andrea swerved through a series of S-turns, the car like a big oarless boat shooting down the rapids of some wild river, and finally Tierwater found himself breaking the silence with a pointed question: 'Where're we going?'

She gave him a wild glance, her eyes extruded and hard. 'Out of here, what do you think? You're the one – if you hadn't pushed it, if you didn't – you had to see her, didn't you? You couldn't leave well enough alone. I told you Fred was going to take care of it, didn't I?'

'Fred,' he spat, all but obliterating the name under the weight of his disgust. His face had come up out of its huddle. The countryside rushed by. He was scared, of course he was, but he was exhilarated too – he'd done something, finally done something – and his heart was racing faster than the Nova's straining engine. He was worked up, shot full of adrenaline, wild and angry and not to be denied. 'All right, sure, let's argue about it. Let's talk about whose idea it was to go into the fucking Siskiyou in the first place, all right? Because that's going to do us a lot of good right now.' A car loomed up on the left and shot by with a soft whoosh. Somewhere behind them the phone lines were busy, very busy. 'But where are we going? You know where you are?'

He watched her shoulders, furious shoulders, as she dug into the glove compartment. It took her a minute, and then she flung a map over the seat. 'You figure it out. You're the lunatic. You're the one they're after.'

That was when Sierra lifted her face from the cavity of his left arm. She'd buried it there when he leapt into the car and held his arms out to her, and through every jolt and dip of the road he'd felt the heat of her breath on his skin, the gentle swaying orbit of her body as the centrifugal forces threatened to pull her away from him. The car hit a bump and he watched her head wobble on the uncertain fulcrum of her neck. She was wearing mascara, and the tears had smeared it across her face in a dark wet paste. 'They took my nose ring,' she sobbed. 'They, they said it wasn't *Christian*.'

He intoned the automatic words – 'It's all right, honey' – and Andrea intoned them too, all the rage gone out of her voice. The car decelerated a moment in sympathy, but then she floored it again.

'I mean, they were horrible people – you wouldn't believe it. They made you sit straight up in your chair like some sort of marine or something, and, and' – she broke down again, and Tierwater felt his stomach sink – 'and they made you *pray* before you could eat!'

That was something, he was thinking – prayer, no less – but before he could absorb this information, before he could chew it over and let his eyes narrow over the implications and ramifications of this particular brand of child abuse ('They didn't touch you, did they, honey? I mean, nobody laid a hand on you in any way, did they?'), Andrea let out a low exclamation of surprise. 'Oh, shit!' she said, and gave the wheel a sudden savage spin. In the next moment he was thrown into his daughter, both of them rocked across the seat in a helpless surge of dead weight and flailing limbs. He snatched at the window crank for support, but it came off in his hand, one more useless scrap of metal.

When he regained his equilibrium he saw that they were on a dirt road now, the car fishtailing from one side to the other, tires spewing gravel, a contrail of dust spinning out behind them – and what else? What was that sound? It came to him with a jolt of recognition: it was a siren – a *siren!* – screaming in the distance. Andrea fought the wheel and the car skidded to a stop in a clump of weed just off the road, and they all three turned to stare out the back window at the intersection behind them. Tierwater saw a pall of sunstruck dust, a tunnel of pine, the natural world reaching out to them. His heart was pounding. The siren screamed, and screamed again. And then he saw it, a red streak flashing past the mouth of the dirt road, hook and ladder, men in T-shirts and hardhats – one glimpse and it was gone. 'It's a firetruck,' he said, and he couldn't seem to catch his breath. 'It's only a firetruck.'

The sky had begun to close up, a low dirty rug of cloud stretched out on a line and beaten till the bright corners went dark. Tierwater lay on his back in a nest of grass, the wadded-up plaid shirt supporting his head, the 49ers cap perched on his chest like a sleeping pet, and watched the clouds unravel. He smelled chlorophyll, mold, the vague tangy scent of wildflowers he didn't know the names of. In half an hour, it would be raining.

Twenty feet away, Sierra and Andrea were busy scooping mud out of a culvert alongside the road and flinging it at the car. They were aiming for a Jackson Pollock effect, an intricate web of abstraction that would somehow transmute the car into something harmless and inconspicuous, something a local might drive, with plates so muddied you couldn't tell at a glance whether they'd been issued in California or Oregon – or Saskatchewan, for that matter. Tierwater could have told them they were wasting their time – the rain would wash the car clean, no doubt about it – but he didn't want to dampen their enthusiasm. Besides, it gave them something to do, good healthy activity to while away the hours till dark, when they would make a run for the California border and get lost in the traffic that swept down out of the north in dense hurtling clots of steel and glass.

Andrea was making a game of it, and Sierra, with her mother's moon face and churning awkward legs, was laughing, actually laughing, as the mud flew and Robin Goldman's Chevy Nova became a work of art. This was good – she'd been scared, no doubt about it, scared and confused, the slab-faces whispering in one ear, the cops and her lawyer in the other – and if the past month had been hell for Tierwater, he could only imagine what it must have been like for her. But Andrea was the charm. Andrea took her in her arms and they sat down and talked it out, sharing a stale sandwich and a can of tepid root beer, and Tierwater was right there, his arms around both of them, so moved he could barely speak.

'I know there's no way we can ever make it up to you, honey,' Andrea said, 'and it's my fault, my fault entirely, you have to understand that. Your father didn't want to take you – he was right, and I should have listened, because you know we would never do anything to consciously hurt you or even if we thought there was the slightest risk . . . but I never dreamed . . . These are real sons of bitches we're dealing with here, major-league, and they'll do anything to bring us down. You'll be stronger for this, you will.'

(It was a dubious proposition, and it made no mention of the future, of the safe house, the underground, the assumed names and paranoia and the shuttling from one school to another – but my daughter was only thirteen years old and so glad to be rescued, to be out of the iron hands of the do-gooders, she never questioned it. And how do you give birth to a radical? I could write the manual.)

Sierra ducked her head, the half-eaten sandwich in one hand, her eyes like wolves' eyes, darker than the sky, wild already. 'I know,' she whispered.

But now Tierwater was lying in the grass and the solemnity was over. His wife and daughter were splashing the car with mud, giggling, crying out, feinting at one another with dripping palms, their bare feet black and glistening. He lay back and watched the clouds, smelled the rain, and it shouldn't have surprised him in the least that it was Jane he was thinking of, because she was the one he couldn't rescue, didn't rescue, the one who slipped away from him for good.

How do you want your pancakes – that's what she'd asked him on the morning of the day she died, and he could hear her voice like a half-remembered melody floating through his head – *burned black or semi-black?* He saw her in a pall of smoke – smoke that rose around her and ascended into the trees in thin white coils. She was wearing shorts, hiking boots, a New York Rangers sweatshirt – she was an upstate girl, from Watertown, hockey her passion. He hated hockey – a bunch of pumped-up yahoos slamming each other into the boards and grunting out violent epithets in Qué-becois French while the ice held its breath – but he loved her. That was the fact, though he hardly knew it himself and never expressed it aloud except in moments of erotic confusion. They didn't talk about abstractions, they talked about the baby, his job, her job, they talked about marmots and grizzly bears and what they were going to have for breakfast.

Give her dirty legs – scraped, scabbed, mosquito-bitten – and hands that could have been cleaner. And smoother. A smudge under her left eye that glistened like a scar. Limp hair. Clothes that smelled of smoke and food and her own rich musk. Give her all that, because they were camping, Glacier Park, special permit, and you could wash all you wanted, but you couldn't escape the dirt, not under those conditions.

He wanted his pancakes semi-black, and he communicated that much from the folds of his sleeping bag, which was laid out next to hers on a neoprene pad in the tent that looked like a big amanita mushroom sprung up out of the earth. It was raining, a soft misting rain that stained the trunks and silvered the needles of the trees. The night before, in the brooding black ringing silence of 11:30 p.m., they'd violated the chastity oath they'd taken on entering the park a week earlier: no sex in grizzly territory. No sex. That was common sense, and they'd discussed it dispassionately on the plane into Kalispell, and with real feeling in the motel room the night before they hiked into the back country – she was all skin and heat and hot ratcheting breath and they must have done it ten times against the deprivation to come. But two girls had been killed here – maimed and killed and one of them partially eaten – and they were taking no chances.

This was the wild, or as wild as it got on the planet earth in 1979. Ticrwater's heart beat just a little bit faster to know that there were creatures out there that could and would attack a human being and maybe even eat him, big eight- and nine-hundred-pound bears that could outrun a racehorse and outsmell a pack of bloodhounds, real serial killers, the top of the food chain. It thrilled Jane too. This wasn't Westchester County, where the most dangerous thing you'd run into was a black widow in the shower or maybe the quick-moving shadow of a copperhead sucking itself into a crevice in a fieldstone wall. This was raw. This was nature, untamed and unsanitized. 'You know what the scientific name for the grizzly is?' he'd asked her as the plane dipped its wings and the landing gear thumped into place. '*Ursus arctos horribilis. Horribilis?* Isn't that a gas?'

It was, it was. And he could see it in the sheen of her eyes and the way her face opened up to him. 'And those girls? Is it true they were menstruating?'

'You have to realize these things make their living by smell – they have to sniff out spring beauties, whitebark-pine nuts, carrion that's hardly even dead yet. Because they can never have too much to eat, and their whole life is a trip to the salad bar with a nice piece of meat on the side. So yes. The girls were menstruating, and maybe wearing perfume too. A grizzly could smell it – the blood – from miles away. It's like ringing a dinner bell – '

'Come on.'

'It is. And that's why there's no sex. They can smell the secretions.'

'Come on.'

'No, I mean it. Just last summer, right here in Glacier, a couple was killed in their tent. At night. They were – at least this is what the investigators say – they were doing it.'

So the pancakes. The pan was black, inside and out, soot like paint running right up the handle. Tierwater slapped mosquitoes and choked down the Jane-fried flapjacks that tasted like incinerated wood pulp and watched his wife eat her portion. There was no syrup. Syrup was too potent an attractant for bears. The beverage of choice? Pond water, fresh from the tin cup.

Of course, what was a potent attractant and what was not really hadn't come into play the night before. They'd been out there a week now – one week down, one to go – collecting the scat of the yellow-bellied marmot in Glad sandwich bags. Jane was working toward her Ph.D. in wildlife management, and one of her professors was studying the dietary predilections of the marmot in Glacier National Park for some reason fathomable only to herself. But, for two weeks, Dr. Rosenthal had to be at a Sciuridae/Rodentia/Mustela conference in Toronto, and Tierwater and Jane jumped at the opportunity to spell her, though it meant leaving Sierra with her grandmother in Watertown. That hurt. And yet there was never any real debate about it – this was a chance for Jane to do fieldwork and to score some bonus points with her friend and mentor, Dr. Sandee Rosenthal, the foremost marmot-person in the world, and it was a chance for Tierwater and his wife to be alone together, romantically alone, in a romantic setting. A second honeymoon, nothing less.

No sex, though – that would have been crazy.

Still, when Jane lit up a joint and slid bare-legged into his sleeping bag, he couldn't seem to keep his hands from making a mute appeal to her – and she seemed to be having the same problem he was. She pulled him to her. They kissed, long and hard, and then, panting and hot, they forced themselves apart. They lay there under the canopy of the tent, fighting for self-control – 'We can fool around, can't we? Maybe just a little?' – listening to the condensation drip from the trees as the fire outside settled into its embers, and what with the stillness and the pot and the electricity of their bodies, things got out of hand. They hadn't seen a grizzly, hadn't heard one, hadn't seen tracks or scat or stumps gutted for ants. They took a chance. They couldn't help themselves. And it was all the more intense for the danger of it – for the fractured resolve, for the tease – and when it was over they made themselves get up out of the sleeping bag and follow the beam of the flashlight down to the pond, where they slipped into the icy envelope of the water to scrub themselves with scentless soap till their teeth chattered and their lips turned blue.

Tierwater chewed the cud of his pancakes, the atomized rain collecting in his hair, and stared up into the canopy of the trees, opening up to everything there was. He was feeling rich, feeling blessed, and – he was only twenty-nine then, so you'll have to forgive him – feeling all but invulnerable. When Jane cried out he almost laughed, it was so comical. 'Oh!' she said, and that was all – just 'Oh' – as if she'd been surprised in the dark or fallen out of bed. It wasn't 'Oh, shit!' or 'Oh, fuck!' – just 'Oh.' Jane didn't curse, couldn't bring herself to it, and though they'd played at being street-smart and tough when that was the thing to do and smoked countless bowls with countless stoners and shouted their lungs out in dark overheated clubs and reeling outdoor arenas, Jane clung to her core of small-town propriety. Tierwater always thought that if it weren't for him she would have grown up to be the kind of woman who sat on the PTA board and went to church in a veiled hat and white gloves. And he loved that, he loved that about her. The world was full of obscenity, full of hard cases, antichrists and nutballs – he didn't need that. Not at home. Not in a wife.

'Oh!' she cried, and she jumped up from the dish of pancakes as if she'd been stung. *As if,* he says – but that was exactly what had happened. A bee had stung her. Or not a bee – a yellow jacket, *Vespula maculifrons,* the gold-and-black-banded wasp the locals called a meat bee because of its love for burgers, steaks and chops fresh off the grill. Not to mention carrion.

It was almost funny. A bee sting. But the incredible thing was that Jane had gone through an entire life, all twenty-five years of it, without ever having been stung before – or not that her mother could remember anyway. So this wasn't funny, wasn't the casual mishap it might have been for 99 percent of the species, the lucky ones, the nonallergic and resistant. It was death, that's what it was. Though Tierwater, fully engaged in the bliss of natural being and chewing his cud of semi-blackened buckwheat meal, didn't yet realize it. He got up, of course, set down the tin plate and went to her, the fire smoking, the trees dripping, the swatted yellow jacket lying on its back in the dirt and kicking its six moribund legs as if it could live to sting another day.

Jane's face went red. Her eyes sank into their sockets and bounced back at him like two hard black balls. She couldn't seem to stop blinking. She couldn't catch her breath. All this, and still he had no idea, no conception, not the vaguest hint that the plug had been pulled on everything he'd known as life to this moment. 'What is it,' he said, trying to laugh it off, 'a bee sting? Is that it?'

She couldn't answer him. He held her – what else could he do? He'd never heard of anaphylactic shock, never heard of epinephrine or histamines, he knew from zero to nothing about first aid and CPR, and he was twelve miles from the nearest road. And, besides, *it was only a bee sting.* Yes, but her heart was trying to tear its way out of her chest even as he held her, and she wet herself, hot urine down her leg in a smear of dirt, the smell of it like vinegar burned in a pan, and here she was on the ground, on her side, vomiting up the blackened paste of the pancakes. Water, he brought her water, and cleared the hair away from her mouth, but there was nothing in her eyes and she was as cold as the dirt she was lying in.

He didn't know how long he sat there with her, alternately

feeling for a pulse and trying to force air down her throat through the ache in his lungs, trying to make her breathe, stir, get up and walk it off, for Christ's sake. Prayers came back to him then, the faces of the dead, *ora pro nobis,* and though he was panicked – or because he was panicked – he couldn't bring himself to move her, even after the mist turned to drizzle and the drizzle to rain. Finally, though – and it must have been late in the afternoon – he pulled her up out of the mud and slid her over one shoulder, nothing heavier in the world, nothing, not stone or lead or all the mountains marching off in neat ranks to Canada. Down the trail then, down the trail to the trailhead, and out to the road and the car and the hospital in Whitefish. He brought her back, all the way back, out of the tall trees and the wet and the sting of the everlasting day, but it didn't matter to him or to anybody else, because he didn't bring her back alive.

PART TWO

Progress Is Our
Most Important Product

Santa Ynez, November 2025

I **CAN'T SLEEP**. Christ knows I'm tired enough, my knee throbbing, my back gone into permanent retirement, every muscle in my body stretched to the tearing point and both my shoulders hanging on threads like a puppet's. I'm beat, whipped, done in and played out. It's been a day. I'm in bed, in Mac's place, in a room bigger than a bus station, staring up at the ceiling in the dark. Andrea is here beside me, curled up like a question mark and snoring so softly I can barely hear her, and Mac's pink satin sheets are flowing like bathwater over and under my grateful old man's feet. Do you want to define cozy? This is it.

Outside, it's different. Outside is the wind, the horizontal rain, the rending and the howling, outside is the wreckage of the place I've called home for the past ten years and all the pens and cages we contrived to design and build for the greater welfare and happiness of the animals. Gone. Just like that. Where the guesthouse used to be there's a river now, all roiling muscle and deep-brown ribs, no more Rancho Seco, no more Lupine Hill condos, nothing but sirens and searchlights and people clinging to one piece of wreckage or another.

But that's not what's keeping me awake. I've been through the list of the animals twice already, and I'm satisfied on that score, and Andrea managed to salvage most of my personal belongings (yellowing boxer shorts, the food compressor, the toaster, my beat-up copies of *The Rise and Fall of the Third Reich* and *The Dharma Bums,* the odd bottle of *sake* and assorted foodstuffs). Things are nothing to me anyway. I could rebuild, pack up and move on, live in a ditch or a teepee – or a six-by-eight platform in a redwood tree, for that matter. No, the problem here seems to be my brain – it just won't shut down. For a while I tried to trace the

whole convoluted chain of my thoughts back to the first image –
that works most of the time, because sooner or later I forget what
the point of the exercise is and then it's six o'clock in the morning –
but perversely, and maybe because there's been such radical
change in my staid and limited sphere here in the past few days,
new thoughts kept spinning out of the recovered ones, so that, in
going back from the idiosyncrasies of Andrea's snoring to my
mother's when she fell asleep on the couch with a quilt pulled up
to her chin and her drink gone to water in her hand to the way the
light came through the kitchen window in the house in Peterskill
to Anthony's Nose and Dunderberg and all the hikers coming
down with Lyme disease on the Appalachian Trail, I found myself
wondering about the new breed of nature-lovers who take their
TV attachments every place they go because the real thing has
nothing to offer anymore. Then I got stuck on TV, my boyhood
in front of the tube, and before I knew it I was reprising the entire
CBS, NBC and ABC schedules for a given week in 1959 or so.
That's how I got to Ronald Reagan. I went through each of the
weekdays like beads on a string, got to Saturday night and *Have
Gun, Will Travel,* then Sunday, Ed Sullivan, eight to nine,
followed by *The General Electric Theater,* hosted by the future
governor of California and fortieth president of the United States.

I'd stretch out on the rug that smelled of carpet cleaner with my
school books scattered round me, and watch the jugglers, come-
dians and dancing horses that made up Sullivan's pretty dull affair,
and then, if I wheedled and pled, I'd get to stay up half an hour
more to watch the drama that followed, because anything was
better than bed. And there he was, Ronald Reagan. I was nine
years old and I had no idea who he was – I'd never heard of *Bedtime
for Bonzo* or *Hellcats* or the Gipper or any of the rest of it. I just saw
him there, bland and anonymous but for the amazing glistening
meatloaf of hair glued to his head and the motto of the company
he shilled for: *Progress is our most important product.* Sure. Of course it
is. That makes sense, doesn't it? We move forward, conquer and
foster and discover – plug it in, tune it up – and life just gets better.
And what about that house they built for him and his wife in the
Pacific Palisades? An intercom in every room, electric switches to
close the drapes, electric barbecue and hedge clippers, three TVs,

two ranges, two ovens, three refrigerators, two freezers, heat lamps, electric eyes, washers, dryers, a retractable canopy roof for al-fresco dining. That's progress. And so is naming James Watt your secretary of the interior.

My guts are rumbling: gas, that's what it is. If I lie absolutely still, it'll work through all the anfractuous turns and twists down there and find its inevitable way to the point of release. And what am I thinking? That's methane gas, a natural pollutant, same as you get from landfills, feedlots and termite mounds, and it persists in the atmosphere for ten years, one more fart's worth of global warming. I'm a mess and I know it. Jewish guilt, Catholic guilt, enviro-eco-capitalistico guilt: I can't even expel gas in peace. Of course, guilt itself is a luxury. In prison we didn't concern ourselves overmuch about environmental degradation or the rights of nature or anything else, for that matter. They penned us up like animals, and we shat and pissed and jerked off and blew hurricanes out our rectums, and if the world collapsed as a result, all the better: at least we'd be out.

In between gusts the volume comes up on the rain and I can hear it patiently eroding the lashed-down tiles of the roof (two years ago Mac had steel mesh welded over the entire thing and so far it's held up – no splootching buckets here). *Sssssssss,* the rain sizzles, fat in a fryer. Andrea snorts, mutters a few incomprehensible syllables and rolls over. More rain. An unidentified flying object hits the side of the house with a thud, a dull booming reverberation that sets tinkling the flesh-toned figurines in the display case (each of the guest bedrooms is decorated after an era in rock-and-roll history – we're in the Grunge Room, replete with replicas of Nirvana, Soundgarden and Pearl Jam in action, as well as a framed lock of Kurt Cobain's hair over the legend 'A Lock of Kurt Cobain's Hair'). This is crazy. How can I sleep through this? How can anybody sleep through it? How can Andrea, April Wind, Mac, Chuy, Al and Al?

More to the point: how can the animals? And yes, I admit it, I *am* concerned about them, or concerned all over again, because that's the way it is with insomnia – the brain, diligent organ that it is, will always manage to come up with something to forestall the inevitable shutdown. Very still now, Andrea between breaths, the wind making a snatch at the rain, and I swear I can hear one of the lions coughing two floors beneath me. I'm not imagining this – there it is again. Sounds like Amaryllis. I can picture them down there, exploring their new quarters, scent-marking the walls, gutting the furniture, ripping up carpets, settling in.

The amazing thing is, no one got hurt.

All those claws, all those teeth, all those hundreds of pounds of irascibility and recalcitrance, the wind blowing up a tornado, the water waist-deep and running slick and fast, and me at seventy-five with my bad knee, savaged back and chewed-up arm and nobody to help but Chuy and five conscripts: this is a recipe for disaster. I didn't need April Wind, I needed the Marine Corps. But Chuy, never to be mistaken for a genius, especially since the pesticide seemed to have annulled most of the cognitive functions of his brain, really came to the rescue. He did. He saved the day and no doubt about it. Because his idea of roping the cats (and, ultimately, Lily and Petunia) and forcing them to swim for it, as ridiculous as it might sound, was the one thing that ultimately worked. While Mac and the women went off to hood the Egyptian vultures and prod the honey badgers into their carrying cages, I unlocked the gate on the chain-link fence and stepped into the lion compound, Chuy right beside me with a coiled-up rope. Al and Al sat in the Olfputt, flexing their muscles and looking very small in the face: they wanted no part of this, and who could blame them?

I never liked darting the animals. Too risky. We were using a mixture of Telezol and Xylazine, and it worked like a charm – if you got the dosage right. Too much, and you had a dead animal on your hands; too little, and you ran the risk of becoming a dead animal yourself. I'd worked out the dosage as best I could under the conditions (duress, flooding, excitable women and a hysterical Mac, inundated kitchen, floating table, that sort of thing), and I figured I'd try half a dose for starters – enough to make them groggy, but not so much that they couldn't swim behind the Olfputt and find their way through the open basement door to where dry accommodations, some hastily scattered straw and the freshly drowned carcass of an emu awaited them.

The water was waist-deep – did I mention that? – and slipping by at a pretty good clip. Plus there were the damned catfish crawling up on every horizontal surface in their little gift-wrapped packets of slime. And how did the lions feel about it? Pissed off. Definitely pissed off. They were hungry and tired and sick to death of being wet and cold and clambered over by fish that had no right to exist in this environment at all. Dandelion fixed his tan eyes on us and let out a belly-shaking roar of complaint from his perch atop the lion house.

'All right, Chuy,' I said, 'I'm going to dart Dandy first, and when you see him go down on his haunches, fling that rope around him. That lasso, I mean. You can use it, right?'

'*Sí,* Mr. Ty, I can use, *no hay problema.*' (Among his many former occupations, Chuy listed 'bronco-buster' and 'vaquero.' When he was in his twenties, before he came north, he'd worked in a Mexican rodeo, roping dogies, whatever they were – calves, I take it.) 'No worries,' he said now, grinning out of the wet mask of his face. The wind screamed, flapping the hood of the slicker against my elongated old man's ears, and I could hear Lily harmonizing in the distance: *oooo-whup, oooo-whup!*

'And if the other two come for us, I'm not going to dart them, so we're just going to have to back out of the cage and lock the door, okay? They're not all that fond of the water, so they'll probably stay put – '

'That is what I am thinking *también,* Mr. Ty,' Chuy said, wading forward with deep thrusts of his legs till he was twenty feet from the gate and maybe thirty from the lions. And they were roaring now, all three of them, ears flattened, lips pulled back, tails twitching, their eyes locked on Chuy as he whirled the lasso over his head in the wind and driving rain. 'Yippee!' he shouted. 'Yippee-yi-ki-yay!'

I was worried, I admit it. I'm a worrier and cynic at heart, always have been – at least since Earth Forever! came into my life. Or before that even, when a stinking little half-inch wasp that couldn't have weighed more than a quarter of an ounce took Jane away from me for good. I expect the worst, and I'll have to say that my expectations have been abundantly fulfilled through the seventy-five years of shitstorms and bad luck that constitute my life to this point. At best I expected three drowned lions; at worst, I pictured Chuy with his limbs separated from his body and me with my intestines rearranged in a way that would have caused real consternation down at the emergency room. That's why I had Philip Ratchiss' Nitro Express slung over my shoulder in addition to the Palmer dart gun.

My hands were trembling as I sighted down the barrel of the dart gun (old age, palsy, the *sake* shakes, undiluted terror – you name it), and the first dart took off like a guided missile, streaking high over the lions, out of the pen and into the dense fabric of the wind-whipped sky. The lions roared, Chuy yippeed and yahooed and twirled the rope over his head. I took my bifocals off and wiped them on the handkerchief in my breast pocket, the only reasonably dry thing on me, and then I lined up a second shot with the tip of my nose spewing water like a fountain and my fingers befuddled and the catfish crawling up my pantlegs, and let it go out of desperation, frustration and something very much like hate – hate for the animals, for Mac, for the U.S. Weather Service and all the polluters and ravagers and industrialists who had brought me and Chuy and the lions to this absurd and humiliating moment in the history of interspecies relations.

There was a sound like the final blow in a pillow fight – a soft *whump!* – and there it was, the dart, dangling from Dandelion's flank like a – well, like a big yellow jacket. He turned and snapped at it, whirling round two or three times with a snarl more bewildered than fierce, and in the process inadvertently knocked Amaryllis off the roof and into the cold swirl of the muddy water. She didn't like that. Didn't like it at all. Thankfully, though, she didn't take her displeasure out on Chuy – or me – but instead scrabbled back up on the roof of the enclosure and gave Dandy a swat that would have crushed the spine of a zebra or wildebeest (if such things existed), but only managed to operate in concert with the drug and knock him off his feet. That was when Chuy's rope work came into play. He was a master, no doubt about it, the lasso snaking out, catching the wind and riding it in an elliptical trajectory right over Dandy's head, where it came down soft as a snowflake.

The rest was easy. (I'm speaking relatively here, of course – relative to a week ago, when all I had to worry about was what I was going to read on the toilet and which can of soup to open for supper, it was the seventh circle of hell.) Chuy cinched the rope, waded back to me and stood at the open door of the enclosure to watch the result – and slam shut the door if anything went wrong. I backed up, the current snatching at my old man's feet, the wind slamming at me in gust after gust, and slowly made my way back to the Olfputt, where I climbed into the back seat and fought the door closed. The two Als were up front, giving me the sort of look they reserved for anybody who got within five feet of Mac. They looked fierce and suspicious, puffed up like bullfrogs, the slabs of their shoulders rising titanically out of the black slickers Mac had provided them with. They also looked scared. 'What now?' the one at the wheel said.

I glanced over my shoulder to where Chuy, partially obscured by a scrim of wind-driven rain, was giving me the thumbs-up sign. A gust rocked the truck. 'Put it in four-low,' I said, still watching Chuy, 'and start up the hill, nice and easy.'

The truck moved forward and the line fastened to the trailer hitch went taut, and in the next moment I saw the distant form of Dandelion pitch forward off the roof and plunge awkwardly into the water, all four paws spread like landing gear. For an instant, he was gone from sight, but then his head bobbed up and I could see his front paws churning – he was swimming! But the miracle didn't end there. In the next moment, both the other lions followed suit, flopping into the water with looks of weary resignation and paddling right along with him, through the open gate and on up the hill behind the Olfputt. 'Right up to the door!' I shouted at Al. 'Right on up to the door!'

Now, there are many forms of disaster that could have spun out of this – three full-grown, ill-tempered and half-starved African lions loose among the condos, and how big a check would Mac have to write then? – but the newborn river that had taken possession of Rancho Seco had split round Mac's hill. His place was an island now, and though the cats could have swum off to wreak havoc of the worst and bloodiest sort, I really did think they would have the sense to come in out of the rain and settle down to the breast of feral emu we'd so thoughtfully provided for them. And that's exactly what they did. I leaned out the back window and cut the rope, and Dandy, wobbly from the drug, had to sit

125

down twice in the mud before he could follow his nose – and his two unencumbered companions – through the open door and into the vast recesses of Maclovio Pulchris' paneled and carpeted basement. All that was left was to close and secure the door, and I had Al the First nose the Olfputt in over the flowerbeds and right up to the door, and then Al the Second jumped out and put his shoulder to it in a very definitive way. Then it was the planks and six-inch nails, and all three of us put our energy into that, even as Chuy, triumphant, staggered up to us with a four-foot grin. 'Now we go for Lily, *verdad,* Mr. Ty?'

So this is why I can't sleep – the animals. It was the animals all along. Lions in the basement, vultures round the indoor pool, the hyena in the gift-wrapping room on the second floor. It's crazy, that's what it is. And all the while the water rising.

What are we going to feed them? How are we going to clean up after them? And when the waters recede – if they ever do – will Mac have the energy to start all over again?

I don't know. But Andrea rolls over suddenly, her face right beside mine on the pillow, and in the watery light of dawn I watch her eyes flash open, dreaming eyes, the eyes that pull me down and into her inescapable arms. 'Sleep well?' she whispers.

I try to avoid perspective as much as possible. Perspective hurts. Live in the present, that's what I say, one step at a time, and forget nostalgia, forget history, forget the sketchy chain of loss, attrition and disappointment that got you into bed last night and out of it this morning. It's hard, though, when you've got Andrea Knowles Cotton Tierwater sitting at your elbow and sectioning your grapefruit for you because you can barely lift your arms your back hurts so much, and April Wind the toad worshipper mooning at you from across the table. And Mac. I've known him for ten years, ever since I got out of prison for the last and final time, and here he is skating through the door in a gauze mask that scares the living hell out of me. 'Morning, morning, morning!' he chimes, whirling round on the balls of his feet as if he's onstage, the two bodyguards shadowing him with their big heads and sleepy eyes. One more shock: they're wearing masks too.

I gape. I blink. I fish my glasses out of my shirt pocket. 'All right,' I say finally, 'come on, Mac – what's with the mask? And don't tell me it's the *mucosa* again, because I don't want to hear it, not with the weather and the animals and all the rest of it, uh-uh, no way.'

Andrea's out of her chair already, and screw the grapefruit, screw her ex-husband, nobody exists in the world but Mac. 'It is, isn't it? April and I were trying to tell Ty, but he wouldn't listen. Go ahead, tell him, Mac – '

But let me back up a minute to give you a view of the scene unfolding here. Here's Mac, worth I don't know how many millions, fiftyish and lean to the point of being skinny, bandy-legged in a pair of black jeans, some sort of drum major's jacket with gold piping over a black *Barbecue You!* tour T-shirt clinging to his emaciated torso, his face swallowed up in fedora, shades and mask; and here's Andrea, worth nothing, a hot old lady in a print hippie dress that drops to the toes of her boots, striated bosom exposed, golden eyes agog, taking hold of Mac's forearms in real earnest while the bodyguards shift uneasily from one cloddish foot to the other. And where are we? We're in one of the three dining rooms in the mansion, this one called the Motown Room, perched high over the north wing, looking out the reinforced picture window to the roiling mess of the flatlands beneath us. It's still raining. And the wind is still cutting up.

'I've got masks for everybody,' Mac pipes, shrugging out of Andrea's grip and waving a sheaf of them over his head, 'so there's no reason to get excited. Just a precaution, that's all. Everybody's my guest for as long as this keeps up, and don't you worry, Mac'll take care of you. We've got plenty of food and Al's had the generator going ever since the power went out day before yesterday – '

I'm on my feet and I'm angry and I don't know why. 'So what is this, "The Masque of the Red Death" or something? We all wore masks and kept strictly to ourselves the last time, remember, Mac? And it didn't do Lori a whole lot of good, did it?'

'That was then. We didn't take it seriously at first. We fraternized. Let the maids go home every afternoon. The parties, remember the parties, Ty? But I got out of the Carolinas the minute I heard this time. Siege mentality, folks. And, really, I'm going to have to insist that everybody wear a mask till we hear different – if you want to stay here, you play by my rules. And Dr. Deepit says to stay inside because of the mosquitoes, the ones that carry the – what do they call it, Ty?'

'Dengue fever. They call it dengue fever, and the mosquito that carries it is the *Aedes aegypti,* formerly known to occur only in the tropics. They call it bonebreak fever too, because your bones feel like they're snapping in half when you've got it. But we can stay inside all we want – shit, we could go around day and night in beekeeper's outfits – but what are we going to feed the animals, that's what I want to know. Everything got washed away yesterday, and all of them except for the lions have had to go without.'

Andrea's face is – joyful. Or nearly joyful. And April Wind, dressed in some sort of serape with a clay likeness of Chaac, the Aztec rain god, dangling on a suede cord from her throat, looks ecstatic too. It takes a minute, and then I understand – the storm is raging, the plague afoot, and they're locked in with Maclovio Pulchris: mission accomplished.

I don't like it. I don't like it at all. The *mucosa* is a nasty business all the way round, a sort of super-flu, spread by casual contact, that inflames the mucous membranes of the sex organs, the respiratory canal and the eye until they begin to hyperfunction and you literally drown in your own secretions. It's painful. It's lingering. And it's not pretty.

'It might surprise you to know, Ty Tierwater, that there's meat in this house,' Mac is saying, and he skates playfully across the room to pose beneath a rippling electronic portrait of Gladys Knight and the Pips, performing for the little audience gathered in the dining room. I'd describe his look as sly, but for the fact that he has no look at all – hat, shades and mask, that's all I see.

'Meat?' April Wind is offended. 'But you're a vegetarian, aren't you? You of all people – I mean, I've read all the bios and the magazines too, everything . . .' She's gaping up at him from a plate of chapatis, lime pickle and eggs-over-easy prepared by Mac's invisible cook and served up silently by a masked Pakistani woman who disappeared the minute the plate hit the table. 'You're a vegetarian. I know you are.'

Andrea's left in the middle of the enormous room, looking as if she's been deserted on the dance floor between tunes. 'He probably just keeps it for his guests, for the parties – *Barbecue You?* Right? Isn't that it, Mac?'

Mac. She met him two days ago – through me, because of me – and already it's Mac this and Mac that and could I get you another soda, Mac, or peel you some grapes, and what do *you* think, Mac?

He's smiling – I can tell because the corners of the gauze mask lift just under the plastic rims of the sunglasses, where the muscles of his fleshless cheeks would be. He's looking at me – or at least his head is turned my way. 'Come on, Ty, don't be such a crank – come on, I'll show you,' and there's movement now, Maclovio Pulchris, the ex–pop star who hasn't had a hit in sixteen years sliding across the room on spring-loaded joints to take hold of my aching and angry arm, the two Als stirring and exchanging nervous glances over the dangerous proximity of their employer to another human being, Andrea closing fast and even April starting up from her congealed eggs. 'Down in the basement, Ty – the east basement, locked off from those sweet tawny lions, and you know I love them, man, so don't give me that look. Shit, I've got a whole meat locker full of stuff – steaks, rump roasts, strings of pork sausage, lamb chops, corn dogs, filet mignon, you name it. We could feed fifty lions!'

I've never believed in vegetarianism myself, except as an ecological principle – obviously, you can feed a whole lot more people on rice or grain than you can on a feed-intensive animal like a steer, and, further, as everyone alive today knows, it was McDonald's and Burger King and their ilk that denuded the rain forests to provide range for yet more cows, but, still, I don't make a religion of it. Meat isn't the problem, people are. In prison, they gave us spaghetti with meat sauce, chili con carne, sloppy joes, that sort of thing, and I forked it up gladly and didn't think twice about it. It's a Darwinian world – kill or be killed, eat or be eaten – and I see no problem with certain highly evolved apes cramming a little singed flesh between their jaws every now and again (if only there weren't so *many* of us, but that's another story). Besides, I didn't really come to the environmental movement till Andrea got hold

129

of me, and I'd gone through thirty-eight years as a carnivore to that point. Top of the food chain, oh, yes, indeed.

My daughter saw things differently.

It started when she was eleven. She came back from an outing in New York with Jane's sister, Phyll, which I'd assumed would be a Radio City Music Hall/Museum of Natural History sort of thing, and announced to me that meat was murder. They hadn't gone to the Hall of Mammals after all. No, Phyll had taken her to the Earth Day rally in Washington Square, where she'd been converted by a dreadlocked ascetic and a slide show depicting doe-eyed veal calves succumbing to the hammer and headless chickens having their guts mechanically extracted on a disassembly line. I'd had a catastrophic day at the office, my biggest tenant – a national drugstore chain, the anchor for the whole shopping center – threatening to relocate in the mall down the street, and I was sipping scotch to anaesthetize my nerves and defrosting a fat, dripping pair of porterhouse steaks for dinner. Sierra stood there in the kitchen, five feet nothing and eighty-eight pounds, lecturing me about the evils of meat, the potatoes dutifully baking, the frozen string beans in the pot and the steaks oozing blood on the drainboard. 'That's disgusting, Dad – it is. Look at that meat, all slimy and bloody. Some innocent cow had to die just so we could eat like pigs, don't you realize that?'

I wasn't humorless – or not entirely. But I'd had a rough day, I was a single parent and a cook of very limited resources. Meat was what we had, and meat was what we were going to eat. 'What about last week?' I said. 'What about the Chicken McNuggets I get you every Saturday for lunch? What about Happy Meals?'

The kitchen we were standing in was a fifties kitchen, designed and built by my father after he'd finished the first seventy-five houses in the development. Things were breaking for him, and he spared no expense on the place, situating it on three acres at the very end of the road, with a big sloping lawn out front and an in-ground pool in back, then buffering the property with another hundred acres or so of swamps and briars and second-growth forest – the haunt of deer and opossum, toads, frogs, blacksnakes and the amateur biologist and budding woodsman who was his son. The kitchen, with its built-in oven and electric range,

Formica counters and knotty-pine cabinets my mother insisted on painting white, had been the scene of any number of food rebellions in the past (macaroni and cheese particularly got to me, and wax beans – I couldn't even chew, let alone digest them), but this was unique. This wasn't simply a matter of taste – it was a philosophical challenge, and it struck at the heart of the regimen I'd been raised on.

Her gaze was unwavering. She was wearing shorts, high-tops and an oversized T-shirt Phyll had bought her (*Lamb to the Slaughter?* it asked, over the forlorn mug of a sheep). 'I'll never go to McDonald's again,' she said. 'And I'm not eating school lunch either.'

I took a pull at my drink, the scotch swirling like smoke in a liquid sky. 'What am I supposed to give you, then – lettuce sandwiches? mustard greens? celery sticks? bamboo shoots? You don't even like vegetables. How can you be a vegetarian if you don't like vegetables?'

She had nothing to say to this.

'What about candy? You can eat candy, can't you? I mean, candy's a vegetable, isn't it? Maybe we could base your whole diet around candy, you know, like eggs with fried Butterfingers for breakfast, peanut brickle and baked Mars Bars on rye for lunch with melted chocolate syrup and whipped cream on top? Or ice cream – what about ice cream?'

'You're making fun of me. I don't like it when you make fun of me. I'm serious, Dad, you know, really serious. I'll never eat one bite of meat again.' She pointed a condemnatory finger at the steaks. 'And I'm not eating that either.'

I could have handled it differently, could have humored her, could have applied the wisdom I'd gained from all the little alimentary confrontations I'd had with my mother when I was Sierra's age, not to mention my father and his special brand of militant obtuseness. But I was in no mood. 'You'll eat it,' I said, looming over her with my scotch and the beginnings of a head-ache, 'or you'll sit at that table over there till you die. Because I don't care.'

The steaks were in the pan, inch-thick slabs of flesh, and I looked at them there and for the first time in my life thought about where they'd come from and what the process was that had made them available to me and my daughter and anybody else who had the $6.99 a pound to lay down at the A&P Meat Department. Cattle suffered, cattle died. And I ate burgers and steaks and roasts and never had to contemplate the face of the creature who gave it all up for me. That was the way of the world, that was progress. I shrugged, and shoved the pan under the broiler.

Sierra had retreated to her room at the end of the hall, the room that had been mine when I was a boy, and she wasn't listening to her tapes or doodling in her notebook or whispering dire secrets into the phone – she was just lying there facedown on the bed, and her shoulders were quivering because she was crying softly into the pillow. I'd seen those quivering shoulders before, and I was powerless before them. But not this night. I had my own problems, and I didn't take her in my arms and tell her it was all right, she could eat anything she wanted, Fruit Loops in the morning, cupcakes for lunch and Boston cream pie for dinner – no, I took her by the arm and marched her into the kitchen, where a baked potato sat slit open on the plate beside a snarl of green beans in melted butter and a slab of medium-rare steak the size of Connecticut.

I poured her a glass of milk, set my drink down and settled into my chair across the table from her. I plied knife and fork. I lifted one chunk of meat after another to my mouth, patted my lips with my napkin, vigorously tapped the inverted pepper shaker over my plate, chewed green beans, slathered my potato with sour cream and butter. There was no conversation. Nothing. I might have said, 'Good meat,' or something along those lines, some little dig at her, but that was about it. She never moved. She just bowed her head and stared down at her plate, the potato and beans no doubt contaminated by the juices from the steak, and the milk, which she'd never much liked but only tolerated in any case, entirely ignored. Even when I got up from the table to rinse my plate and dump the rest of my drink down the drain, she never so much as glanced up. And later, when the phone rang and rang again, her friends on the other end of the line anxious to communicate their own dire secrets, she never flinched. She sat there rigid at the table as the daylight faded from the windows, and when I found her sitting there in the dark an hour later, I flicked on the counter lights.

I couldn't look at her face or focus too long on the back of her bowed head and the sliver of white that was the perfect parting of her hair, because I was determined not to waver. Let her get away with this and she'll rule me, that's the way I felt, and then it'll be junk food and candy, then it'll be stunted growth and rotten teeth and ruined skin, delinquency, early pregnancy, bad debts, drugs, booze, the whole downward spiral. At eleven, I crept into the kitchen and saw that she was asleep, head cradled in the nest of her hands, the plate pushed to one side, untouched, preserved like a plate under glass in some museum of Americana: *Typical American meal, circa 1987*. I lifted her in my arms, no weight to her at all, as if the forfeit of one night's meal had wasted her, and laid her gently into bed, covers to the chin, a kiss to the cheek, good night.

Pork chops the next night, breaded, with German potato salad, sauerkraut, hot apple sauce and reheated green beans. She wouldn't even look at it. What did I say? Nothing. She sat there at the table doing her homework till she fell asleep, and this time I left her there. On the third night it was pizza, with anchovies and mushrooms, her favorite, but she wouldn't touch that either. I gave vent to my feelings then. I roared and I threatened, slammed things, stretched her over the rack of guilt and stretched her again – did she think it was easy for me, with no wife, to come home from a numbing day of work and put on an apron, just for her? Huh? Did she?

On the morning of the fourth day of her hunger strike, I got a call from the school nurse: she'd fainted during gym class, halfway through the rope climb, and had fallen twelve feet to the gym floor. Nothing broken, but they were taking her to the hospital for precautionary X-rays, and by the way, had she been eating right? The windows were beaded with rain. Sevry Peterson, owner of the failing stationery store in the shopping center, was sitting across the desk from me in the hopeless clutter of my office, explaining how she'd come to be six months behind in her rent. I waved her off, grabbed my jacket and made the Mustang scream all the way to the hospital.

Sierra was sitting in the waiting room when I got there, looking glum in her leggings, big socks and Reeboks and the oversized fluorescent pink T-shirt she insisted on wearing every third day. Mrs. Martini, the school nurse, was sitting on one side of her, a hugely fat man in sandals and a dirty white sweatshirt on the other. The fat man periodically dabbed his forehead with a bloody rag and moaned under his breath, and Mrs. Martini sat stiff as a cadaver over a copy of *People* magazine. Sierra's eyes leapt up when she saw me come through the door, but then they went cold with the recollection that meat was murder and that I, her father, was chief among the murderers. And then what?

Then we went home and she never touched another scrap of meat in her life.

Mac's house – his Versailles, his pleasure dome, his city under a roof – was built during the nineties, the last age of excess in a long line of them. It has three dining rooms, eighteen bedrooms, twenty-two baths, the aforementioned gift-wrapping room, a theater, spa, swimming pool, gymnasium and bowling alley, not to mention the twenty-car garage and a scattering of guest-houses set amongst the remains of what were once formal gardens. There's plenty of room for everybody – Andrea, April Wind, the ghost of Sierra, Dandelion, Amaryllis and Buttercup, refugees from the condos (though none have showed up yet and the winds are still raging), the two Als, Mac and his collection of gauze masks, even Chuy, who insists on sleeping beneath the vintage Dodge Viper in the garage. And, as I'm about to discover, there's food too. Mac pulled me out of the dining room by the arm, and now I'm following his sloping shoulders down a long corridor to an elevator with hammered brass doors. 'It's down two,' he says, pulling a gauze mask from his pocket and holding it out for me.

What can I say? I take the mask and loop it over my head without a word. My role here is to play the angry old man, and I let my eyes, fully stoked, do the talking for me. Down we go, and then the doors part on another hallway, magenta carpets, recessed lighting, some of the last mahogany paneling ever installed any-where on this earth. In the confusion of yesterday we herded the warthogs and peccaries into the bowling alley, and that's down along here somewhere, I think, and though I can't hear them, I can smell the lions. No doubt they're asleep – even in nature, when there used to be nature, that is, adult lions would sleep something like twenty hours a day. I can picture them laid out like corpses amongst the rags and tatters of the dismantled furniture, only the slow rise and fall of their rib cages giving them away. (It's a crazy picture, I know it, this whole thing is crazy, but welcome to life in the twenty-first century. And who am I to complain – I'm surviving, aren't I? If that's what you want to call it.)

Mac's shoulders work, the fedora rides. We follow a corridor to the right, make a left up another corridor, then pass through the swinging doors of the lower kitchen. Mac fumbles for the light switch and a world of kitchen implements bursts into gleaming view: saucepans, colanders, whisks and graters depending from the ceiling above stainless-steel worktables, a big industrial-sized dish-washer, the polished doors of a walk-in freezer. 'Check this out,' Mac says, his voice muffled by the gauze, and then he pulls back the door on the right and we're engulfed by a creeping cloud of super-refrigerated air. Another light switch illuminates the interior and we can see the carcasses arrayed on their hooks and casting their frozen shadows.

'To be a host – to be *the* host of *the* baddest, hippest and grooviest parties – you just have got to have meat, you know what I mean?' Mac is saying. 'Plus, these poor things were already dead and slaughtered, and it's like, if you're going to have a wine cellar, why not a meat cellar too? I mean, it's an investment. I've got the last Argentine beef in here, you know that? Buffalo tongue, elk, mutton, spicy salsiccia from Palermo – I don't know what-all. And fish. Two whole bluefin tuna, maybe the last ones on earth, and you know what the Japanese would pay for them? For just a slice as long as your little finger?' A wave of his hand. 'They're back in there somewhere. Or at least they used to be.' His breath is steaming through the mask in a weird billow of light, shadows everywhere, the naked beasts on the naked hooks, meat with a vengeance. 'Some of this stuff is twenty years old.'

We've both edged into the locker. Here's something right next to me, frozen like granite, and with a hoofless leg at the end of it. 'So you're saying we can maybe feed some of the older stuff to maybe the fox, the hyena, the lions – in a pinch, that is? You don't mind?'

Mac gives me an eloquent shrug. His shades are frosting over. I can feel the ice crystallizing round the white hairs in my old man's nostrils. 'We've got to save the animals,' he says finally. 'You know that, Ty.'

The Sierra Nevada, August 1989

TIERWATER SAT PERCHED on the edge of an Adirondack chair, a sketchpad in his lap and a tall vodka and tonic within easy reach, watching his wife and daughter shake dice in their fists and move tiny silver markers around a Monopoly board. The temperature was in the low seventies, the sky a clear omniscient blue, the aspens unruffled, the pines, cedars and redwoods silently climbing one atop another to the distant horizon. Andrea was seated in the lotus position on the weathered planks of the veranda, her breasts swinging free behind the thin cotton screen of her T-shirt, her own drink cradled between her thighs. Just below her, on the steps down to the pale needle-strewn duff, Sierra knelt barefooted in a wide stripe of sunlight, contemplating the construction of a hotel on one of her more favorably located properties. There was no sound but for the reiterative knock of a woodpecker from deep in the forest and, closer at hand, the high-pitched complaint of a chickaree from the canopy of a huge ponderosa pine that rose up like a wall outside the bedroom window. There were no bugs. There was no wind. And the smell — it was the smell of a sauna, clean and astringent, the sun slowly baking the scent out of the pines.

Tierwater wasn't much of an artist anymore (though he'd once had vague ambitions along those lines), and he would have been the first to admit it. Still, he liked the feel of the stick of charcoal between his fingers, the easy, faintly rasping strokes, the suggestion of the real in an abstraction — vertical strokes became trees; horizontal, branches; and then there was the quick scrawl to represent the shadows on the tumbled granite that erupted from the earth at the foot of the big pine. The exercise was calming. Deeply calming. And it was more than that too — it was an expression of the love affair he was having with these mountains. Never mind the panic, the police, the warrants, the assumed name (they knew him here as Tom Drinkwater, his wife as Dee Dee, and his daughter as Sarah) – he was in love. Turn by turn, minute by minute, as they'd come up out of the San Joaquin Valley and the staggering heat of late July, he'd felt it growing in him. Each switchback brought him closer to it, a landscape of liberation, light like a bombardment, a forest of trees ten times bigger around than anything he'd known in all his years of hiking the hills of the scaled-down East. And more: this was wild country, haunt of puma, black bear, coyote, ouzel, golden trout and golden eagle. Yes, he'd seen trees in Oregon, magnificent trees, but they were the palisades of his nightmares now, they were the cut and sharpened and fire-hardened pikes of Sheriff Bob Hicks and Judge Duermer as they poked and prodded and held him at bay. This was different. This was landscape as embrace. This was peace.

Sierra let out a squeal. 'Ha!' she said. 'That'll be, let's see – one thousand one hundred and fifty dollars.'

'Killing her, huh, honey? Show her no mercy, that's what I say.'

'Come on, Ty,' Andrea said, raising the glass to her lips and rattling the ice cubes, 'you don't have to be so bloodthirsty, or mercenary, or whatever. What about the spirit of friendly competition, mother and daughter, all the rest of it?'

She was joking, of course, because she was as much in love with these mountains and this moment as he was. 'Call me Tom,' he said.

'All right, Tom, after I obliterate Sarah here and make her mortgage all her properties and squeeze her till she bleeds, how about a little hike out to Kramer Meadow before dinner?'

'You wish,' Sierra said, cupping the dice in her palm. 'Watch out, because here I come!'

Sure, he would say, sure, they'd take a little stroll through the trees and out to the meadow, which was in reality a sort of alpine bog nurturing arrowhead and sedges and tiny tree frogs, good for the appetite, he'd say, and then they'd come home to the eggplant casserole in the oven and have another drink and play Scrabble and maybe even put a log on the fire if the night turned cold. And the nights did turn cold here, perfect sleeping weather, September in the air and then October and November and snow enough to bury every fugitive in the country. To say sure to all that was to say that life was a good and great thing, that life was normal, and a man could love his family and nature too and love them in peace. But that wasn't the way it was, not for Tierwater, not then. And if he needed a reminder, it appeared at that moment at the far end of the dirt drive that wound through the naked legs of the trees and on up to the dead spot – no needles, no pine cones, just dirt – to the left of the graying wooden steps on which his daughter was perched.

Philip Ratchiss' silver Toyota Land Cruiser caught the light and threw it back at them, there was the sound of the big all-terrain tires eating up the ruts, then the glittering boxy machine was settling into its springs over the dead spot and a fine brown dust, the dust of mountains gone down, hung like a trembling nimbus in the air. 'What ho!' Ratchiss said, stepping out of the car and flicking a finger to the brim of his safari hat. He was an American, born and raised in Massapequa, Long Island, but he'd lived twenty years in East Africa, and he had one of those accents that drop somewhere in the no-man's-land between Nassau County plumber and member of the House of Lords – and he loved to quote Shakespeare, not in any apposite or meaningful way, but in the little phrases, the 'What ho!'s and 'Zounds!'s and 'Do you bite your thumb at me, sir?'s. How old was he? Tierwater wasn't sure, but he looked to be in his mid-fifties, a strangely muscled man – muscled in all the wrong places, that is, ankles, wrists, the back of his head – with a bush-ravaged face and a stingy hook of a red and peeling nose stuck in the middle of it as if noses were purely accidental. He'd killed whole herds of animals. He drank too much (gin and bitters). In his blood, he harbored the plasmodium parasites that gave rise to malaria. He was loud, boastful, vain, domineering. He was their host. And this was his cabin.

Tierwater was never quite certain just how to respond to 'What ho!,' so he lifted a lazy palm in greeting as Ratchiss took the three steps to the front deck in a single bound, both his arms laden with groceries, the hat shoved back to expose his retreating hairline and dead-white scalp. 'Hot as a bitch down below,' Ratchiss said, easing open the door to the house with a tentative finger, the paper sacks shifting in his arms with a crunch of glass on glass. 'More things in the car,' he grunted, and then the screen door slapped shut behind him.

Andrea gave him a look, and Tierwater drained his glass and ambled down the steps to the car. He reached into the back seat and extracted three bags more – pickles, relish, buns, condiments to go with the meat Ratchiss was forever grilling on a rack out back of the house. That was all right. There were fresh greens too, and Sierra had enough soy burgers in the freezer to last till Christmas. He hefted the groceries, pinned the bags to his chest and went up the steps and into the house.

Inside, it was dark and cool, with a lingering smell of woods-smoke, burnt bread and mouse urine wedded to the sweet chemical scent of the kerosene lanterns lined up on the mantel above the blackened stone fireplace. The cabin itself had begun as an A-frame, with a grand room just off the veranda and a sleeping loft with two bedrooms and a kitchen tucked under it, but Ratchiss had cobbled an addition onto the back of the place to give it two more rooms, a second bath, and a hot tub cut into the redwood deck and open to the sun and stars. Tierwater wouldn't want to call it a conventional mountain cabin, because at this point he'd had precious little experience of cabins, mountain or otherwise, but it was pretty much standard issue. Except for the views, of course – and for Ratchiss' interior-decorating scheme. There were no deer's heads over the mantel or lacquered trout affixed to the walls on wooden plaques, no sentimental acrylic renderings of alpine grandeur or stark black-and-white photos of El Capitan or the Half Dome – no, inside Ratchiss' cabin, it was Africa.

The furniture – couch, loveseat and two matching chairs – was made of rock-hard *mopane* wood and upholstered in zebra hide. There was a lion rug on the floor instead of the orthodox bear, and the walls bristled with spears, shields, tribal masks and the mounted heads of kongoni, sable, oryx, leopard and bushpig – and one monumental rhino that looked as if it had burst through the paneling directly over the fireplace. But the pièce de résis-tance was the rearing lion – eight feet tall at least, with drawn claws and a stupefied snarl – that stood guard over the entrance to the kitchen. Ratchiss identified it fondly as the Maneater of the

Luangwa, killer and devourer of seventeen hapless men, women and children.

And here was the very man who'd put an end to the lion's existence, the odd band of muscle flashing under his shirt as he alternately tossed cans of beans and piccalilli relish onto the shelf and poured himself a drink from the half-gallon jug of Beefeater's on the counter. 'Heard from Teo,' he said. 'Saw him, in fact, down at my place.'

Ratchiss was referring to his primary residence, a house in Malibu with unobstructed ocean views, two swimming pools and a gallery of African art and trophies that would have put the Smithsonian to shame. He'd left Mag (or Mug) in charge of the place for a few days so he could do a little grocery shopping for his guests and see how they were adapting to their new surroundings. Tierwater merely grunted, but the grunt had a faint interrogative lift to it: Ratchiss had heard from Teo, and he had something to communicate.

'Yeah, we had a couple drinks together and then went out to this place I know in Santa Monica. He's looking good, doing well – E.F.! took in nearly eighty thousand dollars in contributions and new memberships last month alone. Oh, and before I forget, he gave me this, uh, for you – '

Tierwater set down the groceries and took the thick white envelope Ratchiss held out to him. He stuffed it in his pocket without looking at it, but he knew what it contained: hundred-dollar bills, a hundred and fifty of them, paid out of his business account by his secretary and channeled to him through a post-office box in Calabasas; the box was rented by an E.F.! volunteer who gave over the envelope to Teo, who in turn transferred it to Ratchiss. Byzantine precautions, but necessary. The FBI was almost certainly in on this now: Tierwater had jumped bail, violated a court order, committed assault and battery, abduction, child abuse and God knew what else – and he'd fled across state lines to avoid prosecution. He was a criminal, a desperado, a fugitive from justice facing actual prison time, years maybe, years behind bars, and what had he done? He'd stuck his feet in some wet cement. Pissed off a few people. Tried to save the planet. Christ, they should be giving him awards –

But there was no going back now. Sierra was already registered for the eighth grade in the Springville public schools – a mere twenty-eight miles away, down a twisting mountain road – and he and Andrea were in permanent hiding, ready to strike back when the opportunity presented itself. Nobody knew them now, and nobody cared. But they were going to become a *cause célèbre*, that's how Tierwater saw it, heroes of the environmental movement. Like the Arizona Phantom. Or the Fox. People who'd struck back, done something, mattered. People who didn't just take up space and draw breath and consume so many pounds of food and pints of liquid a day and produce nothing in their whole oblivious, cramped and contaminated lives but waste and more waste.

The Phantom was a case in point. He'd appeared along the Arizona/New Mexico border in the early seventies, an anonymous avenger who took on Peabody Coal and its federal allies in the fight over the Four Corners power stations and the mine planned for Black Mesa. Eight-hundred-foot smokestacks. Air like soot. Burn coal and light up L.A. so the megalopolis can creep even farther into the desert – that was the idea. Peaceful protests had no effect. Lobbying failed. The Black Mesa Defense Fund ran out of money. But stealthily, methodically, without ever revealing his identity or coming close to apprehension despite an army of guards and watchmen lying in wait for him, the Phantom went to work on the tracks of the Black Mesa Railroad and every piece of heavy equipment he could find. Ultimately, the mines were gouged out of the ground and the smokestacks went up, but the Phantom – one man, acting alone – showed the world what commitment was. Or could be.

To Tierwater's mind, the Fox was even better, because he was visible – or at least he made himself visible at certain crucial and dramatic moments, like a kind of Zorro of the ecodefense movement. Legend had it that he was just a concerned citizen – a weekend fisherman, a biology teacher, a jogger – who took matters into his own hands after watching local industries pollute the Fox River in northern Illinois. He plugged illegal drains, capped smokestacks, left taunting notes at the scenes of his crimes and once was even interviewed (albeit in a mask) by a local television crew. But most dramatically – and this was what really fired Tierwater's imagination – he appeared one afternoon in the offices of a U.S. Steel executive and proceeded to pour a fifty-gallon barrel of sludge on the carpet. You people keep telling us you're not polluting our water, he said. So, if that's the case, this shouldn't hurt the carpet one bit. And then he disappeared.

'Said he's coming up next week – wants to talk to you.'

Tierwater had the refrigerator door open. He was extracting heads of lettuce, carrots, broccoli from the paper bags and dropping them into the vegetable crisper. 'Who?'

'What do you mean, "who"? Teo. Who're we talking about?' Ratchiss was giving him a look, lips pursed over the bite of his drink, eyes narrowed to slits.

All right, look at me, Tierwater was thinking, belligerent suddenly. If Teo came up, somebody might follow him. And if somebody followed him, it wasn't Ratchiss who was going to jail, it was Tyrone O'Shaughnessy Tierwater. And his wife. And his daughter. 'Isn't that dangerous?' Tierwater said, backing away from the refrigerator, all the peace gone out of the day like air from a hissing balloon.

'Bloody hell, you don't think he's going to *drive,* do you?'

'How else is he going to get here – by parachute?'

There was a moment of silence, Ratchiss studying him, the squirrels chittering in the trees outside the window, a soft exclamation of despair or joy – he couldn't tell which – drifting in from the grudge match on the porch. 'He's no fool – he's hiking in. Having some friend drive him to the trailhead at Camp Orson, and you know Teo – I'd bloody well like to see some lawman try to keep up with him on the trail. No, not to worry, Ty: these people are professionals. *We're* professionals, I should say.' He took a step forward, set his drink down on the counter and held out his hand – a callused, hard, sinewy hand, chilled by cold gin – which Tierwater duly took in his own. 'Nobody's going to give you up, don't you worry.'

Andrea was committed to the cause – one of the charter members of Earth Forever!, a paid, full-time proselytizer and rabble rouser – but Tierwater could see she hadn't counted on this. Living underground, living anonymously, living as Dee Dee Drinkwater in a place as remote from the bright lights as you could get, beautiful scenery, sure, but where was the action? Her forte was traveling the enviro circuit, making contacts over the cocktails and hors d'oeuvres, showing the slides, giving the peroration and passing the hat. She looked good up there onstage, tall and commanding, with her low-cut blouse and scorching eyes, very persuasive, very seductive – as Tierwater could testify. She hadn't said anything yet, but he sensed she was looking for a way out, a deal maybe, a way to cut their losses and generate some publicity. Teo was coming. He wanted to talk. And what did that mean? More lawyers? More Freds? Tierwater didn't want any part of it – he was Tom Drinkwater now, faceless and hidden, and if he was going to go down he was going to go down in flames.

He was in the kitchen, half an hour after his chat with Ratchiss, helping Andrea dice vegetables for the salad that would complement the casserole and the mighty slabs of meat Ratchiss was incinerating on the grill out back, when he broached the subject of Teo's visit. 'Teo's coming up next week, you know.'

He turned his head to study her in profile, the hard bump of her nose, the slash of her cheek, hair falling to her shoulders in laminated coils. 'Philip told me.'

Outside, in the gathering shadows, Ratchiss hunched over the fire, drink in one hand, tongs in the other. He was whistling something, faint and atonal, something maddeningly familiar – 'Seventy-six Trombones'? The theme from *The Magnificent Seven?*

'He did?' Tierwater was surprised. And somehow – he couldn't help himself – annoyed.

She was watching her hands, the knife that deftly julienned the carrots on the chopping block. 'He gave me a letter from him too, E.F.! business mostly.' She shot him a sidelong glance. 'Robin Goldman? Remember her? The one that loaned us the car? Well, she quit. Didn't say a word to anybody, just quit.'

'No lawyers,' Tierwater said, 'and no deals. They pushed me, and I'm going to push back. You want to see sabotage, you want to see destruction like nobody's ever seen, well, that's what I'm devoting the rest of my fucking life to, and I don't care – '

'You want to see the letter? It's up on the night table, right by the bed.' The heel of the knife hit the board, slivers of carrot flew, chop, chop, chop. 'Go ahead, read it yourself.'

'I don't want to read it. Just tell me what the deal is, because I'm getting pretty stressed out here – I mean, every step I've taken since we, since I met you, has been a fucking disaster, one fucking disaster after another, and I want to know what's going on.'

Down went the knife. She turned to face him, wiping her hands on the flanks of her shorts. 'Nothing,' she said. 'Nothing's going on. And it was you who couldn't control yourself, slamming into that goon out in the Siskiyou, breaking out of the hospital, going up there to Sierra when I told you – '

'Yeah, you told me, all right.' He pinched his voice in a mocking falsetto: ' "You think I'd take Sierra along if I wasn't a hundred percent sure it was safe?" If Sierra doesn't go that night, then we're not here now, then my life isn't fucked, ever think of that?' He was shouting, he couldn't help himself, though he knew Ratchiss was listening, and, somewhere, Sierra too.

'All right. I made a mistake. What do you want me to do, bleed for it?'

'I just want to know one thing,' he said, and he got his voice under control, or tried to. 'Did you ever have anything going with him?'

'What are you talking about? With who?'

He dropped his voice, way down low, so low he could barely hear it himself: 'Teo.'

Later, at dinner, after Sierra had expressed her disgust over the bleeding mound of sliced tri-tip Ratchiss had set down in the middle of the table ('What do you call that – carpaccio?'), and Ratchiss had told a pungent, sweltering anecdote about tracking down a wounded leopard in thick bush and removing its head with a double blast of his shotgun as it hung in the air two feet from his face, Tierwater began to feel better. It wasn't so much Teo that was bothering him as what Teo represented. Intrusion. The outside world. Business as usual. These past three weeks had been an idyll, and Tierwater knew it, but he wanted the idyll to go on forever. He looked at Andrea, at her hands and arms and the way she cocked her head first with amusement and then intrigue and finally something like fear as Ratchiss spun out his story, and wished he could freeze the moment.

'You know, really,' Ratchiss was saying, 'my life's come a full three hundred sixty degrees.'

'One eighty,' Andrea said automatically. 'From one pole to the other. If you'd gone three sixty, you'd be back where you started.'

'That's just what I mean: I'm back where I started.' Red-faced, his skin baked to the texture of jerky, Ratchiss took a gulp of Pinot Noir and looked round the table. 'You see, I started out loving animals – and, by extension, nature – then, suddenly, I hated them and wanted to kill everything with claws and hoofs that moved across the horizon, and now I'm as committed a friend of the earth and the animals as you'd want to find.'

Sierra had been toying with her utensils, filling up on Diet Coke and chips. She didn't really care for eggplant, and salad was salad. 'How could anybody *hate* animals?' she said.

'Oh, it's easier than you might imagine. Ever think of what our ancestors must have felt when Mummy was snapped up by a big croc while washing out her loincloth in the river? Or when they glanced up from the fire to see Grandpa dangling from the jaws of some cave bear the size of that tree out front? Or, more to the point, the thousands of poor Africans taken by leopards every year? You think they love leopards? Or do you think they want to exterminate them ASAP?' He leaned back to light a cigarette, and Sierra made a face. 'Let me tell you a story, a true story, about why I came to hate wild animals – why I gave up my desk job to go to Africa. It was because of something that happened to me when I was little, or not so little – how old are you now?'

'Thirteen.'

'Thirteen. Well. Maybe I was a year or two younger, I don't know. But, anyway, my father took the family on a vacation, to see the country, he said, all the way from Long Island, where I grew up, to Pikes Peak, the Grand Canyon and Yosemite Park – not far from where we sit right here tonight, in fact. I had a sister then, Daphne, and she must have been about four at the time, a little girl with bangs and dimples and a barrette in her hair, and for the last two hundred miles all we talked about was the bears. Would there really be bears in Yosemite? Wild bears? And could we see them? Would we? My father was a solid man in his fifties – he married late and my mother was twenty years younger – and he'd got rich during the war in the canning business. He had one of those little masking-tape mustaches then, I remember, the kind you see on the dashing types in the old movies. Anyway, he just turned around in his seat and said, Sure, of course we'll see them. That's what the park's famous for. Bears.

'This was in the forties, by the way, just after the war. We had a Packard then, big as a hearse, in some deep shade of blue or maroon, I can't remember . . . And the bloody bears were there all right, a hundred of them, lined up along the road into the park like peanut vendors at Yankee Stadium, bears of all colors, from midnight black to dogshit brown and peach, vanilla and strawberry blond. You see, those were the days when the Park Service was actively trying to encourage tourism, and so they encouraged the bears too, by dumping garbage instead of hauling it out, because people wanted to see Bridalveil Falls and all that, sure, but if they were going to experience nature, they figured, *really* experience it, well, bears were the ticket.

'Every car was stopped, and every car had a bear at the window, and people were photographing them up close – from inches away – and feeding marshmallows and bologna sandwiches, candy bars, whatever they had, right into their mouths, as if they were just big shaggy dogs. Some people had their windows rolled down, leaning halfway out of the car to offer up a morsel of this or that, and the bears played it up, sitting on their rumps, doing tricks, woofing in that nasal, back-of-the-throat way that always makes me think of a trombone played in a closet. This was the thrill of my life. I was so excited I was practically bouncing off the ceiling of the car, and my sister too, but for some reason all the bears were occupied and none of them came up to us, or not right away. What's the matter, Dad? I whined. Why won't they come to us? And my father rolled down the window – we all rolled down our windows, even my mother – and he leaned way out and tossed a packet of American-cheese slices out onto the blacktop about ten feet from the nearest bear, all the while making these mooching noises to attract it. I remember the bear. It was medium-sized, black as the car tires, with too-small eyes that seemed to melt into its head.

'Well, it must have heard my father – or the soft wet thwap of the cheese hitting the pavement – and it turned, sniffed and vacuumed up the cheese, wax paper and all, and then it ambled up to the car, swinging its head to catch the scent, and it was like two huge dogs wrapped in an old rug. I remember the smell of it – still, and after all these years and all the animals I've tracked and shot and skinned. It was rank and wild and it engulfed us as if the car had suddenly rolled down a hill and into a swamp or a cesspool, and it made me afraid, but only momentarily, and not so afraid I didn't hang out the window and feed it a whole bag of popcorn, kernel by kernel, and the marshmallows we were going to roast over the fire that night.

'By this time, people were getting out of their cars all up and down the line, so many people you could hardly see the bears for them. They all had cameras, and some of them were offering the bears more elaborate things, like hot dogs on a stick and jars of peanut butter – one guy even held out a pineapple to a bear, and though I'm sure the bear had no idea what it was, it ate it, prickly skin and all. That was when my father closed in on our bear – the black one with the melted eyes, a thing that barely came up to his waist – and decided he wanted a picture with one of us kids mounted on the thing's back.'

'You've got to be kidding,' Tierwater said. Sierra darted a glance out the window. She was hunched over her plate, rhythmically knocking her knees. She didn't say a word.

Ratchiss just shook his head. 'I was too big, obviously, so he got my mother to hold the camera and he lifted my sister up into the air, thinking to swing her over the bear's shoulders for just an instant as it nosed at the popcorn on the pavement. My sister was wearing a white dress, with pink roses on it, that's what the pictures show, and a ribbon, I remember a ribbon.' He pushed back from the table, drew on his cigarette and let out a long slow exhalation. 'And that was it. My father was six months in the hospital. My sister, what was left of her, we had to bury.'

Andrea leaned forward, both hands cupped over the rim of her wineglass. 'You must have been devastated – '

'I saw the whole thing, my mother screaming, my father wrestling with this snarling bolt of stinking primitive energy, my sister, and I didn't do a thing, nothing, just stood there . . .

It took me half my life, looking at my father's disfigured face and the looping white scars down his back every time we went to the beach or the pool, to understand that it wasn't the bear's fault.'

'She died?' Sierra said, but nobody answered her.

After a suitable pause, during which Ratchiss stared down at the juices congealing on his plate and they all took a moment to listen to the silence of the woods brooding over the house, the conversation moved on to other things. There was coffee, and hot chocolate for Sierra, and then they retired to the big room to throw a log on the fire and sit watching the flames chew away at it. At some point, Andrea and Ratchiss talking in low tones about gut-shot buffalo and wild dogs, Tierwater poking through Emerson and Sierra hunched in the corner over a magazine, the telephone rang – but it didn't just ring; dropped into that well of silence, it was like an explosion. On the first ring, Tierwater felt as if he'd been hit in the back of the head with a hammer; on the second, he wanted to leap up and tear the cord from the wall. He was jumpy, and who wouldn't be? They could come for him at any moment.

Ratchiss answered it. 'Yeah,' he said. 'Oh, hi. Just talking about you. Uh-huh, uh-huh.' He cupped a hand over the mouthpiece. 'It's Teo, calling from a phone booth. Change of plans – he'll be up tomorrow. He wants to know if you want anything – '

Tierwater just shook his head, but Sierra rose out of her seat and threw down the magazine. 'Tell him I want magazines, books, video games, anything,' she said, advancing on Ratchiss as if to snatch the phone away from him. 'Tell him I want friends. Tell him I'm bored, bored, bored – '

'Yeah,' Ratchiss whispered into the phone. 'Uh-huh, yeah.' Then he put his hand over the receiver again and gently replaced it in its cradle.

Sierra was left standing in the middle of the room, her hands spread in extenuation. She was grimacing, and Tierwater could see the light glint off her braces – and that was another thing, an orthodontist, and how was he going to explain the fact that somebody had twisted those wires over her teeth and kept meticulous records of it but that that somebody's name and records were unavailable? 'I mean it,' she said, and he thought she was going to start stamping her foot the way she did when she was three. 'I don't want to be trapped up here with a bunch of old people and hicks, and I don't want to be Sarah Drinkwater either – I want to be me, Sierra, and I want' – her voice cracked – 'I want to go home.'

'You see this?' Teo was standing at the edge of a dirt road deep in the woods, hands on his hips. He gestured with a jerk of his chin. 'This is a culvert, twelve-inch pipe, nice and neat, keeps the creek from flooding out the road at snowmelt. If they don't have a culvert they don't have a road, and if they don't have a road they can't get the logs out.'

It was a day of high cloud and benevolent sun, a Saturday, and the trees stood silent around them. They weren't real trees, though – not to Tierwater's mind, anyway. They weren't the yellow pines, the Jeffreys, ponderosas, cedars and sequoias that should have been here, but artificial trees, hybrids engineered for rapid and unbending growth and a moderate branching pattern. Neat rows of them fanned out along both sides of the road, as rectilinear as rows of corn in the Midwest, interrupted only by the naked rotting stumps of the giants that had been sacrificed for them. Tree farming, that's what it was, tree farming in the national forest, monoculture, and to hell with diversity. Tierwater didn't see the long green needles catching the sun, didn't smell the pine sap or think of carbon-dioxide conversion or the Steller's jay squawking in the distance – he just gazed with disgust on the heaps of frayed yellow underbranches the timber company had pruned to make the job of harvesting all the easier. There was even a sign down the road – a sign in the middle of the forest, no less – that read *Penny Pines Plantation*. It was no better than graffiti.

One night, against his better judgment, he'd gotten into a debate with a logger at the local bar, an old man so wizened and bent over you wouldn't have thought he'd be able to lift a saw, let alone handle it, but as it turned out, he was a trimmer, part of the crew that shears the branches off the trees once they've been felled. Tierwater had said something about clear-cutting, and the old man, who was sitting at the bar with two cronies in plaid shirts and workboots, took exception to it. 'Let me ask you this,' he said, leaning into the bar and fixing Tierwater with a stone-cold crazy look, 'you live in a house or a cave? Uh-huh. And what's it made out of? That's right. You use paper too, don't you, you got some kind of job where you don't get your hands dirty, am I right? Well, I'm the one that give you the paper in your nice clean office, and I'm the one that cut the boards for your house — and if I didn't you'd be living in a teepee someplace and wiping your ass with redwood bark and aspen leaves, now, wouldn't you?'

Tierwater had felt something rise up in him, something born of impatience, truculence, violence, but he suppressed it — he was trying to keep a low profile here, after all. There weren't more than fifty cabins out there in the woods, with a couple of blacktop roads connecting them to the combination lodge, gift shop, bar and restaurant he was now sitting in, and everybody knew everybody in Big Timber. So he just turned his back, picked up his beer and went off to sit at a table in the corner. He'd felt bad about that, about letting the running dogs of progress have the last say, but now, out here under the sky, in the midst of their plantation, he saw a way to answer them all.

'And this' — Teo was grinning, squatting over his big calves to rummage through his backpack and produce a scuffed rag of leather that looked like a deflated volleyball — 'is a deflated volleyball. All you have to do is stuff it in the pipe, inflate the piss out of it and toss some debris up against it for camouflage. Soon as the water starts to flow — goodbye, road.'

'Perfect for ten- or twelve-inch pipe,' Andrea added. She was in a pair of khaki shorts and a T-shirt, her legs and arms tanned the color of iced tea, plastic wraparounds for sunglasses, Angels cap askew, halo and all. This was her hiker's disguise — that and the map in her hand — and she stood at the edge of the road shuffling her feet and grinning as Teo produced a bicycle pump and bent to his work. 'Of course,' she continued, 'for bigger pipe we use a drill and those little eye screws? You know what I mean, Ty — the kind of thing you use for hanging plants? You just screw four of them in, or maybe six, depending, and then stretch some chicken wire across the gap.'

'Right, and for really big pipe, pipe you can walk through' —

Teo was off the road now, down in the gully, wedging the ball deep into the culvert – 'you use a pickax, just punch holes in the bottom of the thing, I mean really tear it up, because eventually the water'll seep in underneath and undermine the whole business.'

'It's really pretty easy,' Andrea said. She was enjoying this, a little field trip, she the professor and Tierwater the student. Call it Ecodefense 101, or Monkeywrenching for the Beginner.

Teo's face, peering up from the culvert, a grin to match hers, the sun glancing off the shaven dome of his head: 'Not to mention fun. You're having fun, aren't you, Ty?'

'I don't know – am I? What if somebody comes, what then?'

'We're hikers, Ty, that's all,' Andrea said. 'Here, look at my map. Besides which, there's nobody within ten miles of us, and all the loggers are hunkered around watching the game – '

'What game?' Tierwater said. 'Is there a game on today?'

'There's always a game, football, basketball, hockey, championship bowling, whatever – and they're all watching it and getting liquored up so they can go out on the town and get into a brawl someplace. We don't even exist. And nobody'll know about this till spring runoff.'

Fine. But would it save the forest? And beyond that, would it save the world? Or would it only serve to provoke the timber company all the more, like the Oregon fiasco? Where had that gotten them? What had that saved? Even the press was bad, portraying Tierwater as a subspecies of violent lunatic (two of the flattopped kid's teeth had been knocked loose, and the building inspector claimed he'd suffered a bruised windpipe), and Earth Forever! as a collection of unhinged radicals dedicated to killing jobs and destroying the economy. Still, as he shouldered his pack and moved on up the road, Tierwater understood that he didn't care, not about the press or the organization or the trees or anything else: all he cared about now was destruction.

'You see, Ty, what I wanted to tell you is you're in a unique position.' Teo shifted his own pack with a twist of his shoulders and took two quick steps to catch up. 'My hands are tied – I mean, they're watching me day and night, phones tapped, the works – but you're Tom Drinkwater now, you're nobody, and you can have all the fun you want. Right here, for instance, where the road narrows by that bend up there? See it? Perfect place for a spike-board.'

'What's a spikeboard?'

'Maybe a four-foot length of two-by-four, studded with sawed-off pieces of rebar, set at a forty-five degree angle. You anchor the thing in the road with two L-shaped strips of the same rebar – invaluable stuff, really, you'd be surprised – maybe a foot and a half, two feet long, so the board doesn't shift when they run over it. Then you just kick some dirt on top of it and it's practically invisible.'

Andrea, loping along, all stride and motion, hands swinging, eyes electric with excitement: 'That slows them down all right.' She let out a barely contained whinny of a laugh that rode up into the trees and startled the whole world into silence. And then Teo laughed along with her – a soft nasal snicker that sounded as if someone were drowning a cat – and Tierwater joined in too.

An hour later they arrived at their destination, a bald spot carved out of the mountain at the end of the road. On one side was the unbroken line of shadow that was the forest; on the other there was nothing but a dome of rock and debris that fell away into the valley below. There were machines everywhere, naked steel and scuffed paint glinting in the sun. It was dry underfoot, the duff scattered and pulverized, crushed twigs poking out of the soil like bones, dust like a second skin. In the center of the bald spot, a thin coil of smoke twisted up into the air where a heap of charred branches, crushed pine cones and other debris had been swept up by the Cats and left to smolder over the weekend.

They scouted the place as thoroughly as they could from the cover of the trees, then stepped out into the open. 'Don't worry, Ty, we're only hikers, remember?' Andrea said. 'And it's not like we're trespassing. This is still the Sequoia National Forest, and whether the Freddies would admit it or not, we have as much right to be here as the – what does that say on the loader over there? Can you read that?'

'Cross Creek Timber Co.,' Teo read.

'Right – as the Cross Creek Timber Company.'

They walked right up to the machines, Teo and Andrea

alternately lecturing about the most effective way to disable them, pointing out the salient features of a Clark scraper, a shovel loader and a pair of Kenmore log trucks parked nose to tail at the mouth of the road. Tierwater didn't like being out in the open in broad daylight, even if there was no one around. He kept looking over his shoulder, expecting to catch the quick glint of the sun flashing off a pair of binoculars from the cover of a blind, or worse – a couple of forest rangers, with sidearms, ambling across the burned-over field. Or cops. Or FBI agents. And this was yet another movie, and he the reluctant star of it. What did FBI agents look like? Robert Stack? Tommy Lee Jones?

'See, they burn it over to put something back in the soil,' Teo was saying, squatting to sift the blackened dirt through his fingers. 'Gets rid of the debris too. Then they come in and plant in their neat rows and twenty more acres of old growth become a plantation.'

They were in the shadow of the shovel loader, a big cranelike thing that heaved the logs up onto the trucks once the Cats had knocked them down and the trimmers had removed the branches. Andrea slipped on a pair of cheap cotton gloves and unscrewed the filler cap on the crankcase. 'Right here, Ty – this is where you pour the sand, tonight, when it's dark. Medium-grit silicon carbide is even better, but obviously we're not going to haul anything extra all the way out here. And don't forget your boots.'

All three of them, at Teo's insistence, had slipped sweatsocks over their hiking boots before they emerged from the woods – to cover up the waffle pattern on the soles. It was daylight, and they were hikers – only hikers, nothing but hikers – but they were taking no chances. 'I won't,' Tierwater promised. 'But I tell you, I don't know if I can wait till dark. I'm here, the machines are here, the fucking artificial pines are down the road – I wouldn't mind torching the whole business, plantation, Cats, the whole fucking thing.'

'I know, Ty,' Andrea said, and her hand was on his arm, a gentle hand, a persuasive hand, a wifely hand that spoke volumes with a squeeze, 'but you won't.'

When the lesson was over for the day, the three of them retired to a creek bed half a mile away and Andrea spread out a picnic lunch – smoked-duck sausage, Asiago cheese, artichoke hearts, fresh tomatoes and baguettes, replete with a stream-chilled bottle of Orvieto. They drank a toast to Tierwater's first covert action – coming action, that is – and then Andrea and Teo shouldered their packs and headed up the streambed to the trail that would, in three hours' time, take them back to Ratchiss' cabin. And Tierwater? He settled in to feel the sun on his face, read a book, watch the sky and wait till the day closed down and the moon rose up over the bald spot on the mountain.

It was past nine when he woke. Something had crossed the stream not fifty feet from where he lay, something big, and it startled him out of a dreamless sleep. The first thing he thought of, even before he fully recalled where he was or why, was Sierra. He checked his watch, listened again for the splashing – it was a deer, had to be; either that or an FBI agent – and pictured her dangling her big feet over the arm of the *mopane* easy chair, reading *The Catcher in the Rye* under the dull, staring gaze of the kongoni head in Ratchiss' living room. She wasn't here tonight, and she wasn't going to be present – ever again – for any nighttime activities of any kind. He was determined that she was going to have a normal life – or as normal a life as you can have living under an assumed name in a museum of African memorabilia in an A-frame in the hind end of nowhere. She was going to go to school, learn about the Visigoths and prime numbers, go to dances, acquire a new squadron of evil friends, experiment with pot and booze, become passionate about affectless bands, debate meat-eaters, rebel and recant, have her nose ring reinserted and drive a convertible at a hundred and ten. In five years – four and a half, actually – she could even have her identity back.

As for Teo, there was never any question of his participating in anything like this, not for real, not anymore – he was Earth Forever!'s poster boy now, the big fund-raiser, and he couldn't afford to get caught in a covert action. He could chain himself to nuclear reactors and tree-sit and preach and publish all he wanted to, but his tire-slashing days were over. 'Really, Ty,' he said, working the corkscrew with the sun flattening his face and the butt of the wine bottle clenched between his thighs, 'you understand why I can't risk any extracurricular activities anymore, don't you?' The cork slid from the bottle with a wet oozing pop of release. 'But I envy you, I do.'

And Andrea. She'd paid her fine, like Teo, and gotten off with probation for the Siskiyou incident – she hadn't assaulted anybody. And who knew it was her in that turd-brown car? Or at least that's what Teo was thinking. Maybe they'd let her back in, maybe Fred could do something . . . 'About the kidnapping. Or abduction, or whatever. The Sierra thing.'

Tierwater watched her. She'd tugged the brim of the baseball cap down to keep the sun out of her face and it immobilized her hair as she sliced cheese and portioned out the wine. She didn't say anything, but Tierwater could read the look on her face. Second thoughts. She was having second thoughts.

'Look,' he said, 'there's no reason I can't do this myself. How hard can it be? In fact, I insist. I know the drill. I know the trail out of here better than either of you.' Andrea looked up. The brim of the cap threw a shadow over her face. 'Right, hon?'

'I don't know,' she said. 'I don't feel right about it.' That was what she said, and she might even have meant it, or thought she meant it, but she was already looking for a way out of the whole mess, whether she realized it or not. 'You sure you want to do this by yourself, Ty?'

She'd asked him twice. Once over the wine and duck sausage, and then when she bent to kiss him just before she and Teo packed up and left.

'It's all right,' he told her. 'Hey, the Fox always worked by himself, didn't he?'

But now it was dark, and he was alone, and something was splashing in the creek. When he'd fallen asleep, it was on a scoured pan of granite just above the high-water mark, in a place where the spring floods had scooped out a hollow in the rock, and he lay there as if in the palm of a sculpted hand, the water continuously butting up against it and rushing by with the white noise of infinity. A minute passed, and then another. Whatever it was that had wakened him was gone now. He listened for a minute more to be sure, then pushed himself up and flung the pack over his shoulder. Before he knew it, he was weaving through the debris of the clear-cut, his footsteps muffled by the sweatsocks stretched over his boots, a gibbous moon showing him the way with a light as pale and cold as the ambient light of a dream.

(And what was I carrying in that pack? The tools of my new trade. Pipe wrench, socket wrenches, gloves, wire cutters, hacksaw, flashlight, plastic tubing and plastic funnel, a couple of granola bars, bota bag, sheath knife, matches. I was equipped to wreak havoc, no excuses, no regrets. The least of those machines was worth fifty thousand dollars, and I was prepared to destroy every working part I could locate – but subtly, subtly, so they'd see nothing amiss and run their stinking diesel engines till they choked and seized. I only wished I could be there to see it happen, see the looks on their faces, see the trees I'd saved standing tall while the big yellow machines spat and belched and ground to an ignominious and oh-so-expensive halt.)

Tierwater scouted the place twice – no one and nothing moved; the silence was absolute – and then he slipped on the black cotton gloves and began servicing the machinery. He hit the shovel loader first, unscrewing the filler cap on the manifold as Andrea had showed him, neatly inserting the plastic tubing and then pouring cup after cup of sand (or decomposed granite, actually) into the funnel. It sifted down and into the innards of the engine with a soft gratifying swish, and it was that sound, the sound of sand in a plastic tube, that he would forever identify with nightwork – and revenge.

He went to each of the vehicles in succession, working not only on the engines but on all the lubrication fittings he could find, and when he was done with the heavy machinery, he turned his hand to the two trucks. Tinkering, tapping, murmuring directions to himself under his breath, he lost all sense of time. When finally he thought to check his watch, he was amazed to see it was past three in the morning. He had to get going, had to get out of there and head down the moonlit trail that would take him back home to the safety and anonymity of his bed, and already he could see ahead to the next day, a late-afternoon drink at the bar, his ears attuned to the buzz of drunken conversation ebbing and flowing around him. Sabotage? What do you mean, sabotage? Where? When? You're kidding. Now, who would do a thing like that?

The night breathed in, breathed out. He stood there looking up into the nullity of the sky, and for a long moment he didn't move at all. What was he feeling? Satisfaction, yes, the special charge that comes of knowing you've done your best, the true sweet exhaustion of a job well done, but something more – anger. He was angry still. This was nothing, the smallest pinprick in the web of progress, the death of a few machines – maybe, if he was lucky, of a logging company. But what about the trees? What about all those artificial pulpwood trees in the Penny Pines Plantation an hour down the road? They were there still, weren't they, and until they were gone, eliminated, erased from the face of the mountain, there was no forest here. No forest at all.

He found himself walking. Not down the path, not toward the cabin and Andrea and his bed, but toward the place where the planted pines ran on as far as the eye could see. The air was cool – temperature in the low sixties, or fifties even – but he was sweating as he walked, and even as he sweated he stepped up the pace. Fifty minutes later he was in the middle of the plantation, down on his knees in the dry, yielding, friable dirt, and in his hands, the matches. There was the sudden sizzle of the struck match, the bloom of light as he touched it to one of the random heaps of shorn branches, and then the quick fingers of flame racing through the desiccated needles. He watched it take, watched the first tree explode in violent color against the black of the night, and even as he ran, even as he fought down the pain in his knee and the screaming of his lungs, the world at his back was transfigured, lit so spontaneously and so brightly it was as if the sun had come up early.

Andrea murmured something, a snippet of dream dialogue, and rolled over. The windows were infused with the green light of seven-thirty in the morning, and when Tierwater lifted the covers and slid in beside her, the tranquil hot familiar odor of the nesting animal rose to envelop him, the smell of his wife's body, her beautiful naked slumbering body, rich in all its properties and functions. He nuzzled at her ear and worked an arm underneath her so he could cup her breasts in both hands. He was excited. Burning up with it. She murmured again, moved her buttocks against him in a sleepy, precoital wriggle. 'You're back,' she said. 'I am,' he whispered, and felt her nipples harden. He was thinking of Jane and Sherry and half a dozen other girls and women he'd known, and then she turned to face him, to kiss him, and he was thinking of her, nobody but her.

Afterward, they lay side by side and stared up into the rafters as the house began to stir beneath them. There was the sound of a flushing toilet, then the wheeze of the refrigerator door and the low hum of Sierra's tape deck as the muted throb of gloom and doom filtered up through the floorboards. Voices. Sierra's, Teo's. The swat of the screen door, and then Ratchiss' 'What ho!' and Teo's whispered response.

'You smell like smoke,' Andrea said.

'Me?' Tierwater knew he'd gone too far, knew they'd suspect arson once the machines went down, and he'd heard the first of the planes rumbling in to attack the fire even as he legged it on up the trail home. The lookout at Saddle Peak or the Needles must have been up early, because the helicopters were in the sky before he'd had a chance to catch his breath, and within the hour the drone of the bombers saturated the air and he looked up to see three of them scraping overhead with their wings aglow and their bellies full of fire retardant.

She was up on one elbow now, watching him. 'You didn't start a campfire out there last night, did you? Because that would be stupid, really stupid – '

'Are you kidding? It went great, every minute of it. I was like the Phantom and the Fox rolled into one, so efficient it was scary. It was a rush, it was.'

He could feel her eyes on the side of his face, the eyes that brooked no bullshit and reduced every complexity to the basics. She was sniffing – first the air, and now him – hovering over him, her breasts soft on his chest, ruffling his hair, sniffing. 'I don't know,' she said, 'but you smell like you spent the night in the chimney.'

'Maybe that's it,' he lied – 'I started a fire when I came in, just to take the chill off the morning.'

That seemed to satisfy her, at least for the moment – until she heard the bombers for herself, that is, and walked down to the mailbox and smelled the smoke on the air and saw the Forest

Service buses rolling down the highway crammed to the windows with the impassive dark-faced immigrants they hired at minimum wage to beat back the flames bush by bush and yard by yard. Then she'd know. And Teo would know, and Ratchiss. He could hear them already – *Are you crazy? Right in our own backyard? You think these people are stupid? You want to jeopardize everybody and everything – the whole organization, for Christ's sake – just because you're out of control? Huh? What's your problem?*

Suddenly he was exhausted. He'd been up all night, hiked nine miles each way, destroyed hundreds of thousands of dollars' worth of heavy equipment. His knee ached, and his upper back, which he must have strained somehow – probably fighting one fitting or another. He was no mechanic.

'You want to get some rest?' Andrea said, and already she was in motion, the bed pitching like a rubber raft in deep water, a lingering glimpse of her nude body, and then she was shrugging into T-shirt, panties and shorts.

'Yeah, that would be nice,' he said, 'but you never answered my question.'

'What question?'

'About you and Teo. All those nights on the road, Connecticut, New Jersey, wherever. You slept with him, didn't you?'

'What does it matter? It was before I even met you.'

'You did, didn't you?'

Somewhere, far overhead, there was the thin drone of an airplane. The wind must have shifted, at least temporarily, because he could smell the smoke now too, as if the air had been perfumed with it. 'I'm not going to lie to you, Ty – we're both grownups, aren't we? You want to know the answer? Did I sleep with him?'

He closed his eyes. He'd never been so tired in his life. 'No,' he said. 'No, forget it.'

Santa Ynez, December 2025

MAC HAS ALWAYS made a big deal of the holidays – glitter, he just loves it, cookies in the oven, blinking lights, fa-la-la-la-la, that sort of thing – and this year is no exception. So what if conditions are a little extreme? So what if we live on what amounts to an island and can't get out to the supermarket, hospital, sushi bar or feedlot? So what if the basement is full of shitting, snarling, pissed-off and dislocated animals? Let's decorate, that's his thinking. Two years ago he brought in a crew of fifty to string lights in parallel strips up and down the walls of the house so the whole place looked like a gift box on a hill (or, more accurately, a huge electric toaster as seen from the inside out), something like twenty thousand bulbs burning up electricity nobody has and nobody can afford, and he wasn't even here. Last year a crew nearly as big showed up on the first of December, but the winds were so intense the workers kept getting blown off their ladders and out of their cherry pickers, while the lights they did manage to string just slapped against the side of the house till there was nothing left but a long chain of empty sockets chattering in the breeze. Mac wasn't here then either. He's here now, though, here with a vengeance, and if we can't have Christmas outside because of the unremitting meteorological cataclysm that seems to be lashing away day and night at everything that isn't buried ten feet underground, then we're going to have it inside.

Which to my mind is purely asinine. What's to celebrate, that's what I want to know? That we had a forty-eight-hour respite from the rain last week? That April Wind has started her Sierra-the-martyr book with me as the chief and captive source? That Lily seems to have adjusted to her new surroundings as if she'd been born between paneled walls and that the rock-hard pendulous corpses of cattle, pigs and turkeys look to tide us over right on through the next millennium? Piss poor, that's what I say. The end is nigh. What fools these mortals be.

We're wearing masks still, all of us, though we might as well be on a coral atoll for all the contact we've had with the outside world, and when I'm not disinterring the past with April Wind or watching Andrea cozy up to Mac, I try to stay busy with the animals. Chuy and I are doing a creditable job of feeding them, I think, but feeding isn't the problem. Captive breeding, and that's been our biggest goal here, right from the start, is nothing less than impossible under conditions like these. We have no real access to the animals – it's just too risky to try to tiptoe up to a reinforced wooden door and surprise any creature that isn't deaf, blind and comatose. And forget the cleaning, it's just too dangerous, particularly with Lily, Petunia and the lions – and you'd be surprised how cantankerous and subversive even a warthog can be. Open the door of the bowling alley, and you hear nothing, not so much as a snort or whimper; half a heartbeat later you've got two angry pairs of tusks swiping at your gonads. Someday, in the dry season, if it ever comes, Mac will have to rip up the carpets, tear out the pissed-over paneling and burn it, that's all. And then we can start again, with new pens and new animals – or some new breeding stock, at least.

But back to Christmas, because Christmas is what's happening here, floods, *mucosa* and irate quadrupeds notwithstanding. The two Als, left with no discernible use or employment since there's no one within half a mile to protect Mac from, have been co-opted by the interior-decorating department (Mac and Andrea, working in concert) to string lights and pin tinfoil angels to the walls. It all feels – I don't know – *vestigial* somehow. And sad. The empty ceremony of a forgotten tribe. Christmas means nothing to me, except maybe as a negative, the festival of things, of gluttony, light the candles and rape the planet all over again. Even the Japanese got in on the act at the end of the last century, but they saw the Yule season for what it was – wall-to-wall shopping and nothing more.

I know, I know. We had Christmas when I was a boy, because

of my mother, and there was magic in the world then – there was redemption. Hope. And more than that: there was a reason, for us and the beasts and the plants and everything else. That's all gone now. Long gone. And though I'm utterly practical and unsentimental, as stripped of illusion as any captive of the Mohawk, the first time I come down the hall and spot those silverfoil angels crowding the ceiling on their crimped and glittering wings, it's all I can do to keep from blubbering into my gauze mask. And how do you like that for a confession?

In fact, I'm standing there in the downstairs hallway, overcome with emotion, ten o'clock in the morning and eight more shopping days to Christmas, when Chuy materializes from behind a lifesize marble statue of Elvis, chopping along the Persian runner in his quick purposive way. I can see from his body language – head down, shoulders bunched up around his ears, feet snipping at the carpet like lawn shears – that he's looking for me, and that he's looking for me because something has gone suddenly and irremediably wrong. 'Mr. Ty,' he calls, his eyes already running away from him, 'I don't want to tell you, but *la puerta del cuarto de regalos?* – the gift room? – this is open. Open wide.'

What am I thinking? Lily, that's what. She's over six feet long from snout to tail, weighs a hundred and sixty pounds, with a big gray head shaped like an anvil and black stripes on her legs. The bulk, the fur, the collapsible rear and ungainly legs – don't let appearances fool you. This is an animal that can run better than thirty miles an hour in a burst, and run all night long, designed by evolution as an eating machine, pure and simple. No codes, no ethics. See it, kill it, eat it – that's the motto of the family Hyaenidae. And now the door's open, open wide, and the hoped-for, prayed-for, one-in-a-thousand-chance miracle – that's she's snoring and sated in a midden of gnawed bones and foil gift wrap – is not a thing I'm counting on. She's too smart for that. Too devious. Too wild.

My first impulse is to fly up the stairs on my seventy-five-year-old feet and see for myself, maybe even slam the big mahogany door and turn the key in the lock, but I suppress it. That's what an impetuous forty-year-old would do – or even a headstrong fifty- or sixty-year-old. Sure. And have his head crushed and his bowels ripped out in the process. No, the wisdom of age speaks in my ear (life might be shit, but why curtail it here, before the end of the story?), and my aching feet take me down the corridor in the direction of the back stairway, Chuy hurrying along beside me with an inscrutable look. Is he concerned, frightened, excited? With Chuy, it's hard to say. His eyes are like trick mirrors and he never loses that loopy, gold-inlaid smile, no matter what happens. We're being stealthy, though, both of us – we're in lock-step on that score – and we slip down the hall to the Grunge Room as quietly as possible.

Ten feet from the door, both of us stop dead: something isn't right. Something, in fact, is very wrong: the door is ajar. What I'm feeling all of a sudden is nothing less than panic. My heart is pounding, my eyes are burning – vinegar, somebody's poured vinegar in my eyes – and I can't seem to swallow. It's me. My fault. I'm old, forgetful, a fool and worse, because I'm the one who must have left that door open when I slipped into my jeans and boots and staggered down the corridor to breakfast. Andrea, I'm thinking, Andrea, even as I lean into the howling depths of that still and silent room and fumble for the light switch on the wall inside the door. I can't find it, at least not right away, because I'm just a guest here, because my fingers are trembling and I'm old and I want to be back in my own house, amid my own things, and away from all this.

The room is deep, high-ceilinged, cavernous. I can't see a thing. The weather has been so bad it's hard to tell morning from night anyway, but Andrea keeps the big brocade curtains drawn to squelch any hint of daylight till she drags herself out of bed, usually about noon. She's there now, a hyena-sized mound in the center of the bed, all the stories of African witches shape-shifting and taking on the form of the sneaking graveyard robber come back to haunt me ('And what big teeth you have, Grandma') till she rips off a sudden burst of crackling old-lady snores and I can breathe again.

Then the light, and I see that the room is empty, but for Kurt Cobain's hair and the heap of molding artifacts that represent my worldly wealth, the salvage of the guesthouse rudely dumped in the far corner. In amongst the junk, though, duly cleaned and lubricated with a rag soaked in 3-in-1 Oil, is the .470 Nitro

Express rifle that once belonged to Philip Ratchiss. I've never hunted a thing in my life, not to kill it – I'm with Thoreau: *No humane being, past the thoughtless age of boyhood, will wantonly murder any creature which holds its life by the same tenure that he does* – but I go straight to the gun, force the cartridges in the chamber and sight experimentally down the length of the barrel.

Andrea (half awake): 'Ty?'

Me: 'Yeah?'

Andrea: 'You're not – ? What are you doing? Is that a gun?'

Me (hard, cold, tough as the callus on the heel of a fakir's foot): 'I'm going hunting.'

It's all a pose. Because I'm not that tough. Nobody is. Except maybe Ratchiss. Or Teo – the *late* Teo, and why does it give me such satisfaction to turn that phrase over on my tongue? I have no illusions here: Lily is going to have to die, the soft-point bullets tearing a hole in her you could stuff an encyclopedia into, and Lily is one of – what, two, three hundred? – of her kind left on earth. She's been with me since the beginning, a scruffy yearling we got from the L.A. Zoo before it went under, and she was here for me when Andrea wasn't. How many morsels have I tossed her in the space of ten years, how much roadkill, how many chicken backs? (And if you've never tossed a chicken back to a hyena, how can I begin to describe the satisfaction of hearing the snap of those iron jaws, the gorge descending, the efficiency of the animal, my animal, as it consumes and thrives and grows into the very image of the shaggy wild-eyed thing that trotted across Olduvai Gorge when we were still toolless apes bolting our own meat raw?) This is Lily we're talking about here, *Lily* – I'd as soon have to shoot Old Yeller.

Out in the hallway, stalking now, Chuy at my back: 'Mr. Ty,' he whispers, 'you *quiere* for me maybe to get the wire net, I think maybe?' And then, when I don't answer: '*No le vas a disparar* – you no shoot Lily, Mr. Ty?'

I just grit my teeth – or what's left of them, anyway.

'The dart gun, *por qué no* we just dart her?'

I'm busy stalking. Crouched over my screaming septuagenarian lower back muscles, the gun as heavy as a hod of bricks in my weak wet hands, eyes watering, hearing shot, I haven't got the energy to respond. You don't dart an animal like this, not at close quarters – even if you did manage to hit her, she'd have removed your face before the drug began to take the spring out of her legs, and she'd have her head deep in your intestines by the time she felt a yawn coming on. This is no Patagonian fox. This is no stitch job at the local hospital. This is finality. Good night, all she wrote, sheet-over-the-face time.

Upstairs, there's nothing. The bedroom doors are all firmly shut, the fluorescent energy-savers glow in their sconces, silence reigns. I say nothing to Chuy, and he says nothing to me. It's all we can do to breathe, the air thick in our nostrils, almost solid with the stench of hyena, urine, excrement, rotting meat. The gift-wrapping room is up ahead on our left, three doors down. What I want more than anything in the world is for that door to be closed, for Chuy to have mistaken it for another one, for all this to be nothing more than a false alarm, a joke on me, the smallest little inconsequential miscue to laugh about over coffee and crullers. But it's not, and that's an affirmative, Captain, because we're close enough now to see that the door is indeed open, open wide, flung all the way back on its hinges like a big toothless mouth.

That freezes me up, all right. My legs feel as if they've been sawed off and put on backward, my fingers are rigid, I think I'm having a heart attack. And the gun – suddenly the gun weighs as much as a howitzer. 'The chair,' I whisper, jerking my chin first at Chuy and then at some priceless antique from the nineties, all molded black plastic and chrome, until Chuy catches my meaning and inches the chair away from the wall and into my purview. Now I'm resting the gun on the back of the chair, finger on the trigger, the barrel trained on the open door at optimal hyena height, and now Chuy – the most tentative man in the world, an acrobat on a wire stretched high over a pit of snakes – is inching toward the door.

I've had a lot of bad moments in my life, bad moments like little missives from the Fates, whole truckloads of them, but this is one of the worst. I am ready for anything – or as ready as a mostly broken-down young-old man with deteriorating reflexes and a serious loss of faith can expect to be – but it's not Lily that comes sailing through the door, it's Mac. *Mac.* He's wearing the usual getup, half drum major, half hood from a forties B-movie, his legs gliding on silk strings, a stack of gift-wrapped boxes in his arms, and he's whistling – actually whistling – some Motown tune of the sixties. It takes me a minute, and then I've got it – The Supremes, 'Stop in the Name of Love.'

I can't seem to find my voice. But Chuy, who doesn't seem capable of construing things with the same degree of complexity as I do, has no trouble finding his. 'Mr. Mac,' he says, waving his rope-walker's arms for balance, 'I think you better maybe look out. *Cuidado,* you know?'

As I've said, my hearing could be better, the vestigial buzz of Hendrix's 'Voodoo Child' forever vibrating in the cochlea of my left ear, and I can't make out Mac's gauze-muffled response. 'Muffins on marmalade,' he seems to be saying, or maybe it's the other way around. He's arrested there in the doorway, not ten feet from the barrel of the gun, and I can see that his lips are moving behind the gauze film of the mask. Meanwhile, my hands are trembling so hard I'm afraid I'm going to squeeze the trigger in some sort of involuntary reflex, so I let go of it, rise up to my full height (which is two full inches less than it was when I was middle-aged, another of the humiliations of longevity), and tear my own mask off. 'Mac, for Christ's sake, will you get out of the way!'

No response.

'It's Lily!' I shout. *'Lily!'*

In pantomime now, the spilling legs, floating packages, eyes bugging behind the silver lenses of his shades: a glance over his shoulder, a glance for me, and then the packages are left to the mercy of gravity and Mac is at the door, flinging it shut like the lone defender at the gates. He's so stunned, so consternated, so much at a loss, he forgets all about cool and contagion and strips off both his shades and the gauze mask in one frantic motion. 'Holy – ,' he says, searching for the expression, because Mac doesn't curse, 'I mean holy crap! What was I thinking? I wasn't, Ty, that's just it, I wasn't thinking. It's just like I mean it was Christmas and I – she didn't get out, did she? Is she loose?'

I shrug. 'How would I know? But my guess is yeah, sure, she's loose. Long gone, in fact.'

The three of us take a minute to look both ways up and down

the long corridor, as if we expect to see her scrag of a tail poking out from beneath one of the memorabilia cases that line the walls on either side. (No suits of armor or crossed halberds here – this is nothing less than a shrine to the genius of Maclovio Pulchris, and I don't mean that sarcastically. He *is* a genius. Or was. Maybe he's gone a little bit overboard with the self-deifying aspect of it, I won't deny that. It's a question of proportion, I suppose, because it's all here, Pulchrisized for the ages. Not only has he got photos and oil portraits of himself staring out from the walls wherever you look, but every record and CD he's ever recorded is on permanent display, not to mention tour souvenirs, ticket stubs, T-shirts, yellowing press releases and fanzine articles, even the outfits he's worn onstage, all of it meticulously arranged according to release dates, artistic period and hairstyle.)

'I don't know,' Mac says, 'it was only a minute. Maybe she was asleep or something.'

I'm shaken. I'm angry. And though he's my employer, though he's my lifeline in the dark churning Social Security–less waters of the perilous young-old life, I let him know it. 'What do you think, you can just leave the door wide open and she's going to curl up like some fat lapdog?'

Mac wants to answer – I can see a response gathering itself in his naked, faintly yellowish eyes – but the opportunity dissolves into the sudden ringing of the doorbell. Or it doesn't ring exactly, but chimes the opening bars of Mac's biggest hit, 'Chariots of Love,' from the *Chariots of Love* album. It's a curious thing, the ringing of that bell – because no one rings the bell, ever. No one, even in normal (or less *ab*normal) times, can get through the big gates out front and past the surveillance cameras and Al and Al and even me and Chuy and the day-workers and gardeners and all the rest to arrive at the door and find the button to depress in the first place. And as if that isn't enough of a feat under ordinary conditions, now we're even further isolated by the flooding. So who's ringing the bell? Lily? God? The Ghost of Christmas Past?

Down the stairs we go, judiciously of course, the Nitro Express and I shielding Mac from the front, Chuy and his Dursban-saturated hide screening him from the rear, and then we creep cautiously down the first-floor hallway and out into the vestibule even as the bell chimes again and the two Als materialize grimly from the surveillance-control room to the left of the main entrance. The taller Al, after giving his employer a warning glance, pulls open the door.

There, in the strange subaqueous glow of the storm, stands Delbert Sakapathian, the cat-lover, he of the cueball head and overinflated gut. He's lost his slicker and his rain hat, his clothes cling wetly and what hair he has left is painted to his skull. But that's not all: beside him, wrapped so tightly in a black slicker he looks as if he's been extruded from a tube, is an old man – or maybe an old woman. It's hard to tell, because this person is one of the old-old, the ancient old, the antediluvian, artifactual, older-than-knowledge old, so old that he/she has been rendered utterly sexless. We see the tube of the slicker, the monkey hands, the face like a peeled grape, toothless, chinless, cheekless, a scraped and blasted black hole of humanity. Neither of them is wearing a gauze mask.

'Mr. Pulchris,' Delbert Sakapathian says, addressing Mac with all the awe and humility of a communicant in the church of celebrity, 'we need help. I – this is Old Man Foley, from the Lupine Hill Retirement Home? – and there's nothing left over there but wreckage, and he needs shelter, I mean, if you can spare it, just till they can get the emergency crews in there to rebuild or take people to a gymnasium somewhere or something. He's been wet through to the skin for days now.'

The rain keeps up its steady sizzling. And the smell is there, so sharp it makes me wince – the smell of the underside of things, of decay, of death.

'Look, I'm not asking for myself – Lurleen and me are okay, I've got my canoe out there tied to the railing and they can condemn the condos all they want but they're going to have to shoot me to get me out of there, at least till the rain stops . . .' He looks at me now, at the two Als and Chuy, making a mute appeal.

Finally, Mac, in his sweetest voice, says no. Shakes his head wearily, the eel whips slipping across the slick surface of his restored shades. 'I'd like to help,' he says, 'I really would, but I just can't – we can't – risk it. It's the *mucosa*. You understand, don't you? I want to help. I do. Money's no problem. You want money?'

I'm watching Delbert Sakapathian's face. His expression says, *Shit and die, all of you, you fools on a hill, you animal lovers and epicene rock stars;* it says, *I'm worth ten of you because I'm a human being still and you're just things in a cage.* Chuy gives me a look. The two Als brace themselves. And that is the precise moment when Lily appears.

The noise she emits – a low chuff of warning or surprise – is so faint as to be barely audible over the sibilance of the rain, and anybody who hasn't watched her eat, sleep and scratch round her pen for ten years probably wouldn't have recognized it as an animal vocalization at all. I turn my head. That's all – just turn it, a simple flexion and release of the appropriate muscles – and Lily is gone, a brownish streak, black stripes, gray head, dodging past Delbert Sakapathian and the extruded old man to vanish into the storm.

For a moment, nobody moves. Then a breeze comes up, and that smell with it, and one of the tinfoil angels scratches its wings against the ceiling. That's when I step forward, not a word for Mac or Chuy or the two men standing on the doorstep. The doorknob is in my hand, the rain hissing like static, the smell of it, and then the door somehow swings closed till it hits the frame with a shivering thud.

And then? Then I bolt it.

A week later, I find myself sitting in front of a faux fire, rain spitting at the windows, April Wind crouched on a footstool at my feet with a tape recorder the size of a matchbox. She's wearing a denim dress with thin two-inch strips of material sewn randomly to it, fringed suede boots and a belt of what looks to be at least two boxes of Kleenex knotted together. The overall effect is of a big unfledged bird with buck teeth and a head too small for its body. Have I mentioned that I have no use for this whittled-down little stick of a woman? That I hate the past, have limited tolerance for the present and resent this or any other form of interrogation? That I'm sitting still for it for one reason only and that that reason is spelled A-n-d-r-e-a?

'So,' April Wind breathes, setting the tape in motion with a practiced flick of her index finger, 'tell me about the whole tree-sit thing, from the beginning, because I didn't join E.F.! till after Sierra – well, till after she was already up there in the arms of Artemis. What I wanted to know is, whose idea was it – was she pushed into it by Teo? Or Rolfe? Or what's-his-name, Ratchiss?'

We're in the James Brown Room, surrounded by images of the godfather of soul, his sunken eyes, glistening pompadour and thrusting chin replicated over and over till the walls seem to shift like the walls of a planetarium and his multiplied eyes become the stars in the sky. It's quite a trope, I know, but then I'm suffering from indigestion, the gauze mask is like a smotherer's hand clamped over my mouth and my mind is already playing tricks on me. *Papa's got a brand new bag,* oh, yes, indeed.

'Or was this her own thing, something spontaneous, something she just had to do? For love of the earth, I mean?'

I'm fumbling around for an answer, suddenly ambushed by an image of my daughter that's as palpable as the portrait of the Famous Flames leering at me from the place of honor over the fireplace. She's twenty-one, long-limbed and lean, with the cleft chin she inherited from her mother and her mother's heat-seeking eyes, wearing running shoes, cut-off jeans and a thermal T-shirt. Her hair is in a braid as thick as a hawser, and there's no trace of the makeup she used to baste herself with when she was fourteen and terminally angry. I see a whole tribe of tree-huggers and vegans and post-hip hippies gathered round her, pounding on bongos and congas, somebody playing a nose flute, the spice of marijuana in the air and the big ancient trees rising up out of the duff like the pillars that keep the sky from crashing down. It's the first day, the day of the ascension, and her feet are on the ground still. And me? I'm in the picture too. I'm there to see her off.

'Well?' April Wind wants to know.

I try to shrug, but the catch in my shoulders makes me wince. It's the weather. It makes me feel twenty years older than I already am. 'For love, I guess.'

'Nobody put any pressure on her? You didn't, did you?'

I shake my head, and even that hurts. Pressure her? I tried to talk her out of it, tried to remind her what peaceful protest had got us in the Siskiyou and the whole sorry downward spiral that had spun out of that, but of course she wouldn't listen. She was fresh from

Teo's Action Camp, in love with the idea of heroic sacrifice and so imbued with the principles of Deep Ecology she insisted on the ethical treatment not only of plants and animals, but even rocks and dirt. *'Rocks?'* I said. *'Dirt?'* She just nodded. She was lit up in the glow of all that attention, the cynosure of the Movement, the sacrificial virgin who was going to dwell in a tree while the rest of them went home to their TVs and microwaves, and I looked into her eyes and barely recognized her.

'Everything in the ecosystem has its integrity,' she assured me, leaning back against her tree and sipping a concoction of papaya, wheatgrass and yogurt from a glossy red plastic mug with the Earth Forever! logo stamped on it (another of Teo's ideas, and he was a marketing genius, all right, never doubt that. If there was an angle, Teo would exploit it). 'Really,' she said, glancing up as the drummers shifted into another gear and the dancers swayed round the trees with their goat bells and tambourines ajingle, 'it's not just about wolves and caribou and whooping cranes – it's about the whole earth. I mean, you have to think about what right do we have to dig up the ancient soil and disturb the fungus and microbes, the springtails and pill bugs and all the rest, because without them there'd be no soil, and we have even less right to manufacture and mutate things into new forms – '

'Like that mug in your hand,' I said. 'Or that shirt that's going to keep you warm tonight.'

'Compromises,' she said, 'everything's a compromise.'

This was in December of 1997, just outside of Scotia, in Humboldt County, California. I was an ex-con at the time, a jailbird, an absentee father, a name on a card in the mail, and I hadn't seen much of her over the course of the past four years. I didn't want her up in that tree – Teo wanted her there, Andrea did, all the northern-California Earth Forever! tribe and their ragtag constituency were clamoring for it – but I was there to give her my love, unconditionally, and to worry over her and maybe tug on the long cord that had bound us together through all the years of her life and convince her to let somebody else – some other virgin princess or square-jawed dragon-slayer – deliver themselves up to the enemy. I knew this: once she set foot in that tree, she was theirs.

Deep Ecology – Adat – says that all elements of a given environment are equal and that morally speaking no one of them has the right to dominate. We don't preserve the environment for the benefit of man, for progress, but for its own sake, because the whole world is a living organism and we are but a humble part of it. Try telling that to the Axxam Corporation when they're clear-cutting thousands of acres of old growth to pay down the junk-bond debt accrued in their hostile takeover of Coast Lumber, and you find yourself in a philosophical bind. They're going to cut, and Earth Forever! is going to stop them, any way they can. Hence Sierra, up in the tree.

I hugged her to me, held her for as long as she could stand it. Then I pressed a knapsack full of granola bars, dried fruit, books and toilet paper on her, and walked away from her, through the crowd and into the trees. I couldn't afford to stick around for the denouement – all this noise was designed to bring on the goons, and all these people were going to jail – but I waited long enough, on the fringes, to watch them haul her up the tree to the platform that already awaited her, one hundred eighty feet above the ground.

It was cold. There was a smell of rain on the air. A thickening mist clung like gauze to the high branches and a pair of birds fled through it as if they'd been shot out of a gun. How can I say what I felt? The pulleys creaked, the drummers drummed and my daughter rode up into the mist, higher and higher, till the pale-white bulb of her face was screened from view, and the last things visible – the dark, gently swaying soles of her running shoes – finally disappeared aloft.

That night it rained. But this was no ordinary shower or even a downpour, this was an El Niño event, evil harbinger of the apocalyptic weather to come, and it was accompanied by high winds and a drop of twenty degrees inside of an hour. I was in a motel room in Eureka at the time, working my way through a bag of Doritos and a six-pack of Black Cat malt liquor (choice of environmentalists everywhere), while watching Humphrey Bogart grimace in black and olive on a pale-green motel TV screen and waiting for Andrea and Teo to be set free on bail. The wind came up out of nowhere, flinging a hail of rubbish against the door and rattling the windows in their cheap aluminum frames. A framed list of motel do's and don'ts fell from the wall and landed face-up on the bed, right about where the back of my head would have been if I'd been asleep. I went to the door first, then thought better of it and brushed aside the curtains to peer out the window just as the rain exploded across the parking lot.

The fall of water was so violent it dimmed the lights across the street, and within seconds it was leaping up from the pavement in a thousand dark brushstrokes, as if gravity had been reversed. I had three beers in me and three to go, and when the next gust bowed the window, I backed away and sat on the bed, thinking of Sierra in her tree. What if a branch tore loose? What if the tree fell – or was struck by lightning? And what of her fear and desolation? There were no painted renegades out there now, no nose-fluters or drummers, nobody making lentil stew or chanting slogans – no one at all, not even the enemy. Who would haul away her bucket of waste, already overflowing with all this excess water, who would talk to her, comfort her, keep her dry and warm?

She was twenty miles away, on property owned and jealously guarded by Coast Lumber – a hypervigilant and enraged Coast Lumber, awakened now to the undeniable fact that my daughter was occupying their turf, high up in one of the grandest and most valuable of their trees, thumbing her nose at them, making a statement, saving the world all on her own – and even if I could get that far in the storm and locate the place to park the car off the public highway and find my way through the big trees to her, what then? She wasn't just rocking in a hammock – she was a hundred and eighty feet up, and there was no way for me to reach her. On a clear, calm day, sure, maybe – bring on the harness and jumars, and I'll do my best, though I have to admit I've never been one for heights (roller coasters leave me cold and ski lifts scare the living bejesus out of me). And with the wind and the crash of the rain, she probably wouldn't even be able to hear me shouting from down below. But I would be there. At least I would be there.

I left a note for Andrea, fired up the black BMW she'd bought while I was putting in my time at Vacaville and Sierra was doing the same at another state institution (not to worry: it was UC Santa

174

Cruz), and headed off into the storm with my three remaining cans of Black Cat. It wasn't a night to be out. Trees were down, and they'd taken power lines with them, and though this was the first heavy rain of the season, the roads were already running black with water and debris. I dodged logs, fenceposts, bicycles, boogie boards, cooking grills and a ghostly dark herd of cattle with tags in their ears. And I fought it, fought through everything, forty-seven years old, nearsighted and achy and already hard of hearing, the radio cranked up full, a sweating can of malt liquor clenched between my thighs, the headlights illuminating a long dark tunnel of nothing.

Three times I went by the road I wanted and three times had to cut U-turns in a soup of mud, rock and streaming water, until finally I found the turnout where we'd parked that afternoon. It had been compacted dirt then, dusty even, but now it was like an automotive tar pit, a glowing headlighted arena in which to race the engine and spin the tires till they stuck fast. I didn't care. Sierra was up there on top of the ridge before me, up there in the thrashing wind, scared and lonely and for all I knew dangling from some limb a hundred and eighty feet in the air and fighting for her life. I had five beers in me. I was her father. I was going to save her.

What was I wearing? Jeans, a sweater, an old pair of hiking boots, some kind of rain gear – I don't remember. What I do remember is the sound of the wind in the trees, a screech of rending wood, the long crashing fall of shattered branches, the deep-throated roar of the rain as it combed the ridge and made the whole natural world bow down before it. I was ankle-deep in mud, fumbling with the switch of an uncooperative flashlight, inhaling rain and coughing it back up again, thinking of John Muir, the holy fool who was the proximate cause of all this. One foot followed the other and I climbed, not even sure if this was the right turnout or the right ridge – path? what path? – and I remembered Muir riding out a storm one night in the Sierras, thrashing to and fro in the highest branches of a tossing pine, just to see what it was like. He wasn't trying to save anything or anybody – he just wanted to seize the moment, to experience what no one had experienced, to shout his hosannas to the god of the wind and the rain and the mad whirling rush of the spinning earth. He had joy, he had connection, he had vision and mystical reach. What he didn't have was Black Cat malt liquor.

I spat to clear my throat, hunched my shoulders and hovered over the last can. I was halfway up the ridge at that point, sure that at any moment a dislodged branch would come crashing out of the sky and pin me to the ground like a toad, and when I threw back my head to drink, the rain beat at my clenched eyelids with a steady unceasing pressure. Three long swallows and my last comfort was gone. I crushed the can and stuffed it into the pocket of the rain slicker and went on, feeling my way, the feeble beam of the flashlight all but useless in the hovering black immensity of the night. I must have been out there for hours, reading the bark like Braille, and the sad thing is I never did find Sierra's tree. Or not that I know of. Three times that night I found myself at the foot of a redwood that might have been hers, the bark red-orange and friable in the glow of the flashlight, a slash of charred cambium that looked vaguely familiar, the base of the thing alone as wide around as the municipal wading pool in Peterskill where Sierra used to frolic with all the other four-year-olds while I sat in a row of benches with a squad of vigilant mothers and tried to read the paper with one eye. This was her tree, I told myself. It had to be.

'Sierra!' I shouted, and the rain gave it back to me. 'Sierra! Are you up there?'

I don't really remember what the past few Christmases were like. One year – it might have been last year or five years ago, for all I know – Chuy and I went up to Swenson's and had the catfish boat with gravy and stuffing on the side, and another time we sat in my living room and watched the buckets splootch while sharing one of the last twelve-ounce cans of solid white albacore on earth. We ignored the expiration date and ate it with capers and pita bread and a bowl of fresh salsa Chuy whipped up, and I remember we washed it down with *sake* heated in a pan over the stove. And what was on the radio? *Ranchera* music and a trip-hop version of 'God Rest Ye Merry, Gentlemen.' This year is different. This year it's Andrea and April Wind and Yuletide cheer chez Pulchris.

Christmas morning I'm awake and waiting for the dawn as

usual, Andrea snoring lightly beside me, the concept of a good night's sleep as foreign to me now as jogging or biting into an apple sans forethought or even bending to tie my shoelaces without a whole string section of pain playing up and down my spine in a mad pizzicato. Sleep at my age comes like a blow to the back of the head, any time of day or night, and you'd better have a couch or an easy chair handy when you go down for the count (and don't even ask about the old-old – they're nothing more than zombies, staggering around on bird's bones with twenty or thirty years' accumulation of sleep deprivation bleeding out of their eye sockets). Anyway, the first thing I notice is that the rain has stopped. No rattling, no whooshing, no white noise like a lint screen inside your head, nothing but a profound early-Christmas silence, not a creature stirring, not even a Patagonian fox.

Up out of bed and into the clamminess, a pair of powder-blue boxer shorts climbing up my glabrous old man's legs and cradling the brindled spectacle of my old man's sexual equipment. Then the jeans, the plaid shirt and the rinsed-out jeans jacket, Grunge all the way, yes indeed. I'm thinking of Andrea's present – and I know she's expecting one, though every other breath out of her body for the past week has been a pro-forma denial ('Oh, no, no, Ty, you don't have to bother, really') – wondering what totemic object to dig out of the water-logged mound of my possessions or to beg or borrow from Mac that would express what I'm feeling for her. Because what I'm feeling is gratitude, what I'm feeling is an affection so deep for this big-shouldered oblivious old lady in the bed at my feet that it's verging dangerously close to love, and beyond love, to forgiveness and even – dare I say it? – bliss. I'm in love all over again. I am. Standing there in the dark, the silence so profound it's beating in my veins with an unconquerable force, the force of life undenied and lived right on down to the last tooth in the last head, I'm almost sure of it. On the other hand, it could just be indigestion.

There's no newspaper, of course, what with the flooding, and since magazines are scarce because of the lack of stock – paper, that is – I retreat to the lavatory with a mold-splotched copy of Muir's *The Mountains of California*. This is a big room, by the way, a room the size of the average condo, with a six-person Jacuzzi and a tiled shower stall with dual heads, recessed lighting and a built-in bench for comfort, and it smells of Andrea, of her perfume and powders and skin rejuvenator. The walls are painted to resemble the aluminum garage doors of old, in honor of garage bands every-where, the detail true right on down to three-dimensional handles and glittering rust spots (the portrait of Eddie Vedder, all eyes and teeth, I've long since turned to the wall, so as to be able to conduct my business in peace). In any case, I stoop to the faucet for a drink, just to rinse the night-taste out of my mouth, and then settle in for a long pre-Christmas-dinner bout with my comatose digestive tract. Relaxing, or trying to, I flip back the page and read of fantastical forests: *The trees of the species stand more or less apart in groves, or in small, irregular groups, enabling one to find a way nearly everywhere, along sunny colonnades and through openings that have a smooth, park-like surface, strewn with brown needles and burs. Now you cross a wild garden, now a ferny, willowy stream . . .*

I don't know how long I'm lost in those memorial forests – the better part of an hour, at least – moving on from the unconquered trees to the adventures of the water ouzel and the Douglas squirrel, not even the faintest stirring of a movement down below, when Andrea raps at the door. 'Ty?' she calls. 'You in there? I have to pee.'

'Just a minute.' I lurch up off the seat with a jolt of pain in both hips and my left knee, hoist my pants, flush, and close the book on my index finger to mark the place.

'Ty?'

'Yeah?'

'Merry Christmas.'

The phrase takes me by surprise, the novelty of it, and beyond that, the novelty of the situation. We didn't wish one another a merry Christmas in prison, and, as I say, Chuy and I have been on our own the last few years. Nobody has wished me anything in a long time, not even hate, despair or a lingering death. I'm moved. Moved almost to tears, as I'd been with the tinfoil angel in the hall. I'm halfway to the door, but then I remember to go back and wash up at the nearest of the four sinks, so I have to raise my voice to be heard through the solid plank of the door. 'You too,' I call, my voice echoing in the tomblike vastness of the place. 'Merry Christmas.'

The Sierra Nevada,
May–August 1990

TIERWATER WAS FEELING his age. He'd
turned forty at the beginning of the month, an occasion
memorialized by a discreet party out on the redwood
deck. It was a small gathering, as it would necessarily have to be if
FBI agents were to be excluded, consisting of his wife and
daughter, Teo, Ratchiss and Mag (or Mug). Everyone, even
Andrea, seemed to be in good spirits. They drank a California
Viognier without worrying about the oak trees and other native
species the vineyards had displaced, and as the evening turned chill,
they disported themselves in the redwood hot tub without a
murmur about the ancient giants felled for their momentary
pleasure. Sierra – Sarah Drinkwater, that is, the cynosure of the
junior high in Springville – went in to write an essay on ancient
Mesopotamia after the birthday cake had been set ablaze, wished
over, sliced up and divided, while the rest of the party lingered in
the hot tub, global warming be damned, at least for the duration of
the night. Mag, in a high energetic voice, volunteered the story of
how he'd lost his face, with Ratchiss filling in the supporting
details *(He creep on me, because I am profound inebriate with the strong
savor of palm wine on my lips, and I am dreaming of the long rains and
millet when he come and snap him jaw),* Teo and Andrea hatched plans
for her covert participation in a coordinated series of protests along
the northern-California coast and Tierwater got so drunk he'd had
to go off in the woods and commune with nature a while – it was
either that or vomit in the recirculating waters of the hot tub.

Tonight, though, he was only mildly drunk – just drunk
enough to take the sting off. He'd twisted his bad knee and nearly
fractured an ankle stumbling into a hole while trying to outrun the

beam of a watchman's flashlight up in Del Norte County two nights ago, and he was sitting in front of the fireplace, his leg propped up, judiciously anaesthetizing himself. The house was quiet. It had been quiet since the fire last summer, which had sent a ripple – no, a tidal wave – through all the West Coast chapters of Earth Forever! Thirty-five thousand acres had burned, and spokespersons up and down the coast fell all over themselves denying any involvement – E.F.!ers might have marched in the street and shouted slogans like 'Back to the Pleistocene!' but they strictly eschewed any illegal activity; it was only the disaffected fringe that sometimes, out of frustration and an overriding love of the earth, spiked a grove of ancient redwoods or blocked a culvert, but certainly the organization was there to protect the forests, not burn them down. And where did that leave Tierwater? Right where he wanted to be, on the unraveling edge of the disaffected fringe.

Teo, back safe in Tarzana, was especially vocal, deploring everybody and everything, even while the Tulare County Sheriff's Department expanded its investigation and Coast Lumber hired a pair of shuffling retirees from the local community to stand watch over the gleaming new Cats, wood-chippers, loaders and log trucks the insurance money had provided. (In their generosity, the insurers also provided a private investigator by the name of Declan Quinn, a shoulderless relic who sat permanently hunched over a pack of Camels at the Big Timber Bar and Mountain Top Lodge, chain-drinking Dewar's and water and asking endlessly in a cancerous rasp if anyone had seen 'anything suspicious.') At the first whiff of smoke, Ratchiss had lit out for Malibu, and Andrea, though she stayed put and went through the motions of mothering and housewifery, devoted her every waking minute to roasting Tierwater for his lack of judgment, juvenility and criminal stupidity. Even Sierra weighed in. 'It was really like mega-dumb, Dad,' she said one night over home-made manicotti and the steamed vegetables she kept pushing from one corner of the plate to another. 'What if they catch you? What if you go to jail? What am I supposed to do then – change my name to Sarah *Dork*water or something?' The idyll was over. Definitely over.

And then it was his birthday, and both Teo and Ratchiss showed up. It was dusk, and they were out on the back deck, charring meat, when Teo ambled out of the woods in a pair of shorts and hiking boots. Ratchiss had arrived an hour earlier, the silver Land Cruiser packed to the ceiling with gifts and goodies, and he looked up from the grill and raised his gin and bitters in salute. 'All hail,' he said. And then: 'Methinks yond Teo has a lean and thirsty look. How about a drink, my friend?'

Teo dropped his backpack on the planks and accepted a glass of iced gin with a splash of vermouth. He was shirtless, though the evening had begun to take on a chill (there was still snow out there in the woods, especially on the north-facing slopes), but then that was his pose: the insensible, the indefatigable, the iron man of the Movement. 'It's been a while,' he said, ducking his head and taking Tierwater's hand, 'but hey, happy birthday, man.' He nodded democratically at Mag, who stood behind the grill in a torpedoed freighter of smoke, basting the meat with his secret sauce, and then he was embracing Sierra and digging into his pack for the plain-wrapped gift he'd brought her. There were the usual exclamations – 'You're as tall as me now' and 'Let's get this girl a basketball scholarship!' – and then Andrea, who'd gone into the house for a sweater, stepped out onto the deck.

It was just a moment in a history of moments, but it bore watching. She was buttoning the sweater up the front, her hair swept forward, barefoot in a pair of jeans. 'Teo,' she exclaimed, and Tierwater saw the anticipatory smile, the quickened stride, watched them embrace, the tall woman and the short man, and he knew the answer to his question as surely as he knew it would be dark in half an hour and the sky would spill over with stars: of course she'd had sex with him. Fucked him, that is. Of course she had. Any fool could see that from the way they moved around each other, the familiarity of one organism with the other, all those dark and secret places, the commingled breath and shared fluids and supercharged emotions. But so what? So what? That was before he'd even met her – so what if she'd fucked whole armies? Tierwater was no puritan. And he wasn't jealous. Not a bit.

After the meat and before the cake, there was a lot of discussion of strategy – of the upcoming 'Redwood Summer' campaign, of Andrea's dyeing her hair or wearing a wig and coming down off the mountain to work behind the scenes and, eventually, of her coming in out of the cold altogether. Fred was working on it. A plea bargain, no time, just maybe community service, something like that. 'And what about me?' Tierwater had said. 'Am I just supposed to stay here forever? And won't it look a little fishy here – I mean, if my wife suddenly ups and deserts me?'

Teo just gave him a blank stare. Ratchiss looked away. And Sierra, who'd adjusted to her rural surroundings by ritualistically re-embracing the Gothic look (graveyard black, midnight pallor, ebony lipstick, the reinserted nose ring that drained all the remaining light from the sky), set down her soy burger and pitched her voice to the key of complaint: 'And *me?*'

'You're out of the loop, Ty, at least for now,' Teo said, flashing Sierra a quick smile of acknowledgment, and then coming back to him. 'You've got to be patient. And nobody's deserting anybody. I just think Andrea can be more effective if she – '

'And what does *she* think?' Tierwater said, cutting him off and turning to his wife. 'Isn't that what matters here? Isn't that what we're talking about?'

Andrea wouldn't look him in the eye – or she did look him in the eye, but it was the sort of look that flickered and waned and said, I want no part of this. She'd been unusually restrained all night, except when she was buzzing with Teo over tactics and the campaign to mobilize college kids for the protests, and now she just said, 'It's complicated, Ty. Beyond complicated. Can't we talk about it later?'

And Ratchiss said, 'Yeah, isn't this supposed to be a celebration?'

It was. And Tierwater, itching with his insecurities and angers, drank himself into celebratory oblivion.

Now, two weeks later, he'd almost forgotten about it. Teo was gone, as were Ratchiss and Mag, and Andrea was still here, still playing Dee Dee Drinkwater to his Tom. It was night. All was calm. Tierwater had his leg propped up, a drink in his hand, four good chunks of wind-toppled pine on the fire, no sound but for the snap of the flames and the doomed doleful wail of Sierra's Goth-rock leaking out of her speakers and through the locked door of her room like some new and invasive force of nature. He was just about to lift the drink to his lips when there was the dull thump of footsteps on the front deck, followed by a light rap at the door.

That altered things, all right.

He was transformed in that instant from the bruised eco-warrior taking his ease to the hunted fugitive living under a false name and called suddenly to task for his multifarious crimes. He froze, his eyes as glassy and dead as the eyes of the butchered animals staring down at him from the walls. The knock came again. And then a voice, gruff and hearty at the same time: 'Tom? Tom Drinkwater? You in there?'

Where was Andrea? 'Andrea!' he shouted. 'Can you get that? Andrea! There's someone at the door.' But Andrea couldn't get it, because she wasn't in the house, a small but significant piece of information that rose hopelessly to the surface of his consciousness even as he called out her name. She'd gone out half an hour ago with the flashlight and a sweater. Where? To walk the mile and a half to the bar and sit outside in the phone booth and await a call from Teo, very secretive, hush-hush, E.F.! business, Ty, so don't give me that look –

'Tom?'

'Just a minute, I – ' Tierwater's gaze fell on the rack of big-bore rifles Ratchiss kept mounted on the wall just inside the door, and then he was up out of the chair and limping across the room. 'Hold on, hold on, I'm coming!'

At first he didn't recognize the figure standing there at the door. The weak yellow lamplight barely clung to him, and there was the whole brooding owl-haunted Sierra night out there behind him, a darkness and fastness that was like a drawn shade and this man on the doorstep a part of its fabric. 'Tom – Jesus, I didn't mean to scare you . . . Don't you recognize me?'

The man was in the room now, uninvited, and it was the nagging raspy wheeze of the voice that gave him away, even more than the boneless face and dishwater eyes. It was Declan Quinn, the insurance investigator, all hundred and ten bleached alcoholic pounds of him, and Tierwater saw why he hadn't recognized him right away: he was wearing some sort of camouflage outfit, buff, khaki and two shades of green, and his face was smeared with a dully gleaming oleaginous paint in matching colors. Greasepaint, that's what it was, the very thing Tierwater himself employed on his midnight missions.

'Jesus, Tom,' he repeated, and the very way he said it – *Jaysus* – marked him for an immigrant, if not a recent one, and why hadn't Tierwater noticed that before? 'You look as if the devil himself had come for you.' And then he let out a laugh, a quick sharp bark that trailed off into a dry cough. 'It's the getup, isn't it? I completely forgot myself – but I'm not intruding, am I?'

'Oh, no, no, I was just – ' Tierwater caught a glimpse of himself in the darkened window and saw a towering monument to guilt, staved-in eyes, slumped shoulders, slack jaw and all. He'd been caught in a weak moment, taken by surprise, and though he was as articulate as anybody and fully prepared to act out his role onstage before a live audience, if that's what it took, he couldn't help wishing Andrea were here. For support. And distraction. This man was an investigator, a detective, and what was he doing in Tierwater's living room, if Tierwater himself wasn't a suspect?

Quinn laughed again. 'Completely forgot myself. You see, I've been out back of your place the last three days, not four hundred yards from where we now stand, tracking a sow with two cubs. Out of her den now, but it's right there, right out back, so close you wouldn't believe it – but, Lord Jesus, you've got some heads here, haven't you?' He was pointing to the kongoni. 'What is that, African? Or maybe something out of the subcontinent? It's no pronghorn, I know that much.'

'Well, it'd have to be African,' Tierwater was saying, though the phrase *out back of your place* was stuck in his head like plaque on an artery, 'because as far as I know that's the only place Ratchiss really hunted – '

'Ah, yes, yes, Philip. Prince of a man, really. The Great White Hunter. Not many of them left in the world, are there? But a prince, a real prince. And look at this lion, will you? Now, that's impressive. That's the real thing, eh?'

'The Maneater of the Luangwa,' Tierwater said, shifting the weight off his bad leg.

'Yes, sir, mighty impressive.' Quinn had his back to Tierwater now, gazing up at the lion. 'Had a bear once,' he said, 'nothing as impressive as this, of course, but I'd put the arrow in her myself, if you see what I mean, and I was attached to it. The taxidermist represented her couchant – lying there like a big spaniel, that is – which was all right, I suppose, though I would have preferred her rampant myself. Mavis, my first wife, hated the sight of her, and that was a sad thing, because she wound up taking her to the dump when I was off in Tulare on an arson investigation.' He sighed, swung round on the rotating pole of one fleshless leg. 'But I see you're having yourself a drink there, and I was just wondering – ? Because I'd love one myself. Scotch with a splash of water, if it's not too much trouble. And if you've got Dewar's, that'd be brilliant.'

Tierwater had seen this movie too, a hundred times – the self-righteous criminal and the unassuming detective – and yet he was playing right along, as locked into this role, this new role, the one he'd never auditioned for, as if it had been scripted. So he poured the man a drink, not so much nervous now as on his guard, and curious, definitely curious. Was this a friendly visit, one yokel neighbor rubbing up against another? Or was it about the gutted Cats and all the rest, was it about the fire? Because, if it was about the fire, he'd already said all he had to say on that subject – months ago, on a barstool – which is to say, no, he hadn't seen anything suspicious.

'No, sir,' Quinn wheezed, poking round the room like a tourist in a museum while Tierwater stood at the counter, pouring scotch, 'I'm up here enjoying myself now,' and he might have been talking to himself – or answering Tierwater's unasked question. 'My family's had a cabin here for twenty-some-odd years, did you know that? Up in back of the Reichert place? We got in when they first passed the bill allowing them to develop this little tract – lucky, I guess.' A pause. He looked Tierwater dead in the eye. 'To get in before the environmentalists started raising holy hell about it, I mean.'

'Ice?' Tierwater asked.

'Just a splash of water, thanks.'

Tierwater saw that he had a magazine in his hand now – *The New Yorker* – and he seemed to be examining the address label, but Tierwater (or Andrea, actually) had thought of everything, and that label read Tom Drinkwater, Star Route #2, Big Timber, CA 93265. 'But, no, I'm not up on business this time – though the fire and all that vandalism still dogs me, it does, because I don't feel I've done my job till those skulking cowards and arsonists are behind bars, where they belong; no, I'm just tracking a little bear. For when the bow season opens up – in August, that is. I just like to pick out a sow and follow her around till I know her habits as well as I know my own. Then I know I can get her whenever I want her.'

So he was a hunter – what else would you expect? A killer of animals, a despoiler of the wild, a shit like all the rest of them. Insurance investigator. Yes. And what did they insure? The means of destruction, that's what.

Tierwater handed him his drink and gave him the steadiest look he was capable of under the circumstances. And how had he felt about the fire? In reality? Good, he'd felt good. And more: he'd felt like an avenger, like a god, sweeping away the refuse of the corrupted world to watch a new and purer one arise from the ashes.

Thirty-five thousand acres, Ty, Andrea had cried, had shouted, so close to his face he could feel the aspirated force of each syllable like a gentle bombardment, *thirty-five thousand acres of habitat, gone just like that. What about the deer, the squirrels, the trees and ferns and all the rest?* He'd turned away, shrugged. *Fire's natural up here, you know that – the sequoia cones can't even germinate without it. If you did a little research or even picked up a nature book once in a while instead of plotting demonstrations all the time, you'd know it's the most natural thing in the world.* Coming right back at him, she said, *Sure, sure, but not if you start it with a match.*

'Cheers,' Quinn said, as Tierwater handed him the drink. 'But what happened to your leg – or is it your ankle?'

Tierwater picked up his own drink – careful now, careful – and settled into the *mopane* armchair before he answered. 'Just one of those things. We were out for a walk the other day, Dee Dee and me, right on the road here, and I wasn't looking and stepped off the shoulder. Twisted my ankle. No big deal.'

'Hah!' Quinn cried, and he was as wizened as a monkey, all spidery limbs and one big bloated liver. 'Getting old, is what it is.

Reflexes shot, muscles all knotted up. And your knees – they're the first thing to go. Then this.' He pointed to his crotch and arched an eyebrow. 'Oh, I could tell you, believe me.' Sinking into the chair across from Tierwater, he paused to gulp at his drink – a double, in a glass the size of a goblet, because Tierwater was taking no chances: get him drunk and see if he tips his hand. And then, into the silence that followed on the heels of this last revelation, Quinn dropped his bomb: 'So how's the book coming?'

(I was within an ace of saying, What book?, half cockeyed myself at that point, but panic does wonders for the mind, better than neuroboosters any day, and I barely fumbled over the reply. Which was, 'Fine.' This was our cover, of course – I was an aspiring novelist, working on my first book, and we'd come up to the mountain, my wife, Dee Dee, and my daughter, Sarah, and me, to rent our old friend Ratchiss' place so I could have some peace and quiet to work in.)

'Well, I'm glad to hear it,' Quinn said, setting the glass down on the coffee table. 'I don't know how you people do it – writing, I mean – it's just beyond me. People ask me, do I write, and I say yes, sure: checks.' He had a laugh over that one, wheezed and coughed something up, then took a restorative gulp of Tierwater's scotch. Or Ratchiss', actually. 'A novel, right?' he said, cocking his head and pointing a single precautionary finger. 'Would that be fiction or nonfiction?'

'I, uh, well, I'm just in the beginning stages – ' Tierwater lifted his own glass to his lips and drank deeply.

Quinn leaned forward, all eagerness. 'So tell me, if it's not a secret – what's it about?'

There was a pause. Tierwater went for his drink again. A hundred plots, subjects, scenarios crowded his brain. He could hear each individual flame licking away at each molecule of the split and seasoned wood, breaking it down, converting matter to energy, murdering the world. 'Eskimos,' he said finally.

'Eskimos?'

Tierwater studied the bloodless face. He nodded.

Quinn sat stock-still a minute. All this time he'd been in motion, pressing, probing, snooping, rocking back and forth in his chair as if he were hooked up to a transformer, and now, suddenly, he was still. 'Well, now, that's a charge,' he said finally, and gave a low whistle. 'Now, isn't it?'

'What do you mean?'

'I mean it's your lucky day, Tom. You're staring at a man who spent two years in Tingmiarmiut among the Inuit – back in the days when I was working for British Petroleum, that is. You spend much time up there?' Suddenly he slapped his knee and gave out a strangled cry. 'By Jesus God, I'll bet you we know some of the same people – '

Salvation comes in many forms. This time it came in the form of Sierra. The door of her room flew open and the whole house was suddenly engulfed in a world-weary thump of drums and bass and the scream of a single suicidal guitar rattling round an echo chamber. She was dressed in black jeans with distressed knees, high-heeled boots and a blouse so small and shiny and black it could have been torn out of a baby's casket. But for the black lipstick, she might have been a young Victorian widow, in mourning for her husband, the late industrialist. 'Dad,' she said, 'have you seen my gum – you know, that bag of Plenti-Paks we bought down the mountain the other day?'

The room reverberated. It shook. Sierra was already halfway to the fire when she noticed Quinn huddled there in the chair in his face paint and his fatigues. 'Oh, wow,' she said, caught in mid-step, 'I didn't know we had company.' She gave the insurance investigator a look and a tentative smile. 'Are you guys going to a costume party or something?'

Andrea passed out red berets all that summer, sold T-shirts imprinted with the raised red fist of the E.F.! logo and, in a wig that made her look like Barbara Bush's love child, advised accounting majors, aspiring poets and premed students how best to bicycle-lock their heads to bulldozers, log trucks and the front doors of the Axxam Corporation's headquarters in Severed Root, Kentucky. Teo started up an action camp for neophyte protestors and led marches on half a dozen lumber mills on the North Coast, and Ratchiss stayed at home in Malibu, watching the Discovery Channel and marveling at the way the sun glittered off the water at cocktail hour each day. Tierwater brooded. He dug up everything he could find on Eskimos, lest he should run into Declan Quinn over a plate of runny eggs and home fries at the lodge, played endless games of pitch and Monopoly with his daughter and went vengefully out into the night at least twice a week to beat back the tireless advance of progress.

In mid-July, almost a year to the day after the Siskiyou fiasco, Tierwater was taking his ease on the rear deck one afternoon, studying the configurations of the clouds from the nest of his hammock and feeling as Thoreauvian as he was likely to. He and Sierra had got up early, driven down the highway and hiked out into the burn, and he'd been gratified to see how many of the big pines and redwoods had resisted the fire. They were scarred, certainly, raked from the ground up as if mauled by a set of huge black claws, but the winter's snows had already worked the ash into the soil and seedlings were sprouting up everywhere. Better yet: the Penny Pines Plantation was no more, and there were no carved wooden signs announcing the largesse of Coast Lumber — or anything else, for that matter. And where the sawmill trees had stood in all their bio-engineered uniformity, there were now fields of wildflowers, rose everlasting, arnica, fireweed, mountain aster and a dozen others their field guide had no illustrations for. He picked a bouquet for Andrea, and felt he'd sown and nurtured each flower himself. This was nature as it was meant to be.

Andrea was still in bed, snoring lightly, her hair spilled across the pillow, her mouth sagging open to reveal the glint of a gold-capped molar on the upper left side. Tierwater had stolen into the room an hour earlier and set the vase of flowers on the night table, then retired to the deck. His wife was worn out. She'd been away for the better part of a week, stirring up demonstrators and clandestinely visiting her former dentist, and had gotten in late. Tierwater had waited up for her, and they'd traded gossip and made love in the silent, still shell of the house that floated like a ship in the dark sea of the night. Now he was waiting up for her again. Sky-watching.

It was no ordinary sky — rags and tatters of cloud unraveled across it like a scroll you could read if only you knew the language — but it put him to sleep nonetheless. When he opened his eyes, Andrea was there, sitting in the chair beside him, cradling a cup of coffee. The shadows had leapt over him. It must have been three in the afternoon.

She said, 'You're awake.'

'Yeah,' he said. 'I think so.'

Her hair was wet from the shower, ropy and robbed of its sheen, and she bowed her head to work a comb through it. 'You see anything of that little snoop while I was gone?' He watched her fingers, her hands, the snarl of hair. 'You know, what's-his-name – the drunk.'

'Quinn?'

She threw her head back and ran both hands through the wet hair, shaking out the excess moisture; it was so still he could hear the whisper of the odd droplet hitting the deck. 'I can't believe you let him in that night. He's not as stupid as he looks. Or as drunk either.'

'What was I supposed to do?'

'Tell him you had a headache. Heartburn. The flu. Tell him your wife was in a mood and your father just died. Tell him anything. You think if I was home he would have got two feet inside that door?'

Tierwater offered her a grin, but she wasn't receiving it. She'd dipped her head again and the comb was working furiously at a dark knotted tangle. 'You're tougher than I am. Everybody knows that.'

She threw her head back and the hair with it. Now she was glaring. 'It's no joke, Ty. He's on to us – if you can't see that you're nuts. And I tell you, we're not moving again, not with Sierra in school and – '

'Who said anything about moving?'

'I did. It's that or go to jail, isn't it? It's that or the FB-fucking-I kicking down the door at four in the morning.'

Tierwater felt a chill go through him. Did she really think that? How would anybody know anything? There was no evidence, not a scrap of it. And any sort of background check would just turn up the clean, sweet, uncomplicated and lovingly fabricated record of Tom Drinkwater, ex-schoolteacher, budding novelist, family man. 'You've got to be kidding.'

She wasn't kidding. 'I warned you,' she said, and then she launched into a neat little prepackaged speech, one she must have been rehearsing all the way up the coast. She'd been back to Oregon. She'd seen Fred. 'He's put in something like two hundred hours on this, Ty – he's practically bent over and kissed the DA's ass, not to mention the feds – and he's got us a deal. No more false names, no more worrying about every knock at the door.'

Tierwater looked beyond her to where the aspens caught the first hint of a breeze coming in out of the west. It was warm in the sun and the woods were silent but for the drone of the meat bees – the yellow jackets – that nested in the ground every ten feet in every direction for as far as you could see. 'I'm going to jail,' he said, 'right?' He swung his legs out of the hammock, set his feet down on the deck. 'But you're not.'

'That's right, Ty: I'm not. But I didn't assault anybody or break out of jail either. Hey, but let's not argue, because this is right, you know it is, and it's going to be the best thing for Sierra.'

He wanted to tell her about the Eskimos, how they had no jails or laws and lived within the bounds of nature – they didn't even cook their meat, because they had no wood or coal or oil, which is why they'd been called Eskimos in the first place: Eaters of Raw Flesh. And when they had a dispute, they didn't need lawyers to settle it for them – the injured parties would sing insults at each other till one of them lost his composure. The one who broke down first was the loser, simple as that. Of course, by the same token, Tierwater understood that he wouldn't fare any better under their system than under Fred and Judge Duermer's – not with his temper.

'It's all set,' Andrea said. 'The DA – he's new to the job, a man by the name of Horner, a younger guy? – he understands that all this arose out of a peaceable demonstration and that you were just trying to protect your daughter – '

'How long?'

'What do you mean?'

'You know what I mean – how much time do I have to do?' She looked away, fussed with her hair. 'Six months,' she said.

'To a year. But, listen, I get off with probation only – and we get Sierra back. That's the important thing. I mean, isn't it?'

At first he wouldn't listen. Wouldn't even consider it. Give himself up? Go to jail? For what? This wasn't Nazi Germany, was it? This wasn't Pol Pot's Cambodia. Jail? He was outraged. So outraged he'd punted a chair into the hot tub, hopped the railing and stalked off across the yard and into the trees. He sat out there in the woods all afternoon with the meat bees, each a perfect replica of the one that had done Jane in, turning it over in his mind. He had a yellow pine for a back rest, and he crossed his outstretched legs at the ankles, brought back down to earth – no more cloud-gazing today. He studied his clasped hands, the scatter of pine cones, the carpenter ants scaling his boots. Every few minutes, as the sun fell through the trees and the ravens called and the chipmunks flew across the duff like skaters on a pond, a yellow jacket would land on his exposed forearms or the numb monument of his face – not to sting, but to taste, to see if he was indeed made of meat, rent meat, meat sweet with the taste of fresh blood. Finally, at cocktail hour, when all the trees were striped with pale bands of sunlight and the birds began to hurtle through the branches in their prenocturnal frenzy, he got up, brushed himself off and ambled back to the house.

Andrea was sitting at the kitchen table with Sierra, both of them intent on the fashion magazines she'd brought back with her from the world below. There was something in the microwave, revolving endlessly – macaroni and cheese, from the smell of it. Three places were set at the table, and a bowl of salad, garnished with slices of tomato and avocado, stood on the counter. Tierwater said nothing, aside from a grunt of acknowledgment in response to Andrea's muted greeting, but went straight to the liquor cabinet and poured two tall vodka-tonics with a squeeze of lime. He took a long swallow from the nearest one, then crossed the room and handed the other to his wife. 'Okay,' he said. 'Okay, you're right.'

Sierra was absorbed in the page in front of her, gloss and color, some band, some actress, some model. Without looking up, she said, 'About what?'

Andrea signaled him with her eyes. 'Nothing, honey,' he said automatically, and then he wandered out onto the deck, leaving the sliding door ajar behind him. A moment later, Andrea joined him, drink in hand. He turned to watch her as she slid the door closed.

'Good, Ty,' she said, 'it's for the best. We can get out from under all this.'

He dropped his eyelids, shrugged, felt the sting of the ice as he lifted the drink to his lips.

She was in his arms, hugging him, her face pressed to his. 'But you haven't heard the best part yet, and this is great, you're going to love this – '

'Sure,' he said, pushing away from her and stepping back to the edge of the deck, 'I'll bet. But don't tell me: you're going to bake me cookies every week while I'm in jail, right? You're going to knit me a sweater for those frosty nights on the cellblock when the sons of bitches won't turn the heat on – '

Her face was cold. 'It isn't funny, Ty. This is the best we can do, and we're going to make the most of it. When we give ourselves up it's going to make the news coast to coast.'

He said nothing. He didn't know where this was leading, but he didn't like it.

'Get ready,' she said, and now she was animated, all right, effervescent, lit up like a self-contained power source, the three-hundred-watt smile and radar eyes. 'You remember my great-grandfather?'

'Never met him.'

'I mean, his story?'

He remembered. She was the great-granddaughter of Joseph Knowles, one of the archetypal eco-nuts. On a gray spring day in 1913, in the Maine woods, he did a striptease for a gaggle of reporters, emptying his pockets, setting aside his watch and wallet and penknife, neatly folding his jacket, vest, trousers and shirt, until finally he was down to his long underwear. Ultimately, he shed that too, to stand pale and naked before them. He then reiterated the credo that had drawn the journalists in the first place – that nature was to be preserved for its own sake as the nurturer of mankind – and plunged into the woods to live off the land. Two months later, hard and brown and considerably thinner, not to

193

mention chewed, sucked and drained by every biting insect in the county, he emerged at the same spot to an even larger crowd and proclaimed that his God was the wilderness and his church the church of the forest. 'No,' Tierwater said. 'You've got to be kidding. Tell me you're kidding.'

There was the world, there were the trees, there was his wife. The light was perfect, held in that fragile moment between light and dark, the highest crowns of the trees on the ridge behind them on fire with it. She came to him again, and all he could see were her eyes and her lips, her glowing lips, her red, rich, persuasive lips. They kissed. He held her. The sun faded from the trees. 'Think of it, Ty,' she whispered, 'think of the statement we'll make.'

Tierwater had never been good with crowds. Crowds made him nervous; crowds made him think of the degradation of the planet; crowds showed him what humanity was, and he didn't like what he saw. This crowd, the one he, Andrea and Teo were the current focus of, must have consisted of a hundred or more. There was a good contingent of E.F.!ers out there, conspicuous in their red berets and the power-red T-shirts of the clan, thirty or forty of them, dispersed through the crowd like poppies in a field. You couldn't miss them. They were there to provide moral support – and to mob Tierwater and Andrea if any law-enforcement types showed up, in uniform or otherwise. The general public was in attendance too, at Andrea's express invitation – journalists, mostly, turned out in two-hundred-dollar hiking boots, pressed jeans and disc sunglasses in sixteen different earth-annihilating colors, as well as a scattering of the curious, the nearsighted and the bored. The day was golden. The mountains lay all around them, folded into one another like ripples in meringue. Teo had given his speech, and Andrea had given hers. There was nothing left now but to get to it.

Tierwater eased himself down on a section of wind-smoothed rock and began unlacing his boots; Andrea, bare-legged in an airy dress the color of salt-water taffy, shucked off a pair of beaded moccasins. There was no wind, and the sun stood directly over-head, hot on his shoulders and the back of his neck. He gazed out over the mountains, his heart pounding, embarrassed already – and how had he ever let her talk him into this one? – and then he glanced up at Andrea. She was staring placidly at the onlookers, making eye contact with one after another of them, milking the moment for all it was worth. Tierwater stood abruptly. The quicker they got this over with, the better, that was his thinking, and he unbuckled his belt, unzipped his pants, and stepped out of them, one leg at a time.

No one said a word, the whole crowd holding its breath. Tierwater was in good shape from all that hiking and his nighttime activities, six one, a hundred eighty pounds, too skinny in the legs, maybe – and he hated showing off his legs in public, and his feet too – but all in all, a fair match to play Adam to Andrea's Eve. He folded up his pants and handed them to Teo (who, incidentally, was dressed all in white, in a muscle shirt, shorts and sandals, like some sort of priest of the Movement). Everyone was staring at him, and he did his best to stare back, but then Andrea reached behind her for the zipper to her dress, and a hundred pairs of eyes went to her. He watched her arms bow out as she worked the zipper down to the base of her spine, and then the big hands come up and pull the dress over her head with a quick shake of her perfect hair, which fell perfectly into place. She was wearing crimson underwear – the subject of intense discussion that morning at breakfast, Tierwater fiercely opposed to it, Teo all for it – and the cups of her brassiere, right over the nipples, were imprinted with the raised black fist of the Movement. A smile for the crowd, and then she handed the dress to Teo. Defeated, feeling more foolish and more enraged by the moment, Tierwater tore off his shirt, dropped his briefs – his plain white briefs, $3.99 a pair at J. C. Penney – and stood there naked for all the world to see.

All right. And they were quiet now, E.F.!ers, newspaper hacks, birdwatchers and Winnebago pilots alike. This was a spectacle. This was nudity. And Andrea – Andrea Knowles Cotton Tierwater, the Earth Forever! firebrand and environmental fugitive – was next. Again the bowed arms, as she worked at the catch of the brassiere, again the hundred pairs of eyes deserting Tierwater to embrace his wife. *(Come on, Ty,* she'd said, *it's the human body, that's all, nothing to be ashamed of. You're beautiful. I'm beautiful. This is the way we were born.)* Then her breasts fell free and she stepped out of her panties — and handed them, silken and still warm, to Teo, Teo who'd seen all this before, up close and personal. And the rest of them? They saw that she was a natural blonde, for what it was worth.

There was a spatter of applause, and then Tierwater had her by the arm — grabbed hold of her before she could take a bow, because he was sure it was coming, and *Why not,* she'd insist, *why not?* — and they turned their backs and hobbled awkwardly over a spew of distressed granite on feet that weren't nearly hardened enough. He couldn't see the picture this made, because he was at the center of it, but Tierwater was reminded of nothing so much as Raphael's depiction of the expulsion from paradise. But that wasn't right. It was paradise they were entering, wasn't it?

For the next three hours, Tierwater focused his attention on his wife's buttocks, though the glutei were only the most prominent of the muscles in operation here. He studied her thighs, calves and ankles too, and the dimple at the base of her spine. Her shoulders dipped and arms swung free with the easy rhythm of her stride, and her hair — newly washed, brushed and conditioned — lifted and fell with a golden shimmering life of its own. He admired the sweet triangulation of her scapulae, the exquisite grip and release of the muscles of her upper back, and her heels, he loved her heels. This was all new to him, a revelation, bone and muscle working beneath the silk of the skin in a way that was nothing less than a miracle. He'd seen plenty of women with bare shoulders in his time, women playing tennis and wearing evening gowns, women in swimsuits and tank tops, women in the raw, active women, ballerinas and gymnasts, porn queens on the receiving end of a zoom lens and Jane giving birth to his daughter in the flesh, but he'd never followed a naked woman through the woods before. It was something. It really was. And it moved him somehow, the grace and good sense of it, even more than it excited him — and it did excite him, so much so that he was hard-pressed to keep from planting her in the ferns at the side of the trail and expressing his wonder in the most immediate and natural way.

Of course, he couldn't do that. Not with Chris Mattingly moving along lightly behind him. And 'lightly' was the word – the man kept a discreet distance, the only indication of his presence the occasional scrape of boot on rock or the rustle of cooking equipment packed loosely in the outer flaps of his backpack. This – Chris Mattingly, that is, and picture an Eagle Scout all grown up and rejected by the Marines, twenty-eight years old, regular haircut clipped to fishbelly-white arcs around the ears – was another of Andrea's inspirations. We've got to bring a journalist along, she insisted. Somebody impartial – or at least impartial enough to see that we don't cheat. How else would anybody know we don't have a cache of jerky or candy bars or even filet mignon out there in the woods – or a cabin with a satellite dish? Or how would they know we didn't just slip away to Maui for a couple of weeks? We need to record this, Ty, if it's going to do any good.

So Chris Mattingly was going to shadow them for a month (thirty days, yes, because there was no sense in challenging Great-grandfather Knowles' record, and, besides which, by September first it could get pretty frigid in these mountains). He would be sleeping in a tent, on an inflatable mat, and feasting on freeze-dried lobster thermidor, scallop enchiladas and power bars, while they made do with bark and pine boughs for bedding, and scraped watercress out of the muck and toasted grasshoppers and fresh-water mussels on a stick – if they could manage to start a fire, that is. *Think of it as an adventure,* Andrea said, and it was an adventure, Tierwater saw that immediately, the sort of thing that would make the two of them more notorious than all the Foxes and Phantoms combined. Of course, when Andrea first mentioned it, he bitched and moaned, argued, pleaded, employed all the specious reasoning of the Sophist and the third-year law student, but it was for form's sake only – secretly, he was pleased. To go out into the wilderness with nothing, to hunt and gather and survive like the first hominids scouring the African plains, that was something, a fantasy that burned in the atavistic heart of every environmentalist worthy of the name. And he was one of them, as far now from the shopping center and the life of the living dead he'd been enduring all these years as it was possible to be. And though his feet hurt and he ached with lust for his wife and he was already feeling the first stirrings of hunger despite the staggering mounds of ham, bacon, flapjacks and eggs he'd forced down for breakfast, he was feeling at peace with himself, feeling fulfilled, feeling lucky even.

They hiked all that afternoon, following a trail that led them out of the national forest proper and into a remote wilderness area (entry by permit only, no hunting, no logging, no motorized vehicles, no traps, snares, seines or gigs, all fishing on a strict catch-and-release basis, beer cans, chain saws and boom boxes strenuously discouraged). This was old-growth forest, the redwoods gathered in groves along steep stream courses, the pines rising up out of the hills like bristles on a brush, the silence absolute but for the screech of a jay or the breeze that would announce itself with a long echoing sigh in the treetops. It was dry. And warm. Very warm. Tierwater had begun to feel the sting of the sun on the back of his upper thighs and his own lean buttocks, and he watched his wife's shoulders and backside turn first pink and then a freshly spanked red as the day wore on (and this despite the fact that they'd put in at least an hour of nude sunbathing each day over the course of the past two weeks as a precautionary measure). But you couldn't guard against the sun, not if you were going to live in nature, or any of the other vicissitudes of natural life either – insects, snakebite, the elements – and both of them were prepared to make the sacrifice. Still, what he wouldn't give for a tube of sunscreen or even a palm-full of Hawaiian Dream tanning butter.

But they didn't have sunscreen. They didn't have toothpaste or dental floss, aspirin, Desenex, matches, knives, crockery or silverware, they didn't have down pillows or blankets or cell phones or even so much as a ring or bracelet to decorate their bodies with. All those things he'd accumulated in his life, all that detritus from his parents and his house and office and even the little he could call his own at Ratchiss' – it was gone now, irrelevant, and he was like one of the roving Bushmen of the Kalahari, blackened and bearded little men who accounted themselves prosperous if they had an empty ostrich shell to haul water in. Sure. And what else were he and Andrea going to have to do without? Coffee, English muffins, canned tuna, chocolate, vodka. Books, music, TV. Band-Aids. Mercurochrome. A snakebite kit.

And this last was important. Vitally important. Indispensable, even. Because their destination was a stretch of the upper Kern River, deep in the gorge it had carved out over the eons, and there were whole tribes of snakes there – or so Tierwater had been informed by three-quarters of the residents of Big Timber, none of whom had ever actually set foot in the place. And it wasn't as if they had hiking boots and sweatsocks and stiff thick denim jeans to protect against the savage thrust of the naked fangs. Or scorpions – what about scorpions? Ticks? Mites? Cougars, bears, rabid skunks? What about them?

(Ultimately? The way I felt that day? I welcomed them, welcomed them all: Here's my flesh, I murmured – said it aloud – here's my flesh. Come and get it.)

They didn't have a permit either.

We don't want to look hypocritical, Andrea had argued, because what are people going to think if we go out there and violate the rules like the Freemen and the Phineas Priests and all the rest of the self-righteous back-to-the-earth yahoos? But Tierwater knew they would have to violate the rules systematically if they were going to get through this – let alone make a statement. What kind of statement would they make if they gave up? Or, worse, died? This was an experiment, and the wilderness was the laboratory. They would do what they had to do to survive – that was the point, wasn't it? *Catch and release.* Did the Bushmen practice catch and release? And what about Great-grandfather Knowles – had he lived on air while wandering the Maine woods?

It was past six and getting cool in the gorge by the time they found a likely-looking place to make camp, a tongue of sand thrown up against a wall of rock on the far side of the river. They waded across, the river no more than thirty feet wide and two or three feet deep at this juncture, and the frigid racing water felt good on their battered feet and sunburned legs. They'd agreed that their main priority the first night would be constructing a shelter – food they'd worry about in the morning. And so, dutifully, Tierwater and his wife had begun gathering brush and leaves to construct a debris shelter according to the instructions in one of the wilderness-survival manuals they'd found on Ratchiss' shelf. It was a pretty rudimentary affair: just prop a pole up on a stump or rock three feet off the ground, lay sticks against either side of it and cover the whole business with leaves and brush. Then line the interior with four or five armloads of spare leaves for bedding, and presto, you've got an insulated shelter for the night.

Dusk fell. A wall of cold air worked its way down the canyon foot by foot, settling into the low places, probing corners, retarding the metabolism of all those hidden snakes and scorpions and prickling the skin of Tierwater's chest with goosebumps. He was bent over a fireboard – a fragment of sun-bleached driftwood, that is – vigorously spinning a long, thin, very nearly straight drill of the same material. Andrea knelt beside him, fragments of brush in her hair, her breasts nicked and blemished from cradling armfuls of river-run debris, her big hands working in her lap. 'Harder, Ty,' she urged, 'it's starting to smoke.' And it was, it was, the spindle working in the groove as he furiously kneaded it between his palms, the faintest glimmer of a coal reddening the tip of the thing, friction, more friction, and Andrea blowing now, puffing for all she was worth. There it was – a coal! And the coal fired the kindling for the briefest, most desperate moment, before it died out in a faint little ribbon of smoke. By Tierwater's count, this was the twenty-seventh time the same scenario had played itself out in the course of the past hour. He was exhausted. His palms were raw. He sat heavily and let the cold air settle over his shoulders like the mantle of defeat.

It was then that the smell of a clean-burning campfire came to them, sharp and somehow delicious on the chill air. And the scent of food – some sort of sauce, tomato sauce, and the unmistakable aroma of fresh coffee. Tierwater drew his wife to him and held her in his arms, and it was the saddest moment of the whole adventure. They turned their heads in unison to gaze through the snarl of scrub willow in the riverbed to a point a hundred yards upstream. Through the screen of the bushes, they could just make out the figure of Chris Mattingly, crouched lovingly over his fire. And then, as faint as the first tentative murmur of the birds on a cold spring morning, a sound came to them, pitched low and melodic. He was singing. Cheered by the blaze and the wildness of the place and the intoxicating smell of the freeze-dried entrée he raised to his lips, bite by savory bite, Chris Mattingly was singing at the fall of day.

It got better, and then it got worse. In the morning, with a pain in his gut that twisted like the blunted stone head of a Bushman's arrow, Tierwater managed to get a fire going. He squatted beside it, his testicles dangling in the cool sand, and nurtured the weak dancing flame till it danced higher, into the nest of twigs and bark he'd prepared, and there it was: fire. It was a hungry little fire, and it chewed contentedly at everything he fed it, till finally he was dragging branches the size of coat racks out of the piles of river-run debris scattered along the spit and slamming them hard against the standing trees till they yielded the fuel he wanted, in convenient three-foot sections. He didn't know what time it was – only that it was light and that the chill had begun to lift – and he did a naked capering dance of triumph round the fire, kicking up his heels in the sand. They had fire. Fire!

While Andrea slept on, oblivious, her slack limbs encrusted with leaf mold and all the small but ferocious things that lived within it, Tierwater gathered firewood. He combed both sides of the river, keeping an eye out for fish or bird's nests or even snakes – and, yes, he'd be pleased and honored to indulge in a little roast rattlesnake for breakfast – and by the time the sun had climbed up over the eastern ridge of the gorge, he had enough fuel for a hundred fires stacked up round the shelter. But he wasn't done yet – no, this shelter would never do; it wasn't much more imposing than a suburban mulch pile, and all night, as insects crawled over him and fragments of leaves worked their way into his private parts and maddened him with itching, he envisioned a larger, airier shelter, a model of cleanliness and efficiency. Something you could stand in, with pine boughs spread inside over the soft, clean sand. The thought of it made his spirits lift and soar, as if a fierce-eyed bird of prey had emerged from his body – climbed right up out of his throat – and shot into the sky. He'd never felt anything like it. Never. And then he was crouching in the hut, leaning over his wife to kiss her awake, the smell of her like some fermenting thing, like vinegar or curdled milk spilled on a patch of damp ground, bits of leaf mold stuck to her lips and forced up her nostrils, a scurry of insects frantically hopping and burrowing out of his calamitous way. 'Wake up, baby,' he said, pressing his lips to hers, the leaves rustling and fragmenting beneath them, and she woke to the smell of him, to the smell of smoke on him, and they made love in the twisted thrashing way of animals in the bush – for the third time since the hut had gone up the night before. 'I made fire,' he told her, over and over, and she clutched at him with her big hands and powerful arms, pulling him into her with a furious urgency the hut couldn't withstand. It rattled, it swayed, it fell, and they hardly noticed.

It was erotic, the primitive life, Tierwater was thinking – all those naked pot-bellied tribes in the jungles of South America and New Guinea, bare breasts, loincloths, penis sheaths, doing it in the hut, on a log, in the stream as the water sizzled round you – but it only took a day or two to disabuse him of that notion. The fact was that lust consumed calories, and in the final analysis calories were the only thing that mattered. Once their cells had been burned clean of fats, nitrates and cholesterol, once they understood that the odd fish, indifferently charred on a green stick, or a fistful of manzanita berries *au naturel* was it for the day – hold the butter, please, and no, I think I'll pass on the napoleons this evening – their erotic life came to a screeching halt. He saw his wife crouched there by the new and improved hut, weaving sticks into a primitive weir, her breasts pendulous, her skin so burned, abraded and chewed over it was like a scrub pad, and he barely glanced up. There's a naked woman, he thought, in the same way he might have thought, There's a tree or a rock.

In the beginning, it had all seemed possible. They were enthusiasts, pumped up with confidence and what they'd distilled from the pages of a book, so simple really, the diagrams still resonating in their heads (attach x to y to z and *voilà*, there's meat in the pot). Tierwater spent hours constructing deadfalls to lure the unsuspecting skunk or raccoon, but it proved to be a fruitless endeavor, because nothing, as far as he could see, ever went near the baits he left out – except flies. Andrea sat cross-legged in the sand and fashioned snares from the thin whiplike branches of the willows, yet they snared nothing but air, and both of them spent the better part of a long morning digging mouse bottle pits (two and a half feet deep, with a wide bottom and narrow neck, hidden beneath a flat rock propped up on both ends to provide access), only to discover that no mouse, if mice even existed this far afield, had been generous enough to tumble into one of them. After inspecting the empty traps three days running, they looked each other in the eye beneath the tall trees, amidst the glorious but inedible scenery, searching for signs of the inevitable breakdown. There was frustration in the air. There was anger. And more than that, there was hunger – desperate, gnawing, murderous.

'A mouse,' Andrea spat, arms akimbo, her skin burned to the color of boiled wiener, 'we can't even catch a mouse. And how many calories you think we wasted digging these pits, Ty? Huh? And even if we did catch one, or even ten of them, what good would it do? What are they, the size of a marshmallow, once you skin and gut them?'

But Tierwater was in the grip of something – a delusion, that's what it was – and out here, where there were no microphones or high heels or E.F.! contributors to woo, he was in charge. 'Bears eat them,' he said lamely, staring down into the dark, mocking aperture of the empty hole at his feet.

'Yeah,' she said, 'and people eat bears. Why don't we catch a bear, Ty? You know any good bear recipes?'

They spent the rest of the day haunting the streambed, darting after the elusive shadows that were the fish, but it was an unlucky day, and finally they were reduced to turning over stones to pluck beetles, salamanders, earthworms and scorpions from their couchettes, the whole mess, two handfuls of pulped and writhing things, singed in the cup of a rock Tierwater set in the middle of the fire. 'I don't care, Ty,' Andrea sang, huddled over her naked knees as the sun clipped off the rock wall above them and the ambrosial smell of whatever it was Chris Mattingly was cooking drifted down the gorge, 'I'm not eating anything with the legs still attached. I'm not.' So Tierwater mashed the whole business together with the blunt end of a stick, pounded it and pounded it again, till they had a dark paste sizzling there in the scoop of rock. They ate it before it had cooled – 'It has a kind of nutty flavor, don't you think?' Tierwater said, trying to make the best of it – but fifteen minutes later they were both secreted in the bushes, heaving it back up.

The next morning, Andrea was up at first light, a cud of twig and leaf working in her mouth. He was tending the fire when she rose up suddenly out of the dirt and took hold of his arm. 'I want meat,' she said. 'Meat. Do you hear me?' Her eyes were swollen. Her nails dug into his flesh. 'Can't we at least hunt? Isn't that what people do when they're starving? Isn't that standard operating procedure?'

Tierwater didn't bother to answer, because if he'd answered he would have asked a question of his own, a question that was sure to bring some real rancor to the surface – *Whose idea was this, anyway?* Instead, he said nothing.

'What about marmots? Aren't there marmots out here?'

The fire was snapping. It was early yet, the sun buttering the ridge before them, the canyon still sunk in shadow. Tierwater had always been one to eat breakfast – and a substantial breakfast, at that – as soon as he arose in the morning. *It's the most important meal of the day,* his mother used to say, and she was right. He wanted coffee, with heavy cream and lots of sugar, he wanted eggs and thick slices of Canadian bacon, buttered sourdough toasted till it was crisp, but he heaved himself up with the picture of a marmot – a fat yellow-throated thing like a giant squirrel and so stupid it wasn't much smarter than the rocks it lived among – planted firmly in his head. 'I used to collect marmot shit,' he said, the smoke stabbing at his eyes. 'I guess I ought to know where to find them – up there, I would think,' he said, gesturing at the ridge behind them.

They looked at one another a long moment, their bodies smudged and battered and all but sexless, and then they turned as one and started to climb. It was no easy task. Already, after a mere five days, they could feel the effects of starvation, a weakness in the limbs, a gracelessness that took the spring out of their step and made their brains feel as if they were packed with cellulose. They gulped air like pearl divers, left traces of themselves on the rough hide of the rocks. Every bush poked at them. They tasted their own sweat, their own blood. And when they got to the top of the canyon, they discovered more scenery, a whole panorama of scenery, but nothing to eat. 'We've got to look for their burrows,' Tierwater said, snatching the words between deep ratcheting breaths.

Andrea just stared at him, her chest heaving, the whole world spread out behind her. Burrows, they were looking for burrows.

They spread out and combed the ridge, chasing incidentally after lizards that were so quick they couldn't be sure they'd seen them, chewing bits of twig and the odd unidentifiable berry that might or might not have been poisonous, but they found no scat, no burrows, no sign that marmots or anything else lived there. Tierwater, the tender skin of his back and shoulders baked to indelibility, was making some sort of excuse, flapping his hands, dredging up marmot lore, when the two of them suddenly froze. There was a sound on the air, a high chittering whistle that seemed to be emanating from the next ridge over. 'You hear that?' Tierwater said, and his face must have been something to see – give him a loopy grin, the look of the mad scientist, the cannibal turning a corner and bumping into a sumo wrestler. 'That's a marmot. That's a marmot for sure.'

Guided by the sound, they moved through the brush and into the cover of the tall pines till they came to a clearing dominated by a tumble of rock; in the center of the tumble, its broad flat rodent's head jerking spasmodically as it sang or screeched or whatever it was doing, was a marmot. A yellow-bellied marmot, fat and delicious. Tierwater glanced at Andrea. Andrea glanced at Tierwater. He put a finger to his lips and bent for a stout branch.

For an hour, crouching, creeping through a bristle of yellowed grass and pine cones on their stomachs, Tierwater and Andrea converged on the animal from opposite directions. It was hot. Tierwater was white with dust and itching in every fiber of his torn and abraded flesh. He watched Andrea's head bob up from behind a fallen log ten feet in back of the marmot, then he swallowed his breath and charged the thing, stick flailing in the air – and she, taking his signal, rose up with a whoop, her own stick clutched tight. It was a careful stalk, a brilliant stalk from a tactical standpoint, but, unfortunately, the marmot was unimpressed. With a single squeak that was like the first faint exhalation of a teapot set on to boil, he – it – disappeared down its hole.

'All right,' Tierwater said, 'all right, we'll dig him out, then.'

And so they dug, with brittle pine sticks instead of a pick and shovel, in dry, rocky soil, their stomachs creaking and crepitating and closing on nothing. They dug wordlessly, dug mindlessly, earth and stones flying, sticks shattering, the vision of that stupid, dull-eyed, buck-toothed animal constantly before them – meat, meat spitted on the grill – until they gradually became aware of a noise behind them, a high chittering whistle. They turned as one to see the marmot watching them from the neck of a burrow twenty feet away, its head bobbing in complaint. Tierwater picked up a stone; the marmot disappeared. 'No problem,' Tierwater said, turning to his wife, and she was a mess, she was, her hands blackened, a fine grit glued to her with her own sweat, 'you just stay here, at this burrow, and I'll dig him out over there.'

And so they dug again, with renewed vigor, watching the distance between them shrink as Tierwater traced the burrow back along a meandering line to where Andrea dug forward to meet him. Half an hour passed. An hour. And then, finally, though they were exhausted – tense, exhausted and angry – the end was in sight: there were no more than five feet separating them. 'I'll force him out,' Andrea whispered, her voice gone husky, 'and you club him, club the living *shit* out of him, Ty.' Yes. And then they heard the whistle behind them, and there was the marmot, the fat, stupid thing, on the lip of yet another burrow.

Thirty days is a long time to play at nature. An infinity, really. But they learned from their mistakes, until finally, with coordination and the fiercest concentration, they began to eke out a starvation diet, all the while marveling at Great-grandfather Knowles and the sheer grit he must have had. Eventually, they caught things and ate them. They herded fish into shallow pools and scooped them out with a sort of lacrosse stick Tierwater fashioned one afternoon (the protected golden trout, *Salmo agua-bonita,* mostly, but chub and roach too); they gathered crickets, grasshoppers and berries; they extinguished a whole colony of freshwater mussels that tasted of mud and undigested algae. They foraged for bird's eggs, chewed twigs to fight down the hunger that tormented them day and night, lingered round Chris Mattingly's camp like refugees choking on their own saliva. At night, wrapped in their leaves and detritus, when the stillness descended and there was no sound but for the trill and gurgle of the river digging itself deeper, they dreamed of food. 'Reese's Pieces,'

Andrea would murmur in her sleep. 'Cheeseburger. Doritos. Make mine medium rare.'

The days stretched on, each one an eternity unto itself, animal days, days without consciousness or conscious thought. No books. No TV. No sex. Every waking moment consumed with a sort of ceaseless shifting and wandering in search of food, and no set time for meals either, not dawn or high noon or dusk. No, they just fell on whatever they managed to catch or forage – berries, forbs, a brace of lizard smashed to pulp by a perfect strike right down the middle of the plate – and ate greedily, no time for manners or self-abnegation or even civility, no time but primitive time. Andrea had grown up in the outdoors. She'd hiked, fished, camped, ridden horseback for as long as she could remember, and she had the blood of the mad anchorite Joseph Knowles in her veins, but, still, this was too much for her, Tierwater could see that before the first week was out. And it was too much for him too, too much suffering to prove a point, though there were moments when he stared down into the rolling liquefaction of the waters or up into the starving sky and felt washed clean, no thought of Sierra ensconced on Lake Witcheegono, New York, with her Aunt Phyll, no thought of Sheriff Bob Hicks or the awesome weight of the prison door as it slammed shut behind you or the busy wars of accumulation and want that raged through the world with the regularity of the seasons.

Tierwater lost twenty-five pounds, Andrea nineteen. They were stick people, both of them, as hard and burnished as new leather, and they barely had the strength to drag themselves up and out of the canyon on the last day of their exile. Chris Mattingly led the way with his loping vigorous strides, a man who dwelt deep inside himself, and nobody said a word the whole way back. The path rose gradually out of the gorge and into the higher elevations, and Tierwater had to stop every ten minutes to refocus his energy, Andrea tottering along on the poles of her legs like a furtive drunk, the sky overhead expanding and contracting at will until both of them had headaches so insistent they could barely see. But it was worth it, it was, because when they got there – to the big exfoliated dome of granite where it all began – there was a crowd of five hundred gathered to greet them and they roared like a crowd twice the size.

Teo was there, newspeople with minicams and flashing cameras, children, dogs, E.F.!ers, potters, crystal and totem vendors, and every last resident of Big Timber, turned out in flannel shirts and jeans. Declan Quinn was at the front of the press, nodding the parched bulb of his head like a toy on a string, and two cops in uniform flanked him. 'That's the man,' he rasped, 'that's him,' and the cop to his left – the one with a face like the bottom of a boot – stepped forward.

It was funny. Though he was making a spectacle of himself in a penis sheath he'd constructed of willow bark and rattlesnake skin, a man of sticks barely able to stand up straight while his wife, the thousand-year-old woman, limped along gamely at his side in a crude skirt and top made of woven grass, though it was over now and they were going to shut him up in a cage, Tierwater felt nothing but relief. He was as calm as Jesus striding out of the Sinai after his thirty days and thirty nights of temptation, and when he felt the cold steel grip of the handcuffs close over his wrists, he could have wept for joy.

Santa Ynez, April 2026

AND THEN, ONE day, the rain stops for good. There it is, the sun, angry and blistered in a sky the color of a bleached robin's egg, steam rising, catfish wriggling, eighty-seven degrees already and it's only eight in the morning. I'm outside, squinting in the unaccustomed light, my feet held fast in the muck of the yard, a flotilla of crippled-looking geese sailing by in the current of what we've dubbed the Pulchris River. What am I feeling? The faintest, tiniest, incipient stirring of hope. That's right. Hope for the animals – and they've suffered, believe me, cooped up in the house like that, no breath of fresh air or touch of the earth under their hoofs and paws, filthy conditions, irregular diet, lack of exercise – and hope for myself and Andrea too. Mac's promised to rebuild on higher ground, state-of-the-art pens and cages for the animals, a bunker for me and Andrea, with two bedrooms, a kitchen and a living room. Of course – and this is the sad part – for a good third of our specimens, it's already too late. The warthogs, all fourteen of them, have slipped into oblivion (a swine flu, we think, passed by the peccaries or maybe Chuy, but then I'm no veterinarian), Lily's vanished, the spectacled bear poisoned herself after she broke through the wall into the garage and lapped up a gallon of antifreeze, and there's been a whole host of other calamities I don't even want to get into.

Anyway, I was up at six, the astonishing wallop of the meteorological change registering insistently in my back and hip joints, the pillow gummy with sweat, my glasses misted over the minute I clapped them on the bridge of my nose. Global warming. I remember the time when people debated not only the fact of it but the consequence. It didn't sound so bad, on the face of it, to someone from Winnipeg, Grand Forks or Sakhalin Island. The greenhouse effect, they called it. And what are greenhouses but pleasant, warm, nurturing places, where you can grow sago palms and hydroponic tomatoes during the deep-freeze of the winter? But that's not how it is at all. No, it's like leaving your car in the parking lot in the sun all day with the windows rolled up and then climbing in and discovering they've been sealed shut – and the doors too. The hotter it is, the more evaporation; the more evaporation, the hotter it gets, because the biggest greenhouse gas, by far and away, is water vapor. That's how it is, and that's why for the next six months it's going to get so hot the Pulchris River will evaporate and rise back up into the sky like a ghost in a long trailing shroud and all this muck will be baked to the texture of concrete. Global warming. It's a fact.

But right now my spirit leaps up: I'm here, I'm alive and the sun is shining. Spring has sprung, and my brain is teeming with plans. I haven't even had breakfast yet or labored over the toilet and already I'm pacing off the rough outline of the new lion pen on a prime piece of high ground, a good half-acre of ochre muck and devilweed wedged between the garage and the gazebo. It's the lions that are suffering most – their hair is falling out, they're too depressed even to cough, let alone roar, and Buttercup seems to have lost most of her carnassial teeth, which makes chewing through all that partially defrosted prime rib a real chore – and I'm determined to get them fixed up first. Besides, they're the most dangerous things in the house (except maybe for Andrea, but who's complaining?), and though we've barricaded the doors and taken every precaution, I shudder to think what would happen if one of them got loose.

So this is how it is, the sun up there in the sky, me down here thinking lions, the wind out of the southeast ripe with a smell if not of redemption then at least of renewal – and isn't it supposed to be Easter soon? – when I hear Andrea calling my name. And this is remarkable in itself, because we're shy of noon by nearly four hours and she hasn't been up this early since she reinserted herself into my crabbed life back in November. She's wearing a white flowing dress, low-cut, and half a dozen strings of multicolored beads that bring to mind hippie times, and she's lifting the hem of the dress to keep it out of the muck and moving in her gum boots with the kind of lightness and grace you wouldn't expect from an old lady. I watch her pick her way to me, and I know I must have an awestruck look on my face (for a minute there I'm not even sure who I am or what lifetime this is), and then I watch her lips moving and notice her lipstick and hear her say, 'So there you are.'

I lift one of my boots from the grip of the muck and point to it: 'I'm pacing off the new lion compound.'

She's got a hand to her forehead, screening her eyes from the sun. 'Did you remember your sunblock?' And before I can answer: 'You should be wearing a hat too. How many carcinomas have you had removed now – what was it, twenty-two, twenty-five?'

Andrea isn't wearing a gauze mask, by the way, and neither am I. Nor is Mac or Chuy or April Wind or anybody else in the house. We gave up on all that nonsense back in January, when the screen informed us that the *mucosa* scare was just that – a scare. It seems there was a localized outbreak of a new and especially virulent strain of the common cold on the East Coast (people died from it, mostly the old-old, but still, it was only a cold), and a certain degree of hysteria was inevitable. Mac insisted on the charade for a week or two after the news became definitive, but we were all relieved when finally, one afternoon, he appeared at lunch with the bridge of his nose and thin, pale, salmon-colored lips revealed for all to see. I remember the sense of liberation I felt when I tore off my own reeking mask and buried my dental enhancements in a thick, chewy chili-cheese burrito without having to worry about getting a mouthful of gauze with every other bite.

'Is that what you came out here to tell me?' I say, and I'm irritated, just a little, because I know she's right.

'No,' and her voice is soft as she moves into me with a slosh of her boots and wraps her big arms around me, 'I just wanted to tell you we've got eggs for breakfast this morning.'

'Eggs?' We haven't seen anything even vaguely resembling an egg since the storms started in, and forget the cholesterol, I can already picture a crisp golden three-egg omelet laid out on the plate – or, no, I'm going to have mine poached and runny, so I can really taste them. 'Where'd you get them?'

She pulls back to give me a sly smile, then lifts her chin toward the wreckage of the condos across the way. The two buildings that collapsed back in November have gradually subsided into the muck, a spill of ruined sofas, exercise equipment and video attachments littering the far shore under the glare of the sun. 'The good old barter system,' she says. 'There's a kid over there – a kid, listen to me; I mean, he's got to be forty-five or so – who says he's a big Pulchris freak, went to all the shows, lifted all the performance tracks off the Net, that sort of thing – '

I smile. 'And he's got chickens.'

'He wouldn't take money, but April gave him a couple of old tour T-shirts – with Mac's permission, of course.'

'Nothing like living off the past,' I say, and then I loop my arm through Andrea's and we slog off across the yard to the house, awash in sunshine.

I remember there wasn't much sun the winter Sierra climbed into her tree. El Niño really took it out on us that year, one storm chasing another down the coast, the rivers flooding and the roads washed out, mudslides, rogue waves, windshield-wiper fatigue, drip, drip, drip, everybody as depressed as Swedes. Nobody liked it – except maybe the surfers. And Coast Lumber. Coast Lumber loved it. Coast Lumber couldn't have been more pleased if they'd ordered up the weather themselves. A tree-hugger by the name of Sierra Tierwater, twenty-one years old and a complete unknown – nobody's daughter, certainly – was trespassing in one of their grand old cathedral redwoods and the press was waiting for them to send a couple of their goons up to haul her down, as brutally as possible. But they weren't about to do that. Why bother? Why give her anything? All they had to do was sit back in their paneled offices and let the weather take care of her. And then, quietly, while the eco-freaks and fossil-lovers were hunkered in their apartments watching the rain drool across the windows, they could take that tree down, and all the rest like it, and put an end to the protests once and for all.

The first night, the night I drove up there to rescue her from the storm, I was so disoriented I couldn't have found her if she were standing behind the cash register of a 7-Eleven lit up under the trees. All I managed to do was add to my quotient of suffering, inhabiting yet another dark night of the soul, face to face with my own dread and loss of faith. Drunk, I stumbled around through the graveyard of the trees while the wind screamed and the branches fell. I don't know how long I was out there, but it was a relief when I finally found my way back to the car, though the car was stuck to the frame in mud and there was no hope there either. My head was throbbing, my throat so dry it was as if somebody had been working on it all night with a belt sander, and my clothes were wet through to the skin. I felt dizzy. Nauseous. I was racked with chills. I stripped off my clothes, socks as wet as fishes, underwear like something that had been used to swab out toilets, and then, thinking *Sierra, Sierra,* I wrapped myself up in Andrea's mummy bag, and in the next moment I was asleep.

The morning wasn't much different from the night that had preceded it. Rain fell without reason or rancor, an invisible creek blustered somewhere nearby, the car settled into the mud. There may have been a quantitative difference in the light, a gradual seep of visibility working its way into the gloom, but it wasn't much. I pulled on cold wet socks, wet jeans, wet boots and a wet T-shirt, sweater and windbreaker, and went off to find my daughter. This time I walked straight to her tree.

There were eight redwoods in her grove, two conjoined at the base and blackened by the ancient fire that had scarred the trunk of her tree, and the forest of cedar, fir, ponderosa and other pines was a maze of trunks radiating out across the hillsides from there. Except to the west, where the skin of the earth showed through and there was nothing but debris and stumps as far as you could see. This grove was scheduled next, and my daughter – if she was alive still and not a bag of lacerated skin and fragmented bone flung out of the treetops like a water balloon – was determined to stop the desecration. I was proud of her for that, but wary too. And afraid. I leaned into the wet, dark trunk and peered up into the sky – her platform, the shadowy slab of plywood lashed across two massive branches with nylon cord, was still there. I pushed back from the tree to get a better angle, blinking my eyes against the fall of the rain, and saw the bright aniline-orange flash of her tent trembling in the wind like a wave riding an angry sea. She was there. She was alive. 'Sierra!' I shouted, cupping my hands.

A gust shook the treetops, and Sierra's tree quaked till I could feel the recoil of it in my feet. I looked up and there she was, her face a distant, drawn-down splash of white in a welter of rocketing green needles. And then her voice, buffeted by the winds and assaulted by the rain, came drifting down like a leaf: 'Dad!' she called. 'Dad!'

My heart was breaking, but she was smiling, actually smiling, if I was seeing right – and even in those days, my eyes were nothing to brag about. 'Sierra!' I called, feeling as if I'd been turned inside out. I didn't want her up there. I wanted to be up there with her. I wanted to bomb Coast Lumber, neutralize their heavy machinery, throttle their stockholders. 'Honey,' I shouted, and my voice broke, 'do you want to come down?'

It seemed as if it took an hour for her answer to drift all the way back to me, the tree quaking, the rain thrashing, my heart like a steel disc in the back of my throat, but her answer was no. 'No!' she cried, cupping her thin white hands round her mouth to make it emphatic. 'No!' And the message fell with the rain.

I was her father. I knew what she was like, heard the determination in her voice, the fanaticism: she wasn't coming down, not today, and there was no use arguing. 'Tomorrow maybe?' I shouted, my neck already strained from flinging my head back to gape up at her. 'Till the storm stops, anyway? You can always go back up – when the weather clears!'

Again the answer drifted down, this time in a long-drawn-out bleat of protest: 'Nooooo!'

All right. But did she need anything? 'Do you need anything?' I shouted.

Rain trailed down my back. I was shivering spasmodically. My throat was sore. My head ached. In time, she would need all sorts of things: a chemical toilet, books, magazines, art supplies, a cell phone, fuel for her camp stove, a special harness so she could descend to thirty feet like a big pale spider and conduct the endless press interviews her crusade would generate. But now, on the first morning of her life as an arboreal creature, an evolutionary oddity, a female *Homo sapiens* of breeding age whose feet never touched the ground and whose biological imperative would have to wait, she needed nothing. Except a favor. 'Can you do me a favor?' she called out of the drifting white flag of her face.

'Yeah,' I shouted, digging at the back of my neck and pushing away from the tree for a less inflammatory angle. 'Sure. Anything!'

214

'Take these,' she called, and suddenly two objects, oblong, pale gray and streaking white, came sailing down out of the tree. It took me a minute to identify them, even after they landed separately in the duff not more than two feet from me. Thump, came the first of them, and then the second, slapping down beside me with the sound of finality. They were her shoes. Her shoes. Her running shoes, walking shoes, walking, breathing and living shoes, the very things that connected her to the earth. But she flung them down to me on that first morning, because she wouldn't be needing them, not anymore.

Eggs. Such a simple food, the sort of thing we used to take for granted, the mainstay of every greasy spoon in every town in America, scrambled, soft-boiled, over easy with home fries on the side. I grew up on eggs, in the time before we realized what they did to the arteries, and my daughter grew up on them too, simply because she had to get her protein somewhere. But as I say, eggs have been scarce at Chez Pulchris during the siege. The cook – her name is Fatima, by the way, and her husband is Zulfikar – served up omelets and fresh-baked bread for a week or so after we all moved in, but then the eggs were gone and it's been meat, rice and canned vegetables since. Oh, the tall Al managed to make it across the Pulchris River once or twice in the beginning, but the supermarkets had been stripped down to the bare shelves – nothing left but cornstarch and pickled beets – and after that even the Olfputt couldn't breach the floods and we all just stayed put and made do with what we had. So I'm looking forward to a plate of eggs, even if I do have to sop them up with chapatis instead of toast, and I kick off my boots on the doorstep and go in to wash up, change my shirt and slip into the black-and-gold satin tour jacket Mac gave me when I ran out of clothes a month back. Sun floods the windows, and I'm actually whistling – *Ride your pony, Ride your pony* – as I gaze into the mirror and slap on some of Mac's three-hundred-dollar-an-ounce aftershave.

We're gathering on the third floor, in the Gangsta Rap Room, as it turns out, for a formal brunch – Mac has an announcement to make. As Andrea and I step into the elevator, her arm tucked neatly into the crook of my elbow, I can already guess what he's going to say: he's leaving. Going north for the summer – Fairbanks, Winnipeg, maybe one of the big Hokkaido resorts. He'll climb into a helicopter, and he'll take the Als with him (and none too soon for the shorter one, who must have put on a good thirty pounds of flab since the rains started). That's all right. I don't mind. As long as I have his commitment to rebuild, he can be on the far side of the moon for all it matters to me, not that I don't enjoy his company, don't get me wrong, but Mac is going to be Mac, and that means globe-trotting. That means excess. That means Mac in Edinburgh or Reykjavík, bent over the gaming tables or squiring some starlet round the tony eateries where they serve tuna garni or twenty-year-old monkfish at three thousand dollars a plate. I'm used to it.

At any rate, I'm feeling good as we glide through the door and into the dining room, the sun shining, eggs on the menu, the future looking bright. The table has been set for six (Chuy never joins us for meals, though Mac, I'm sure, would have no objection, being the democrat and humanitarian he is) and we're the first to arrive, followed shortly by April Wind. 'Hellooo, Ty!' she chirps, as if she hasn't seen me in months, and she bends to peck a kiss to Andrea's cheek before seating herself at the far end of the table, next to Mac's place. She's had an exciting winter, the dwarf woo-woo woman in the size 2 dress, rattling away at her Sierra book (tentatively titled *For Love of the Trees*) and romancing Mac. That's right. They found common ground in the Zodiac, Pantheism, holistic medicine, yin yang and the androgynous universe, and crystals, and since she was the only woman under sixty-seven washed up on Pulchris Isle, I guess it was inevitable that she caught Mac's eye. Not that he isn't discriminating, just practical.

Orange juice is on the table (fresh-squeezed, in a stone pitcher), a plate of chapatis and dishes of lime pickle and mango chutney, two bottles of champagne in iced buckets, kiwi fruit, bananas and kumquats from our own inundated orchards. I pour myself a glass of orange juice, twist off the wire and pop the cork on a bottle of Mumm's Cordon Rouge, 1999, from the Pulchris cellars. 'So how's the book going?' I say, giving April Wind a look.

'Let me have a little of that, Ty.' This is Andrea speaking. She wants champagne, and who can blame her after all that rotgut *sake,* but she also wants to deflect my question. She leans forward, tipping her wineglass under the lip of the bottle while I pour. It's hard to say what she's thinking, but my guess is that, if she had to choose between me and April, I'd be out the door. And that hurts. It does.

'April?' I ask, lifting my eyebrows and proffering the bottle.

'No, thanks.' She has the look of a decrepit child, the limp black hair, the vaguely Asian eyes, the lipstickless mouth. She seems to be hugging her shoulders, which makes them appear even narrower, her miniature hands clasped before her, the totem dangling from her throat in its pathetic little sack. What could Mac possibly see in her?

I smack my lips over the champagne, dilute it with a splash of orange juice. 'So the book?' I repeat, and I hear my father's voice, the half-mocking tone he'd use when he came into the kitchen at night to refill his drink and saw me sitting there at the table with my homework spread out before me like so much refuse. 'So *nu?*' he'd say.

April Wind ducks her head. She shrugs. Holds out her glass for orange juice. 'As well as can be expected.'

'No big publishers beating down the door?'

'Come on, Ty,' Andrea says, exchanging a look with April Wind. The look says, Forgive him, he's being a jerk, and I am being a jerk, of course I am – that's my blood on those pages, and my daughter's.

'What's the celebration?' April Wind wants to know in her tiny piping kindergartner's voice, and I can't resist saying, 'Mac's going away,' just to watch her face fall.

'You don't know that, Ty –' There's an edge to Andrea's voice, and whose side do you think she's on here?

'Want to bet? You might think you know him, after, what – four, five months? – but I've been with him ten years, and I know he's getting squirrelly, has to be. If it wasn't for the weather and the *mucosa* business, he'd have been out of here months ago, believe me.'

And then the door swings open, right on cue, and there he is, Mac, in hat, shades and eel whips, flanked by the two Als. 'What's happening, people?' he sings, spreading his arms wide. 'Don't you just love this groovy sunshine? Isn't this just a *day?* Do we deserve it or what?'

The Als have seen better days. Their eyes are haunted by visions of blackjack tables, cocktail waitresses, the track, and their skin is the color of the growth medium in a petri dish. The taller one was a professional wrestler back in the time when people cared about such things, and the shorter one, as I say, has put on so much weight he doesn't even look human. They take their places heavily, and without joy.

Mac is grinning. Mac is overflowing with all the emotions his bodyguards lack, and for a minute there I think he's going to snatch the bust of Chuck D off its pedestal and waltz round the room with it, but he slips into his chair at the head of the table and unfurls his napkin with a practiced snap of the wrist. 'Eggs today, that's what I hear,' he crows, treating us to his famous smile, 'just like Mama used to whip up when there was eight of us growing up in Detroit, yes, absolutely, eggs for breakfast, lunch and dinner – and now they're a treat, how do you like that?'

Before anybody can respond, April Wind draws in an audible breath – a stabbing, shrieking, stifled-in-the-cradle sort of breath – and asks, 'Is it true, Mac?'

Mac turns his head to me, the shades flinging off the light of the chandelier in a poisonous silver flash, then comes back to April Wind, and I can't help thinking of the tight little smile of satisfaction on her face the first morning I saw her slipping out of Mac's room or the time he held her in his lap like a ventriloquist's dummy all through a showing of *Soylent Green* in the screening room. Good, I think, let her get her comeuppance. Who is she anyway, and how did she weasel her way in here?

Mac's response is so soft, so sweet and lispingly breathy, my old man's ears can barely pick it up. 'If you mean what I think you mean, baby, then, yes, it's true, we're out of here – Al and Al and me – this afternoon. Business, that is. Up north. You all can stay on, and everything's going to be built back again, so don't you worry, Ty – you know I wouldn't sacrifice those precious sweet creatures down there for anything in the world.'

April Wind wants to say a whole lot more, I can see that, she wants to call on the spirits of the trees and the other animist gods, wants to talk crystals and auras, wants to marshal all the forces of woo-woo to bind Mac to her, to us, but she just gives him a plaintive look and stockpiles her words for later, when she can get him alone. I'm not a betting man, but I give her less than a ten-percent chance of finding a seat on that helicopter when it rises up out of the muck with our resident god aboard. Goodbye, Mac, I'm thinking, and let's get on with it.

Events to this point are still pretty clear in my mind, the champagne, the promise of eggs fried in butter, Mac, April Wind, Andrea, the two Als – all that's been preserved in the hard drive of my old man's memory. But the rest of it, I'm afraid, suffers from gaps and deletions. It's the shock factor, I suppose, selective memory, repressed material, events so naked and grisly you can't admit them. For better or worse, here's what I *can* bring up:

Fatima, all in black, shoving through the swinging doors to the upper kitchen, which is really just a warming room, connected by dumbwaiter to the main kitchen on the first floor and the incinerator in the basement, and Zulfikar right behind her in his white toque and spattered apron. Both of them carrying big silver chafing dishes and a familiar ambrosial aroma that takes me back to my mother, my grandmother, the kitchens of old, but I can't taste those eggs now, so I don't think we got that far. I see the big silver dishes in the center of the table, Fatima's pitted black eyes peering out of the gap in her yashmak, and then I'm seeing Dandelion, incongruous as that may seem, scraping his way up the dumbwaiter from the basement with a kind of grit and leonine initiative I'd have had to admire under other circumstances. And that's a picture, four hundred–and–some–odd pounds of deter-mined cat, the yellow fire of his eyes, the mane swinging from the back of his head like an ill-fitting wig, the spidering limbs and grasping claws. He defies gravity. He is silent, absolutely, no sound but for the rasp of those hooked claws digging for purchase. Dandelion. Climbing.

The door swings open again, right on Fatima's heels, as if there's another server back there, more to the feast than just eggs – curries and lamb *tikka,* defrosted halibut in a cardamom sauce, unexpected delicacies and further delights – but no human agency has pushed open that door. I don't know who becomes aware of it first. I remember looking up, heads turning, the motion of the door, and then seeing Dandelion there. And smelling him. A lion in the doorway might have been a trick of the light, slip off your glasses and polish them on your sleeve, get a new prescription ASAP, but there was no arguing with that smell. That smell was immemorial. That smell was the smell of death.

In the wild, when there was a wild, lions would kill their prey through suffocation. They would bring down a zebra or a wild-ebeest or even a cape buffalo, and then clamp their jaws on the throat or, more typically, over the mouth and nose, until the animal lay still. And when they took humans, they would most often attack at night, biting through the walls of a tent or hut and seizing the victim by the skull, crushing it instantly. If the victim awoke or the lion missed its stroke, things would get nasty. Then the claws would come into play, and the victim would be dragged off screaming into the night. Of course, in a chance encounter in the bush, all bets were off. The lion would do what lions do.

Is there a snarl? Or a woof? I don't know, but I have a hand on Andrea's arm and I'm dragging her awkwardly down into the vacancy beneath the table, chairs scraping, somebody shouting, God Himself invoked by one of the Als, the one who's about to be sliced open like a watermelon and flung across the room even as Dandelion, spitting and roaring, homes in on Mac. Why Mac? I'm thinking, as I scramble for the door with Andrea in tow and April shrieks and the surviving Al tries to draw a ridiculous little pistol from the leather holster under his arm, but thinking isn't something you do a lot of under circumstances like these. The roaring alone is enough to seize your heart – and I've never seen Dandelion like this, so wrought up and nasty, whirling, biting, slashing – and then there's the sight of the blood. And worse, the sight of Mac – our benefactor, Dandelion's benefactor, the provider of meat, money, health care, companionship, a true and caring friend of the animals – lying there so still in the cradle of his overturned chair. His hat is gone, the shades are crushed, the eel whips drawing the blood out of his scalp like the bright-red tips of a painter's brushes. Andrea is screaming something in my ear and the door to the hallway is closing on the scene, closing firmly, Ratchiss' big gun all the way down on the first floor and no hope for anybody or anything left in all this world.

PART THREE

Wildlife in America

Lompoc/Los Angeles, September–October 1991

IT HAD TO be one of the stranger transformations – from a penis sheath and limitless horizons to prison-issue cotton and a twelve-foot chain-link fence with concertina wire strung across the top. Tierwater let his legs dangle from the upper bunk in the room (not cell, *room*) he shared with Bill Driscoll, stock swindler, scam artist and interstate bilker of the elderly, and turned it over in his mind. Most offenders, white-collar or blue-, were either taken in the act or surprised in their own beds at 4:00 a.m., but how many went from a state of nature to civilization and incarceration in one fell swoop? Tierwater pictured some Wild West desperado hunkered over a jackrabbit stew one day and tossed into the Yuma Territorial Prison the next. Or the Bushmen themselves, run down on horseback and converted to slaves by their Boer masters. Or, even more poignantly, an animal captured in the wild, one of Uncle Sol's orangutans torn from the trees and fitfully gnashing at the alien mesh of the wire cage, the elephant trapped in the *kraal* and chained to a stake, the eagle with its wings clipped.

But if he felt like an animal, it wasn't a wild or even a feral one – no, he felt like a domesticated beast, a child's pony with its nose in the feedbag, the bloated dog curled up on a rug in front of the fireplace. For thirty days last year he'd subsisted on roots, insects and fish no longer than his index finger, and when they locked him up in here, he ate like three men, fried chicken and mashed potatoes, Boston cream pie, sloppy joes, pizza, spaghetti, french fries and onion rings, three scoops of ice cream with chocolate syrup and a can of root beer to wash it down. He was in possession of a belly for the first time in his life, and he'd even developed something resembling buttocks to fill out his prison-issue trousers. There was that, and the fact that this place – Club Fed, they called it – wasn't much more rigorous than Boy Scout camp. But Boy Scouts got to go home, and, however you sliced it, Tierwater was still in jail – locked up, incarcerated, separated from his wife and daughter and his checkbook and his cause – and he hadn't done a thing to deserve it.

They'd wanted to pin the fire on him – and the destruction of all that costly equipment belonging to Coast Lumber – but he got angry, got incensed, and denied everything with the self-righteous rage of the falsely accused, and, of course, they had no proof. Not a shred. Though they let Quinn in on the interrogation, and Quinn, rasping and nodding and scratching, was certain he was guilty, and did everything he could to prod the state and federal investigators into extending the list of charges. They didn't. Tierwater pled guilty to interstate flight and kidnapping, as per the plea bargain worked out by Fred and his team of wild-eyed paper-shufflers, the other charges against him dropped in both federal and state courts. He was sentenced to three hundred and sixty days at the Federal Prison Camp in Lompoc, the state sentence to be served concurrently with the federal.

At first he'd been glad to come in out of the cold, happy just to find himself in a bed at night or following his nose to the dining hall three times a day. He was dead to everything else, as if he were recuperating from a serious illness. He didn't even see the other inmates, didn't see their shuffling feet or their faces frozen in fear, lust, rage and hate. All he saw was the plate, the food, the Twix bar and the Milky Way at the prison commissary. That didn't last long. Four or five days maybe. A week. Then he began to notice the guards as if they'd materialized out of a dream, he saw the fence, the barred windows, the sly and all-knowing faces ranged round him like masks on a wall. He was a criminal. He was in jail. And though the other inmates learned to stay out of his way, though there were classes to attend in everything from Zen to auto mechanics to poetry writing and there were three blacktop tennis courts and a workout room at his disposal, the fact of his incarceration began to gnaw at him till he could barely sleep at night. This was what the system had done to him. The machine. Progress.

Each day was eternal, but not in the way of those shimmering, unconscious days in the wilderness when all his senses were on fire and every least rustle of the leaves screamed *food* in his brain, but in the way of stupefaction, of boredom so black and viscous it was like sludge poured through a funnel into a very small container. He read, he slept, he watched TV with the other emasculated idiots. Out of desperation, and because Fred said it could reduce his sentence (it didn't), he took a class called 'Salutary Self-Expression and the Paradox of the Me' from an embittered unpublished poet who taught part-time at the local community college and confessed that he was 'attracted to the criminal mind.' He worked in the prison printshop, turning out government forms. He played cards, checkers, chess, Parcheesi, chewed gum, put model airplanes together from kits Andrea brought him. Three times a week he played savage stinging sets of tennis with a young bankrobber by the name of Amaury Benitez, who'd been arrested on his doorstep twenty minutes after passing a note to the teller scrawled on the back of one of his own deposit slips. At night, when Bill Driscoll's breathing derailed itself and fell away into the twisting tunnels of deep sleep, he thought of Andrea, naked in the wild, and masturbated in a slow dream, making it last as long as he could.

Well, he was at the end of all that now, due for release in twenty-six days. Twenty-six days. And then he could go back to his normal life, meeting with his parole officer every Monday and slipping out in the wee hours to do his bit to bring the whole system crashing down, and don't think he hadn't had plenty of time to draw up an exhaustive list of key players – the very props and supports of the machine – with Sheriff Bob Hicks, Judge Duermer and Siskiyou Lumber right at the top. Ah, yes: freedom. And what was the day like out there beyond the barred windows and the chain-link fence? Sunny and cool, with an ocean breeze that smelled of sea wrack and clams – geoducks – dug wet from the sand and minced for chowder.

As Tierwater eased himself down from the bed so as not to wake Bill Driscoll, who seemed intent on sleeping out his sentence, he felt good, renewed, ready for anything. This was Saturday, visiting day, and he was expecting Andrea and Sierra in the early afternoon. He'd kiss his wife – once at the beginning of the visit, and once at the end, as sanctioned by the regulations – and he'd pat his daughter's hand and listen to her go on about school, boys and the mall and how she was *so totally glad to be out of that hick town and the whole Sarah Dorkwater thing*. He wanted to open up to her, to tell her how much he missed her and how he was going to make everything up to her as soon as he got out, but he couldn't; she always seemed so muted in the visitors' hall, intimidated by the place – and, he began to suspect, by her father too. He stared across the table at her, and didn't know what to say.

He saw her once a month, and each time she was a new person, nothing like the scrawny red-faced infant he'd thrown over his shoulder like a rug, or the little girl slashing away at the out-of-tune violin while the sun crashed through the trees, or even the loose-limbed teenager playing Monopoly on the steps of Ratchiss' cabin. She was growing up without him. She was fifteen now, nearly as tall as Andrea, and with the flowering figure of a woman, and he had so much to tell her. Or he thought he did. But when she was actually there, sitting across the table from him, and Bill Driscoll was complaining in a thunderous voice about the food to the bob-nosed little exercise freak who was his wife and Amaury Benitez's mother was sobbing into a handkerchief the size of a beach towel, he couldn't seem to summon any advice, fatherly or otherwise.

But now, now he hitched up his pants and ambled down the hall and out the door into the courtyard, stunned all over again by the reach of the sky and the feel of the sun on his face, and he didn't have a worry. Twenty-six days. It was nothing. He'd move into the house Andrea had rented for them in Tarzana and mow the lawn and take the trash out, and he'd drive Sierra to school in the morning and be there for her in the afternoon, and he'd take her shopping, for ice cream, to the movies, and it would be like it used to be, before Teo and Sheriff Bob Hicks came onto the scene. Yes. And then there was Andrea. He'd love her in the flesh – all night, every night – and not in the pathetic theater of his mind.

A couple of the inmates were sunning themselves against the south wall of the dormitory – Anthony Imbroglio, a small-time gangster from Long Beach, and his muscle, a perpetually smirking fat-headed goon by the name of Johnny Taradash – and Tierwater gave them a noncommittal nod, not friendly exactly, but not disrespectful either. That was the thing here, respect. Even though the place was for nonviolent and first-time offenders – nothing like the maximum- or even medium-security prisons, where your fellow inmates were armed robbers, killers and gang members and you were locked in cells on a cellblock just like in an old George Raft movie – you could still get hurt here. For all the overweight accountants, pigeon-chested scam artists and inside traders with flat feet and staved-in eyes, there were drug offenders too, muscle-bound high-school dropouts, ethnic groups with gang affiliations – black, Latino, Native American – and all of them were angry, and they all pumped iron instead of worrying about their investment portfolios.

At the end of Tierwater's first week, Johnny Taradash had come to him and suggested he might want to have Andrea deposit a hundred dollars a month in Anthony Imbroglio's account at First Interstate in Los Angeles. For his own protection, that is. Tierwater was weak still, skinny as a refugee, but his temper – that un-containable flood of rage that came up in him like Blitzkrieg at the most inopportune times – was as muscular as ever. He told Johnny Taradash to fuck off, and Johnny Taradash let out a weary sigh and began tearing up the room in a slow methodical way, ripping the covers off books, crumpling magazines, that sort of thing, and he left Tierwater gasping for breath on the concrete floor. The next day Tierwater smuggled a wrench and screwdriver out of the printshop and spent the better part of the afternoon removing a dull-gray scuffed metal leg from the desk in his room. He lingered in the doorway that evening, while Bill Driscoll turned to the wall and moaned in his sleep and the shadows solidified in the trees beyond the window, till he caught sight of Johnny Taradash's big head floating down the hall from the TV room, just behind the sleek, neatly barbered form of his boss. He waited. Held his breath. Then stepped out and hit Johnny Taradash flat across the plane of his face, swinging for the fences with everything he had. After that, there was respect.

He'd almost reached the visitors' hall when Radovan Divac, the Serbian chess fiend, came at him out of nowhere, demanding a game. Divac was a gangling, morose-looking character with a nose like a loaf of French bread and a pair of negligible eyes who'd tried to rob a federal credit union with a water pistol. 'Come on, Ty,' he pleaded, 'I give you queen and, and – knight's bishop. Fi' dollar, you beat me.'

'Sorry, Rado,' he said, brushing past him, 'I've got visitors.'

The Serb held up a fist choked with black pieces. 'And the rook – I give you both rook. Fi' dollar, come on!'

Tierwater gave his name to the guard at the door of the visitors' facility and went on into the long low rectangular room with its wrung-out light, its smell of flooding glands and the dust that hung eternally in the air. A segmented table divided the room: on one side were women in dresses, makeup and heels, accompanied by the occasional squirming infant or fiercely scrubbed toddler; on the other were the prisoners. Tierwater took one of the only two seats available – on the far end, next to a guard named Timson who must have weighed three hundred pounds. They were like umpires, the guards – bloated, titanic men with dead faces who called all the strikes balls and the balls strikes, enemies of the game and the players alike. Tierwater had learned not to expect much from them. He was listening to one of the new inmates tell his wife or girlfriend how thoroughly he was going to fuck her when he got out in six months – *Right on down to the spaces in between your toes, baby* – when Andrea and Sierra came through the door.

Andrea was wearing heels and a tight green dress with spaghetti straps that showed off her arms and shoulders. Sierra, in baggy jeans, high-tops and a sweatshirt that featured the name of her high school stamped across the front of it, stood against the wall just inside the door while one of the guards – another flesh-monster born of doughnuts and Kentucky Fried – frisked Andrea for contraband. Up and down her front with the portable metal-detector, both sides, now turn around, the wand re-creating each dip and bulge, the hair falling across her face in a shimmering, fine white-blond sheet, every prisoner watching with that starved prison light in his eyes, even the ones with their pregnant sixteen-year-old girlfriends propped up across from them like tombstones. Then Andrea was crossing the room, everything in motion, and Tierwater stood to place his hands flat on the table and lean into her for the kiss.

The kiss was the big feature of every visitors' hall encounter, and every inmate lingered over it, dreaming of another place and another time, savoring the female smell and the female taste as long as humanly possible. Tierwater was no different. Three hundred and thirty-four days without sex. That was paying your debt to society, all right. With interest. He clung to her with his lips as long as he could, and then they were sitting on opposite sides of the table, his erection throbbing insistently, and they talked about the things that counted for nothing, the mundane things, the things of the world outside the wire. 'The deal's all but done,' she said.

'What do you mean – the shopping center?'

'Uh-huh. Teo knew somebody back east – remember I told you last time? – and he came in and got it closed. No reflection on that realtor you were stuck on, but she was a low-grade moron with about as much chance of selling that place as I've got of being named premier of China – '

'Elsa was a friend of my father.'

'Yeah, well, she couldn't have sold that place if it was the last piece of property on the East Coast. She was tired. She was *old*, Ty – I mean, what is she: Sixty? Seventy?'

'What'd we get, just out of curiosity? I mean, this is what we're going to be living on for the rest of our lives, that's all. No big deal.'

She pursed her lips. Shifted her buttocks. Let her hair fall and then swept it back again. 'One three,' she said.

For a vivid moment he saw the place he'd abandoned, the Mongolian barbecue that used to be a dry cleaner that used to be a notions shop, the dirty-windowed vacancy of the deserted drugstore, the model shop he'd haunted as a brainless teenager, the yarn store, the pet shop with its grimy aquariums and enervated birds and its smell of superheated death. It was a prime property, or at least it used to be, back in the sixties, when his father built the place. One three. Well, one three was better than nothing, and who would be crazy enough to buy the place anyway – even for half the price?

'That doesn't include the office building and all that parcel,' she was saying.

He was doing the math. One three minus the six-hundred-thousand second mortgage and the forty-odd for the realtor's fee and the taxes on top of that — it would still leave them a nice piece of change. How many flyers could they print up with that? How many culverts could they block?

'Or the house, though we did get one low-ball bid on that, and the property out back of the development is something we — you — should sit on. That's going to go through the roof one of these days, I know it is . . .'

Then there was Sierra. Andrea got up and Sierra took her place, slouching across the room and dropping into the chair as if she'd been struck by paralysis, the other inmates moistening their lips and shooting her covert glances — she was a woman, she was, and for half the pedophiliac bastards it wouldn't have mattered anyway. Flesh, that's all they cared about it, flesh and orifices. He wanted to get up and punch somebody. Hurt them. Make them pay.

'Hi, Dad,' she whispered.

Bill Driscoll had apparently roused himself from his dreams in time for visiting hours. Tierwater heard him before he saw him — he was three seats down, leaning into the table with both elbows while his wife, Bunny, sat across from him, her posture so rigid she might have been nailed to the seat. 'Some of those, what do you call them, caramels?' he boomed. 'Like you get in the supermarket with the little scoop? And those other chewy things I like, with the three layers and the coconut shreds? A pound bag. Of each.'

'What,' Tierwater said, 'no kiss?'

Sierra glanced down at her lap, and her face was a legitimate miracle, the silken eyelids, the lashes thick and dark and mascara-free, his mother's nose, Jane's eyes. Then she stood, and he stood, and they placed their hands flat on the table, and pecked their mutual kisses. 'No makeup,' he observed, settling back into the chair. 'Is it because of' — he nodded at the long row of chairs and the inmates, mostly young, crouched over them and leaning into the table as if into a wind that would suck them out the door to freedom — 'because of them?'

'I'm a vegan now,' she said.

'So?'

'That means no animal products of any kind, no eggs, no milk even. And makeup – you know what they do to those poor lab animals just to test it? I mean, *eyeliner* – you really think a rabbit, hundreds of rabbits, should have to die just for us to smear up our eyes? Ever hear of the Draize test? Did you?'

He shrugged.

'They put these chemicals in the animals' eyes – the stuff they're going to use in mascara and eyeliner? – and they superconcentrate it to see what would happen if some lady like used twelve tons of it on her face, just to see if the rabbits and white mice'll go blind. You think that's right?'

Nothing was right. Not injecting chimps with the AIDS virus or creating mice with human immune systems or clear-cutting the Sierras. Of course it wasn't right. But none of that mattered in here. 'No more gloom-and-doom?' he said. 'What about the Cure? And all your black clothes – did you donate them to the vampire club or something?'

'Dad,' she said, and he knew it was all right.

'You walking the dog?' Bill Driscoll's voice, heavy with bass, rose above the general clamor. He should have been a radio announcer, Tierwater was thinking, one of those gonzo morning-drive types. Or, better yet, a TV evangelist. He certainly had the background for it. 'Twice a day like you promised? Because, I'm telling you, she needs it, for her bladder, and I swear I'm not paying the vet bills – '

'Everything okay at school?' Tierwater said. 'At home? You getting along with Andrea?'

Sierra nodded.

'Because you're one lazy-ass bitch, Bunny, you were born lazy, and if I'm stuck in here and you can't get your skinny ass off the couch twice a day – '

'I'm getting out soon, you know – twenty-six more days – and then it's going to be just like it used to be, you and me – '

' – and Andrea.'

'Yeah, and Andrea.' He ducked his head and drew in a breath. 'But I know I've done some things I shouldn't have, and I really should have paid more attention to you, your needs, I mean – I should have put you first – and I'm going to do that as soon as I get out of here. I promise.'

She was watching him now, the gray eyes, the sweet full-moon of her face, hair pulled back in a braid, her hands clasped in her lap. 'You don't have to apologize to me, Dad. I think what you're doing – and Andrea and Teo too – is the greatest thing anybody could do. The only thing.' She glanced up as Bunny Driscoll stifled a sharp sob, then came back to him. 'I think you're a hero.'

(What's the first thing you do when you get out of prison? Scoot your wife over and get behind the wheel of the car. What car? Any car. In my case, it was the new Jeep Laredo Andrea had bought me on the promise of real-estate cash, and the simple prosaic act of driving – of going where the whim takes you, of opening it up on 101 South and watching the hills and the trees roll by and all the law-abiding motorists fall away from you like leaves in a gutter – was the sweetest thing I'd ever known. I hammered it, pedal to the metal all the way, windows down, radio cranked, the sun stuck overhead and the ocean spread out on the right, freshly spanked and blue as a gun barrel. Then it was the restaurant, a real restaurant, with prissy waiters and fish on the menu – and wine, wine in an iced bucket right there at hand. We ate outside, in the sun, then went to a movie, my wife and daughter and I, like real human beings. Finally, it was home, the new house, twelve-month lease, big lawn, pepper trees along the street, isn't this nice. Then bed. And sex.)

But Tierwater had to face a gauntlet of reporters before he could get to the car, minicams whirring, mikes thrust in his face: Mr. Tierwater, Mr. Tierwater, hey, Ty, over here, Ty, *Ty*. Do you think the forests can be saved? How did they treat you in there? What about the spotted owl? Are you planning any new protests? Do you believe in nudism? Vegetarianism? Crystal power? He squeezed his daughter, squeezed his wife, kissed them both for the cameras, and he stood there outside the gates for half an hour giving speeches and pontificating and posing with Teo and the E.F.! Santa Barbara chapter president, famous birdwatchers and nationally known tree-huggers till Andrea whisked him away and he had the car keys in his hand and the car was rolling down the blacktop road to the freeway. 'Tell me,' he said, swinging round to rest his eyes first on his grinning wife and then on his worshipful daughter in the back seat, 'did the Fox ever have it this good?'

No, the answer was no. Because there was no feeling like this, nothing in his vocabulary to express it. He was supercharged with emotion, dancing in his socks, rocking in his seat. Touch the accelerator and watch the car go, hit the brakes and feel it stop. In the morning, he sang in the shower and let the water run till it went cold. The toaster was a miracle, the smell of rye toast, the light in the windows. Every ordinary moment of every ordinary day made him want to cry for the beauty of it. Pushing the start button on the dishwasher, flicking the remote to bring the TV to life, standing under the walnut tree out back and watching the crowned sparrows flit through the branches: these were the expressions of the inestimable richness of his newly anointed life. The microwave made him weep. Beer in a six-pack. The bed-spread.

Still, for all that – for all the exhilaration of those first few days and the steady trickle of interviewers at the door with their mikes and tape recorders and yellow pads, and for all his prison vows about overseeing Sierra's book reports and attending parent/teacher conferences and seeding and mowing and fertilizing and mulching like any other suburban drone – Tierwater was bored right on down to the hems of his socks before the week was out. Or it wasn't just boredom – prison was boring – it was more a restlessness, a feeling of emptiness and impotence, a growing certainty that all this was a charade. The animals were dying, the forests falling. There were scores to be settled.

He didn't say a word to anybody. Just waited till Andrea went off to work the phones at the E.F.! office half a mile up the street and Sierra was safely deposited at school, then rummaged through the garage for the watchcap and face paint, the crowbar, bolt-cutters and wrenches wrapped in black electrical tape to dull the kiss of metal on metal and the flashlight with the red nail polish smeared across the lens. And what were the terms of his parole? To remain within the city limits of Los Angeles, to report to his parole officer once a week, to protest nothing, demonstrate against nothing, abjure all tree-huggers and -spikers, and above all to steer clear of illegal activity of any kind. No extracurricular activities. No nightwork. No monkeywrenching. The judge made that abundantly clear.

Yes. Well, fuck the judge.

Black jeans, black T-shirt, black hiking boots: Tierwater looked like any other middle-aged Angeleno climbing aboard the RTD bus at the end of the block. He set the backpack – black and logoless – on the seat beside him and watched the mini-malls, restaurants, discount houses and tire shops scroll by the crusted windows till Budget Car presented itself amid a field of humped and gleaming automobiles. Inside, he was transformed into Tom Drinkwater, and though he knew it wouldn't wash if he was caught, he handed the man at the counter a Tom Drinkwater Visa card and showed him Tom Drinkwater's California driver's license, replete with a stunned-looking portrait of himself fixed in the lower left-hand corner.

There wasn't much on the radio all the long way up through the Central Valley – country or Mexican, take your pick – but somewhere around Stockton he picked up an oldies channel featuring the hypnotic noodling of Jerry Garcia, followed by an eternal raga of the sort Ravi Shankar used to inflict on audiences in the sixties. That was all right. The guitar climbed the stairs and came back down again, then climbed them, and came down, and climbed them, and the sitar jumped like a nervous bird from branch to branch of a spreading tree. He felt the music – he saw it – and it took him back to a time when he and Jane wore flowered shirts and pants so wide they were like flapping sails, a time when they subscribed to everything and never thought twice about it. Drugs were part of his life then. And protests. Political protests. Flag-burning. Jeering. Painting your face for the sheer hell of it.

There was none of that in what he was doing now. What he was doing now – in this car, on this highway – was the prelude to an act of revenge. It was as simple as that, and he had no illusions about it. He drove with the calm that comes of purpose, sticking to the slow lane except to squeeze past the hurtling caravans of trucks, not daring to push the wheezing crackerbox of a rental car much more than ten miles over the limit: it wasn't worth the risk of getting pulled over. There was no point in having people see his face either, so he stopped only for gas, and when he got gas he picked up a chili-cheese dog or a microwave burrito and a Coke or a cup of coffee, one more anonymous traveler in a whole nation of them. He drove through the high-crowned afternoon and into the evening and the fall of day, and then it was the stars and the headlights until he crossed the Oregon border in a kind of trance in the unsteady light of dawn. His stomach was queasy – all that grease – and the caffeine had turned to sludge in his veins, so he steered his way off the interstate and down a series of increasingly small roads till he found a place where he could pull over and sleep beneath the trees.

It was past four in the afternoon when he woke. He thought of Andrea briefly, and of Sierra. They'd be worried, and in Andrea's case angry – he could hear her voice already, *You idiot, you jackass, what are you thinking? Enough, Ty. Enough already. Let it go.* The voice was in his head, the argument as familiar as any litany, but he was unmoved. He drifted off into the woods, chewing the cold stub of a bean burrito and swilling from a plastic bottle of water. When he was finished with breakfast, he made his ablutions in a stream, relieved himself (properly, with every thought and care to contamination and the stream's drainage), and spent the rest of the daylight hours in a bed of pine boughs, watching the sky.

For long stretches, he thought nothing, but then he was thinking of Chris Mattingly, and the article he'd written about the Tierwaters' venture into aboriginal life. It had made the cover of *Outside* magazine, and it put them on the map, that was for sure. After that, practically every publication in the country, from *People* to the *New York Times* to the *Enquirer,* wanted to know what he and Andrea thought about the rain forest, the holes in the ozone layer, the decline of frogs worldwide, what it felt like to live naked and make love in a hut. The article had run to twelve pages, with photos, and each line added another layer to the myth till the canonization was complete: they were the saints of the Movement, and forget the Fox, forget Abbey and Leopold and Brower and all the rest. Tierwater must have read it twenty times, lingering over the photos as he lay in his bunk in prison, remembering the texture of the rock, the smell of the night air and the taste of water fed on alpine snow. And the cover photo – he could see it now – of him and Andrea from the waist up, their faces reddened and smudged, the sun-bleached ends of her hair blowing across her face, both of them healthy still and sleek, looking like naked rock stars on the cover of *Rolling Stone*. It was a charge. But what, he wondered, would Chris Mattingly think of this, of what was going to come down tonight? Would that be a saintly thing? Would that be worthy of the cover?

He drifted off, and then darkness came, attached to a fine drizzle, and he sat in the car to get out of the wet, listening to the radio and letting his mind go numb. It was too early yet to get down to business – he'd wait till twelve at least, maybe later. He tried to sleep – it was going to be a long night, and a longer day, because he was driving straight through the minute he was done, and he would be sitting right there in the living room in front of the TV when Jimmy Chavez, his parole officer, came round to ask him if he'd heard anything about what had gone down in Oregon last night.

At quarter past twelve, he put the car in gear and followed a snaking series of back roads to Grants Pass. It was nothing to find addresses for Judge Harold P. Duermer and Sheriff Robert R. Hicks – they were both listed in the phone book – and he already knew where the police station was. He drove by the judge's house twice, then parked round the corner, on a street so dark it was like the inside of a cave. The drizzle had turned to a persistent shower by this time, and when he came up the judge's long macadam drive, it shone like a dark river in the light of the gas lamp over the garage door. There was no sound at all, but for the hum of a transformer on the telephone pole overhead: no crickets, no frogs, not the hoot of an owl or the soft *shoosh* of a passing car. Tierwater stuck to the shadows and reconnoitered.

The judge lived well, in a big colonial-style place that stood on the crest of a hill, surrounded by lawns and flowerbeds, and with a swimming pool and clay tennis court out back, and Tierwater didn't begrudge him that. The man was a tool of the machine – why wouldn't he live well? All he had to do was toss a bunch of protestors in the slammer, break up families and terrorize little girls, and somehow, with the good grace of the timber company, convert all that ponderous legal activity into something tangible, the yacht in the harbor, the white Mercedes 500SL, the condo in Aspen and a good month here and there in Cancún or Saint-Moritz, maybe a shopping spree in the Big Apple for Mrs. Justice Duermer herself.

No lights on in the house, no dogs, sleeping or otherwise. Tierwater tried the door at the back of the garage, barely a creak of the hinges, and then he was inside. The pinkish glow of the flashlight revealed three cars, and what was this – a Lexus? Two Lexuses – Lexi – one silver, one black, his and hers. And some sort of sportscar, an old Jaguar, it looked like, big wire wheels, running boards – lovingly, as they say, restored. Imagine that – imagine Judge Duermer, robeless, a porkpie cap pulled down over his fat brow, wedged into the puny leather seat of the roadster, Sunday afternoon, *roaaaaarrrrrr,* hi, judge, and a safe sweet taste of the bohemian life to you too. But Tierwater wasn't there to imagine things, and it took him less than five minutes to locate the cars' crankcases, lovingly tap a few ounces of silicon carbide into each and close the hoods with a click as soft as the beat of a moth's wing.

There were lights on at the police station, some poor drone – Sheets, maybe it was Sheets – putting in his time by the telephone, waiting for the call from the old woman who'd lost her glasses or maybe the one with the raccoon in her kitchen. The town stood still. The rain fell. Tierwater could see his breath steaming in front of his face. He couldn't get at the hoods of the two cruisers parked out front of the place, but they hadn't thought to put locking caps on the gas tanks. It hurt him to have to settle for slashing the tires, jamming the locks with slivers of wood and pouring diatomaceous earth into the gas tanks, but there wasn't much more he could do, short of firebombing the station itself, and he didn't want to alert anybody to what was going down here, especially not Sheriff Bob Hicks. Because Sheriff Bob Hicks (wife, Estelle), of 17 Spruce Lane, was next on the list.

This was where things got tricky. Sheriff Bob Hicks lived outside of town, on a country road fringed with blackly glistening weeds and long-legged shrubs, no other house in sight, rainwater gurgling in the ditches and no place to pull over – at least no place where the car wouldn't be seen if anyone passed by. It was getting late too – quarter past four by Tierwater's watch – and who knew what hour people around here got up to let the cat out, pour a cup of coffee and stare dreaming into the smoke of their first cigarette? Tierwater found the mailbox set out on the road, number 17, the house dark beyond it, and drove on by, looking for a turnout so he could double back, do what he had to do and head back to the bosom of his family. But the road wasn't cooperating. It seemed to get progressively narrower. And darker. And the rain was coming down harder now, raking the headlights in sheets so dense he could barely see the surface of the road.

For a minute he thought about giving it up – just getting out of there and back to the interstate before he got the car stuck in a ditch or wound up getting shot at or thrown in jail. What he was doing wasn't honorable, he knew that, and it wasn't stopping the logging or helping the cause in even the most marginal way – Andrea was right: he should let it go. But he couldn't. What they'd done to him – the sheriff, the judge, Boehringer and Butts (and he'd like to pay them a visit too, but life was short and you couldn't settle every score) – was no different from what Johnny Taradash had done. Or tried to do. Just thinking about it made the blood come up in him: a year in jail, a year listening to Bill Driscoll moan in his sleep, a year torn out of his life like a chapter from a book. And for what? For *what?* When he saw a driveway emerge from the vegetation up on his left, he jerked the wheel and spun the car around, and so what if he took some stupid hick's mailbox with him?

The rain was blinding, absolutely, and where was the damn house anyway? Was that it up there? No. Just another bank of trees. He swiped at the moisture on the inside of the window with an impatient hand, fumbled with the defroster. And then he came around a bend in the road and saw a sight that shrank him right down to nothing: there was Sheriff Bob Hicks' mailbox, all right, illuminated in the thin stream of the headlights, but a long, flat, lucent object had been coughed up out of the night beside it. It might have been a low-slung billboard, a cutout, the fixed reflective side of a shed or trailer, but it wasn't: it was a police cruiser. Sheriff Bob Hicks' police cruiser. And Sheriff Bob Hicks, a long-jawed, white-faced apparition in a floppy hat, was frozen there at the wheel, as if in an overexposed photo.

Tierwater's first impulse was to slam on the brakes, but he resisted it: to stop was to invite disaster. Windshield wipers clapping, defroster roaring, tires spewing cascades of their own, the rental car crept innocuously past the driveway, Tierwater shrinking from the headlights that lit up the front seat like a stage – and would the sheriff be able to see the slashes of greasepaint beneath his eyes, the watchcap clinging to his scalp? Would he recognize him? Was he looking? Did he wear glasses? Were they fogged up? And what was the man doing up at this hour, anyway? Had he gotten a call from the station, *Better get on down here, Chief, some asshole's gone and slashed the tires on two of the squad cars,* was that it?

Sheriff Bob Hicks could have turned either way on that road – he could have backed up the driveway and gone back to bed, for that matter – but he turned right, the headlights of the patrol car shooting off into the night and then swinging round to appear in Tierwater's rearview mirror. Heart in mouth, Tierwater snatched off the watchcap, cranked the window enough to wet it and used the rough acrylic weave to scrub the greasepaint from his face. He was doing, what, thirty, thirty-five miles an hour? Was that too fast? Too slow? Weren't you supposed to drive according to the conditions? The rain crashed down; the headlights closed on him.

For an instant, he thought of running – of flooring it and losing the bastard – but he dismissed the idea as soon as it came into his head. He didn't even know what kind of car he was driving – the cheapest compact, some Japanese piece of crap that wouldn't have outrun an old lady on a bicycle – and besides, nothing had happened yet. There was no reason to think he'd be pulled over. He just had to stay calm, that was all. But here were the headlights looming up in his mirror and then settling in behind him, moving along at the same excruciatingly slow pace that he was. His hands gripped the wheel as if it were the ejection lever of a flaming jet. He tried to project innocence through the set of his shoulders, the back of his head, his ears. He sped up ever so slightly.

The worst thing was Andrea. Or no, Sierra. How was he going to explain this to her? Out of jail a week and a half, and back behind bars already? He hadn't even attended a parent/teacher conference yet. And Chris Mattingly and all the rest of them – what were they going to think? He could see the headlines already, ECO-HERO TARNISHED; E.F.! TIRE-SLASHER; TIERWATER A PETTY VANDAL. Then he had a vision of Lompoc, Judge Duermer, Fred: this time it wouldn't be prison camp. Oh, no: this time it would be a cell on a cellblock, gangs, rape, intimidation, level two at least, maybe worse. Violation of parole, in possession of burglary tools, breaking and entering, destruction of private and public property, use of an alias in the commission of a crime –

But then a miracle happened. Slowly, with all the prudence and slow, safe, peace-officerly care in the world, Sheriff Bob Hicks swung the cruiser out to the left and for the smallest fraction of a moment pulled up even with Tierwater before easing in ahead of him. Through two rain-scrawled side windows and the inter-mediary space of the rain-thick night, Tierwater caught a glimpse of the man himself, the incurious eyes and pale bloated face that was like something unearthed from the ground, the quickest exchange of hazy early-morning looks, and then the sheriff was a pair of taillights receding in the gloom.

Santa Ynez, April 2026

THE FIRST ONE to show up, aside from the county sheriff and the coroner, is a lawyer, and if that isn't emblematic of what we've become, then I don't know what is. He's about the size you think of when you think of regular, with a pillbox of kinky hair set up high against a receding hairline, teeth that look as if they've been filed and a pair of five-hundred-dollar fake-grain vinyl shoes so encrusted with mud he's had to remove them and stand there on the doorstep in his muddy socks. His suit is soaked through. His tie is twisted up under his collar like a hangman's noose. And his briefcase – his briefcase is just a crude clay sculpture, with a long trailing fringe of pondweed. In the confusion of that house, in the shock, horror and trauma following in the wake of Mac's death, there's nobody to answer the door, and while the sheriff and his men are prowling around upstairs and the coroner's people zipping up the body bags, I'm the one who responds to the 'Chariots of Love' theme and swings open the door on the eighteenth repetition of that unforgettable melody. 'Good afternoon,' he says, as if we're standing in the hallway at the county courthouse, 'I'm Randy Bowgler, of Bowgler and Asburger? I represent Jasmine Honeysuckle Rose Pulchris. May I come in?'

Jasmine Honeysuckle Rose: that'd be Mac's third wife, the real-estate heiress, the one with eyes like two cold planets glittering in the night.

I'm looking out over the hill in front of the house, the ambulance and police cruiser stuck up to their frames in the muck of the receding river and the media vans beginning to gather on the horizon like the vanished herds of old. It must be a hundred and fifteen degrees out there. 'I don't think so,' I say.

'I'm here to protect my client's interests, Mr., ah – I didn't catch your name?'

'I already gave at the office,' I tell him.

His lips curl into a tight, litigious smile. 'I'm afraid I'm going to have to insist.'

'Yeah,' I say, and my heart is still jumping at my ribs four hours after the fact, 'well, fuck you too,' and I slam the door in his face.

What's going on here is chaos of the worst and blackest sort. Dandelion, as best we can tell, is back down in the basement with Amaryllis and Buttercup. What he did to Mac is worse, far worse, than anything I'd heard about in rap sessions in prison or seen in the old nature clips of the Serengeti. Mac's insides – heart, liver, lungs, intestines – are the first thing the lion apparently consumed, and then, before Chuy and I could get back up the stairs with the Nitro and the dart gun, he dragged the meatier of the Als to the dumbwaiter and disappeared into the basement with him. The other Al was sprawled across the sofa with one arm bent the wrong way at the elbow and his scalp torn back so the parietal bone showed white beneath it, and both the servants had been swatted down like insects, Zulfikar crumpled in the corner in a dark pool and his wife draped over a chair with her throat torn out. April Wind we found whimpering inside one of the compartments in the sideboard. We helped her out, boarded up the dumbwaiter on all three floors and called 911.

No sooner do I shut the door than the 'Chariots of Love' theme starts up again, and then again, and I'm wondering, how in Christ's name did this ghoul find out already? Did he have a direct hookup to 911? Had he paid somebody off? Was he circling the house on leather wings? No matter. The Nitro is propped up against the wall behind me, and I just pluck it up, aim it letter-high and swing open the door again. I admit it – I'm agitated and maybe not entirely in my right mind, whatever that is. Anyway, I level the thing at him and growl something out of the corner of my mouth and he actually takes a step back, but by now a very wet crew with a minicam is sprinting across the lawn and flashbulbs are popping in the distance, and I figure it's a losing proposition. Down goes the gun. In comes the lawyer.

Mac's death is big news. Not as big maybe as McCartney's or

Garth Brooks', but it's really something. Within the hour, the HDTV screen is showing images of the death scene intercut with clips of Mac at various stages of his career and the shock and disbelief registering on the faces of fans from Buenos Aires to Hyderabad and Martha's Vineyard (now largely under water, by the way). I'm sitting there in the Grunge Room, trying to catch my breath, cops, journalists and lawyers flitting back and forth like flies dive-bombing a plate of custard, when April Wind appears on the big screen across from the bed. She's squinting into the camera not two hundred feet from where I'm sitting, a dazzled look on her face, the dwarf become a giant. Like all Americans, she was born with the ability to talk to a camera. 'It was horrible,' she's saying, 'because we were eating eggs, or we were just about to, and then there's this like roar, and I, I – '

The camera never wavers, April Wind's face revealed in every pixil and particle, a sorrowful face, the face of tragedy and woo-woo gone down in flames, but a voice slips in over her own, lathered with concern: 'You were his last lover, isn't that right?'

Of all the journalists there that afternoon and late into the night – young hotshots, most of them, scud studs and the like – only one of them has been around long enough to take a second look at me. He's maybe fifty, fifty-five. Short, glasses, frizz of a beard gone white around the gills. It's getting dark out by this time, and we're all gathered in the Motown Room – even Chuy – for what I suppose you'd call a press conference, though there's precious little conferring going on. 'You're – ' he sputters, police everywhere, the lions roaring from the basement, film rolling, Andrea and April Wind pinned in the corner with two dozen microphones jabbing at them like the quills of a porcupine (*Erethizon dorsatum*, now endangered throughout its range) – 'you're Tyrone Tierwater, aren't you – the eco-radical?'

My back hurts. My feet. I have a headache. My gums are aching round the cold porcelain of my dental enhancements, I could use a drink and I'm hungry – we never did get those eggs, or anything else for that matter. I wave a hand in deprecation. 'Eco-what?'

'You're him, aren't you?' There are lights everywhere, heads talking, sound bites crackling from every room of the house. 'What was it – twenty years ago? The Cachuma Incident, right?'

The man's a historian, no doubt about it, and right here, right now, in the midst of all this chaos, he takes me back to a dark, pitching lake and a boat that trembled under my feet like a false floor that drops you headlong into the infinite. *The Cachuma Incident*. What can I say? There's no excuse or exculpation for what I did, or tried to do. My daughter was dead and my wife may as well have been, and the names of the animals were on my lips day and night – six billion of us at that point and how many gorillas, chimps, manatees, spotted owls, Amboseli lions?

It was my darkest moment – skull-and-crossbones time, hyena time. I was fighting a war, you understand, and maybe I lost my judgment, if I ever had any. In the company of an FBI agent posing as a disaffected scientist from BioGen and a shit by the name of Sandman (more on him later), I found myself out on those windswept waters with eight big plastic buckets of tetrodotoxin at my feet. The lake was in the Santa Ynez Valley and it constituted the water supply for the city of Santa Barbara. The toxin, the very same concentrated in the liver of the puffer fish – fugu, that is – was produced by the *Alteromas* bacteria, it was twelve hundred and fifty times more deadly than cyanide, and it had been mutated in the lab to adapt itself to fresh water. Or so it appeared, but appearances can be deceiving.

In truth, Sandman and the FBI agent (tattoos, tongue stud, the true look of the transgenetic nerd) had set me up, hoping, I think, to use me to get to the leadership of E.F.!, but by then Andrea and Teo and all the rest of them had turned their backs on me, so it was this or nothing. And when it came right down to it, when it was time to tip the buckets and begin evening the score in favor of the animals, I couldn't do it. Though I'd steeled myself, though I seethed and hated and reminded myself that to be a friend of the earth you have to be an enemy of the people, though Sandman and I had agreed a hundred times that if a baby and an anteater fell in a drainage ditch at the same time the baby would have to be sacrificed, though this was the final solution and I the man chosen to administer it, when it came right down to it, I faltered. I did. Believe me. Give me that much at least.

'Am I right?' The man's face is anxious, blistered, peeled back like a skinned grape. 'You're the one they called the human hyena, aren't you?'

I'm in a chair in the front hallway. I can hear Andrea's cracked, vinegary old lady's voice going on for the hundredth time about Dandelion and how 'he was just suddenly there, as if he appeared out of thin air.' I've never seen so many cops – in plain clothes, in blue, in the dun of the highway patrol. Down in the basement, sniffing warily, is a SWAT team from San Luis Obispo, ready to do what needs to be done. My heart is broken – or, no, it's smashed, laid out on the chopping block and beaten with a mallet till all the fibers have been reduced to paste. Mac is gone. And the animals are next in line. I don't bother to answer.

'But what are you doing here?' the man says, and he's got a microphone too, a slim black thing like the barrel of a gun pointing at my face. 'Do you know Maclovio Pulchris? Or did you, I mean?'

I'm thinking about that, about Mac and how he gave me a break when I got out of prison for the last time – me, a nobody, one of five or six lackeys charged with looking after the Vietnamese pot-bellied pigs, the emus, horses and dogs, no job more menial on the whole estate. But it was a beginning, and I was glad for it. And it wasn't long before he singled me out and we began to talk – about the pigs and their diet at first, but then about other things too, far-ranging things like the weather and the death of the planet and the possibility of God and who I really was – my name wasn't Tom Drinkwater, was it? He recognized me. Behind those shades and eel whips and all the rest, Mac went deeper than you might think. He'd known all along. Known who I was and taken a chance. After that, well, the others fell by the wayside, all except for Chuy, that is, and Mac and I hatched our scheme to do what nature and the zoos were incapable of – and we almost succeeded too. But, of course, to say 'almost' is meaningless. We could have succeeded, let's put it that way – if things had been different. Vastly different.

The first of a series of muffled shots sounds from deep in the bowels of the house. 'Were you here when he died? Can you tell me anything about that, what it was like, I mean?'

'Because of the storms,' Andrea is saying from the far side of the room, a hint of exasperation in her voice, 'because of the flooding –'

And Chuy, fencing with his own circle of microphones: 'No, man, I'm *corriendo,* you know, up out of *el garaje,* and Dandy, he's *muy malo* – '

Pop. Pop. Pop-pop. That's what I'm hearing, but what I'm seeing is dead lions, dead peccaries, jackals, vultures, living flesh converted to so much furred and feathered meat, extinction in a wheelbarrow.

'There are wild animals in the house,' the reporter is saying, and he's trying to work a little moral outrage into his voice, 'living right here in the rooms and wandering the halls. Isn't that right?'

Pop. Pop-pop. I nod my head. Wearily.

The sheen of his glasses, the thrust of the mike. 'Maybe you can explain it for me, because I think I'm missing something here – isn't that dangerous?'

After the cops, after the scribblers and the talking heads, after the lawyers, bereaved fans, curiosity seekers and relic peddlers, the book editors start dribbling in from New York, Berlin, Los Andiegoles. Mac's been buried three days when the first of them shows up (the funeral was in Detroit, televised of course, and it was built around a six-hour memorial concert featuring pop stars of the past, distant past and present hammering out ensemble renditions of Mac's big hits while legions of weeping fans swayed in place and held up candles and cigarette lighters in a blaze so prodigious it must have added half a degree to the average temperature of the globe). Our position here – mine, Andrea's, April Wind's, Chuy's, the surviving animals' – is tenuous, to say the least. Mac died intestate, and the lawyers representing his four wives, real and putative mistresses, children legitimate and il-, not to mention the various record companies that claim rights in various songs and recordings, are fighting a battle royal over his estate. I have no claim on anything. I don't even have an income. Or health care. The animals – we've still got a few peccaries left, a pair of honey badgers, three Egyptian vultures and Petunia – have even less.

What I'm trying to say is, I'm scared – rudderless, incomeless, Social Security–less and soon to be homeless too, no doubt – and I'm ready to welcome this editor with open arms (not to be mercenary about it, but if there's money in it I'll do an as-told-to account of my years with Mac and my life as a monkeywrencher and push April Wind's hagiography of Sierra on him too). And who is he? Ronnie Bott, of Bertelsmann West, the biggest – the only – publishing house in New York. He comes the way of Randy Bowgler and the rest of the parade of lawyers, journalists and deranged fans (several of whom are even now peering in at the windows, despite the efforts of the rent-a-cop outfit Mac's first wife's lawyer hired to keep them at bay): across the all-but-dried-up Pulchris River, currently breached by a crude bridge of whorled imitation-plywood slabs laid out in the mud. It's 9:00 a.m. and a hundred and ten degrees, with a screaming wind out of the southeast, when the 'Chariots of Love' theme re-echoes through the house. Andrea's in bed, of course, and April Wind, who's arranged this whole thing, is locked in her room doing her Tantric exercises, so it's Ty Tierwater, aching knees and all, to the door again.

What do I do? I fix the man a tall glass of iced tea and settle him down in the Motown Room, just under the glowing electronic portrait of the Four Tops. He looks to be no more than fourteen (though I know he must be older), sporting one of the wide-collared shirts and patterned vests that seem to have come back into fashion, along with the bell-bottoms and high-heeled boots. As for the rest: long hair, no hint of musculature or even a beard, a spatter of what could only be acne clinging to his right cheek. I ease into the chair across from him, clutching my own sweating glass of iced tea, and give him a look of wisdom and ready access.

'So,' he says, shifting in his seat and crossing, then uncrossing, his legs, 'you ran Maclovio Pulchris' private menagerie, is that right?'

'Ten years of shoveling shit,' I say, and look down at the wedge of lemon floating round the rim of my glass.

'You were in charge of the lions, then?'

'That's right. They required plenty of shit-shoveling too. And meat. Of course, with the world the way it is, it was no easy thing keeping them fed and reasonably healthy, and if it wasn't for the permanent fucking El Niño we've got going here they'd be' – and here I have to pause to deal with a sudden constriction in the back of my throat that just about chokes off my windpipe – 'they'd be fine still. And so would Mac.'

The editor – what was his name?, because I've lost it – he just nods.

'You know who I am,' I say, 'right?'

He nods again.

I lean into the platform of my bony old man's knees and give him my cagiest look, and I can see myself in shadowy reflection in the sheen of Marvin Gaye's portrait, hanging opposite. I look like a Yankee horse-trader, a used-car salesman – or, worse, a funda-mentalist preacher. 'You want a book, I'll give you a book. Not just about Mac or my daughter, but about me and what I've been through trying to save this woebegone planet and the, the' – there it is again, the involuntary contraction at the back of my throat – 'the animals.' And here I have to pause a minute to collect myself. My heart is heavy. My mind is numb. There's moisture gathering in the desiccated corners of my old man's eyes and I have to pinch it away with two trembling fingers.

'That's what we were trying to do here, Mac and me,' I say, and I'm pleading with him, I can't help myself, 'save the animals. It's too late for the earth. Or for us. But the animals, if only we can keep them from extinction until we're gone – they'll adapt, they will, and something new will come up in our place. That's our hope. Our only hope.'

I guess by this point I've got to my feet and I'm trying to marshal my thoughts to tell him about extinction, about how we're at the very end of the sixth great extinction to hit this planet, caused by us, by man, by progress, and how speciation will occur after we're gone, an explosion of new forms springing up to fill all the vacated niches, a transformation like nothing we've known since the Cambrian explosion of five hundred seventy million years ago, but he's not listening. It's 9:15 a.m., he's come all the way from New York and he's stifling a yawn on Mac's couch beneath the undulating portrait of the Four Tops in the Motown Room. He doesn't want to hear about the environment – the environment is all indoors now anyway, right on down to the domed fields that produce the arugula for his salads and the four-walled space he calls home. The environment is a bore. And nobody wants to read about it – nobody wants to hear about it – and, for all April Wind's machinations (and Andrea's), nobody wants to hear about Sierra either. Or me. No, what they want – and it comes to me with a clarity I can only attribute to the neurobooster cap I popped earlier this morning – what they want is to know if the weather will ever go back to normal and what Maclovio Pulchris' sex life was like.

And here, right on cue, is tiny, cute little not-so-young April Wind, baby-stepping across the room like some idol of the Ituri pygmies, to tell all.

If Ronnie Bott and Bertelsmann West don't give two shits about my daughter and the sacrifices she made or the world beyond their computer screens, I do, I still do, and I can't help myself. Call it the intransigence of age. Call it nostalgia. But after skirting April Wind for five months and resenting the hell out of her wheedling questions and the whole idea of a Sierra Tierwater biography, now that it's gone I want it back more desperately than I wanted it to disappear in the first place. Does that make sense? All right, call it senility, then. Call it hope, resentment, despair, call it anything you like, but I want to testify, and I will, even if I have to slip into April Wind's room, filch the manuscript and finish the thing myself.

Sierra gave up everything for an ideal, and if that isn't the very definition of heroism I don't know what is. Once she was up in her tree, that was it, her life was over. She never had children, never had a house, a pet, an apartment even, she never again went shopping, bought something on impulse, watched TV or a movie, never had a friend or a lover. She was separated from her father by six hundred and thirteen horizontal miles and one hundred and eighty vertical feet, and she might as well have been in prison too. For three years, through the refrigerated winter and the kiln that was summer, she never bathed. Her clothes stank, her skin burned, she ate rice and vegetables six days a week and lentil soup on Sundays. She squatted over a bucket to move her bowels. Her fingers and toes felt as if they were going to fall off, her back ached worse than her father's, she had a cavity in one of her upper molars and it threatened to bore right through her head. She never went to Paris. Never went to grad school. Never stretched out on a couch in front of a fire and listened to the rain on the roof.

Coast Lumber tried to ignore her at first, but after El Niño failed to dislodge her, she became an embarrassment – and, worse, a liability. Because the longer she held out, the more people began to take notice. No one had been up a tree more than twenty days before Sierra climbed up into Artemis, and as she reached the one-month mark the press started to converge on her dwindling grove in the Headwaters Forest. Teo, never one to miss an opportunity, led them to the base of the tree himself, and even helped hoist some of the hardier ones up to the lower platform (she had two by then, one at a hundred feet, which she used for interviews and cooking; the other at one eighty, which was her private space, for meditation and sleep). Andrea gave her a cell phone too, and by the end of the second month, she was spending two or three hours a day on it, chatting with her father and stepmother sometimes, sure, but mainly giving interviews, educating the public, throwing down a gauntlet in the duff.

The other two tree-sitters – a skinny girl with a buzz cut and a sad-eyed, bearded nineteen-year-old known only as Leaf, each perched in a neighboring grove – had given up after the first week of unappeasable rain and fifty-mile-per-hour gusts, and Coast Lumber, I'm sure, felt vindicated. Sit on your hands, that was their policy. Avoid force. Squelch bad press before it can poke its ugly head out of its hole and bite you in the foot. But my daughter was something they hadn't reckoned with. She wasn't your ordinary body-piercing neo-hippie college kid chanting slogans and chaining herself to the bumpers of corporate town-cars on her summer vacation, she was a shining symbol high up in the tower of her tree, she was immovable, unshakable, Joan of Arc leading her troops into battle, with nothing to lose but the bones of her flesh. They had to get rid of her. They had no choice.

Pick a morning, midway through the second month. Seven a.m. A light rain falling with the slow, shifting rhythm of the infinite, the serried trees, the sky so close it seems illuminated from within. Sierra is asleep. Encased in her thermals, wrapped in her mummy bag, stretched out on her insulated mat beneath the roof of her Popsicle-orange tent on her cramped wooden platform one hundred and eighty feet above the ground. The forest breathes in and out. A marbled murrelet perches on a branch fifty feet below her. She's dreaming of flying. Not of falling – that's a dream she refuses to entertain up here in a bed this high above the earth, even in her unconscious – but of sprouting wings and diving off the platform to swoop low over the lumber mill and then rise up aloft until the forest falls away and then the hills and even the ocean, higher and higher until she's dodging satellites in the glittering metallic bands of their orbits and can gaze down on the earth unobstructed. The blue planet. It's there in her half-waking mind, right there behind her eyelids, sustained in nothing but the cold black reaches, when, suddenly, the platform shudders.

She wakes. Looks through the aperture at the south end of her tent. And sees a hand, a human hand, tensed there on the corner of the platform like a bird-eating spider hatched in the forests of the Amazon. She's dreaming. Surely she's still dreaming, asleep and awake at the same time. There's a grunt, and then another hand appears – and in the next instant a head pops into view, presumptive eyes, the sliver of a mouth, a face framed in a beard the color of used coffee grounds. It is a face of insinuation, and it belongs to Climber Deke, a twenty-eight-year-old employee of Coast Lumber who specializes in ascending trees and escorting trespassers to the ground, where they can be duly arrested and charged.

One hundred and eighty feet above the ground. From that height, looking down, it might as well be three hundred feet. People are the size of puppets, the squirrels and chipmunks rocketing through the duff all but invisible, downed branches, manzanita bushes and boulders like the pattern in a tribal carpet. Sierra disdains ropes, harnesses or any other sort of safety devices. She goes barefoot, the better to grip the bark, and she relies on Artemis – her tree, the spirit of her tree – to sustain her. 'Who – ?' she says, and can't get the rest of it out.

He's got a knee on the platform now, and his eyes have never left hers, no diffidence here, no higher feelings about slipping into a girl's bedroom while she sleeps or invading a stranger's space. And the thing is, he's not bad-looking: every hair in place, the beard neatly clipped, the sliver of a mouth widening in a smile, the eyes friendly now and warm. 'Good morning, Sierra,' he says, and she likes his voice too, wondering if he isn't one of the new support people from E.F.! or maybe a truly intrepid journalist, but then, in the same moment, she's annoyed. They know she doesn't give interviews this early – and they should know enough to call first, too. Her hair is a disaster. She claps a knit cap over it, sits up and kicks her legs out of the sleeping bag. And Climber Deke? He's crouched at the end of her platform in his spiked shoes – six-by-eight, that's all she's got here, two sheets of plywood, and he's halving her space, she can feel the weight of him, can feel her platform adjusting itself to accommodate him. 'You know who I am?'

Under the orange canopy, her feet bare and already cold, sweats and a parka and thermals on underneath. Is this some sort of quiz, is that what it is? She looks into his eyes and watches them go cold, even though he's smiling still. 'No,' she says, her breath hanging there as if the single syllable were concrete. Everything is wet. And slick. It can't be much more than forty degrees.

He's wearing a flannel shirt, wet with sweat or the rain or a combination of the two, jeans, a thermal T-shirt the color of dried blood visible at his open collar, some sort of elaborate tech-pro watch, and suspenders – red suspenders. 'My name's Deke,' he says, 'Climber Deke is what they call me, actually,' and his smile has become a grin, as if this were the world's richest joke. She knows who he is. Now she knows. The suspenders would have told her if he hadn't. 'I'm here to bring you down. And we can do it the easy way – the civilized way – or we can get rough, if that's how you want it. But you're coming down out of this tree, little lady, and you're coming down now.' He pauses to shift his weight to his knees and the platform trembles. 'And don't look to your friends for help, because we just happened to detain and arrest three of them on their way in here from the road this morning – trespassing, that's the charge – and I'm afraid I had to dismantle your lower platform, the one with all the food and your camp stove? Yeah, honey, you'd just starve up here anyways, so why don't you just dump what you want to take over the side here and we'll be on our way.'

'Okay,' she says – that's what my daughter says, 'okay' – and her voice is so soft he can barely hear her. But he nods – she really hasn't got any choice, she's breaking the law up here and he'd strap her to his back if it came to that, and handcuff her too – and settles down on his flanks to give her time to bring down the tent and roll up her sleeping bag and get rid of the damned New Age hippie mural of a butterfly she's painted on a piece of canvas as if this were a walkup on Ashbury or something. Sierra crawls out of the tent – six by eight – and rises to her feet so that she's standing over him, just inches away from his crossed ankles, and she makes as if to loosen the cord at this end of the tent.

Makes as if. That distracts him a moment – he's in command here, and who is she but a slim moon-faced young woman with a braid of a hair like a hawser and dirty feet and clothes that stink – and that moment is all she needs. Before he lets out a breath and breathes in again, she's gone. In a single motion, she grips the branch above her and flips herself up like a an acrobat, and then, her feet gripping the slick, corrugated bark, she climbs high up into the crown of the tree, even as he struggles up after her, and there are no safety lines here, not for her or for him. 'Come back here, you little bitch!' he shouts, digging his spikes in, thrusting upward. His reward is a faceful of redwood bark, threads and splinters kicked up by her feet and sifting down into his eyes, his nostrils, his mouth.

Climber Deke is a lumberman. A timber person. He's agile and muscular and cocksure. If she wants to play, he'll play. She goes higher. So does he. And what's she going to do – ultimately? Sprout wings and fly away?

He doesn't know my daughter. She finds a limb and she goes out on it. And when he gets to that limb and he's facing her over a gap of maybe ten feet or so, he stops. Redwood tends to shear. The trees are forever dropping branches as the crowns rise higher and the lower limbs become expendable. The limb Sierra is crouched on won't support two people – in fact, from Climber Deke's perspective, it doesn't look as if it'll support one much longer. And what does he say, face to face with my daughter, two hundred feet above the ground? 'You cunt,' that's what he says. 'You tree-hugging cunt.'

'Go ahead,' she says, 'curse all you want.' The rain has picked up now. Far below them a pileated woodpecker (*Dryocopus pileatus*) flits through layers of light, its wings extended and then drawn down and up again with an audible snap of its crisp black feathers.

'But even if there were fifty of you, you couldn't get me down from this tree.'

The rain has picked up now, the needles letting go of it, the rough recessed bark a conduit for a thousand miniature rills and cascades. The moisture flattens Climber Deke's hair, clings in droplets to the pelage of his face. He curses again, his voice flat and hard.

'Fifty of you,' my daughter spits. 'I'd rather die up here than have some pathetic gutless bastard like you even touch me.'

'Then die,' he says. 'Die. Because we're going to cut this tree whether you're in it or not.'

Our eviction notice comes within the week. We – Andrea, April Wind, Chuy, the animals and I, that is – are to vacate the premises in thirty days. The interested parties and their platoons of lawyers have agreed on a conservator, and the conservator wants us and our menagerie out, 'in order to prevent further damage to the property and assets of Melisma House, Santa Ynez, California.' Melisma House. I didn't even know the place had a name. Certainly Mac never used it – he just called it 'the Ranch,' if he called it anything. But there it is: it's got a name, this place, and we're no longer welcome in it.

I'm in possession of this information because I'm the one standing in the yard risking heat stroke in hundred-and-ten-degree heat when the messenger arrives (yes, messenger: they hand-deliver the thing as if it's a subpoena). It's just past eleven in the morning, the sun has never in this lifetime been anywhere but directly overhead, and Chuy and I, incurable fools and optimistic pessimists that we are, are trying to construct cages for the honey badgers, Petunia and the peccaries out of the flotsam left along the banks of the now officially dry Pulchris River. 'Yo!' a voice cries out, and here's one of the young-young in a suit of clothes the size and color of a life raft (very hip, I'm told), with one of those haircuts that eliminate the need of a face. 'Yo,' he repeats. 'You Tierwater?'

I am. And I shake out my glasses and read the notice in silence while Chuy wrestles with a twenty-foot strip of artificial wood (think plastic, resins and the pulverized remains of shredded tires) that used to grace the façade of the condos across the way. This is the final blow, the last nail in the coffin of my useless life on this useless planet, but I'd be a liar if I said I wasn't expecting it. Still, it strikes fear in my heart – fear of inanition, the uncertain future and the inevitable end. I'm lost. I'm hurt. I've got no income and no place to go and my only remaining ambition at this juncture is to be one of the old-old. *Andrea,* I think, *Andrea'll know what to do,* and then I'm following my feet across the bleached yard with its browning devil grass and the twisted, gummy clots of flesh that used to be walking catfish scattered round like dark pellets thrown down out of an angry sky. A mutant lizard (two heads, one foot) slithers under a rock to escape my shadow. My throat is dry. 'Mr. Ty,' Chuy calls, 'where you are going?' And what do I say, what do I croak like a parched old turkey cock on his way to the chopping block? 'Be back in a minute.'

Andrea is stretched out supine on the bed in the Grunge Room, naked. And sweating. She looks good, very good, especially in those places where the sun hasn't had much of a chance to wreak havoc with her epidermis, and for the briefest fraction of a second I'm wondering when we last had sex – or made love, as we used to say – and then I'm waving the eviction notice in her face.

She won't even look at it. 'The heat,' she says. 'This is worse than Arizona. Be a sweetheart, will you, Ty, and go get me something cold to drink – a Diet Coke, maybe? With lots of ice?'

What am I supposed to say: Sure, honeybun. Want me to give you a sponge bath too? Rub your feet with alcohol? I don't know, because this is not an ideal relationship and this is not an ideal planet and we don't live in a sitcom reality. Check that: maybe we do – but this has got to be the sit- part of it, because it's very far from funny. I wave the notice till it generates the least part of a cooling draft and she murmurs, 'Oh, that feels good, that's sweet, don't stop – '

'It's an eviction notice,' I say, nothing in my voice at all. 'We have to be out in thirty days.'

Andrea sits up, and that's a shame, because her breasts, which had fanned out fetchingly across her rib cage as she lay there sweating atop the sheets, now have no choice but to respond to gravity and show their age. She snatches the notice from my hand, swings round to bend to the page (no glasses for her, reading or otherwise – radial keratotomy corrected her to 20/10 in her left eye, 20/20 in the right, and don't think she doesn't lord it over me).

When she turns back round, she lets the notice fall to the floor and gives me a long look, as if she's deciding something. 'I know where we can go,' she says finally, and the plural pronoun makes my heart leap up: sure, and we're in this together, aren't we?

'Where?'

'Ratchiss' cabin.'

It takes me a minute. 'Isn't he dead?' (The question is strictly rhetorical – or maybe strategic. Ratchiss has in fact been dead for twenty-odd years, a victim of nature and his own apostasy. It seems he'd gone back to hunting finally, having given up on everything else after the meteorological dislocations at the turn of the century. Why bother, that was his thinking, and he got it in his head that he was going to go down in history as the agent of extinction of a given species, one that was barely hanging on by a thread. He chose the California condor, of which there were then a hundred and ten individuals extant, some fifty of those released into the wild from a captive breeding program at the soon-to-be-defunct L.A. Zoo. The way I heard it was that he'd managed to hit two of them as they wheeled overhead in the remote hills of the Sespe Preserve, and he was reloading for a shot at yet another when one of the perforated birds came hurtling down out of the sky, purely dead and extinguished, and hit him in the back of the head with all the force of a soggy beach umbrella dropped from a cliff. He never regained consciousness.)

She purses her lips, gives me the look that used to burn holes in rednecks, polluters and their shills. 'Yes,' she says, 'he's dead. But his cabin isn't.'

'Well, we can't just . . . Who lives there now?'

She's staring off into the distance, no doubt individuating each strand of Kurt Cobain's hair with her surgically enhanced vision. 'Nobody. He left the place to E.F.!, to us, and last I checked, there was nobody there.'

'But we can't just move in, can we?'

'You got a better plan?'

'What about money, food? We can't live on pine needles and duff. I haven't got more than fifteen hundred bucks in the bank – if the bank's even still there.'

And here comes her smile, rich and blooming right up there at the focal point of her naked young-old lady's body. 'We've been selling things,' she says, 'April and me.'

I'm slow. I admit it. Slow and confused and old. 'What things?'

The smile blooms till it begins to lose its petals and she glances away before bringing her eyes back to mine. 'Oh, I don't know,' she says, and she nods in the direction of Kurt Cobain's locks without pulling her eyes back – 'call them relics.'

The temperature must have gone up another five degrees by the time I get back out to Chuy. The heat is like a fist – a pair of fists – boom-boom, hitting me in the chest and pelvis till I can barely lift my feet, and let me tell you, the wind is no help. It's only blowing at about twenty miles per hour, nothing compared with what's coming in the next few months, as the season heats up and the winds suck in off the desert, but still the ground is in constant motion, dust devils everywhere, scorched grains of windborne detritus clogging my nostrils and stinging the back of my throat, all the tattered trees throwing their rags first this way, then the other. Normally I'd be wearing a gauze mask this time of year, but after the *mucosa* fiasco I just can't stand the idea of having anything clamped over my mouth again (except maybe Andrea's sweet, supple young-old lips, and then only once a week, at best), so I just clench my face, squint my eyes and stagger on.

Chuy looks as if he's been slow-cooked on a rotisserie. His skin is prickled, his color bad, his clothes are so shiny with sweat they might have been dredged in olive oil. He's managed to set four posts in concrete, one at each corner of the pen he can envision in the damaged runnels of his mind, yet he's having trouble with the salvaged board he means to nail to them. Or not the board, actually, but the hammer and nails. Each time he steadies the hammer, the nail slips through his fingers, and when he finally gets the nail in position, the hammer fails him. It's the Dursban. I'm no physiologist, but it seems that when he exerts himself too much –

when he sweats, in particular – the nerve cells start to misfire all over again. His eyes are spinning in their sockets and his fingers playing an arpeggio on a single three-inch nail when I lay a hand on his shoulder. 'Forget it, Chuy,' I tell him.

The nail is suddenly too hot to handle, the hammer even hotter, and he drops them both in the dust at his feet. 'Forget it?' he echoes, squinting up at me from his crouch.

I'm not even looking at him, just staring out over the burning landscape, the regular dull thump of reconstruction echoing across the hill from the tumbledown condos, the wind kicking up its miniature cyclones, no animate thing visible, not even a bird. I'm thinking of the dead lions (the carcasses disappeared, and I wonder which of the SWAT-team cowboys has a lion skin draped over his couch), and I'm thinking of Mac and how he wanted to do something for all the ugly animals out there, the ones nobody could love, and I'm thinking of my own eternally deluded self, just out of prison and imagining there was something I could do, something to accomplish, even at my age. 'We're all done here,' I say. 'It's over.'

The next day, at lunch, April Wind is heroically squirrelly. Andrea and I are eating ancient beef from Mac's freezers, along with a medley of steamed vegetables and reconstituted potatoes au gratin, and washing it down with a '92 Bordeaux that's as rich and thick as syrup and with a bouquet as heady as what God might have served Adam that first night in the garden. It's good stuff. Believe me. April Wind, wrinkling her nose at the beef, pushes the vegetables around on her plate the way Sierra used to do when she was a child, and after refilling her glass twice, announces, 'It's been fun.'

I give Andrea a look, but Andrea's look tells me she already knows what's coming. In detail.

'I just wanted to say thank you, Ty,' April Wind says, homing in on the little purse of her mouth with a knuckle of steamed cauliflower, only to have it drop unerringly into her wineglass. The wine reacts by dribbling down the stem of the glass, an ominous red stain spreading across the tablecloth as she finishes her thought: 'For everything. I mean Mac, and all. And the earth too – for loving the earth. And the animals.'

She's leaving, that's what all this means. All right, fine. We've got twenty-nine days to make other arrangements, and the conservator – a skinny, evil woman in a black tube of a dress that looks as if she found it in the back of a surf shop – has already got a dozen people methodically working their way through the house, cataloguing Mac's vast holdings of memorabilia, jewelry, artwork, furniture and Les Paul guitars. I'm relieved, I am. And I don't say a word.

April Wind fishes the cauliflower out of her wine, plops it in her mouth and begins tapping idly at the rim of her wineglass with the dull blade of her butter knife. The wine stain has settled into a definitive shape, something recognizable, like the face of Jesus revealed or Picasso's *Head of a Woman Weeping,* but I can't say what it is. 'I'm going to New York,' she says, giddy with the idea of it, 'with Ronnie. He's sending a car for me at one.' A pause. 'I'm going to meet my co-writer, you know, like the as-told-to guy who did the book on Gywneth Paltrow? And I'm going to be on the *Wes Starkey Show* and everything – '

I don't know whether to congratulate her or commiserate with her, so I just nod, sip my wine and wonder what it is about this moment that makes me feel old beyond any Baby Boomer's most distant hope or expectation.

But that's that. Goodbye to April Wind, and then comes an evening when the evil woman in the tube dress and her cataloguers are tucked safely away in their beds at the Big Ranchito Motel in Buellton, and Andrea and I, by mutual consent, begin to load up the Olfputt while the sun festers on the horizon and Chuy backs the pimento-red Dodge Viper out of the garage with the fifteen hundred dollars cash I gave him tucked deep in the pocket of his blue jeans. (I gave him the Viper too. '¿*Qué estás diciendo?*' he said, his eyes chasing each other like bugs round his face. 'You say this car is mine?' I signed the registration over to him, imitating Mac's EKG scrawl as best I could. 'Go ahead,' I said. 'You've earned it.')

Andrea didn't have a whole lot with her when she showed up on my doorstep back in November – cosmetics, Indian jewelry, a selection of halter tops and clingy dresses calculated to drive males in the young-old range into a fever of sexual nostalgia – and she doesn't have much more now. What she does have, though, is a healthy selection of Maclovio Pulchris memorabilia, all of it neatly folded away before the lawyers descended and the conservator opened up shop. This we load into the back of the Olfputt, along with the raggedy odds and ends of mine that had survived the inundation of the guesthouse and the ensuing months of rot. We work without talking, work like a team, instinctively, each looking out for the other, and we think to take along a selection of venerable meats in a big cooler and as much fine wine as we can reasonably cram in under the seats (no more *sake* for me, local or otherwise). Is what we're doing strictly legitimate – or even legal? Of course not. But Mac, I like to think, would have no objections. I gave him ten years without complaint, after all, longer by far than any of his wives.

The car is packed. The keys to the house are in my hand. There's one more thing: the animals. I'd determined, the minute that notice of eviction found itself into my hand, to set them free. It didn't matter a damn anymore, and nothing was ever going to get better. Two honey badgers, one male, one female. Where would they go, what would they do? In times gone by, they were native to Africa and India, fierce omnivores that fed on everything from snakes to insects to rats, tubers, fruit and (yes) honey, but the whole world is Africa now, and India, Bloomington, Calcutta and the Bronx, all wrapped in one. The megafauna are gone, the habitat is shrunk to zero, practically no animals left anywhere but for the R–species and the exotics. So why not? Let them go and hope for the best.

I'm standing well back from the cage, with the Nitro cradled under one arm, when I pull the trip wire Chuy rigged up and let them go. They can be irredeemably nasty, going directly for their adversary's sexual organs in any dispute or confrontation, and I suppose I feel a slight twinge about unleashing them on the condos and the put-upon population of Sakapathians and all the rest eking out a living there, but ultimately, as Andrea and I watch their slinking white-crowned forms make their way across the open ground and into the dead brush along the dried-up watercourse, I feel nothing but relief. Maybe they'll find the living easy, feasting on rats and opossums – maybe they'll breed and a whole new subspecies will spring up, *Mellivora capensis pulchrisia*.

The peccaries are easy. They'd once been native to the South-west in any case, and all I have to do is open three doors – the one in the bowling alley, two in the lower hall – and watch them snort off into the fading light until they're no more strange or un-expected than the dust and rocks and mesquite itself. And the Egyptian vultures – they're purely a pleasure. These are the birds, by the way, that used to be featured in the old nature films, cream white with ratty black trailing feathers and hooked yellow beaks, the ones that would drop rocks on ostrich eggs in order to get through the tough outer tegument – when there were ostriches, that is. I hood them individually and make use of a leather gauntlet one of Mac's Saudi Arabian friends left behind years ago. Then we're out on the lawn – or where the lawn will be when the irrepressible landscape architect gets himself back in business.

The heat has died down into the eighties. Everything smells of life. The birds grip my arm and sit still as statues, and then, one by one, off come the hoods, and they lift into the air with a furious beating of their shabby wings. For a long while, we watch them climb into the sky, the night settling in behind them while a deep stippled cracked egg of a sunset glows luminously over the hills and the hint of a breeze finds its way in off the sea.

That leaves Petunia.

'I can't do it,' I say. 'I just can't.'

Andrea considers this as we stand there in the drive, the lights of the house glowing softly behind us. There is no sound, nothing, not the roar of an engine or the wail of a distant siren, and all at once a solitary cricket, incurable optimist, starts up with a creaking, teetering song all his own. She touches me then, her fingers gently stroking the sagging, tired flesh of my forearm and the raised reminder there of my thirty-two stitches and all the wounds I never knew I'd sustained.

She understands. Andrea, my wife of a thousand years ago, and my wife now. Her voice is soft. She says, 'Why don't we take her with us?'

Los Angeles, September 1993/ Scotia, December 1997

TIERWATER CAME HOME shaken from his Oregon adventure, and for a good long while thereafter – nearly two years – he lived the life of a model citizen, exemplary father and devoted husband. Or at least he tried to. Tried hard. He didn't work, not at anything so ordinary or tedious as a job – the only thing he was qualified for was running antiquated shopping centers into the ground, and there wasn't much call for that in southern California, where all the maxi- and mini-malls seemed to have been built in the last ten minutes – and his father's money, the money Andrea and Teo had squeezed out of the stone that had been hanging round his neck all these years, was plenty enough to last for a good long time to come. So what he did was throw himself headlong into suburban life, though suburban life was the enemy of everything he hoped to achieve as an environmentalist, but never mind that: it was safe. And it provided a cocoon for Sierra. She was what mattered now, and what she needed was a regular father, a suntanned grinning uncomplicated burger-flipping dad greeting her at the door and puzzling over her geometry problems after dinner, not some incarcerated hero.

Still, for all that, the days seemed to go on forever. Andrea was at work, knocking down eighty-five thousand dollars a year as a member of E.F.!'s board of directors, and Sierra was at school, maneuvering her way out of the Goth crowd and into the inchoate grip of the makeupless neo-hippie vegan earth-saving contingent. So what did Tierwater do, apart from becoming an inveterate house husband, deviser of three-course meals and underassistant coach of Sierra's rec-league soccer team? He gardened. Or landscaped, actually.

The place was a rental, yes, but they had an option to buy, and Tierwater would have gone ahead with his planting, mulching, digging and trenching in any case – it was a compulsion, or it became one. The house was a classic sprawling ranch dating from the late forties and sitting on a full acre in a decidedly upscale neighborhood. The problem was that all the plantings – pittosporum, wisteria, crepe myrtle, cycad, banks of impatiens, ivy geranium and vinca – were artificial, nonnative, wasteful of water and destructive of the environment. He tore them out. Tore out everything, reducing stem, branch and bole to fragments in a roaring wood-chipper, and began replanting with natives. In the back of the house he planted sycamore, walnut and valley oak, and on the west-facing slope beyond that he put in ceanothus, redshanks, Catalina cherry and big stabbing swaths of yucca. He was equally decisive with the pool. He couldn't live with it – it was as simple as that. There it was, artificially shimmering in the sun, devouring electricity, chemicals, water piped all the way down from the Sacramento and Colorado Rivers. It was obscene, that's what it was. And before the first two months of his tenure were out, and despite Andrea's objections, he'd fired the pool man, drained off the top three feet of water and tossed rocks and dirt and debris into the basin until he'd created a marsh where waterfowl could frolic side by side with the red-legged frog and the common toad.

The next-door neighbor – Roger something or other; Tierwater never did catch the man's surname – questioned the wisdom of this. Roger was an investment broker, and he wore long-sleeved pinstriped shirts even while pruning his roses or overwatering his lawn with a snaking green garden hose. 'It'll breed mosquitoes,' he opined one afternoon, thrusting the stalk of his neck over the redwood fence that separated their yards.

Tierwater had already stocked the pond with mosquito fish (*Gambusia affinis holbrooki*), but he didn't tell Roger that. 'Better than suburban drones,' he said.

The front lawn came up in strips, and where unquenchable grass had been, he created a xeroscape of native plants, and, like any good and true denizen of suburbia, told the cavilers among his neighbors to go fuck themselves. He felt good. Self-righteous. He was doing his part to restore at least a small swath of the ecosystem, even if nobody else was doing theirs. And if they all converted, if they all pitched in, all his Mercedes-driving, bargain-obsessed neighbors, then everything would be fine – if they had the further good sense to go out back to their mulch piles, bury their designer-clad torsos in leaves and grass clippings and shoot themselves in the back of the head, that is.

All right, maybe he was something of a crank – he'd be the first to admit it. But at least he stayed out of trouble, which pleased Andrea and his parole officer, and, he liked to think, Sierra too. But one day, all the trees had been planted – and the bushes and the succulents and cacti – and the frogs cried lustily from the reconverted swimming pool, and Tierwater found himself craving more, craving action. It was an addiction, exactly that: once you'd identified the enemy, once you'd struck in the night and felt the magnetic effect of it, you were hooked. The passive business was fine, restoring an ecosystem, digging up a lawn, handing out flyers and attending rallies, but there was nothing like action, covert, direct, devastating: block enough culverts, destroy enough Cats, squeeze enough blood out of the corporate sons of bitches, and they'd back off. That was Tierwater's thinking, anyway. He'd just about served out his parole, and his daughter was growing up fast, seventeen years old, a senior in high school and already talking about UC Santa Cruz, the cheerful sylvan campus of which he and Andrea had dutifully visited with her during spring break. Two years was a long time to play *Father Knows Best*. And he was sick to death of it.

Of course, there was Andrea to consider. She might have been happy to show him the tricks of the ecoteur's trade at one time, but things were different now. She had a position to maintain – and so did he. And it did nobody any good if he was in jail. He remembered an evening somewhere toward the end of his two-year stint as house husband and suburban drone, when for the first time in a long while he broached the subject of nightwork. It was after dinner and they were lingering over a glass of wine. Sierra was in her room, on the phone, nouveau folkies harmonizing through her speakers like a gentle fall of rain on a still lake. Outside, beyond the window screens, the red-legged frogs were working up a good communal croak to celebrate the setting of the sun. 'No,' Andrea said, 'it's too risky.'

She was responding to a comment Tierwater had just made about the local electric company and its plans – 'plans already in the implementation stage, for Christ's sake, bulldozers, backhoes, habitat loss, you name it' – to bring a new power grid in over the Santa Susana Mountains at the opposite end of the Valley. 'It's nothing,' Tierwater countered, running a finger round the rim of his wineglass. 'I've been up there hiking every afternoon for the past week – did you know that? – and it's nothing. Like what you said about the Siskiyou thing – a piece of cake. But truly. In fact. No guards, no night watchmen, no nothing. They're just whacking away at everything, just another job, guys in hardhats who never heard from ecology and think a monkey wrench is something you tighten bolts with.'

'Uh-uh, Ty,' she said, and there were those ridges of annoyance climbing her forehead right on up into her hairline. She swept her hair back and cocked her head to stare him in the face. 'No more guerrilla tactics. We can't afford it. Every time some eco-nut blows something up or spikes a grove of trees, we lose points with the public, not to mention the legislature. Seventy-three percent of California voters say they're for the environment. All we need to do is to get them to vote – and we are. We're succeeding. We don't need violence anymore – I don't know if we ever did.'

Tierwater said nothing. Eco-nut. Is that what he was now? A loose cannon, an embarrassment to the cause? Well, he was the one who'd done the time here, while she and Teo and all the rest of them held hands and skipped through the fields – and made money, don't forget that. Sure. And what was environmentalism but just another career? He lifted the glass to his lips and let the wine play on his palate. It smelled like mineral springs and fruit fat with the sun, but he took no pleasure in it because the smell was artificial and the grapes that gave up their juice for it had been dusted with sulfur and Christ knew what other sorts of chemicals. Oak trees had fallen to make that wine. Habitat had been gobbled up. Nothing lived in a vineyard, not even nematodes.

'I'm not saying we don't need direct action – especially against people like the Axxam Corporation and the mining companies and all the rest. But it's got to be peaceable – and legal.' The light of the setting sun glowed pinkly off the plaster walls, kitchen fixtures and hanging plants, and it fixed Andrea in her chair as if in a scene of domestic tranquillity – *Seated Woman with Wineglass* – which was what this was. So far. 'We did a great thing up there in the Sierras, Ty, and everybody's tuned in now, you know that. Tuned in to us, to you and me. I'll say it again – we can't afford to slip up.'

'I'm not going to slip up.'

She came right back at him: 'I know you're not.'

He didn't like her tone, heavy with the freight of implication: he wasn't going to slip up because he wasn't going to do anything much more than flap his mouth and wave his hands, that's what she was saying. And further, if he did dare to fish out the watchcap and the greasepaint and bolt-cutters, there would be no more domestic tranquillity, not in this house, and not with this wife. 'Listen to yourself,' he said. 'You sound like some sort of corporate whore. Is that what this is all about – rising to the top of the food chain? Politics? A fat paycheck? Is that what it is?'

She tipped back her head and drained her glass. When she set it down, the base of the glass hitting the tabletop with a force just this side of shattering, he saw how angry she was. 'I was out there on the front lines when I was twenty-three years old – where were you?'

'How many species you think were lost when we were running around bare-assed in the mountains? Tell me that,' he said, ignoring the question. 'How many did we save in those thirty days? And how many roads were built, how many trees came down? Worldwide. Not just in California and Oregon, but worldwide.' Tierwater's hand went for the bottle. The wine might have been poison for the environment, but it sang in his head. 'And while we're on the subject of numbers, how many guys did you fuck while I was in Lompoc?'

It all stopped right there, dead in its tracks.

'Huh?' he demanded, and he felt low, felt like a toad, a criminal, a homewrecker. 'I don't hear you? How many? Or was it just Teo?'

She was on her feet now, and so was he. The look she gave him had no reserve of love in it, not the smallest portion. She was beyond exasperation, beyond contempt even. If she'd been a dog – or a hyena or a Patagonian fox – she'd have snarled. As it was, she just jerked her head to take the hair out of her face, turned her back and stalked out of the picture.

And Tierwater? He hit the wall so hard with the bottle he could feel the jolt of it all the way down to the base of his spine. He stood there a minute, the neck of the bottle sprouting from his hand like a bouquet of hard green flowers, and then he went out to the garage to look for the watchcap.

He didn't get far. Not that night. There was a problem on the freeway, shoulder work, a police chase, chemical spill, furniture in lane two, some maniac blocking an on-ramp with his pickup truck and threatening suicide – take your pick. When wasn't there a problem on the freeway? Tierwater sat there, stalled in traffic, fuming. There were cars as far as he could see in either direction, cars hemmed in by apartments and condos, restaurants, parking lots and auto malls, each of them pumping its own weight in carbon into the atmosphere each year, every year, forever. The radio played talk and scandal. A baseball game. Oldies. He listened to the oldies and felt nothing but old. The traffic crept forward like an army converging on some distant objective and he crept with it, cursing his fellow drivers, squeezing the Jeep over one foot at a time until he reached the nearest off-ramp, which just happened to be blocked, along with the surface streets it fed.

Sierra had the right idea. She refused to drive. Refused even to get her learner's permit. The bus is good enough for me, she said. And boys. Boys'll always take me where I want to go. They're lined up out there, Dad, twenty deep. Boys. Yeah, he said, sure, and he winked, because he wouldn't rise to the bait. But you tell them your heart belongs to Daddy.

That was when – yesterday? A week ago? He was thinking about that, his rage dissipating, the Jeep rolling forward – the whole line moving now, the car at the head of the train lurching into motion, and then the next in line, and the next, motion communicated through hands and feet and gas pedals in an unbroken chain – until he was staring bewildered into the brake lights of the car ahead of him and hitting his own brakes, hard. At the very instant everyone had lurched forward, a boxy little foreign car shot into the gap that opened between the first and second vehicles, and suddenly, all along the line, twenty drivers – the old, the suspect, the drunk, the suffering – were slamming on their brakes in succession. Before he could think – before he could even squeeze his eyes shut or clench his teeth – Tierwater was jerked forward in his seat and wrung back again, as the car behind him rode up his bumper, crumpled the rear end of the Jeep and drove him helplessly into the next car up the line.

He'd never understood what whiplash was until that moment, muscle fibers fraying, the back of his neck and shoulders stinging as if he'd been slammed with a board, blindsided, knocked down for the count, but it didn't prevent him from leaping out of the car to confront the jackass who'd hit him. What was wrong with these people? How could they live like this? Didn't they realize there was a natural world out there?

The smog was like mustard gas, burning in his lungs. There was trash everywhere, scattered up and down the off-ramp like the leavings of a bombed-out civilization, cans, bottles, fast-food wrappers, yellowing diapers and rusting shopping carts, oil filters, Styrofoam cups, cigarette butts. The grass was dead, the oleanders were buried in dust. A lone eucalyptus, twelve thousand miles removed from the continent where it had evolved, presided over the scene like an advertisement for blight. There were shouts in the distance, curses, the screaming, uncontainable blast of one car's horn after another, and sirens, the ubiquitous sirens, playing a thin dirge over it all.

Tierwater wrenched open the door of the car behind him, no need for rationality here, some threshold crossed and crossed again, Andrea, Teo, the shithole that was the human world, and he was capable of anything. Here, here in this ratcheting, stinking, crumpled hulk of steel, was the face of his enemy, an enemy as specific and unequivocal as Johnny Taradash, and he had his left hand on the door handle and his right balled into a fist, all the horns in the world shrieking . . . and then he saw that face and stopped.

She was an Asian girl, seventeen, eighteen, no older than Sierra, with eyes like the bottom of a well and three bright tributaries sectioning her face into a delta of blood, and though he hated everybody and everything, though he had an acetylene torch and a tank of oxygen and a sack of silicon carbide in the back of the Jeep, he reached into the wrecked car, pulled her out and held her in his arms till the ambulance came.

What did that mean to him? Nothing, nothing at all. Sure, there were individuals out there, human beings worthy of compassion, sacrifice, love, but that didn't absolve them of collective guilt. There were too many people in the world, six billion already and more coming, endless people, people like locusts, and nothing would survive their onslaught. It took Tierwater less than a week – the rear end of the Jeep hammered roughly back into shape, his neck immobilized in an antiseptic white brace that would have glowed like a light bulb if he hadn't blackened it with shoe polish – and he was back in action. First, though, he'd had to sit through a dinner with Teo, Andrea and three other E.F.! honchos, at which they discussed things like the electorate, Congress, letter-writing campaigns and ways to attract more green-friendly donors. Teo was wearing a four-hundred-dollar suit. *Teo. Liverhead.* Sitting there like he'd already been nominated for state senator. Plates of Phat Thai, ginger shrimp and glass noodles circulated round the table. Nobody said a word about the earth.

Tierwater excused himself before the dessert came – 'My neck's killing me,' he said, giving Andrea a pathetic look, 'Teo'll drop you off, won't you, Teo?' – and before the hour was out he was parking in a quiet cul-de-sac in a development less than a mile from where General Electric (or the DWP or whoever, it was all the same to him) was rearranging the earth in the name of progress. That was when he got out the shoe-blacking and his watchcap and all the rest. In hindsight, he shouldn't have acted alone. Always work in pairs, that was the monkeywrencher's first rule, because a lookout was absolutely essential, especially if you were wearing welder's goggles and you couldn't move your neck more than half an inch in either direction, let alone look over your shoulder. But he was done with the law now – he'd paid his dues and then some – and he was eager to get back into the game, to act, to do something meaningful. And he was fed up too, terminally fed up, with Andrea and Teo and the rest of the do-nothings. So he took a chance. Who could blame him?

It was just after eleven when he left the car, a few lights on in the houses still, but nobody out and nothing moving, not even the odd dog or cat. He slipped noiselessly down the street, ready to duck into the bushes if a car should happen by – it would be difficult to explain the way he was dressed and just what his mission was, and even if he *was* able to explain himself he could expect little sympathy from the concerned homeowner, who no doubt applauded General Electric and its mission to bring more electricity to the Valley in order to create yet more homes and, by extension, concerned homeowners. He saw himself sitting at a kitchen table trying to explain island biogeography, extinction and ozone depletion in the upper atmosphere to a yuppie homeowner with a never-used .38 Special pointed at his neck brace. No, anybody who caught even the most cursory glimpse of him would mistake him for a burglar, and the passing cop, if cops came out this far, would take one look at him and start shooting.

He skirted a house with its porch light burning, then made his way through the one lot left vacant in the whole creeping five-hundred-home development and on into the chaparral behind it. Here he could breathe. Here were the smells of sage and sun-baked dirt strewn with the chaff and seeds of the plants that sprang from it, desert lives and desert deaths. He sat on a slab of sandstone to draw the heavy black socks on over his boots and saw the San Fernando Valley spread out below him like a dark pit into which all the stars in the universe had been poured. Each light out there, each of those infinite dots of light, marked a house or business, and what would his father think? What would Sy Tierwater, the developer, the builder of tract homes and shopping centers, think about all this spread out beneath him? This was the fruit of ten thousand Tierwaters, a hundred thousand, the city built out beyond any reason or limit. Would he say enough is enough – or would he applaud all those intrepid builders, say a prayer of thanksgiving for all those roofs erected over all those aspiring heads? An owl hooted emphatically, as if in answer, and then Tierwater detected the sound of its wings and lifted his head painfully to watch the dark form beat across a moonless sky.

The answer was self-evident: Sy Tierwater would have loved all this, and hated what his son was about to do.

The night was shrunk down to nothing, the stars glowing feebly through a shroud of smog, the yellow bowl of light pollution halving the sky at his back. He came down off the ridge behind the development and into the moonscape of the construction site on muffled feet, every step sure, not so much as a kicked stone or snapped branch to give him away. He wasn't reckless. He knew what jail was and he wasn't going back, that was for sure, and he knew what Andrea's wrath meant, and her love and attachment too. There could be no slip-ups tonight. The very fact of his being here would outrage her, if she knew about it – and by now, he supposed, she did. He was risking everything, he knew that. But then, what was one marriage, one daughter, one suburban life compared with the fate of the earth?

Sometimes, hiking the trails, dreaming, the breeze in his face and the chaparral burnished with the sun, he wished some avenger would come down and wipe them all out, all those seething masses out there with their Hondas and their kitchen sets and throw rugs and doilies and VCRs. A comet would hit. The plague, mutated beyond all recognition, would come back to scour the land. Fire and ice. The final solution. And in all these scenarios, Ty Tierwater would miraculously survive – and his wife and daughter and a few others who respected the earth – and they would build the new uncivilized civilization on the ashes of the old. No more progress. No more products. Just life.

He turned first to the heavy equipment – the earth movers, a crane, a pair of dump trucks. It was nothing, the routine he'd gone through a dozen times and more: locate the crankcase, fill it to the neck with grit and move on to the next diesel-stinking hulk. He'd waited for the dark of the moon so he could work without fear of detection, and though the shapes were indistinct, he was blessed with excellent night vision, and yes, he took his multiple vitamins every morning and a beta-carotene supplement too. The usual night sounds blossomed around him, the distant hum of the freeways, crickets and peepers, a pair of coyotes announcing some furtive triumph. He felt relaxed. He felt good.

This was the point at which he should have called it a job well done and gone home to bed. But he didn't. He wanted to do something big, make a grand statement that would pique interest out there in the dens and kitchens of the Valley, generate news clippings and wow the hard-core Earth Forever! cadre, the ones who weren't afraid to get their hands dirty. In his backpack was the acetylene torch and an oxygen bottle made of aluminum. This was a heavy-duty torch, the sort of thing that could cut through steel like a magic wand, just wave it at the blade arms of a bulldozer or a section of railroad track and it would do the trick in less than a minute. Tierwater had been instructed in the use of the thing by an Oregon E.F.!er by the name of Teddy Scruggs, a twenty-five-year-old welder with a lazy eye, bad skin and long trailing hair that generated enough grease to lubricate machinery – no more idiocy like the dance around the cement bags in the Siskiyou, not for Tierwater. He was a professional now, a veteran, and he prided himself on that.

The power company had sheared off the top of a hill here and run a dead zone back into the mountains as far as you could see. And they'd erected a chain of steel towers, bound together by high-tension wires, marching one after another on up the hill into the blue yonder – and soon to reach down on the near side into the Valley itself. He'd given some thought to waiting till the project was complete and the power up and running, but bringing down those towers when they were carrying God knew how many megavolts of electricity was just too risky. Not that he meant to cut all the way through the supports – no, he would merely weaken them, slice neatly through the steel right at the base, where it plunged into the concrete footings. Then he'd go home and wait for the wind to blow – as it would tomorrow, according to the newspaper, Santa Anas gusting up to fifty miles per hour in the mountains and passes. Just about the time they'd be wondering what was wrong with the trucks, the towers would come thundering down, each yoked to the other, bang-bang-bang, like a chain of dominoes.

And what was that going to accomplish? He could hear Andrea already, and Teo – though Teo would have to give him his grudging admiration. Oh, yes, and the rest of the armchair radicals too. Because the answer was: plenty. Because all it took was public awareness – if they only knew what that electricity ultimately cost them, if they only knew they were tightening the noose round their own throats, day by day, kilowatt hour by kilowatt hour, then they'd rise up as one and put an end to it. And to make sure that they did know, to make sure they understood just what the environmental movement was all about, Tierwater had drafted a ten-page letter to the *Los Angeles Times,* on a used typewriter he'd bought for cash at a junk shop in Bakersfield and discarded in a Dumpster in Santa Monica, and that letter was his testament, his manifesto, a call to arms for every wondering and disaffected soul out there. He'd signed it, after much deliberation, *The California Phantom.*

It was a good plan. But the problem with the torch, aside from the obvious disadvantage of its awkwardness and the weight of the tanks, was visibility. On a dismal black smog-shrouded night like this, you'd be hard-pressed to find anything much brighter than an oxy-fuel torch, except maybe one of those flares they used to shoot off over the trip wire in Vietnam so they could count how many teeth each of the Viet Cong had before blowing them away in a hail of M-16 fire. Tierwater considered that – he even thought about waiting till dawn, when the big light in the sky would efface the glare of the torch – but he went ahead with it anyway. There was nobody out here, and if he waited till dawn he ran the risk of running into an overeager GE employee or some suburban dog-walker with a photographic memory for license-plate numbers. He bent for the pack, hefted it and ambled up the grade to where the first of the towers stood skeletal against the night.

The stanchions were thicker than he'd supposed. No problem, though – he was ready for anything; hell, he could have taken the George Washington Bridge down if he'd had enough time and enough fuel and oxygen. He did feel a twinge in the back of his neck as he bent to attach his hoses and the oxygen regulator – the brace shoved at his chin and held his head up awkwardly, as if he were about to lay it out flat on the chopping block or into the slit of the guillotine. But the torch took away his pain. He flipped down his goggles, turned up the flame and began to slice through high-grade Korean steel as if he were omnipotent.

Tierwater had always been a careful worker, precise where

another might be approximate, a model of concentration who never allowed himself to be distracted, even when he was a boy putting models together on a noisy playground or sitting at his father's drafting table creating his own blueprints of imaginary cities. His mother praised him for what was really an extraordinary ability in one so young, and his teachers praised him too. There was one in particular, an art teacher in the fifth or sixth grade – what was her name? – he could see her as clearly as if she were standing before him now, a tiny smiling woman not much older than Morty Reich's big sister – who really thought he had a talent, and not just because he'd mastered perspective drawing in a week and could sketch an unerring line, like the one he was drawing now, but –

He never got to finish the thought. Because just then, though the neck brace prevented him from turning round to acknowledge it, he felt a firm, unmistakable tap at his shoulder.

They came down hard on him this time. The State of California arraigned him on four counts of felony vandalism, and then the feds stepped in to charge him with violating parole, and that was the unkindest cut of all, because at the time of his arrest he had less than three weeks left till he was in the clear. Fred – and the defense attorney Tierwater had to hire to replace him when Fred begged off the minute he made bail – could do nothing. The press jumped gleefully on the case – this was Tierwater, Tyrone O'Shaughnessy Tierwater, the nudist radical who'd spent a naked month in the Sierras with his naked and busty wife, Andrea Knowles Cotton Tierwater, the high-flying E.F.! director and spokesperson, and here were the photos of that infamous stunt dredged up out of the files and reprinted with remarkable clarity on page one of the Metro section, nipples and genitalia airbrushed out so as not to offend puerile sensibilities, of course. The DA wouldn't bend, not with all that light shining on him. He made Tierwater plead to the face – plead on all counts, that is – and he was sentenced to two years on count one, the other three eight-month counts to be served consecutively, after which he'd be going back to Lompoc for six months under federal supervision. Tierwater was no mathematician, but no matter how he juggled the figures, they added up to fifty-four months – four and a half stupefying years.

But it got worse. He was ordered to pay restitution in the amount of eight hundred and seventy-five thousand dollars for damage to the vehicles and earth-moving equipment, not to mention the compromised stanchion, which required full replacement of the tower in question. The press wasn't calling him a hyena yet – that would come later – but there wasn't a friendly reporter out there, not even Chris Mattingly, who went on the record condemning any sort of monkeywrenching as anarchy, pure and simple. *Newsweek* ran a feature on ecotage, replete with the usual diagrams, a titillating breakdown of the various techniques employed, from tree-spiking to fire-bombing corporate offices, and a photo of a watchcapped and greasepainted Tierwater in a little box on the front cover. And the good honest law-abiding image-conscious hypocrites at Earth Forever! fell all over themselves denying any involvement. Which was why Fred had to bow out – 'It just wouldn't look right,' he said. 'I hope you understand.'

All right, so Fred was a coward, like the rest of them. But he was there the first day to bail Tierwater out and, along with Andrea, to creatively restructure the Tierwater holdings, both in real property and in the mutual-fund investments into which the shopping-center profits had gone. It was like this: Fred had foreseen the judgment and already had the instrument in hand that would shift all Tierwater's assets to the Earth Forever! Preservation Trust, under his wife's name and control. 'Before the court gets it,' Fred reasoned, pacing back and forth across the living-room carpet of the rented house in Tarzana, the frogs croaking and birds singing obliviously in the trees Tierwater wouldn't be seeing again for some time to come. 'Or GE. You don't want to see GE get everything you have, do you?'

Tierwater was in a state of shock. He held himself rigid against the smudged neck-brace and bent awkwardly to sign the papers. And Andrea, as prearranged, filed for divorce. 'Yes, I'm pissed off,' she said, 'of course I am, and disappointed and hurt too – I can't begin to tell you the harm you've done, Ty, and not just to me and Sierra, but to the whole organization. You're so goddamned mindless and stupid it just astonishes me' – a shadow swept by the window on swift wings, Sierra sat white-faced on the couch, her knees drawn up to her chin, Fred stood by – 'but I'm not deserting you, though no one would blame me if I did. This is just a maneuver, don't you see? We're hiding your assets and hoping the other side won't find out you have anything more than a closet full of old camping equipment, a beat-up Jeep and a rental house. If you don't have anything, what can they take?'

(Speeches. I heard one after the other, everybody so practical, so reasonable, but what it amounted to was the fleecing of Ty Tierwater, once and forever, my father's last hard-earned dollars poured down the funnel and into the money-hungry gullet of Earth Forever!, the incorporated earth-savers, Rallies R Us, rah-rah-rah. Andrea and I never did remarry, although she was there for me, nominally at least, when I got out. Do I sound bitter? I am. Or I was. But none of it matters anymore, not really.)

So Tierwater, officially penniless, shackled at the ankles and handcuffed at the wrists, took a bus ride to the state prison at Calpatria, a big stark factory of a place in the blasted scrubby hills of the Mohave Desert. What can he say about that place? It was no camp, that was for sure. Forget the tennis courts, the strolls round the yard, the dormitory. It was cellblock time. A lockup for the discerning criminal, no amateurs here. Your cell consisted of a metal-frame bunk, a lidless steel toilet, two metal counters with attached swing-out stools, a sink, a single overhead lightbulb and a sheet of polished metal bolted into the wall for a mirror. The guards didn't like to be called guards – they were 'correctional officers' – and they called everybody else 'shitbird,' regardless of race or crime or attitude. What else? The cuisine was shit. The work was shit. Your fellow inmates were shit. You got drunk on a kind of rancid thin liquid made from bread, oranges, water and sugar fermented for four days in a plastic bag hidden in the back of your locker. Drugs came in in the vaginas of girlfriends and wives, tucked into condoms that made it from the female mouth to the male during that first long lingering kiss of greeting. Tierwater didn't do drugs. And he didn't have a girlfriend. His wife – or ex-wife – visited him once a month if he was lucky. And his daughter – to her eyes, and hers alone, he was still a hero – tried to come when she could, but she was in college now, and she had papers to write, exams to take, rallies to attend, protests to organize, animals to liberate. She wrote him every week, long discursive letters on the Gaia hypothesis, rock and roll, fossil love and her roommate's hygienic habits. Once in a while she'd take the bus down to Calpatria and surprise him.

(Sample conversation, Tierwater and his daughter, the table between them, the shriek and gibber of two dozen voices, Fat Frank, the puffed-up guard, looming over them like an avalanche about to happen.

Sierra: Yeah, well, chickens have rights too. They do. It's just species chauvinism is what it is.

Tierwater: What what is?

Sierra: Saying they're just dumb animals as a rationale for penning them up in a space the size of a shoebox for their whole lives, with a what-do-you-call-it – a conveyor belt – underneath it to carry off their waste. Well, they used to say the same thing a hundred and fifty years ago about African Americans.

Tierwater: I'm not following you – you want to liberate the chickens and deep-fry African Americans, is that it?

Sierra: *Dad.*)

Then there was Sandman. Sandman – Geoffrey R. Sandman, the 'R.' signifying nothing, but giving the extra bit of heft to a name that had to look good at the bottom of a bad check – was Tierwater's cellmate during the better part of the thirty-eight months of the state sentence he wound up serving. It was Sandman who kept him sane (if 'sane' was an accurate description, and there were plenty who would debate that), and kept him safe too. Sandman was in for armed robbery – he'd taken down a Brinks guard coming out of the neighborhood Safeway with the day's receipts, then shot the man at the wheel in both feet when he stepped out to come to his partner's aid, and on top of that he wound up stealing the armored car for a glorious two-hour chase on the 605 Freeway – and he was a force to be reckoned with. He was tall, six three or four, and he put in his time in the weight room. Tierwater's reputation had preceded him – the Johnny Taradash incident, a few other minor but indicative things at Lompoc and the sheer craziness of the nude stunt and trying to take out General Electric – and that gave him at least some initial respect on the cellblock. Together, they formed a gang of two.

They were sitting in the cell one night, half an hour before lockdown, playing take-no-prisoners chess for five-dollar chits (Tierwater already owed his cellmate something like three hundred and twenty dollars at that point) and sharing the last of a pack of Camels (a nasty habit, sure, but what else were you going to do in prison?). There were the usual sounds, the jabbering, the cursing, the rucking up of clots of phlegm, the persistent *tuh-tuh* of sunflower seeds spat into a fist or a cup. The usual smells too, the body reek of caged animals, of vomit, urine and disinfectant, cut by the sweet cherry perfume of pipe tobacco or the scent of beer nuts or a freshly cracked bag of salt-and-vinegar potato chips. From the radio that hung from the bars in the exact spot where the reception was best came the low thump of bass and the high breathy wheeze of Maclovio Pulchris rendering the ineluctable lyrics of his latest hit: *I want you, I want you, I want you, / Ooo, baby, ooo, baby, ooo!*

'Christ, I hate that shit,' Sandman said, maneuvering his bishop in for the kill – he still had better than half his pieces on the board; Tierwater was down to his king, an embattled queen and two pawns. 'Every time he opens his mouth he sounds like he's pissing down his leg.'

'I don't know,' Tierwater said, 'I kind of like it.'

Sandman gave him a look of incredulity – what he liked to call his 'tomcat-sniffing-a-new-asshole look' – but he let it drop right there. He had the most malleable face Tierwater had ever seen, and he used it to his advantage, acting, always acting, but ready to underscore any performance with a ready brutal violence that was no act at all. When Tierwater first met him, Sandman was thirty-two, his face tanned from the yard, with a pair of casual blue eyes and a beard so carefully clipped it was like a shadow tracing the line of his jaw and underscoring the thrust of his chin. He was handsome, as handsome as the kind of actor who specializes in the role of the wisecracking world-beater and gets paid for it, and he used his looks to his advantage. People instinctively liked him. And he used their prejudices – no bad guy could look like that, they thought, certainly no con – and turned them upside down. 'I spent years looking into the mirror,' he'd told Tierwater, 'till I got every look down, from "don't fuck with me" to "holy reverend taking the collection" to "would you please put the money in the paper sack before I remove your fucking face."'

'The lyrics might be a little weak,' Tierwater admitted, 'but with Pulchris it's the beat, that's what it's all about.'

Sandman waved a hand in extenuation, then swooped in on the board to replace Tierwater's queen with a black rook that seemed to come out of nowhere. 'Hah, got her, the bitch!'

'Shit. I didn't even see it.'

'Ready to concede? And by the way, speaking of bitches, how's your ex doing?' He leaned forward to collect the pieces. 'I mean, I saw you all tangled up with her there this afternoon, and you didn't look too happy – '

'What about your own bitch of an ex-wife?' Tierwater just sat there, trading grins with him. Andrea was a subject he didn't want to talk about. Or think about. It was like thinking about water when you're out on the desert, or pizza when you're in South Dakota.

'I ever tell you I've been married five times?' Sandman was leaning forward, grinning, the heavy muscles of his upper arms bunched under the thin fabric of his T-shirt. 'Five times, and I'm only still a child yet. But the first one, Candy, Candy Martinez, she was my high-school sweetheart? – she was the worst. Soon as I went up the first time, she turned around and fucked everybody I ever knew, as if it was an assignment or something – I mean, my brother, my best bud, the guy across the street, even the shop teacher, for shit's sake, and he must've been forty, at least, with like those gorilla hands with the black hairs all over them – '

Tierwater pushed himself up off the bunk, took two paces right, two paces left – the cell was fifty-one square feet, total, so it was no parade ground. He just needed to shake out his legs, that was all. 'Thanks, Sandman,' he said, working up his best mock-sincere voice, 'thanks for sharing that with me. I feel a lot better now.'

Prison. Tierwater endured it, and there's not much more to be said about it. Every day he regretted going out there with that torch, but the regret made him harder, and he would have done it again without thinking twice about it – only, of course, as in all fantasies and theoretical models, he wouldn't get caught this time. He wound up serving the better part of his sentence, a block of good days (good-behavior days, that is, two days' credit for every day served in state) subtracted from his record because of an unfortunate incident with two child-sized members of a Vietnamese gang in the prison mess hall, and then he went back to Lompoc, minimum security again, because he wasn't going anywhere with six months left to serve.

And who visited him there? Sierra, sometimes, though it was a real haul for her on the Greyhound bus, and Andrea too, of course, though every time he pressed his lips to hers and felt her tongue in his mouth he knew it was wrong, knew it was over, knew she'd already written him off and was just playing out the game like a good sport. That hurt him. That put the knife in him and twisted it too. And who else visited, right in the middle of that stunned and stuporous time when he walked and talked and thought like a zombie and wondered how he'd ever gone from his father's boy in a clean house in a nice development surrounded by trees and flowers and all the good things of life to this? Who else?

Sandman, that's who. Geoffrey R. Sandman, in a suit and tie and looking like a lawyer or a brain surgeon. 'How the hell are you, Ty?' he wanted to know while the guards edged from one foot to the other. 'Anything you need, you just tell me.'

And then came the day, déjà vu, Andrea waiting for him in the parking lot, the little bag of his belongings, goodbye, Lompoc. He'd served out his sentence, and they unlocked the cage and let him go. Not in time to see his daughter cock the mortarboard down low over one gray, seriously committed eye and accept her degree, cum laude, in environmental science, but that was the way it was when you did the stupid things, the things that put you in their power, the things you swore you would never do again. That was what every prisoner told himself – *I'll never do it again* – but Tierwater didn't believe it. Not for a minute. He knew now, with every yearning, hating, bitter and terminally bored fiber of his being, why prison didn't reform anybody. Penitentiary. What a joke. The only thing you were penitent for was getting caught. And the more time you did, the more you wanted to strike back at the sons of bitches and make them wince, make them hurt the way you did. That was rehabilitation for you.

This time the car was a smooth black BMW – one of the pricey models, 740i, Andrea's car, and who'd bought it for her? 'You did, Ty, and I love you for it. We needed something with a little class for pulling up at the curb when they've got the cameras going, you know? Anyway, I thought I'd surprise you. You like it, don't you?' He did. And this was déjà vu too, hammering the accelerator, the ocean, the wind, outdoors on the patio of the restaurant, waiters, a menu, real food, and then home to bed and sex. Only Sierra wasn't there this time – she was in Arizona, at Teo's Action Camp, undergoing a course of indoctrination in nonviolent protest, as if she hadn't already earned three Ph.D.'s in it – and the sex wasn't there either. Oh, they took off their clothes, he and Andrea, and he built a monument to her body, the smell of her, the taste, her eyes and teeth, the sound of her voice, the simple unadulterated miracle of sitting at breakfast in a sunstruck kitchen and seeing her there across the table in her robe, but it was different. It was like Sandman said, reminiscing in the minutest sexual detail over his third wife and her multifarious betrayals, or maybe it was his fourth: *What do you expect?*

Tierwater kept his head down. He was a blind man given a pair of eyes, and he didn't want to look too hard for fear of going blind again. Andrea took the black BMW to work and he went out in the yard and dug holes and stuck plants in the ground. There was a pair of mallards in the swimming pool, and that pleased him – they'd been flying off in the spring and coming back every fall, Andrea told him – and the red-legged frogs splashed randily in the water while the mosquito fish pocked the surface with thin-lipped kisses. He saw Sandman a couple of times – he was living in Long Beach, working for a biotech firm, 'That's where the money is, bro, and the future too' – but Andrea didn't exactly shine to the man, ex-con and violent offender that he was, and Tierwater let the relationship cool. Teo came back at the end of October, and Andrea seemed to fly south herself, emotionally anyway, and Tierwater was ready to get out the decoys and the shotgun and find out once and for all how things stood, but Sierra came back then too, and he got distracted.

For a month, he and his daughter held an ongoing reunion. They went to Disneyland and Magic Mountain, hiked the San Gabriels, the Santa Monicas and the Santa Susanas, ate out – every meal, every day – and saw *A Doll's House* ('I'll never be like her') and *The Misanthrope* at a theater in Brentwood. She was grown up now, a woman, nearly the age Jane was when they'd first met. Everywhere they went, he watched the men watching her, and that made him feel strange and protective, all those doggy and envious eyes, men of all ages – grandfathers, even – craning their necks for a look at her in her clean-limbed beauty. What did she wear? Shorts, skirts, T-shirts, blouses made of silk or rayon, nothing especially provocative, no makeup, no nonsense, but she had a gift of beauty and every man who wasn't already dead responded to it. One afternoon, over lunch at a place that had the vegan seal of approval – lentil-paste sandwiches, eggplant à la paysanne, peanut-vinaigrette salad and tofu shakes – he asked her about that, about men, that is. 'Rick, wasn't that his name? Whatever happened to him?'

She was chewing, her cheeks full and round, sunlight painting the tiles around a little fountain, a murmur of voices from the other diners, the soft swish of cars on the boulevard. It took her a moment, her eyes tight with some secret knowledge. 'Oh, him,' she said finally. 'That was sophomore year. He was – I don't know, he liked sports.'

Tierwater, puzzled: 'You don't like sports?'

'You know what I mean.' A pause. Somewhere, very faintly, a Coltrane tune was playing, a tune that had ravished him when he was her age. 'I liked Donovan Kurtz senior year, remember I told you? He was in my environmental-issues class? He had a – Do you want to hear this?'

Iced tea, that's what Tierwater wanted. He flagged down the waitress and they both sat in silence while she refilled his glass. 'Sure,' he said, and let the corners of his mouth drop.

'He was a music major and he used to sing to me when we were making love.'

'Let me guess,' Tierwater said, plunging in to cover his

embarrassment, *his daughter making love*, ' "I've Been Working on the Railroad"?'

'Dad.'

' "When the Saints Go Marching In"?'

Was it his imagination, or did she color, just a bit? Coltrane ran distantly up and down the scales, magnificent changes, the ice tinkled in his glass. He said, 'So what happened to him?'

Sierra set down her sandwich, looked away, shrugged. 'He got married.'

Yes, and then she was up in northern California, in Scotia, getting set to trespass on Coast Lumber's property and take possession of one of Coast Lumber's prime trees, and Tierwater was behind the wheel of the black BMW hurtling up 101, Andrea at his side sorting through the CDs ('How about this one, how about *Barbecue You?*'), Teo in back, all that watery sun-pasted scenery scrolling past the windows. The talk was of Washington lobbyists, sanctimonious Sierra Clubbers, the banners they'd be waving when Sierra rose up into the sky – and the speed limit. 'Slow down, Ty – it's fifty-five through here,' Andrea kept saying. 'You don't want to get pulled over, do you? And have to explain to the cop why you're not in Los Angeles?'

'What are you talking about?' He was irritated, of course he was irritated: all he could think about was that trip back from the Siskiyou, more déjà vu, and Sierra left behind in the hands of the enemy. And now what were they doing? Rushing back into the fray, ready to sacrifice her all over again. Because of Teo. Because of Teo and his Action Camp. 'You think some Gilroy yokel is going to know or care who I am or what the deal is?'

'Computers,' came Teo's voice from the back.

'Bullshit,' Tierwater said, but he slowed down.

Then there was the pretense of the motel, Tierwater and Andrea in one room, king-size bed, magic fingers, no sex, and Teo in another, no confessions yet, no avowals or disavowals, something bigger than the three of them in the making, let's focus, let's go team, hooray for our side. Early breakfast. Dim and overcast, fog like the wallpaper of a dream, a smell in the air that was like graves being turned. Tierwater was uneasy. He lit a cigarette, nasty habit, and Andrea told him to go outside.

It was just past nine when they reached the turnoff outside of Scotia and the dusty, compacted lot beyond it that was really nothing more than the result of a pass or two with the Cat during some bygone logging operation. Trees stood tall along the road – the fence, as the timber company called it, to keep motorists from apprehending that the façade was all there was – and there were cars everywhere, sensible cars, Corollas, Accords, Saturns, the faded mustard Volvos and battered VW buses of the Movement. It was a Sunday. There was smoke in the air, a taste of the marijuana-scented past, the chink-chink of tambourines and the skreel of nose flutes. Tierwater pulled a baseball cap down over his balding head and stepped out of the car.

Andrea was dressed down for the occasion in jeans, three-hundred-dollar cowboy boots and white spandex with a red E.F.! sweater knotted round her neck and her hair pulled back in a knot. She had a clipboard in one hand, a bottle of Evian in the other, and she was out of the car before it had come to a halt – Tierwater could see her across the lot, the center of a group of mostly young people with placards, her elbows jerky, one hand fluttering like a wounded bird, already lecturing. There was a quick fusillade of flashbulbs, a knot of journalists sympathetic to the cause converging on her, Chris Mattingly among them. Teo was more deliberate. He took his time gathering his things out of the back seat – pamphlets, copies of the press release, a bullhorn to rally the troops – and then he was standing there, dressed in his muscles, on the far side of the car, giving Tierwater a slit-eyed look over the hump of the sculpted roof. 'You going to be okay with this, Ty?' he asked. 'No violence, no hassles, real low profile, right?' He turned to gaze off at the crowd before he had his answer, and Tierwater understood that he wasn't really asking. 'Oh, and pop the trunk, would you?'

AXXAM OUT! the placards said. SAVE THE TREES! STOP THE SLAUGH-TER!

In the trunk was a picnic basket, a hamper with the ruby necks of two bottles of Bordeaux peeping out of one corner. Tierwater was dumbstruck. A picnic basket. His daughter was going up a tree and they were going to have a picnic. He heard Teo, the surfer's inflection, vowels riding the waves still, 'Would you mind grabbing that basket?'

There were a lot of things here that rubbed Tierwater wrong, too many to count or even mention, but this, this *picnic basket*, really set him off. They were right there, the two of them, shoulder to shoulder at the open trunk of the blackly gleaming car, an excited chirp of voices burbling up all around them like springs erupting from the earth, movement everywhere, dust. 'You're fucking my wife,' Tierwater said.

Teo just looked at him, and he was wearing shades though the day was overcast, two amber slits that narrowed his face and made the gleaming stubblefield of his head seem enormous. 'What? What did you say?'

'I said you're fucking my wife, aren't you, Teo? Be a man. Admit it. Come on, you son of a bitch, come on – '

Liverhead. He flexed his biceps and the muscles that ran in cords down either side of his neck, and he stood there as straight as a post driven into the ground. 'This isn't the place, Ty,' he said, and the pamphlets were bookbagged under one arm, the bullhorn under the other. 'You've been gone a long time. Cut her some slack.'

So this was it. This was the admission he'd been waiting for. Sandman had been right all along – and so had he, so had he. He wanted to hurt somebody in the space of that moment, the picnic basket in his hand, the nose flutes starting up with a shriek, flashbulbs popping – he wanted to hurt Teo, hurt him badly. But then somebody was there, some kid in a tie-dye T-shirt trying to grow into his first beard – 'Teo, Teo, man, Teo' – the kid was saying, pumping Teo's hand and reaching to help with the pamphlets at the same time, and Teo, ignoring the kid, turned to Tierwater and let the extenuation melt into his voice: 'Ty, look,' he said, 'you got to understand – we're all in this together.'

Yes. And then they lifted his daughter up into the shattering light-struck reaches of that tree and everybody cheered, everybody, the whole mad circus, but Tierwater, alone in himself, felt nothing but hate and fear.

The Sierra Nevada, May 2026

IT'S HOT. THAT seems to be the main feature of the experience Andrea, Petunia and I are having as we maneuver the Olfputt over nondiscriminating roads – downed trees, splintered telephone poles, potholes and craters everywhere, anything less than a 4x4 or a military vehicle and you're done for. Sure, there are road crews out there beyond the tinted windows – 131°F. according to the LED display on the dash, and the wind so dirty it's like something out of *Lawrence of Arabia* – but they've got a lot of work ahead of them. Then the rains will come and the roads will wash out again, and they'll have a whole lot more. Andrea's driving. I'm looking out the window. Petunia, restrained by muzzle, harness and leash but otherwise free to roam around the back if she can find a place to stand amid all the provisions, fine wines, relics and household goods we've brought along, is sweating. And stinking.

We're stopped in traffic – ROAD WORK AHEAD – and I'm thinking about the mountains, about the tall trees and the sweet breath of the nights up there and the good times we had, the family times, back when we were the Drinkwaters. At the risk of sounding hackneyed, I'd say the usual, that it seems like an ice age ago, but it was, it *was*. There are squatters up there now, squirrel hunters and the like trying to live off the land, and I hear the trees have really taken a beating after a quarter-century of floods, droughts, beetles and windstorms. At least we don't have to worry about clear-cuts anymore – nothing but salvage timber now.

There's a pioneering stream of sweat working its way down my spine, the inside of the car smells like the old cat-house at the San Francisco Zoo, and the stiff no-nonsense seat of the Olfputt is crucifying my back. We've been on the road for four hours and we haven't even reached Bakersfield yet. 'Crank the air-conditioning, will you?' I hear myself say.

'It's on full.' Andrea gives me a smile. She's enjoying this. For her it's an adventure, one more take on the world and let's see what shakes out this time.

I'm stiff. I'm aggravated. I need to take a leak. Plus, Petunia's got to have a chance to do her business, if we ever hope to leash-train her anyway, and up ahead – we're crawling now, vroom-vroom, up and down over the pits and into and out of a gully the size of the Grand Canyon – I can make out the lights of a restaurant, El Frijole Grande. 'What do you think about some lunch?' I say.

The lot is gouged and rutted and there's wind-drift everywhere, tumbleweeds, trash, what used to be a fence, the desiccated carcass of a cat *(Felis catus)*. I step shakily out of the car – the hips! the knee! – and fall into the arms of the heat. It's staggering, it truly is. The whole world's a pizza oven, a pizza oven that's just exploded, the blast zone radiating outward forever, particles of grit forced right up my nose and down my throat the instant I swing open the door – accompanied by the ominous rattle of sand ricocheting off the scratch-resistant lenses of my glasses. I'm just trying to survive till I can get inside the restaurant, thinking about nothing but that, and yet here's Andrea's face, still floating behind me in the cab of the 4x4, and she seems to be screeching something, something urgent, and suddenly I'm whirling round with the oxidized reflexes of the young-old just in time to catch Petunia's leash as she comes hurtling out the door.

Leggy, stinking, her fur matted till it has the texture of wire overlaid with a thin coating of concrete, she rockets from the car, airborne for the instant it takes to snap the leash like a whip and very nearly tear my abused shoulder out of the socket. But I hold on, heat, age and the exigencies of a full bladder and enlarged prostate notwithstanding. This is the only Patagonian fox left in North America, and I'm not about to let go of her. She doesn't fully appreciate that yet, new to leash protocol as she is, and she goes directly for my legs, all the while snarling like a poorly sampled record and trying to bite through the muzzle while her four feet, sixteen toenails and four dewclaws scrabble for purchase on the blistered macadam.

I'm down on the pavement, born of sweat, and Petunia's on top of me, trying to dig a hole in my chest with her forepaws, when Andrea comes to the rescue. 'Down, girl,' she's saying, jerking at the leash I still refuse to let go of, and all I can think is to apportion blame where blame is due. This was her idea from the start. She didn't want to bring a cage along – 'Don't be crazy, Ty, there's no room for it' – and she reasoned that Petunia was doglike enough to pass. 'They are the same species, aren't they?' 'Genus,' I told her – 'or family, actually. But they still make an awful mess on the rug.'

At any rate, the wounds aren't serious. The back of my shirt is a collage of litter and pills of grit, and two buttons are missing in the front, but Petunia hasn't managed to do much more than break the skin in three or four places before the two of us are able to overpower her. Despite the wind and the heat, we manage to hobble-walk her around the lot until she squats and does a poor, meager business under the front tire of a school bus draped with a banner reading *Calpurnia Springs, State Champions, B-League.* (Champions of what, I'm wondering – desert survival?) After a brief debate about what to do with her next – we can't leave her in the Olfputt in this heat – I decide to chain her to the bumper and hope for the best. Then we're inside, where it's cool, and the hits of the sixties – reconfigured for strings – are leaking through hidden speakers while people of every size, color and shape flock past in a mad flap and shriek.

The place is more arena than restaurant, massed heads, jabbering voices, the buzz and tweet of video games. The theme is Mexican – a couple of shabby parrots and half a dozen drooping banana trees in enormous pots – but the smell is of the deep-fryer, deep-fried everything. I'm bleeding through the front of my shirt. My pants are bound to my crotch with sweat. 'I'll bet they don't have a bar,' I say.

Andrea doesn't respond. She's a ramrod, eyes like pincers, sprung fully formed from the tile in front of the *please wait to be seated* sign. Run five minutes off the clock. Run ten. We're still standing there, though three hostesses in their twenties have managed to seat whole busloads ahead of us. What it is, is age discrimination. We young-old, we of the Baby Boom who are as young and vital in our seventies as our parents were in their fifties, we who had all the power and *invented* the hits of the sixties, have suddenly become invisible, irrelevant, window dressing in an overpopulated, resource-stressed world. What are all these young people telling us? Die, that's what. And quickly.

They don't know Andrea. In the next moment she's got a startled-looking hostess with caterpillar hair in the grip of one big hand and the manager in the other and we're being led to our table right in the middle of that roiling den of gluttony and noise, sorry for the wait, no problem at all, enjoy your meal. I want a beer. A Mexican beer. But they don't have any beer. 'Sorry,' the twelve-year-old waiter says, looking at me as if my brain's been ossified, 'only *sake*.'

What else?

Andrea orders the catfish enchilada and a *sake* margarita, and after vacillating between the catfish fajitas and the *Bagre al carbón* before finally settling on the former, I lift my glass of *sake* on the rocks and click it against the frosted rim of her margarita. 'To us,' I offer, 'and our new life in the mountains.'

'Yes,' she says, a quiet smile pressed to her lips, and I'm thinking about that, about our life together as it stretches out before me, a pale wind-torn sun in the windows, voices roaring around us, and I can't help wondering just what it's going to be like. We could live another twenty-five or fifty years even. The thought depresses me. What's going to be left by then?

'You're not eating,' she says. A dozen kids – children, babies – run bawling down the aisle, ducking under the upraised arms of as many waiters, and disappear into the sea of faces. They are infinite, I am thinking, all these hungry, grasping people chasing after the new and improved, the super and imperishable, and I stand alone against them – but that's the kind of thinking that led me astray all those years ago. Better not to think. Better not to act. Just wave the futilitarian banner and bury your nose in a glass of *sake*. 'Mine's good,' Andrea says, proffering a forkful of pus-yellow catfish basted in salsa. 'Want a bite?'

I just shake my head. I want to cry. *Catfish*.

Her voice is soft, very low, so low I can barely hear her in the din: 'You know' – and she's digging through her purse now, a purse the size of a steamer trunk suspended from two black leather straps – 'I have something for you. I thought you'd want it.'

What do I show her in response? Two dog's eyes, full and wet and pathetic. There is nothing I want, except the world the way it was, my daughter restored to me, my parents, all the doomed and extinguished wildlife of America – the white-faced ibis, the Indiana bat, the margay, the Perdido Key beach mouse, the California grizzly and the Chittenango ovate amber snail – put back in their places. I don't want to live in this time. I want to live in the past. The distant past. 'What?' I ask, and my voice is dead.

The rustle of paper. The strings rumble and then reach high to wash all the life out of a down-tempo version of 'Sympathy for the Devil.' I watch her hand come across the table with it, a sheaf of paper – real paper – and the bands of type that are like hieroglyphs encoded on it. And now I'm holding it out at arm's length, squinting till my eyes water and patting down my pockets for my reading glasses.

'I borrowed it,' she says. 'Stole it, actually.'

I'm about to say, 'What? What is it?,' when the glasses find their way to the bridge of my nose and I can see for myself.

It's a manuscript. A book. And the title, suddenly revealed, stares out at me from beneath the cellophane wrapper of the cover:

MARTYR TO THE TREES:
THE SIERRA TIERWATER STORY
BY APRIL F. WIND

I already know how it ends.

But here it is, a concrete thing, undeniable, a weight in my hands. April *F*. Wind? And what does the 'F.' stand for? I wonder. Flowing? Full of? Forever? I riffle the pages, the crisp sound of paper, the printout, the stuff of knowledge as it used to be before you could plug it in. No need to talk about the inaccuracies here, or the sappy woo-woo-drenched revisionism or New Age psychoanalysis, but only the end, just that.

Sierra set the record. Set it anew each day, like Kafka's hunger artist, but, unlike the deluded artist, she had an audience. A real and ever-growing audience, an audience that made pilgrimages to the shrine of her tree, sent her as many as a thousand letters a week, erected statues to her, composed poems and song lyrics, locked arms and marched in her name till Axxam showed black through to the core. In all, she spent just over three years aloft, above the fray, the birds her companions, as secure in her environment as a snail in its shell or a goby in the smooth, sculpted jacket of its hole.

In the beginning – in the weeks and months after Climber Deke's frustrated effort to dislodge her – the timber company initiated a campaign of harassment designed either to bring her down or to drive her mad, or both. They logged the trees on all sides of her, the screech of the saws annihilating the dawn and continuing unabated till dark, and all around her loggers cupping their hands over their mouths and shouting abuse. *Hey, you little cunt – want to put your lips around this? There's five of us here and we'll be up tonight, you wait for us, huh? And keep the slit clean, 'cause I got sloppy seconds.* At night they set up a wall of speakers at the base of the tree and blared polkas, show tunes and Senate testimony into the vault of the sky till the woods echoed like some chamber of doom. They brought in helicopters, the big workhorses they used for wrestling hundred-foot logs off of remote hilltops, and the helicopters hovered there beside her tree, beating up a hurricane with the wash of their props. It was funny. It was a joke. She could see the pilots grinning at her, giving her the thumbs-up sign, A-OK, and let's see if we can blow you out of there. Do you copy? Roger and out.

They tried starvation too. On the morning after Climber Deke made off with the lower platform and all her cooking gear and foodstuffs, the hired goons established a perimeter around the grove and refused to let her support team in. For three nights running, in the company of a loping, rangy kid named Starlight who haltingly confessed that he was in love with my daughter and wanted to marry her as soon as she came down from her tree, I lugged supplies in to her, and for many more nights than that I wandered the dark woods with a baseball bat, just praying that one of those foul-mouthed sons of bitches would try to make good on his threats. Sierra was unfazed. They couldn't intimidate her. 'Don't worry, Dad,' she whispered one night as she descended as low as she dared to collect the provisions we'd brought her

(Starlight straining against gravity from the top rung of an aluminum ladder while I braced him from below). 'They're all talk.' Her face glowed palely against the black vacancy that was her tree. 'They're scared, that's all.'

Andrea and Teo got the press involved – 'Coast Lumber Starving Tree-Sitter,' that sort of thing – and the timber company backed off. The support team returned, more determined than ever, the lower platform was rebuilt and Coast Lumber turned its back on the whole business. If my daughter wanted to trespass in one of their trees, they weren't going to deign to respond. Because any response – short of suspending all logging and restoring the ecosystem – would be used against them, and they knew it. They would wait her out, that was their thinking. The longer she stayed up there, the less anybody would care, and before long she'd get tired of the whole thing, hold a press conference and leave them to strip every last dollar out of the forest and nobody to say different.

By this point, Sierra had begun to take on the trappings of the mad saint, the anchorite in her cell, the martyr who suffers not so much for a cause but for the sake of the suffering itself. She became airier, more distant. She'd been studying the teachings of Lao Tzu and the Buddha, she told me. She was one with Artemis, one with the squirrels and chickadees that were her companions. There was no need to come down to earth, not then, not ever. She didn't care – or didn't notice – that she was the idol of thousands, didn't care that she was incrementally extending the record for consecutive days aloft till no one could hope to exceed it, and she barely mentioned Coast Lumber anymore. Toward the end, I think, she'd forgotten what she was doing up there in that tree to begin with.

The end, that's right – this is about the end of all that.

Can I tell you this? I was there – her father was there – when it happened. I'd moved out of the house in Tarzana, leaving the mosquito fish and mallards – and my wife – to fend for themselves. Why? I was embarrassed. Ashamed of myself. All along I'd been wrong about Andrea and Teo – there was nothing between them, and after we left Sierra in her tree that first weekend they both sat across the table from me at a Jack in the Box restaurant in Willits with the drawn-down faces of the martyred saints and made me understand that. (Later, long after it was over between Andrea and me, they'd have their time together, and I couldn't help thinking I was the one who'd been campaigning for it all along.) The parole board gave me permission to move to Eureka, where I had a job lined up – a nothing job, clerk in a hardware store, but it was enough to get me out of L.A. so I could be close to my daughter. I packed the Jeep while Andrea was at work. I left a note. I don't know – we never discussed it – but I think she must have been relieved.

My apartment wasn't much bigger than the cell I'd shared with Sandman. A sitting room with a bed and a TV, a kitchen the size of the galley on a thirty-foot sailboat, toilet and shower, a patch of dirt out back with a rusting iron chair bolted to a slab of concrete in the middle of it. I could have had more – any time I wanted I could have drawn on the money we'd invested in Earth Forever! and nobody at GE the wiser – but I didn't want more. I wanted less, much less. I wanted to live like Thoreau.

My chief recreation was Sierra. Four, five, even six days a week, I'd hike out to her tree and chat with her if she wasn't busy with interviews or her journal. Sometimes she'd come down in her harness and float there above me, the soles of her feet as black as if they'd been tarred; other times we'd chat on the cell phone, sometimes for hours, just drifting through subjects and memories in a long, unhurried dream of an afternoon or evening, her voice so intimate right there in my ear, so close, it was as if she'd come down to earth again.

We had a celebration to commemorate her third anniversary aloft – her support team, a dozen journalists, a crowd of the E.F.! rank and file. Andrea and Teo drove up, and that was all right, a kiss on the cheek, a hug, 'You okay, Ty? Really? You know where I am if you need me,' Andrea so beautiful and severe and Tierwater fumbling and foolish, locked into something that was going to have to play itself out to the end. I got her a cake that was meant, I think, for somebody's wedding – four tiers, layered frosting, the lonely plastic figurine of a groomless bride set on top. I was trying to tell my daughter something with that forlorn bride: it was time to come down. Time to get on with life. Go to graduate school, get married, have children, take a shower, for Christ's sake. If she got the meaning of the lone figurine, she didn't let on. She kept it, though – the figurine – kept it as if it were one of the dressed-up dolls she'd invented lives for when she was a motherless girl alone in the fortress of her room.

A week later. Forty-eight degrees, a light rain falling. Those trees, that grove, were more familiar to me than the sitting room in my apartment or the house I grew up in. There was a smell of woodsmoke on the air, the muted sounds of the forest sinking into evening, a shrouded ray of sunlight cutting a luminous band into her tree just above the lower platform – which was unoccupied, I saw, when I came up the hill and into the grove, already punching her number into the phone. It was four-fifteen. I'd just got out of work. I was calling my arboreal daughter.

Her voice came over the line, hushed and breathy, the most serene voice in the world, just as I reached the base of the tree. 'Hi, Dad,' she whispered, that little catch of familiarity and closeness in her voice, ready to talk and open up, as glad to hear my voice as I was glad to hear hers, 'what's up?' I was about to tell her something, an amusing little story about work and one of the loggers – timber persons – who'd come in looking for a toggle switch but kept calling it a tuggle, as in 'You got any tuggles back there?,' when her voice erupted in my ear.

She cried out in surprise – 'Oh!' she cried, or maybe it was 'Oh, shit!' – because after all those years and all the sure, prehensile grip of her bare, hardened toes, she'd lost her balance. The phone came down first, a black hurtling missile that was like a fragment dislodged from the lowering black sky, and it made its own distinctive sound, a thump, yes, but a kind of mechanical squawk too, as if it were alive, as if it were some small, tree-dwelling thing that had made the slightest miscalculation in springing from one branch to another. And that was all right, everything was all right – she'd only lost her phone, I'd get her a new one, and hadn't I seen an ad in the paper just the other day and thought of her?

But then the larger form came down – much larger, a dark, streaking ball so huge and imminent the sky could never have contained it. There was a sound – sudden, roaring, wet – and then the forest was silent.

*   *   *

Petunia is not a dog. She's a Patagonian fox. Above all, I've got to remember that. It seems important. It's the kind of distinction that will be vitally important in the life to come, whether it's on top of the mountain or in a cloning lab somewhere in the bowels of New Jersey. Petunia is not a dog. I seem to be repeating this to myself as we wind our way up the fractured mountain road, the hot glare of the day ahead of me, Andrea nodding asleep at my side. What I'm noticing, at the lower elevations, is how colorless the forest is. Here, where the deciduous trees should be in full leaf, I see nothing but wilt and decay, the skeletal brown stalks of the dead trees outnumbering the green a hundred to one. The chaparral on the south-facing slopes seems true, the palest of grays and milky greens, twenty shades of dun, but each time we round a bend and the high mountains heave into view, the colors don't seem right – but maybe that's only a trick of memory. Just to be here, just to be moving through the apparent world after all these years, is enough to make everything all right.

Of course, there are the inevitable condos. And traffic. This was once a snaking two-lane country road cut through national forest lands, sparsely populated, little-traveled. Now I'm crawling along at fifteen miles an hour in a chain of cars and trucks welded into the flanks of the mountain as far as I can see, and I'm not breathing cooling drafts of alpine air either – wind-whipped exhaust, that's about it. Where thirty-five years ago there were granite bluffs and domes, now there is stucco and glass and artificial wood, condos banked up atop one another like the Anasazi cliff-dwellings, eyes of glass, teeth of steps and railings, the pumping hearts of air-conditioning units, thousands of them, and no human face in sight. Am I complaining? No. I haven't got the right.

Andrea sleeps on, her old lady's double chin vibrating through a series of soft, ratcheting old lady's snores. Petunia, quietly stinking, is licking up a puddle of her own vomit in the space between three cases of fine wine and an ice chest crammed with immemorial beef. I'm whispering to myself, jabbering away about nothing, a kind of litany I began devising in prison as a way of bearing witness to what we've lost on this continent alone – bonytail chub, Okaloosa darter, desert pupfish, spot-tailed earless lizard, crested caracara, piping plover, the Key deer, the kit fox, the Appalachian monkeyface pearly mussel – but I can't keep it up. I'm depressing myself. The top of the mountain looms ahead. Joy. Redemption. The wellspring of a new life. I switch on the radio, hoping for anything, for 'Ride Your Pony,' but all I get is a very angry man speaking in what I take to be Farsi – or maybe it's Finnish – and a station out of Fresno devoted entirely to techno-country. Right. I switch off the radio and start muttering again – just to entertain myself, you understand.

The traffic begins to thin out at five thousand feet, where the narcoleptic community of Camp Orson has been transformed into Orsonville, a booming mid-mountain burg of mobile homes, mini-malls, condos, video stores and take-out pizza (*Try Our Catfish Fillet/Pepperoni Special!*). I keep my young-old eyes on the road, maneuvering around monster trucks, dune buggies and jacked-up 4x4s, and then we're on the final stretch of the road to Big Timber. The road is a good deal rougher here, washouts every hundred yards, the severed trunks of toppled trees like bad dentition along both shoulders, the fallen-rock zone extended indefinitely. But the Olfputt – one hundred and twelve thousand dollars' worth of Mac's money made concrete – is humming along, indestructible on its road-warrior tires. There are only two cars ahead of us now and they both turn off at Upper Orsonville, and whether this is a good sign or bad I can't tell. I have a sneaking suspicion that it's bad – nobody wants to go any farther because the road is so buckled and blasted and there's no there there once you arrive – but it's too late to turn back now. And on the positive side, the temperature has dropped to just over a hundred.

Half an hour later, Andrea wakes with a snort as we creep into Big Timber, where the Big Timber Bar and Mountain Top Lodge still stands – ramshackle, in need of paint and a new roof maybe, and with a dead whitebark pine in the fifty-ton range canted at a forty-five-degree angle over the windows of the restaurant, but there still and to all appearances not much changed since we first stepped through its doors as the Drinkwaters all those years ago. But what has changed, and no amount of footage on the nightly news could have prepared us for it, is the forest. It's gone. Or not gone, exactly, but fallen – all of it, trees atop trees, trees bent at the elbows, snapped at the base, uprooted and flung a hundred yards by the violence of the winds. All the pines – the sugar, the yellow, the Jeffrey, the ponderosa – and all the cedars and the redwoods and aspens and everything else lie jumbled like Pick-up-Sticks. Mount Saint Helens, that's what it looks like. Mount Saint Helens after the blast.

Andrea lets out a low whistle and Petunia's ears shoot up, alert. 'I knew it was going to be bad,' she says, and leaves the thought for me to finish.

I'm just nodding in agreement, as stunned as if I'd been transported to Mars. It's eighty-six degrees out there, accompanied by a stiff wind, and the snow – all of it, the crushing record snow that obliterated everything the winds and the beetles and the drought couldn't reach – is gone. Do I see signs of hope? A few weeds poking through the tired soil at the end of the lot where three weather-beaten pickups sit clustered at the door to the bar, the stirring of buds like curled fingers on the branches of the arthritic aspens, and what else? A bird. A shabby, dusty mutant jay the color of ink faded into a blotter with a wisp of something clenched in its beak. 'I need a drink,' I say.

Inside, nothing has changed: a few stumplike figures in dirty T-shirts and baseball caps hunched over the bar, knotty pine, a ratty deer's head staring out from the wall, discolored blotches on the floor where the roof has leaked and will leak again, dusty jars of pickled eggs and even dustier bottles that once held scotch, bourbon, tequila. And the screen, of course, tuned to a show called *Eggless Cooking* that features a sack-faced chef in toque and apron whisking something vaguely egglike in a deep stainless-steel bowl. If you're looking for the young or even the middle-aged here, you'll be disappointed. I see faces as seamed and rucked as the road coming up here, rheumy eyes, fallen chins, clumps of nicotine-colored hair bunched in nostrils and ears – we're among our own at last. I pull out a stool for Andrea, the only lady present, and await the slow shuffle of the bartender as he makes his way down the length of the bar to us. He's wheezing. He has a coffee mug in his hand. He draws even with us, no hint of recognition on his face, and lifts his eyebrows. 'Scotch,' I say hopefully, 'and for my wife, how about a vodka Gibson.'

'Up,' she says, 'two olives, very dry. And a glass of water. Please.'

There's a murmur of conversation from the far end of the bar, tired voices, a punchline delivered, a tired laugh. Andrea's hand seeks mine out where it rests in my lap. 'My wife?' she says.

I like the look in her eyes. It's a look I once fell in love with, many jail terms ago. 'What am I supposed to say – "Get one for my ex here?"'

The bartender sets down two glasses of murky *sake* and a glass of water, no ice, and I'm trying to pull the years off his face, straighten out his shoulders, erase his gut: do I know him? 'You been here long?' I ask.

He's wearing a full beard in four different shades of gray, the kind that fans out from the cheekbones as if a stiff wind is blowing round his head. He's bracing himself against the bar, and I read half a dozen ailments into that: tender liver, bad feet, bursitis, arthritis, hip replacement, war wounds. 'Nineteen sixty-two,' he says, and throws a wet-eyed glance down the front of Andrea's dress.

She says, 'What happened to all the trees? It used to be so beautiful here.'

There's a moment then, the chef on the screen nattering on about olestra and the processed pulp of the opuntia cactus, a sound of wind skirting the building, pale sun, the jay out there somewhere like a misplaced fragment of a dream, when I feel we're all plugged in, all attuned to the question and its ramifications, the three young-old men at the end of the bar, the bartender, Andrea, me. What happened, indeed. But the bartender, a wet rag flicking from hand to hand like the tongue of a lizard, breaks the spell. He shrugs, an eloquent compression of his heavy shoulders. 'Beats the hell out of me,' he says finally.

No one has anything to add to that, and the bar is quiet a moment until one of the men at the far end mutters, 'Oh, Christ,' and we all look up to see a new red van rolling into the lot, its tires pouring in and out of the ruts like a glistening black liquid. The van noses up to the front steps, so close it's practically kissing the rail, and the bartender lets out a low stabbing moan. 'Shit,' he says, 'it's Quinn.'

Quinn? Could it be? Could it possibly be?

'Drink up, Bob,' one of the stumpmen says, and then they're pushing back their barstools, patting their pockets for keys, groaning, wheezing, shuffling. 'Got to be going, so long, Vince, see you later.'

I'm sitting there rapt, watching the spectacle of the tomato-red door of the van sliding back automatically and a mechanical device lowering a wheelchair from high inside it, when Andrea takes my arm. 'We've got to be going too, Ty – I have no idea what kind of shape the cabin is going to be in – sheets, bedding, the basics. We could be in for a disappointment – and a lot of work too. And I don't feature sleeping in the car tonight, uh-uh, no way, absolutely not.' She's standing there now, right beside me, the handbag thrown over one shoulder. 'I'm just going to use the ladies' – '

Quinn was old thirty-five years ago. A little monkey-man with a dried-up face and a head no bigger than a coconut, the snooping furtive eyes, every walking cell of him preserved in alcohol. He must be ninety, ninety-five. And there he is, outside the window, lowering himself gingerly into the chair and flicking the remote with a clawlike finger as the tomato-red door slides shut behind him. And now the chair is moving and the front door of the bar swings open, and in he comes.

There is no guilt in me, not a shred of it – I'm all done with that. But I'm curious, I am, and maybe a bit angry too. Or vengeful, I suppose. I feel big, I feel notorious all over again, Tyrone O'Shaughnessy Tierwater, Eco-Avenger, the Phantom of California, Human Hyena. 'Hi,' I say, leaning down to smile in his face as the motorized chair pulls him past me, 'how they hangin'?'

Nothing. He's as drawn down and shriveled as a shrunken head preserved in salt with the body still attached, a little man of mismatched parts suspended in the gleaming steel and burnished aluminum of the wheelchair. 'Vincent,' he calls out, and his voice is like the creaking of an old barn door, 'I'll have the usual.'

A bottle of scotch – real scotch, Dewar's, an antique treasure – magically appears, and we both watch as the bartender removes a cocktail glass from the rack over his head, measures out a generous pour and adds a splash of water. Then he comes out from behind the bar, all the way round, and inserts the glass carefully between the old insurance man's crabbed fingers. A shaky ride to the lips, and Quinn takes half the drink in a gulp, then cradles the glass in his lap and turns his battered old face to me. 'So, Mr. New Guy,' he says, 'you're all so friendly with that big smile stuck on your face – but don't I know you from someplace?'

I'm not going to make this easy for him. I just shrug, but I see Andrea out of the corner of my eye, crossing the room in her sensible flats, blusher and lipstick newly applied.

It takes him a minute, the convolutions of a brain even older than the head it's in, and it takes Andrea's appearance at my side too, but then his eyes narrow and he says, 'I do know you. I know just who you are.'

Andrea tries on a smile. She has no idea what's happening here.

He makes as if to lift the drink to his lips again, a stalled grin on his face, a glint of calculation flashing deep in his clouded eyes. His nose – he's fooling with his nose, working a finger up under the flange, and then he fumbles around in his pocket for a hand-kerchief and brings it to his face. We watch in silence as he rotates his head on the unsteady prop of his neck and gives his nose a long deliberate cleansing, and then we watch him fold the handkerchief up and carefully replace it in his pocket as if we've never seen anything like it. 'Tell me,' he says then, 'now that all the years – ' And he pauses, as if he's lost his train of thought, but it's only a game, and I can see he's enjoying himself. But so am I. So am I. 'What I wanted to say is, you did set that fire, didn't you? And destroy all that equipment? Hm? Didn't you?'

The bartender blinks as if he's just wakened from a dream. Andrea puts a hand on my arm. 'Just to satisfy an old man's curiosity,' Quinn wheezes.

I lean in close, Andrea holding tight to me, the bartender dumped over the rail of the bar like a sack of grain, and take some time with my enunciation and the complications of my dental enhancements. 'Yes,' I say, as clearly as I can, so there'll be no mistake about it, 'I set the fire and demolished it all, and you know what? I'd do it again. Gladly.'

Oh, the look. He's the wise man of the ages, the quizmaster, the oracle in his cave. His dewlaps are trembling and the drink, forgotten, is canted dangerously in his lap. 'And what did you accomplish? Look around you – just look around you and answer me that.'

This is it, the point we've been working toward, the point of it all, through how many years and how many losses I can't begin to count, and the answer is on my lips like a fleck of something so rank and acidic you just have to spit it out: 'Nothing,' I say. 'Absolutely nothing.'

Epilogue
The Sierra Nevada,
June–July 2026

THERE'S A PHRASE I've always liked – 'Not without trepidation,' as in 'Not without trepidation, they turn the corner onto what used to be Pine Street and catch their first glimpse of the staved-in, stripped-down and gutted shack in which they will have to measure out the remainder of their young-old lives.' I'm not going to use that phrase here, though it's on my lips as the sun-blasted roof of Ratchiss' place, obscured by what looks like the work of a dozen forty-ton beavers, comes into view. There are so many trees down we can't actually get to the house, though in some distant era somebody came by with a chainsaw and cut a crude one-lane gap into the street itself – and I can see that person, a vigorous young-old man like me, bearded maybe, in a lumberjack's shirt with a lumberjack's red suspenders holding up his dirt-blackened jeans, and I can see that person giving up in despair as one storm climbs atop another and flings down hundred-and-fifty-foot trees as if they were hollow cane.

I stop the car, get a firm grip on Petunia's leash and step out into the late-afternoon glare of the sun. The air isn't so thick here or so hot, and there's a smell wrapped up in it that brings me back, something indefinable and austere, a smell of the duff, aspen shoots, the first unfolding wildflowers – or meat bees, maybe that's it: meat bees swarming over some dead thing buried out there under the tangle of downed trees. All right. But at least Petunia is no problem – she comes out limp as a rag, blinking her canine eyes, and no, Petunia, this is not Patagonia and these are not the pampas – while Andrea, rested and lit up with *sake,* slams the passenger's-side door with real vigor, her chin thrust forward, a look I know only too well burning in her own eyes. Right in front of us, five feet from the bumper of the car, is a fallen tree so big around she has to go up on tiptoe to see over it. 'It doesn't look too bad,' she says. 'Considering.'

'Considering what?' I counter to the accompaniment of Petunia's urine sizzling on the pavement. 'The end of the world? Collapse of the biosphere? Ruination of the forest and everything that lives in it?'

'There's a tree down over the roof, I can see that from here – and it looks like the chimney's gone, or half of it. And the windows. But it looks like – yes, somebody's been here to board them up, most of them anyway.' She turns to me, flush with this latest triumph of her surgically assisted vision, and I wonder if I shouldn't start calling her Hawkeye. 'You think – ?'

'Mag,' I say. 'Or Mug.'

And that's something to contemplate – maybe Mag is in there now, feasting on memories of savannas trodden and gemsbok speared, in no way receptive to our invading his living space. Or no, no, not Mag – he's in a condo someplace, planted in front of the screen in his polo shirt and Dockers, like everybody else. From what I can tell through the refracted lens of a good concentrated squint, the place doesn't look occupied, except maybe by carpenter ants and fence lizards. But there's one way to find out, and Andrea, always a step ahead of me, already has the ax in her hand.

It takes half an hour, but we manage to remove a section of waist-thick branches from the tree in front of us, and then, leaving Petunia tied to the bumper of the Olfputt, I help Andrea over the bald hump of the dead tree and then she helps me. I'm standing on the other side of it, two feet on the ground, fifty yards from the house, and it's as if I've entered a new world. Or an old one, a world that exists only in the snapping tangle of neurons in my poor ratcheting brain. There's the front deck, still intact, the steps where Sierra used to sit over a game of chess or Monopoly, the door Ratchiss shouldered his way through with his bags of groceries. For the first time in a long time I feel something approaching optimism, or at least a decline in the gradient of pessimism. This is going to work, I tell myself, it's going to be all right.

Inside, it's about what you'd expect after fifteen years or more of neglect – or not only neglect, but an active conspiracy of the elements to bring the place down. The tree that rests like the propped-up leg of some sleeping giant across the peak of the roof is the biggest problem – and it's going to be an insurmountable problem when the storms come – but we'll just have to work around it. Andrea, standing there amid the wreckage with all the determination of her squared-off chin and thrust-back shoulders, is thinking along the same lines. 'We'll just have to live out of the back rooms in winter,' she says, bending idly to pluck a bit of yellowish fluff the size of a pot holder from the floor. It takes me a minute, and I have to feel it, rub it between thumb and forefinger, but then I understand what it is – the remains of the lion rug, gnawed upon by generations of wood rats and the like. And birds. Don't forget the birds, because they're still out there, they're still alive, some of them anyway. I get the sudden image of a junco lining its nest with lion fur, and why does that make me want to smile?

For the rest, the sable and bushpig, the tribal shields and rifles have long since been pried from the walls by the looters who seem to have taken everything else of value, including the bathroom fixtures, there are holes in the floor you could drop a bowling ball through, the hot tub is a stew of algae and mosquito larvae, and at least 75 percent of the cedar shakes – the lion's share, that is – have been torn from the roof and flung off over the continent like so many splinters of nothing. And in the wreckage of the kitchen, sprawled out ignominiously on the floor beneath a heap of battered pans, broken glass and dish towels, is the Maneater of the Luangwa himself, still snarling and still affixed to the heavy iron stand via the stake running up his spine. Andrea lets out a little exclamation, and then she's fishing a cold, hard glittering sphere out of the bottom of a frying pan filled with sawdust and mouse droppings. And what is it? The maneater's glass eye, a big golden cat's-eye marble with the black slit of the pupil sunk into it.

That relic, that object, fills me right up to the back of the throat with emotion, and I can't say why. There it is, in my palm, the glittering manufactured thing, succedaneum for the real. All I can think to say is, 'Poor Mac.'

Andrea's rolling up her sleeves, looking for a broom, a mop, heavy-duty garbage bags, yet she pauses a minute to take my hand in hers. She nods in a sad, slow, elegiac way, but she's the optimist here and make no mistake about it. 'As horrible as it was,' she says, 'at least it was, I don't know, *special*.'

'Special? What are you talking about?'

The light through the high, shattered window behind her is like syrup spread over the rafters of the ceiling and the belly of the big tree poking through it, night on earth, night coming down. It's very still. 'Think about it, Ty – of all the billions of us on the planet, he's the last one ever to – to go like that. It's really almost an honor.'

For the rest of it, time takes hold of us and we find ourselves drifting through the days in a pattern as pure and uncomplicated as anything I've ever known – it's almost like being in the wilderness all over again. Up with the sun, to bed at nightfall, no thought for anything but making a life, minute by minute, hour by hour. We bag up the trash and haul it away, scrub the floors till the tile comes back to life and the wood glows under a fresh coat of wax. We crush carpenter ants, battle wasps, chase mice and birds and bats back out into the wild, where they belong. Andrea takes the Olfputt into Orsonville and comes back with sixteen precut and measured windowpanes and wields the putty like a glazier's apprentice, or maybe the glazier himself. Do I know how to mix cement? Sure, I do. And before long I've gathered up the tumble of bricks in the yard and rebuilt the chimney so we can sit around the hearth when winter comes, sipping that fine red wine, gnawing beef, listening to the wind in the hollow places and the whisper of the snow. There'll be no lack of firewood, that's for sure.

The locals are here still, living out there amid the devastation in reroofed cabins, gathering at the lodge on Thursdays for potluck suppers, nothing but time on their hands. With the help of the stumpmen and a few of the others, we're able to restore Pine Street as a viable, if rutted, means of ingress and egress, and we've even got the major portion of the tree off the roof. Even better, Andrea reveals a hitherto unsuspected talent – her father taught her how to split cedar shakes when she was a girl in Montana. 'Nothing to it,' she says, and there she is out in the yard spitting into the callused palms of her big hands and swinging the ax over her head. And don't forget GE. They've hooked us up – the thinnest black cable buried in a trench alongside the street like nothing so much as a long extension cord – and we've got electricity now, the house glowing against the gathering dark like some celestial phenom-enon set down here on earth in a nest of fallen trees and the deep shades of the night.

And there's something else too. The woods – these woods, our woods – are coming back, the shoots of the new trees rising up out of the graveyard of the old, aspens shaking out their leaves with a sound like applause, willows thick along the streambeds. At night you can hear the owls and the tailing high shriek of coyotes chasing down the main ingredient of their next meal. We haven't seen any squirrel hunters yet, or any survivalists either – and that suits us just fine.

Then there comes a soft pale evening in the middle of the summer, wildflowers on fire in the fields, toads and tree frogs in full song down by the creek, and my wife and I strolling down the verge of the open street, arm in arm, Petunia trotting along beside us on a braided leather leash I found in one of the cupboards in the basement. She's adjusting pretty well, Petunia, and so am I, because I'm through with contradictions. We don't need the muzzle anymore, or a cage either. She sleeps at the foot of the bed, curled up on the throw rug, no memory of any other life in her canine brain. 'Come,' I tell her, 'Sit,' 'Stay.'

'See if she'll heel, Ty,' Andrea says, and I dig into my pocket for a Milkbone, pitch my voice low – 'Heel,' I command – and she tosses up her ears and sits right down at my feet on the warm pavement.

That's when the girl appears, dressed all in black, a slight hunch to her shoulders, the long stride, high-laced black boots and hair the color of midnight in a cave. She's got her head down, watching her feet, and she doesn't see us until she's almost on us. 'Oh, hi,' she says, not startled, not surprised, and I can see the glint of the thin silver ring punched through her left nostril. How old is she? I'm a poor judge, but I'd guess thirteen or fourteen. 'You must be the new people, right?' she says, and there's a chirp to her voice that brings me back thirty-seven years.

Andrea's giving her a world–class smile. 'We're the Tierwaters,' she says. 'I'm Andrea, this is Ty.'

The girl just nods. She's looking at Petunia now, the smallest frown bunched round her lips. 'Isn't that a, what do you call them, an Afghan?'

'That's right,' I say, 'that's right, she's a dog.' And then, for no reason I can think of, I can't help adding, 'And I'm a human being.'

A NOTE ON THE AUTHOR

T.C. Boyle is the bestselling author of seven novels: *Water Music*, *Budding Prospects*, *East is East*, *World's End* for which he won the PEN/Faulkner Award for Fiction in 1988, *The Road to Wellville*, *The Tortilla Curtain* and *Riven Rock*. He is also the author of four collections of short stories. His fiction regularly appears in *The New Yorker*, *GQ*, *Playboy* and *Esquire*. He now lives near Santa Barbara in California.

A NOTE ON THE TYPE

The text of this book is set in Bembo. The original types for which were cut by Francesco Griffo for the Venetian printer Aldus Manutius, and were first used in 1495 for Cardinal Bembo's *De Aetna*. Claude Garamond (1480–1561) used Bembo as a model and so it became the forerunner of standard European type for the following two centuries. Its modern form was designed, following the original, for Monotype in 1929 and is widely in use today.